Dead Angels

Also by Glen R. Stott

Heart of the Bison
Neandertal Book One

Spirit Fire
Neandertal Book Two

Search For the Heart of the Bison
Neandertal Book Three

Timpanogos

Robyn

Dead Angels

GLEN R STOTT

Copyright © Glen R Stott

All rights reserved. No part of this book may be reproduced in any form or by any electronic or mechanical means, including information storage and retrieval systems, without permission in writing from the publisher, except by reviewers, who may quote brief passages in a review.

ISBN: 978-1-64669-652-9   (Paperback Edition)
ISBN: 978-1-64669-653-6   (Hardcover Edition)
ISBN: 978-1-64669-651-2   (E-book Edition)

Some characters and events in this book are fictitious. Any similarity to real persons, living or dead, is coincidental and not intended by the author.

Book Ordering Information

Phone Number: 347-901-4929 or 347-901-4920
Email: info@globalsummithouse.com
Global Summit House
www.globalsummithouse.com

Printed in the United States of America

To Chi★Ki

CONTENTS

Acknowledgements ix
Introduction xi

Chapter 1: The Assignment 1
Chapter 2: The Genesis 37
Chapter 3: The Murder 66
Chapter 4: The Gauntlet 99
Chapter 5: The Predator 136
Chapter 6: The Threat 170
Chapter 7: The Detective 208
Chapter 8: The Room 241
Chapter 9: The Penitence 266

ACKNOWLEDGEMENTS

This book took more than a decade to write in its present form. In order to become a writer, I read more than two dozen books on writing and took home study courses. Thanks to all those authors and teachers. I published the first version of Dead Angels in 2000. In spite of everything, it was not good. Since then I have had two professional evaluations, and had it copy edited. Not only did that immeasurably improve the book, it also improved my writing abilities.

A special thanks to my wife, Conchita (Chi*Ki) for her patience and support while I isolated myself in my office and spent the money needed to create me as a writer. In addition, she read through the book with me and provided valuable input.

INTRODUCTION

Since the ninth grade, I had a desire to be a writer and I wrote occasional short stories and some poetry. However, in the 1990s, I was a Civil Engineer in Ontario, California. During that decade, news stories or child molestation were prevalent. Whether it was Catholic Priests on Day Care Centers, it was a problem that impacted the young and innocent of the nation. I wrote a novel titled, Robin, to attack that problem. I found I could not get into the essence of the problem for victims and abandoned it. Then people very close to me, including my own sisters revealed they had been molested. I was so angry that I studied writing and evilest of men; serial killers.

Dead Angels is an angry book written from anger. It focuses on the minds of such men; an extremely evil place to go. This book is not for younger audiences or others who would be uncomfortable looking into this dark hole. Since I first published it in 2000, I have published five other books; two prehistory, one mild science fiction, one romantic literature, and one general literature. Writing, studying writing, and working with professional evaluators and copy editors has improved my writing skills immensely. In 2012, I rewrote Dead Angels. The 2000 version was 489 pages. The 2012 version is 293 lean, hard-hitting pages.

Chapter One

THE ASSIGNMENT

*I*t was all moving one way. And then, an instant snap, everything, a whole life and many more, go another way. The man stepped up to the theater to buy a ticket from the old lady in the booth. *What's an old lady like that doing holding down a job? She should be home,* he thought. He reached in his pocket for the money. The lady smiled; he did not return the gesture.

"One." He slid an oily, crumpled ten-dollar bill through the opening in her glass cage. The old lady pushed a button, and a paper receipt was spit through a slit in the aluminum countertop. She fumbled in her change drawer. *Just give me the change, bitch! I don't want to stand out here on the street all day!* The last thing he wanted was to appear edgy or nervous, but involuntarily he looked up and down the street. The sun of late afternoon danced through the parkway trees and sparkled on glass windows. No one seemed to notice him.

Not paying attention to him, the old lady continued to fumble. *You're too fucking old for this job!* His heart began to race. Finally, the old lady laid some change on top of the receipt and slid it out to the man. "Enjoy the movie," she said in a too-cheery voice.

Fuck you! He scooped the receipt and the change from the counter, put it in his pocket without counting it and hurried through the glass doors. The old theater had a long, wide hallway leading to a small podium. Behind the podium he knew it would open to a large foyer in front of the candy and popcorn concession. All these old theaters were the same. On the walls, in chrome frames with glass doors, were ads for coming attractions, except the ads had not been changed in years. The man stopped in front of an ad for *Bullitt*, starring Steve McQueen. He liked Steve McQueen, but he had died in 1980, seventeen years ago. The carpet had a colorful pattern, like a border around a circus advertisement. Now it was dirty, faded, and threadbare.

A young man stepped to the podium from a wall he had been leaning against. He looked like a college student, probably went to Brigham Young University. "Ticket, please," the usher said as he took the receipt. The usher had no uniform, no flashlight, and he did not offer to help the man find a seat. He was not an usher at all, just a ticket taker. But there should be an usher. *There was a time when going to the theater was an experience. Now it's just a seat and a screen.* He handed the ticket taker his receipt and walked by without looking at him. "Enjoy the movie, sir."

To his left was a wide stairway with a rope across the bottom that held a sign, "Sorry—Balcony closed." The smell of buttered popcorn filled the air, but it did not awaken his appetite. A pretty young girl stood behind the counter, but she did not awaken his appetite. He walked rapidly into the theater. Standing at the back, he let his eyes get accustomed to the dark. Flashes of light on the screen glared, subsided, and then burst again. The volume of the sound was overwhelming. He did not want to be around people. He did not want people to be around him. The theater could seat several hundred people on the main floor, but only about twenty people were silhouetted in front of the screen. He found a seat on an empty row and laid his sweater in his lap. *Why did I bring a sweater? It must be a hundred degrees outside. Everyone will remember a man with a sweater.* All his plans were ruined. *Snap! Everything changed. Why? Snap! One-thou-sand-one. Four syllables—one second. Snap—one syllable. One fourth of a second. Eternity changed in just a fourth of a second. It was the girl's fault.* How he longed for the urine stench of the XXX theaters on Main Street in LA. The movies of wild sex; nothing-left-to-the-imagination sex.

He had made such plans for the girl; today he would finally find the sexual release he had waited for. The girl had ruined it. Some part of him still needed to get the release, but he was not in the mood. One of those movies might help. There was no place in Provo, Utah to see a movie like that. But, truthfully, those movies didn't move him—it was more the atmosphere.

All attempts to create sexy thoughts took him back to the girl. It was no use. As he thought about her, he realized he should go home. He would have to review today and make corrections. He had made mistakes; that could not be tolerated. The stakes were too high now.

The man walked out of the theater. The ticket taker was talking to the cute girl behind the concession counter. The man started for the long hallway. Like a magnet, his gaze was pulled back to the ticket taker. The ticket taker was staring at him. The man could not avert that stare. For just the briefest time he returned it. He knew a connection was made as their eyes met and held each other's. *Damn!* The man walked down the long hallway. *What if he is suspicious? What if he calls the police? What if? Why did I come in here? Maybe subconsciously I was trying to get caught. Fucking psycho-babble! I'm not getting caught! This is all the girl's fault. Now I can't think right. Maybe I should just turn myself in. No, they would send me back. They all think I'm evil, but I'm good. The girl is much better off now.*

* * *

The man drove aimlessly, thinking about the ticket taker. He went to the hunting and fishing department at Kmart. In the display case the man saw what he wanted. He had the clerk remove a sturdy hunting knife. The thick surgical steel blade was four and a half inches long. The handle was bronze, trimmed with black and white inlays. He purchased the knife and a pair of rubber cleaning gloves with cash.

The man parked on a side street near an alley that went behind the theater. He slipped the knife in his belt behind his back and pulled his shirt out to hang over it as he walked to a small parking lot across the alley from the back of the theater. It could hold twelve cars, but only five were parked in it. The sides of the parking lot were bordered by the backyards of houses facing side streets. At the back of the parking lot was a vacant lot overgrown with weeds. Three streetlights gave a soft yellow glow. The man put the gloves on and walked to the back where he crouched in the weeds.

As he sat in the dark thinking, the room came to his mind. He had not been in it for years. The dank, moldy smell and oppressive darkness of the room had terrorized him as a child.

A group of five teenagers came down the alley and left in two cars. Finally, the back door of the theater opened. The girl from the candy counter came out and said something to someone through the open door. He watched her walk to the parking lot, her short skirt swaying from side to side. The man wondered what her panties looked like. He liked pure white. He hated flowered or colored panties that looked like the bottom of a swimming suit. He could kidnap the girl. He could always get the ticket taker another night. He could take her to the room and play games with her. He really wanted to see her panties. *God! If they are white, I'm taking her.*

She approached the car closest to him. He moved just slightly so he could see her get in the car. *She had no idea this morning when she chose her underwear that the choice would be a matter of life and death for her. People never know what might kill them.* His excitement was growing. But as he thought about her and the room, he realized she was not his type.

He still wanted to see what she was wearing. Putting her right leg in the car, she kept her left foot on the ground. The car door was swung wide open, and her short skirt hiked up her legs when she spread them apart. She held that tantalizing position as she set her purse on the seat beside her. Everything was just right, except it was too dark to see up her skirt. *Shit!*

A few minutes after the girl left, the ticket taker came out and started across the parking lot. The man walked toward him. At first his legs were stiff from crouching in the dark. He must have appeared drunk. The ticket taker was walking behind a white four-door Honda to the passenger side, and the car was between him and the theater across the alley. The ticket taker stopped when he saw the man, but he did not seem afraid of a drunkard who could hardly walk. The man walked, partly stumbled, as he moved toward his prey; the knife in his right hand behind his back. About two steps from the ticket taker, he could see the boy recognized him. He felt a powerful, uncontrollable rage. Before the boy could resist, the man smashed his left forearm across the boy's chest and pushed him against the side of the Honda. His right arm drew back like a softball pitcher, and in one fluid, powerful motion he drove it forward with an underhanded arc into the upper abdomen of his victim. He heard and felt a dull thud as the knife went in.

The man's face was just inches from the boy as he held him against the car. He looked into the boy's eyes. He wanted to see death. Instead he saw only surprise. Keeping his elbow pressed against the ticket taker he rotated his arm to put his left hand over his victim's mouth. The ticket taker made a weak attempt to cry out, but it was muffled by the man's hand. He suddenly liked this boy. It would be right to share this moment with him. As he continued to stare into his eyes, the expression changed from surprise to terror and pain. The boy tried to struggle with his arms, but his attempt was weak. There seemed to be little or no strength in his legs as the man felt him begin to slump. He pushed harder with his elbow to keep the boy up.

The man's right hand felt hot. He looked down expecting to see his hand holding the knife; instead, he saw his wrist protruding from the ticket taker's stomach. He must have driven the knife through the boy's body and into the back door of the car. That must have been the cause of the thud. He withdrew his hand, creating a wet sucking sound. He lifted his hand near his face and slowly turned it with his fingers slightly bent and apart. He was fascinated by the blood as it dripped from the glove and ran down his arm.

The boy made another weak attempt to struggle. The man removed his left hand from the ticket taker's mouth. Still holding him up with his elbow and forearm, the man pulled the glove from his right hand, turning it inside out. The boy weakly asked "Why?" just before the man put his left hand back over his mouth. The man took the glove with his right hand, forced it back into the wound and left it. He felt the soft tissue and organs with his hand as he moved it around the hard slippery-wet handle of the knife, staring with fascination into the eyes of the ticket taker with each movement.

"Only your mother could love you like I do. She was there to bring you into the world. I am here to send you out." The terror in the ticket taker's eyes seemed to subside, and his eyes filled with hopelessness and tears.

The back door of the theater opened. The manager of the theater came out and turned his back to the alley as he locked the door behind him. The man pulled the ticket taker from the side of the car. The knife slid out of the boy's back and remained in the car door. He quietly dragged the boy to the back of the parking lot. The manager unlocked the driver's door of the white Honda, got in, started the car, and drove off. The man watched the car leave with the knife sticking out and blood smeared across the side. The man almost laughed out loud as he dragged the ticket taker to the bushes to share this most intimate moment with him. The ticket taker stopped struggling. The man removed his left hand from the boy's mouth.

The man knelt beside him and took the glove from his left hand, turning it inside out. With his right hand he found the open wound again and pushed his right hand with the glove in. The warm softness of ticket taker's insides felt good. He massaged the organs never taking his eyes from the eyes of the ticket taker. He wanted to see death eye to eye as it crept in to take the boy home. The ticket taker whispered again, "Why?"

The man leaned over to his ear. "Because," was all he said. He watched in fascination as the ticket taker's eyes glassed over—the left eye half open and the right eye wide open. They stared past the man blankly into space. The man sighed and removed his hand from inside the boy. Holding his right hand like a surgeon after scrubbing, he walked across the parking lot and down the alley. *I have seen death and stared it down.* His right hand and arm were bloody to the elbow. The front of his shirt and pants were soaked in blood. This was the most exhilarating experience of his life.

* * *

The man stood in the bathroom looking in the mirror. Most of the blood had dried, but in some spots it was still sticky. Some of the dried blood fell off in small flakes when he moved. He took his clothes off and got in the shower. *It was the girl's fault. Snap! Everything got screwed up because of the girl.* He got out of the shower and, sitting on the toilet lid, began cleaning under his nails. He cut the fingernails of his right hand back to the skin, got his toothbrush and peroxide, and started to scrub his hand, arm, and fingertips.

The girl needed a name. The man picked up a book from the bookcase and sat naked on a chair looking for a name. He found two: one for him and one for her. He put the book up, but something was still agitating his brain. He needed to get it out, so he picked up his pen. The words gushed out like the ticket taker's blood.

* * *

Shari Darling walked into the lobby of the Boston Building. She looked every bit the part of a successful businesswoman. The smell of coffee from the kiosk filled the foyer. The heels on her black mid-heel pumps made a hollow sound on the marble floor as she walked to the elevator. She pushed "up" and turned her back to the elevator as she waited. She wore a navy-blue business suit. The skirt came just above her knees, showing off her long, shapely legs. She wore a lacy white blouse. Her jewelry consisted of only a pair of faux pearl earrings.

She put the leather carrying case holding her laptop on the floor beside her as she waited. In spite of the careful way she had dressed, Shari did not feel like a successful businesswoman at all. *Ding-ding*, the elevator bell sounded. Shari sighed, picked up her leather case, and entered. The rush of people coming to work was at nine. It was now nine fifteen, and Shari had the elevator to herself. Once she had liked the excitement of the crowds coming in to start each day, but since the problem with Carl and Tami, she preferred to be alone. The call from Detective Tom DeMayo last night had rekindled the hatred and pain Carl Paskel had caused. Three years was not enough.

The elevator stopped on the third floor, and Shari stepped out. To her right was a door with a frosted glass window with gold letters proclaiming *The Easy Life*. Shari had been a staff writer on the *Easy Life* magazine ever since her divorce from Ralph Darling. Before that she had been a part-time free-lance writer. After the divorce she needed something steadier to take care of herself and Tami. The child support helped, but the income she got as a free-lance writer was not sufficient.

Shari pushed the door open. She shared a work area with the two other staff writers and the secretary/receptionist. Shari's desk was near the south window looking out to the Newhouse Building. The Newhouse Building and the Boston Building were on opposite sides of a narrow street named Exchange Place. The west end of Exchange Place had been closed off at Main Street to accommodate a pedestrian patio between the two buildings. They were not enough alike to be twins, but they could certainly be siblings. The receptionist sat at a desk just inside the door. "Hi, Jane," Shari said.

"Good morning. Oh … uh, Mrs. Johansson had me put a note on your desk." Saundrea Johansson was the owner and editor of the *Easy Life*. Only Jane ever referred to her as Mrs. Johansson. Everyone else called her Saundrea.

"Thanks, I'll check it first thing." *Thanks for nothing.* Her work had been slipping, and a note from Saundrea was not something she wanted to see—especially not today. Karen Troy was not at her desk. Tomorrow was the drop-dead date for this month's article. Karen had probably already filed her article. Shari knew that feeling of being on top of her world, but it was only a memory now. Alfred Longley was working at his desk and probably had been since eight. He always liked to work early in the morning and take the afternoon off. Al was a small, beetle-like man who could be sociable at times, but generally he liked to be left alone. He always wore a brown suit with a white shirt and brown tie. "How's it going, Al?" Shari asked as she walked past his desk. Al grunted, continuing his work without looking up.

Shari's desk was messy—a sure sign she was in the final stages of pulling her article together. She always started an assignment with a neat, orderly desk. Then, when the research and interviews were done, she would spread her notes all over her desk as she developed the final thrust of her article. Shari found the note from Saundrea. "Shari, I need to talk to you. Please see me before lunch today. Saundrea."

Shari had completed the research on the article that was due tomorrow, but she was finding it difficult to put it together. The article was about the Little League in Salt Lake City. It could be done on time, but she knew it would not be the quality of work she had produced before Carl. Shari walked back to Jane's desk. "Jane, is Saundrea free for eleven thirty?"

"Actually she's free all morning." Jane smiled. She had the kind of personality that gloried in other people's trouble.

Shari ignored the not so subtle hint. "Good, put me down for eleven thirty." The digital clock on her desk showed 9:26. She pushed her notes around—shuffled them—organized them—reorganized them. If she could only come up with an angle for the story to show Saundrea she was making headway. It was no use. Carl kept coming to her mind. She had been married to him for two years without knowing what was going on. Two years of suffering for Tami. During the investigation it was discovered that he had been caught molesting another girl before Shari had met him. He got only probation. Shari had pressed charges, and he was sentenced to five years. He was already out on parole! She reshuffled her notes and started a bubble chart. She looked at the clock: 9:31 AM.

Ralph Darling was Shari's first husband and Tami's father. After the divorce from Carl, Shari changed her name back to Darling so she and her daughter would have the same last name.

Only 9:37 AM. She called Tom DeMayo, the detective who had arrested Carl. Since Carl's arrest, Tom had become her closest friend. "Hello? Tom? This is …"

"Hi, Shari. How're things going?"

"Can we get together for coffee?" Shari was not at all surprised he recognized her voice. Although Tom had not said anything, Shari felt he wanted to be more than just friends. After two failed marriages and with a daughter to raise, she was not ready for anything romantic.

"How about ten thirty?"

"Uh … sure. Same place?"

"Yeah." Shari and Tom had lunch together once or twice each week. They usually met at the Royal Eatery on Main Street and Fourth South. It was by the Newhouse Building, a short walk for Shari. Tom's office in the Salt Lake City Police Building on Second East between Fourth and Fifth South was only two blocks away.

★ ★ ★

Detective DeMayo hung up the phone. Shari had been shocked last night when he called her at home to tell her Carl had been paroled. He was not at all surprised she wanted to see him today. He picked up the picture of Shari that he kept on his desk, looked at it, and put the picture back on its spot. He was very particular about his desk. Along with the picture he had a staple remover, a stapler, a desk organizer with a notepad and paperclips, a pencil holder, and his phone. Each had a specific location, carefully marked with a small paper dot stuck to the desk.

DeMayo picked up the poem he had been examining, leaned back, and reread it.

Anahita

Dear Anahita, an immaculate virgin you came to me,
    and I also to you untried.
Gently I would hold you—but you would scream
    so tighter, my hand over your mouth.
Trembling beside me—uselessly afraid.
    Twisting and turning—uselessly fighting.
Oh what plans for you—sensually new.
    Innocent you engage—so innocent after.
I would have been your teacher
    of the animal—carnal joining.
But you taught me!
    A higher law—spiritual joining.
My arm around your head—you twisted right,
    by fate—I twisted left.
In an instant you took me beyond
    Penises—Vaginas—Sex.
In that dying minute we touched immortality
    together—closer than sex or love.
Spirits merging beyond
    mortal thoughts—mortal Love.
An accident—unintentionally done.
    Innocently I engage—so innocent after.
What use this false beard,
    these too-dark sunglasses?
No witness now
    threatens to send me back.

Quietly—gurgling, your sacred flesh
    discharges—soils my car—your clothes.
To a secret stream I carry you—what's left of you.
    Lovingly, tenderly I undress and clean you.
Naked—natural—beautiful—pale white

>   in the grass—beside pure water.
> I love you too much, Anahita
>   to leave your hollow house exposed.
> I return—pulled by? obligation? no, love,
>   to dress you.
> Fresh, clean, pretty, clothes I bring.
>   New clothes—you would have liked them.
> This flesh—never to reach puberty
>   is not you.
> This flesh—never to tempt you
>   is left pure.
> Dear Anahita, my very soul you damn.
>   But innocent you died.
> I send you to the Celestial Kingdom,
>   condemning myself as I do.
>
> Abaddon/Apollyon

The poem appeared to have been printed by an inkjet printer. It had come to the office in the morning mail addressed to "detective hold-the-mayo—personal." His name was pronounced *dee-my-oh*. DeMayo had shown the poem to several other detectives. They thought it was a hoax.

The poem indicated the author had kidnapped a young girl intending to sexually molest her but had accidentally broken her neck first, sending her to the celestial kingdom. According to the doctrine of the Mormon church, the highest degree in the afterlife is named the Celestial Kingdom, and children who died before turning eight automatically went there. Since the poem indicated the victim was sent to the celestial kingdom, DeMayo checked the missing persons list for girls up to eight years old. He found three girls that might fit the poem.

DeMayo called the detectives working on each of the cases. The first girl was Maria Gomez. She had disappeared from a church social at a picnic ground in the mountains near Logan, Utah. The area was rugged, and the evidence indicated she was lost. The second girl,

Terri Sanderson, was the subject of a heated custody battle and had disappeared with her father.

Detective Ralph Thompson of the Provo PD was in charge of the Charlene Gonzales case. He explained that she had disappeared from a local park about a block from her house. The evidence pointed to a kidnapping by a stranger, but there was no ransom note. DeMayo agreed to fax Detective Thompson a copy of the poem, and they agreed to coordinate their investigations.

After DeMayo hung up the phone, Detective Dan Bonner walked over. Bonner had been in Sex Crimes a little over eight months and had already put in for a transfer. The rapes and prostitution were bad enough, but he could not take the things that happened to children. In the Salt Lake Police Department, a detective held the rank of patrolman. This made it easy to rotate between the three divisions: Special Services, Operations, and Investigations. Each division was headed by an assistant chief of police. Sex Crimes was in the Investigations Division. "You still worried about that poem?" Bonner asked.

"I can't get rid of the feeling that there's a young girl out there … dead beside a stream. You know … it's just a feeling I can't shake. Why would the pervert send me a poem about it?" DeMayo stood up as he talked. He did not like to talk up to anyone. At six foot three inches, he usually was not bothered if he was standing.

"It's probably just some sick joke. It's a waste of time."

"Well, there's one girl on the missing persons list who fits this poem. Her name is Charlene Gonzales, and she's seven years old. I don't think she ran away, and the age fits someone before puberty." DeMayo walked to the front of his desk. He towered over Bonner who was five-ten. "Look at the end … here." DeMayo pointed. "He feels he's condemned. The Mormon Church teaches that anyone who harms a child would be better off never to have been born. I think this is a Mormon who feels he has done the girl a favor by killing her before she turned eight."

"I don't know about that. I mean, even if it is real, the poem says it was an accident and so he's innocent." Detective Bonner pointed out the couplet where the author had made that claim.

"My gut feeling from the last line of the poem is that he thinks he's condemned, and he's got nothing to lose. He's telling us something by sending us this poem. I think he's going to rape and kill little girls until we catch him. My guess is that from now on, they will all be under eight."

"Us? We? He sent the poem to you."

"You're right. It must be someone who's got a grudge against me. In the last six months there have been two guys who might fit the bill. I put Carl Paskel away for molesting his stepdaughter. He got paroled a week ago. But he marries the mother and then molests the daughter. Plus, I think a guy would be out a little longer than a week before reverting. Dale Richards got out three months ago. I sent him up for raping and beating an eight-year-old girl. He beat her nearly to death. We couldn't prove it, but there was evidence that he had molested several other girls between the ages of eight to fifteen. He could accidentally kill someone. Both of these guys have a Mormon background."

"But the poem really works only for Richards. It would be pretty stupid of him to send it. You're wasting your time," Bonner said.

"Well, if they find Charlene alive, I'll reconsider. In the meantime, I think I'll pay Richards a visit."

* * *

Shari's blonde, shoulder-length hair bounced as she walked to the elevator. Her eyes were blue green. Her eyelashes and eyebrows were naturally blonde. Even though she wore a lot of makeup to get her eyes to stand out, she was careful to make sure her face looked natural. She wore soft red lipstick to accent her full lips. She walked to the Royal Eatery. Even with all the stress, Shari had not lost the natural bounce to her step.

Shari walked through the glass-enclosed entry area to the dining room of the Royal Eatery. A tile walkway led to the counter where customers could put in and pick up their orders. The walkway went down the middle of black carpet with a design that looked like large bits of confetti had been randomly dropped on it. Light oak tables with matching oak chairs were placed around the eating area. The tabletops were forest green, and the chairs all had burgundy pads on the seats. Except for the carpet, the decor created a feeling of richness. As usual, a local radio station, Oldies 94.1, was being piped in. The station specialized in songs from the '50s and '60s. "True Love Ways" was playing. One of the reasons she liked the Royal Eatery was because of the music they played. Her parents had grown up in the '50s and had married in the early '60s. They had a large collection of the 45 rpm records from that time period which they played constantly around the house when Shari was growing up.

Tom smiled at Shari as he walked in. He wore a dark suit with a white shirt and maroon tie. His face was rugged, but there was something vulnerable there she could not define. His dark-brown eyes with flecks of green seemed capable of seeing into her soul. The smell of fresh coffee and frying bacon was comforting to Shari as he strolled to her. His walk was self-assured and athletic—younger than normal for a man of thirty-eight.

"I still can't believe he's out already," Shari greeted Tom.

"Well, he's not going to try anything." Formal greetings were not necessary. Shari could almost read his mind, and she felt he always knew what she was thinking. It was comforting to be in his presence. They had never actually dated; they just seemed to get together.

"I just can't believe they let him out so early!" Shari said as they walked to the counter.

"Unfortunately, there's just not much we can do," Tom said.

"Can I help you?" The girl behind the counter interrupted.

"I'll have the Italian eggs and sausage with coffee," Tom ordered.

"Just coffee ... and a danish." Shari turned to Tom. "I wish I could afford to have a private detective follow him all the time."

They took a table near the window looking out on Main Street. Across Main Street was the Frank E. Moss US Courthouse. Shari said, "I just want to see him caught and put out of my and Tami's lives forever. But then I guess that would mean he would get another victim. It's a catch twenty-two."

"Guys with that problem cannot be cured. I see it time and time again … repeat offenders back to jail, over and over. I'm not sure that prison is the place for them though."

"Prison is too good for them as far as I'm concerned. I have to deal every day with the damage he did. It's a life sentence to me and Tami. She's only eleven years old, and she's still in therapy, probably will be for several years more. He should be put away for the rest of his life. It should be one time, and that's the end … not parole after one or two years, but life."

"Number thirty-seven," the loudspeaker squawked.

"That's us … I'll get it." Tom brought the tray to the table after picking up cream and sugar for Shari. Tom always drank his coffee back. Shari had only just started to drink coffee. She found it harsh and bitter without lots of cream and sugar.

After arranging the food on the table and taking the tray back, Tom sat down and took a bite of his eggs. "Why did you marry him in the first place?" he mumbled through a mouthful of sausage and eggs.

Shari leaned over the table to respond. "He was different with me. He was … I don't know … considerate, kind … just not like you would expect a child molester to be. They don't wear signs, you know. The worst thing about them is they're so damn good at disguising their true selves." Shari took a sip of her coffee and winced. "That's why I hate it so much that Carl is out." She put sugar and cream in her cup. "He's just going to fool some other unsuspecting woman with a daughter, and then he'll strike like the venomous animal he is. He should be jailed for life, or a brand should be put on his forehead to warn people of the kind of predator he is." Shari had been absently stirring her coffee as she talked, but she stopped to pose a question to Tom. "Do you think he might do something to try to get even with me … you know … for pressing charges and having him put in jail?"

Tom ran the fingers of his hand through his hair and leaned his forehead onto the palm of his hand before looking up. "Well, I know these kinds of perverts. They don't really have the balls to do something like that. Mostly, I think he'll want to make everyone think he's sorry. If he contacts you at all, it'll be to say he's sorry," Tom paused a fraction of a second to take a bite of toast, "to make it seem like he has mended his ways."

"I don't want him to contact me or Tami." Shari pushed her coffee to the side. "I don't want an apology from him, and I don't want to ever hear from him again!"

"Well, I'll see to it that he gets the message in the strongest terms."

Shari leaned back in her chair. "I really would appreciate it if you would do that. He has upset our lives enough." Shari took another sip of coffee. "I have a meeting with Saundrea this morning. I'm a little afraid to go. I have an article due tomorrow, and I haven't even started writing it. Someday she's going to have to do something about my work if I don't get my act together. She's my friend, but now I'm avoiding her." Shari took a small bite of her roll, chewed, and swallowed. "I don't want to go to this meeting today. It's like knowing the axe is going to fall, but just not knowing how hard."

"There isn't much morning left," Tom said.

"I know. I just needed to blow off some steam first," Sheri replied.

"You don't think she would fire you, do you?"

"She runs the magazine at a loss every month. She has run at least five successful publications in her life, but now she just does it for fun ... and maybe out of loyalty to her subscribers. I think she is interested in producing a quality product though, so I don't actually know. But the thing is, I don't want to keep my position solely out of friendship. I want to do a good job. Besides, this magazine is not going to last forever. I need to get a body of good work ... a resume."

"Well, you're going to pull out of this. I know it." The firmness in his voice almost convinced her.

"Thanks for being a sounding board, and thanks for agreeing to get the message to Carl. I don't know what I would do without you."

They visited pleasantly while Tom finished his breakfast. Shari had a couple more bites of her Danish and drank most of her coffee. Tom walked her out the front door. "You know if you need anything you can call me any time."

"I know that, and I really appreciate it." Shari felt better about Carl, but she was still faintly uneasy.

* * *

Shari got back to the office at 11:20. Just time to freshen up and mentally prepare for the meeting with Saundrea. Saundrea was born rich and had lived her life rich. She did not understand the hand-to-mouth way of living Shari was used to. If Shari lost her job, she would lose her house too. There would be no way to meet all of her obligations with just child support and the money she made free-lancing. Her meager savings would be gone in a matter of months. "Hi, Jane. I know I'm a little early. Will you let her know I'm here?" Shari said to the secretary as she walked into the office.

"She's here, and she said to tell you to just go right in."

Shari squared her shoulders and walked to the door and knocked. "Come in," Saundrea's voice called from the other side. Shari noticed a faint odor of Amarige, Saundrea's favorite perfume. Saundrea's office was not large, but it was decorated in very good taste. Her desk was mahogany. It was off to the side and was definitely not the central focus of the room. On the side by the door and taking up more than half of the space was a rectangular table with six comfortable chairs around it. Most of Saundrea's work was done in meetings around the table. She was seated there now with several papers and articles spread in front of her. She wore a simple beige business suit. Her blue eyes generated and aura of enthusiasm that belied her eighty-three years. As Shari came in, Saundrea invited her to sit down, without getting up herself. Saundrea got right to the point. "I've been very concerned with your work ever since that unfortunate thing with Carl. I know it's been very difficult for you, and now I hear they let that rat out. The quality of your work is not something that will make or break this magazine. I'm sure you already know that. But for your own good, I feel it's my duty, as a friend, to tell you that you have been slipping."

Saundrea was basically telling her she would keep her on the payroll, as a friend, even though her work did not merit the pay she would receive. Swallowing the lump in her throat, Shari responded, "I know things have been bad, but ... I don't know what to say. I've been in therapy ... but I can't seem to get beyond the pain and upset Carl put me and my daughter through. And now he's free ... just like nothing happened."

Saundrea got up and walked to her desk. "The only thing I really know for sure is that your life is messed up, and it's going to be up to you to put it back together. I have something here for you." She picked a paper from her desk. "I think this could help." She walked back to the table and sat down. "I have an idea of how to get over what you are stuck on. I don't know if it will work, but I want you to give it a try."

"I'm ready to try anything."

"I've done some reading about trauma. One of the things suggested is that the person needs to face the problem squarely."

"I'm pretty sure I've faced it." Shari tried not to sound contentious. "After all, I did press charges and get him sent to prison."

"I'm sure you have faced the problem in your family, but maybe there is another level of facing it. I got this letter. It's very strange. This is not something we have done in our magazine in the past, but I want you to read this and give me your opinion." Saundrea handed the letter to Shari.

> Dear Ms. Johansson,
>
> I was recently convicted of molesting my stepdaughter when she was sixteen. Perhaps you are familiar with the story. It was a big news item five months ago. My name is Russell Blaine.
>
> I was arrested twenty-seven years ago for voyeurism. I pleaded guilty and was put on probation. I was guilty of those charges, but then I cleaned up my life. I am innocent of this charge my stepdaughter made. She made it because she was angry.

I pleaded innocent, but I put up no defense nor would I allow my attorney to cross-examine my stepdaughter. A lot was made about the fact that I refused to cop to a lesser charge or allow my attorney to make a defense. Since the sentencing, I have had several writers and reporters contact me with requests for interviews. I have turned them all down.

I had expected my stepdaughter's conscience would overcome her by now, and that she would come forward with the truth. However, instead my wife has divorced me, and that is all I have heard from them since the verdict was handed down.

I feel my past experience, and these more current consequences, may be of some value to others. Several magazines have contacted me about doing a story. I have turned them all down. I have read your magazine, and I have a great admiration for the quality of work you do. I have especially admired the work of your staff writer Shari Darling. I am inviting you to send her for an interview if you are interested.

Sincerely,
Russell Blaine

Shari handed the letter back to Saundrea and said, "In my opinion the man is lying. I think he's looking for some way to generate public sympathy, and he wants to use me and your magazine to do it." Shari twisted uncomfortably in her chair.

"I've done some checking, and I've found at least two other larger magazines have attempted to get his story. He is telling the truth on that point."

"So why would he pick your magazine ... and why pick me to interview him?"

"I'm not sure. I think it's worth checking out."

Shari stood up and began to pace. "I'll tell you why. He thinks he'll be able to manipulate a smaller magazine easier than the more sophisticated larger publishers."

"I had thought of that possibility. I think it's something else, and I want you to interview him to find out what it is."

Shari plopped into the chair in disbelief. "You know how I feel about these perverts. There's no way I want anything to do with them!"

"I do know what you have been through, and I also know, too well, how it has affected your professional life. You are a good reporter and a talented writer ... at least you were."

That was a low blow, but Shari knew it was true. "I know my whole life has been upset by what Carl did. I've been trying to get my life together ... mine and Tami's. I think I'm making progress. Getting my life tangled up with another sicko is not the way to make it better."

"This situation is different." Saundrea's tone was firm. "You know what you're dealing with, he's locked up away from you and your family, and you have control. I have discussed this with Dr. Langley and ..."

"You discussed this with my therapist!" Shari shouted. "That's not even ethical. I can't believe Doctor Langley would do that!" Her anger was out of control for just a few seconds. Saundrea and Doctor Debbie Langley were old friends; it was Saundrea who had recommended Dr. Langley to Shari in the first place.

"We did not discuss the details of your case. I merely asked if it would be appropriate for you to take on an assignment like this. She said it could be therapeutic. She did not tell me anything else, and there was no discussion. It was a question and an answer."

"Okay ... let me discuss it with her. I need to talk to her and Tami about it before I make up my mind." Shari left the room, maybe a little abruptly. Something about the letter or the assignment intrigued her. Even as she closed the door, she knew she would accept it. Perhaps it would be good to see and talk to one of those bastards who had gotten his just reward.

★ ★ ★

"Did you read the poem?" DeMayo asked as he came into Captain Harpor's office. Captain Harpor had twenty-two years on the books and was looking forward to retirement. It was well known that he was not willing to take risks at this point in his career.

"Yeah ... I don't think there's anything in it, but let's keep it in case something comes up." Harpor stood up.

"I've given it a lot of thought, and I think it could have come from Dale Richards. Let me follow up on it," DeMayo said.

"What do you mean, follow up on it?" Harpor walked out from behind his desk.

"Let me check on Richards ... pull him in for questioning, search his place ... you know, shake the tree and see what falls out."

"Question him about what? A poem? Sick, but hardly a crime." Harpor remained standing and did not invite DeMayo to sit down.

"He killed that girl."

"What girl? Where's the body?"

"Richards knows. Let me question him."

"The only evidence of a crime is the poem. What if he just denies he wrote it and sues the department for harassment? Even if he wrote the poem ... and there's no evidence he did ... but even if he did, he may have done it just to sucker us into some rash action. I mean, who kills someone and sends a poem pointing to himself? I mean, why not just bring the body and drop it at the front door?"

"Well, my gut feeling is that there's more to it. I want to follow it up."

"Even if the poem has something to it, it's too late to save the girl."

"He may kill someone else."

"There's nothing in here to show that any law was broken. I don't want you to bother Richards without something more to go on."

"But what if ..."

"What if you do what you're told." Captain Harpor walked to the door. "You don't have anything except someone taunting you. My final word is to back off for now."

* * *

Shari stood up as the guard led Russell Blaine into the interview room. He was about five foot ten and weighed about 180 pounds. He was mildly attractive in spite of the bright orange jump suit. Shari remembered his face from the nightly news when his sentence was pronounced. He was better looking in person. Perhaps the expression one has when one is being sentenced to twenty-five years is not flattering. "Hi, I'm Russell Blaine." He put his hand out to her. Shari did not get up nor did she offer her hand. Something about his voice drew her to him. Was there a flaw in her character? Was that why she had been drawn to Ralph and Carl?

"Listen," Shari began, "I didn't ask for this assignment, and I tried to get out of it. My editor showed me your letter. I don't do this kind of article, and I don't particularly want to do it. I don't want to get started in this kind of stuff. I do gardening, Disneyland, camping trips. I just finished an article on the Little League. I just don't understand why you wanted to have me do your damn story. I'm not interested, and I'm not qualified. This isn't even the kind of thing our magazine does. We cater to retirees. I don't know why you wanted me, and I can't understand why my editor wants me to do an article about you and your dirty secrets." Shari knew she was rattling on, but she didn't care.

"I've read some of your articles. They're nice, but wouldn't you like to do something of substance?" It was more a statement than a question.

Shari had never been in a prison before. She did not like it. "That's it." Shari got up from her chair.

"Don't you want to know the real reason I chose you?" Russell sounded almost as if he didn't care. "Plenty of writers want to do my story."

"I don't want to know anything about you, except that you're going to be in jail for the rest of your life." Shari walked toward the door.

"I asked for you because of Carl."

Shari stopped, frozen by that name. She resisted the temptation to knock Russell from his smug, self-created pedestal. "What has Carl got to do with this?"

"You came like, what? about twenty miles? Why waste the trip? Sit down, and I'll tell about Carl."

Shari sat back down mechanically. Her hate for Russell Blaine was palpable, but her curiosity was more powerful. Russell began, "I met Carl here in prison. In fact, he was my cell mate until he was released. They all think he's cured. He's not, you know. Oh, he knows how to play the game and make people believe he's turned over a new leaf, but he'll be back in here someday."

"You're not telling me anything I don't already know."

"I think you should be very careful about Carl." As he spoke, Russell looked straight in her eyes. "He wants to fool someone else into trusting him. It's really unfortunate, but he'll probably succeed and someone else will suffer before he's back."

"Why should I be careful? He'll never fool me again." Shari met his eyes. She sensed real concern in in them.

"He was much more open with me than with the shrinks. He fooled them. With me he talked about how he was going to change his MO. He thinks he's too smart now to be caught again, but he wasn't so smart." Russell looked at his hands.

"What do you mean?"

Russell looked up again. "He told me. Now I know, and I will find a way to stop him."

"So why are you telling me to be careful?"

"I didn't think anything about it ... I mean about the things he said about you. Not until a few days ago. Then something happened." Russell seemed to drift off.

"So are you going to tell me what happened?"

"He was constantly going off about you ... how it was not necessary for you to press charges. He said someone should teach you a lesson." Russell stood up and paced to the door. "This is going to sound crazy, but with all the spare time I have here, I do a lot of meditations trying to get in contact with my cosmic self ...letting my mind carry me to different levels. A couple of days ago, while I was meditating, I got this very strange feeling. I can't describe it, but it really got my attention." Russell sat back down. "It was as if something very evil had suddenly happened. It was like some kind of dam broke ... some pent up evil was released. I don't know what it was—nothing like this has ever happened to me before ... but I know it's important. And in my gut I know it has something to do with Carl. He wasn't violent before, but he is now."

"Am I getting you right? You think you have some kind of psychic ability to know what's going on with Carl?" Shari had knot in her stomach. Shari couldn't tell whether it was fear of Carl or of getting involved with Russell. When she discussed the assignment with Doctor Langley it seemed this could give her a way of facing Carl vicariously. Now, that didn't seem like such a good idea.

"I know how this sounds, but I can't ignore this feeling. That's why I wanted to do this article with you. I mean, I think I have something valuable to give, you know, in the article, but I mostly wanted to warn you. I don't think I'm psychic. But there's something about Carl ... even when I first met him ... just something ... don't ask me what it is; I don't know. I had to let you know ... warn you to keep watch."

"What do you think Carl is going to do?"

"He hates you obsessively. I don't think ... or at least I didn't think he had it in him to do anything about it. Now I'm not so sure."

"Because of this feeling you got?"

"I wish I could explain it. There's something that draws me to him and at the same time something about him that must be stopped ... something only I can sense." Beads of sweat formed on Russell's head, but he looked pale and cool. "He's got it all worked out. He thinks he's too smart to get caught, but he has overlooked something very important."

"What's that?"

"Me."

The silence hung uncomfortably for Shari. "You?"

"I'm in prison for something I didn't do, but I'm glad they're getting tougher. I just wish they had been tougher on Carl. They will the next time they catch him. He knows that. He'll be very difficult to catch. And now I think there's something violent that's been released. He's going to make a mistake, and I'll know about it. Somehow I will get him."

Russell was still leaning across the table. Shari stood up and backed away from the table a step. "I'm glad your sentence is twenty-five years ... I mean that's better than three years. But if I had my way, it would be life for all sex offenders on the first offense."

"That's pretty harsh. I mean, not all sexual crimes are as severe as rape or child molestation."

"It's not the severity of the crime that I'm talking about." Shari stepped forward and sat down, suddenly feeling braver. "It's the certainty that the crime will be repeated. This is not a case of punishment of the guilty, but one of protection of the innocent."

"You see? That's another reason I wanted to talk to you."

"Why?"

"If I consent to do an article, or a series of articles, I want them to be more than one-sided self-justifications. I need to work with someone who hates me."

"There's no question that you have found someone who hates you, but I don't want to do this, and I don't want to work with you. It shouldn't be too hard to find someone else who hates you." Shari got up to leave.

"Okay, but just do one thing." Russell stood up. "Here are some notes for the article. Just read them before you write the project off."

Oh ... so now it's a project. She took the brown manila envelope and walked to the door. "I'll think about it."

"Just be careful about Carl."

"I don't know about your feeling. He's not supposed to be dangerous ... everyone says he isn't." Shari could feel the panic and hated that it might show.

"Maybe those feelings are nothing ... but I'm still worried," Russell said. "At a level he has fooled the people here, plus he knows he won't get another light sentence. At a minimum he will change his MO. He isn't going to marry someone to get to her daughter. I don't know what he'll do; it'll be different. And he hates you. He talks violence, and he dreams violence. He told me that because he thinks I'm some kind of soul mate."

"I'll be watching out for him," Shari assured him. "You can count on that!"

As Shari drove up Interstate 15 on her way back from the prison, she thought about Carl. Then she remembered the rat and the magnifying glass. All the security she had felt after talking to Tom vanished, and her uneasiness blossomed into fear.

★ ★ ★

"You can go in now, Miss Darling," the receptionist announced. Shari walked into Doctor Langley's office. It was a small, about ten by fifteen feet. In the corner, to her right, was Doctor Langley's desk. Two chairs were side by side along the wall to her left, and a third sat in front of the desk facing them about six feet away. Except for a filing cabinet by the desk and a plain wood chair behind the desk, no other furniture was in the room. Most of the time, Doctor Langley sat in the single chair during Shari's visits. Shari always took the chair closest to the door. Doctor Langley was organizing some papers on her desk. "Hi, Shari, how're you doing today?"

"Not so hot." Shari took her accustomed chair. The wall opposite her was covered with framed diplomas and certificates. "Thanks for seeing me on such short notice."

"What seems to be the problem today?" Doctor Langley's voice always sounded comforting.

"I guess you already know I've taken the assignment from Saundrea to do the article with Mr. Blaine."

"Yes, I was aware. I think it will be a good opportunity for you." Doctor Langley walked to her accustomed chair. She wore a professional blue dress with an empire waist and a hemline about an inch above her ankle. The whole effect was ruined by dark-brown leather sandals. She wore no stockings, and her toenails were painted a gaudy red.

"I met with Mr. Blaine yesterday," Shari said. "He knew Carl in prison. He thinks … feels that Carl may want to get even with me in some way."

"How do you feel about that?"

"I couldn't sleep at all last night. I have these weird feelings about Russell. He's a pervert, but at the same time I get the feeling that he's really worried about me. I've been concerned about what Carl might do ever since I first called the police. I thought he would be put away for a very long time. I thought with him in jail, I wouldn't have to worry. But now he's out already."

"What do you think he might do?"

"I don't have a clear idea what he might do. I just think it will be really bad … maybe something like what he did to the rat."

"What rat?"

"It was the first summer we were married. We planted a cherry tomato plant. The tomatoes kept disappearing just before they got ripe. At first we thought it was some neighborhood kids. Carl was prepared to shoot them with a BB gun to teach them a lesson, but then he saw a rat getting in the plant one morning. He grabbed the BB gun and shot at it. The rat ran into the woodpile.

"We bought traps and set them in the woodpile. They were like large mouse traps, you know, with the spring that flips around and hits them in the head. We found dead rats in the traps several mornings, but then one morning one of the traps was gone. We finally found the trap on a walkway behind the garden. There was a rat in it, and it was trying to run away, dragging the trap as it went. The trap had caught it behind the head, but for some reason it hadn't killed it. Carl put on a pair of heavy gloves, took the rat out of the trap, and tied it on its back to a board. When it was tied in place, he got a large magnifying glass. He focused a beam of sunlight about the size of a nail head on the rat. That beam of light created such intense heat that it burned the rat's hair and skin. He burned the rat's testicles off, and then he burned its eyes out. I couldn't bear to watch it.

"I went out once to tell him to kill it and get it over with, but the smell of the burning hair and flesh was so bad I went back in the house. It took several hours before the rat was dead. He did other chores while it was sitting in the sun. I swear he tried to prolong it as long as possible by burning the extremities and pouring water on them. It was horrible. I asked him why he had tortured the rat, and he told me he had to balance the accounts for all the tomatoes it had stolen. If he could do something like that to a rat over just a bunch of cherry tomatoes, what might he do to someone who put him in prison for three years?"

Doctor Langley had taken some notes during the story. "How did you feel about that?" she asked.

"I don't know ... maybe I didn't want to feel. I thought maybe men are like that to a degree. You know ... they hunt deer and hang the bodies up and gut them. A lot of this hunting really has little to do with getting food. It's the hunter instinct. I was thinking that sort of thing back then, but looking at it now, I see it much differently."

"And how do you see it now?"

"It was cruel for the sake of being cruel, of having the power to do something like that, and no one could stop him. And the thing is ... nobody who knew him would have even suspected. He was kind and gentle around others ... a great father ... you know, that kind of stuff. I was the only one who knew the other side of him, and now I'm thinking that was the real Carl, and all the other stuff was the front he put up. Can you imagine everyone thought he was being a great dad to Tami? The real Carl molests children and tortures the helpless to death."

"Are you afraid he will torture you?"

"Me ... or worse, maybe Tami."

"What about your friend Tom ... the policeman? What does he think?"

"He's not as concerned as I am. He thinks molesters like Carl just want to get on to another victim. They don't want to do anything to draw attention. What do you think about that?"

"That kind of behavior is not my specialty. I think, generally speaking, Tom is right, but I'd be pretty concerned about someone who tortures animals. Most serial killers have episodes when they torture animals, but that doesn't mean everyone who tortured animals must be a serial killer."

"That's not too comforting."

"It never hurts to be careful. What about Tom? How are your feelings toward him now?"

"He's my very best friend."

"And how are his feelings toward you?"

"I think I'm getting vibrations that he would like it to be something more."

"How do you feel about that?"

"My first reaction is that I don't want that. I'm not ready for that kind of a relationship yet. I don't know if I ever will be. But it's comforting to have him around."

"And what about Russell?"

"What do you mean?" Shari asked.

"Are these strange feelings about him romantic?"

"Oh no! I don't know what they are, but for sure they aren't romantic."

"Why do you think you might never have romantic feelings?"

"I think if a woman has certain flaws in her psyche she may attract a certain type of person. Ralph had a sexual problem, and it didn't matter to him whom he hurt. I didn't know that when I met him, but I was attracted to him. Maybe at some level I did know what he was, and that's what attracted me to him. The same thing with Carl, only he was worse. I have to figure there's something about me that makes me attracted to men like that, and something about me that attracts that kind of man. So now if I'm attracted to a man, or if a man is attracted to me, I have to wonder. Don't you see?"

"Do you think you are going to take this flaw with you to the grave?" Doctor Langley asked.

"I hope not."

"How would you know if you had overcome it?"

"I guess there would be some kind of revelation, probably from my childhood, that would explain it and, at the same time, let me overcome."

"That does happen ... sometimes. However, very often a person just makes changes in her life and things are better. Not huge, dramatic things but day-to-day living and making better choices. You know you have made a lot of changes. At some point you have to trust yourself to go out and live, otherwise life will just continue to pass you by, and you run the risk of becoming a lonely, suspicious old lady."

"So should I just ignore these feelings?"

"Not necessarily. But perhaps you should be less rigid in thinking that if a man likes you he automatically must be sexually deviant. And the same thing goes if you find yourself attracted to someone. You always have to be careful, but you may be happier if you let these potential relationships prove themselves out."

"That's a lot easier said than done. I know my feelings are sort of an aberration. I guess just knowing that may be a sign of progress. Anyway, I feel much better now. I just wish this Carl thing could be resolved. He's a two-faced, evil man, and I intend to make sure he stays out of my life and out of Tami's."

"I agree with that. There's nothing to be gained by letting him back in your life."

The session relieved some of Shari's concerns. She would not let Russell in her life beyond the assignment. Tom was a different story; she had no reason to distrust him, but she was still not ready for a romantic relationship.

★ ★ ★

Shari met Saundrea at the Royal Eatery for lunch. It had been two days since Shari had given Russell's notes to her. Saundrea had asked her to "do" lunch to chat about the notes and discuss her next assignment. Saundrea was already seated and waiting for Shari when she arrived. "Your Little League article was good."

Shari sat down. "I'm glad you liked it, but this thing with Russell Blaine is not going to work. I just don't see any way to make anything out of his notes … and the interview didn't produce anything useful either. This just isn't anything that would fit this magazine."

"I read the notes you gave me, and I have to agree. I have talked to Mr. Blaine about the project several times in the past few days."

"And you told him to take his story to some other magazine?"

"Why don't you put in your order and we'll talk," Saundrea said in her authoritarian voice. Shari walked to the counter and ordered a junior burger with fries and a medium Diet Coke. When she returned to the table to wait for her order, Saundrea began, "I have an assignment for you that I think will be very interesting."

"Good. I'm ready to get going on something new this afternoon."

"This is something new all right. I want you to take the next seven or eight months to work on it."

"What do you want me to do? Write a book?"

Saundrea leaned forward on her chair. "Yes. I grew up in New York. My father was in publishing, and as his only child it was just natural I would follow in that field. I have never been married; publishing is my family. The last few years running the *Easy Life* has satisfied my interest in the publication field, but I want to do something I've never done before. I want to publish a book, and I want you to write it."

Shari was stunned. "I ... you want me to write a book? Oh sure, I've thought about writing 'The Great American Novel,' but never seriously. I don't even have any ideas."

"I have the idea. This book will be nonfiction, and I want you to be a coauthor."

"You want to coauthor a book with me? What's the subject?"

"I want you to listen to my proposal. Hear me out, and then take a couple of days to think about it before you decide. I want you to work with Mr. Blaine to write abo ..."

"What! You know how I feel about that! I don't want to have anything to do with that pervert."

"Just hear me out. I really think this could be a useful book for many people. I've looked at Russell's notes, and I think they could be the basis for a first chapter of a book."

"Number eighty-nine." The loud speaker startled Shari.

"Excuse me; that was my number."

Shari picked up her order. "You want the fry dip?" the lady behind the counter asked.

"Yes, please." The lady put a container of the dip on the tray, and Shari walked back to the table.

"I've talked to Mr. Blaine. He's also reluctant about doing a book, but he agreed. I want the book to delve into his thoughts and fantasies ... everything that motivated him. I want the book to show how he started, why he kept doing it, what he got out of it, and ... most important ... he claims he overcame it. I want to know if he did, and if he really overcame it, I want to know how. He'll write the book in first person, but I want you to work with every paragraph. I want you to make him look at the things he may try to avoid. He says he's willing to look at everything and reveal his soul. I believe him. He's intelligent, and with some pushing and some editorial assistance, this could be a good book.

"I'll pay your expenses and your regular salary until it's done. I'll split the profits with you at seventy percent for me and thirty percent for you. I don't expect this to be a real money-maker, but in the event it is, I'll up your percentage to fifty percent after I recoup the salary and expenses I pay you during the writing of the book."

"And what does Mr. Blaine get out of this?"

"Well, if he's still in prison, he gets nothing. However, if he does get out, he would get thirty percent from my cut."

Shari had a lump in her chest. "What do mean, 'if he gets out'?"

"He thinks there's a chance that at some point his stepdaughter will tell the truth."

"You believe that crap about her lying? What if she did lie? What did he do to her to make her tell such a lie? Think about that."

"I don't believe him or disbelieve him. And as far as why his stepdaughter would lie about him, I don't know her or what kind of person she is. All I know is that sometimes innocent people go to jail, and sometimes guilty people get off."

"Yeah, but this guy admits he's a pervert."

"He admits he *was* a pervert."

"These guys never change. There's no hope for them, and the best thing is to just remove them from society."

"I'm not sure human nature is so cut and dried. If he wants to pull the wool over someone's eyes, why pick someone who will fight him on it? He did ask for you, even knowing your attitude."

"I'll tell you one thing, I'm not going to help him win sympathy or get public support against the girl he victimized. So if that's his plan, I'll drop this whole thing ... even if I'm in the middle of it."

"You can drop it at any time. You will not have to pay anything back, but I get to keep whatever has been completed to that point. Is that okay with you?"

"You really think there's something to this book, don't you?"

"I'm sure it will more than pay for itself ... but it's not a money thing with me. I think this is a useful project ... for me and you. Here, I have roughed the material out for the first chapter. I want you to review it and decide if you can make it work. I want you to do it ... but I want you to be personally committed to it. You can create something worthwhile for you and many others who need to know what I think we can find out."

Shari took the envelope from Saundrea. It was not fat. "You really think this is important?"

"I don't expect it to change the world, but I am sure there are answers to some questions. Will you do it?"

"Let me look at this, and then I'll let you know."

"You look it over and take your time. If you have any doubts about doing it after you've given it some thought, that's okay. If you decide to do it, I want you to be committed to getting the truth."

Shari knew she had to do something to deal with her fear of Carl. Talking to Russell increased her fear, but facing the fear vicariously through Russell could help her deal with it.

Shari took the folder home and read the notes inside. It was full of self-justifications and evidence that Russell really felt he was basically a good guy in spite of all his sins. Shari rewrote it to clarify it. It boiled down to about a page. Ultimately, she would have to fill it out if it was to become a book. And if it was going to be part her book, it would have her imprint on it from the first chapter, and Russell Blaine—the real Russell Blaine—was not going to hide in it.

Conquering the Ever-Widening Circle
Chapter One: The Problem

Our newspapers scream out to us every day; murder, robbery, rape, drugs, molestation, and destruction surround us and fill the headlines. Why do some humans feel compelled to advance the race and build a better world, while others seem compelled to inflict pain and tear the world down? Some people act as if they are evil with no conscience, while others vacillate from embracing evil to showing regrets for their weakness. The latter group is in a battle where best intentions seem to be easily defeated by a stronger compulsion to act evilly.

This book is an attempt to describe the power and effects of destructive compulsive behavior from the viewpoint of one possessed by this phenomenon. I describe compulsive behavior as an "ever-widening circle," because the behavior starts as small insignificant circles of actions that expand to larger and larger circles, eventually engulfing the life and thinking of the person held in its grip. How does it start? What is the source of its power, and how can one defeat it?

I lived through a personal hell controlled by compulsions I didn't want. This book is not aimed at justifying or minimizing my actions. Rather, it is designed to explain something of what goes on in the mind of the perpetrator.

The act of doing the compulsive behavior was intensely enjoyable for me. However, following the behavior, I felt guilt and shame. These feelings were as powerful as the enjoyment of the act, and as a result, I would resolve never to commit the behavior again. Then the thoughts and fantasies would return, and the circle would turn again. Gradually, the effects of this slowly turning circle became a vicious, all consuming, disgusting, ever-widening circle, which at times devoured me.

When you are really sick, just the thought of food makes you sicker. During the shame and guilt phase of the circle of compulsive behavior, the feeling about the behavior is very similar to being nauseated. The behavior is repulsive and sickening, and it seems possible to overcome it. Being caught causes the deepest repulsion of all, and at such times, you are absolutely sure you will never be tempted again. With time this resolve passes, and the thoughts, the fantasies, and ultimately the actions all return.

I am as revolted and disgusted by my behaviors as any who read this. I battled with myself for over twenty years. Why did I give in despite my best efforts to the contrary? Some researchers say the brain releases an addictive drug, endorphin, when compulsive behavior is being acted out. That may explain why during the acting-out phase I enjoyed doing something that at other times I found repulsive. That does not excuse acting out a compulsion nor does it make the behavior itself any less evil.

I have spent a great deal of time mentally going over all I can remember about what it was I did, how I felt at the time, how I felt after, how it affected my life, and how I was able, ultimately, to overcome the problem.

I experienced three different compulsive behaviors. The first consisted of the destruction of property. There came a time when I replaced the destructive behavior with shoplifting. This became a much larger spiral than the destructive behavior, but it ended abruptly when I was caught. In the background of my actions, the most serious of all my problems was developing. This spiral was near the beginning and was slowly turning and growing.

In the course of this book, I will review each of these behaviors because they are all part of the whole picture.

Chapter Two

THE GENESIS

The man was in the park. It was beautiful, and he felt young. He leaned against a tree as he looked at the pond. Under the sparkle of sunlight playing on lazy waves, the water was dirty and inhabited only by carp. He started walking through the park. It was nice to walk along the meandering pathway bordered by flowers.

He came to the old cinder racetrack where he used to like to race his bike around the banked turns. Once he had jumped one of the turns, out of control, on his friend's bike. He hit a power pole, bending the front wheel and forks. What a beating he had gotten for that! No one seemed to care about the bloody nose and bruises he got from the accident. Pain did not count unless it was administered by his dad.

The racetrack was gone, replaced by a children's playground. A father was pushing his young daughter on the swing. She was wearing a pink jumper and appeared to be seven or eight years old. *I'll bet her panties are white.* The man edged closer.

The girl climbed up the slippery slide, and the father waited at the bottom to catch her. She was afraid, but he encouraged her, and finally she slid down. Her jumper blew up as she came down, but the man was not close enough to see what he wanted. The father caught her as she screamed and kicked in the joy of the moment.

Please — go down one more time. The man would be in just the right place to see by the time she was ready to come down again. *Why didn't my father ever play with me like that?* Just then the little girl noticed him. She was excitedly telling her father something and pointing at the man. He backed away uneasily as the father and the little girl walked toward him. He recognized the girl. It was Anahita! The man with her was his father! *Why is he playing with her?*

"He's the one! He killed me!" Anahita shouted.

"I always knew you were no good!" His father's fingers bit painfully into the man's shoulder as he grabbed him. He dragged him to a sewer manhole at the edge of the park and threw him in! Looking up, the man could see Anahita laughing and singing in a circle of light that was getting smaller and smaller. Suddenly, he hit water. His body slowly turned and twisted. There was a surreal grayness to everything. Gently, he hit the bottom. Without thinking, he turned his feet to the bottom and pushed up. He was dizzy when his head finally splashed free of the water. The air was putrid, but he needed to breathe. He was treading water in a river of sewage. Lumps of fecal material floated around him. He threw up, and his vomit mixed with the sewage circling around his face.

Gradually, he became aware he was in a large dome-topped channel constructed of brick. His father's voice echoed harshly in the distance. "You're good for nothing! You're good for nothing!" Behind that was Anahita's laughter. *She's laughing now—see how long she laughs with him!*

The man spied a landing with a ladder going out of the sewer and swam toward it. The landing was covered with gray slime. He was able to get a partial grip by digging the fingernails of his left hand into the slime, but the nails of his right hand were clipped to the skin and offered no help. Each time he reached with his right hand, he slipped back into the sewage. *The goddamned ticket taker; this is his fault. If I could, I'd kill him again!*

Suddenly, his mother appeared and tried to pull him out. She squatted to reach him. She pulled his right hand as he dug in with his left hand. *I wonder if she is wearing white,* he thought as he struggled up the slippery side of the landing. Just as his face was coming above the edge, his father came from nowhere and knocked his mother backward. She landed on her butt about three feet away. Then his father got down on his knees and put a hand on the man's head. The man asked, "Why?" His father answered, "Because." His father pushed him deep into the sewage. When the man came to the surface, he saw his father slapping his mother. The echo of Anahita's laughter faded as he drifted from the landing. The man knew he had passed his last chance to get out.

★ ★ ★

The man woke up wet and tangled in his sheets. "Thank God, it was a dream! I didn't kill you, Anahita. It was your fault," he said out loud to himself as much as to Anahita. He was dripping in sweat, and the smell of sewage was as real as if he were still dreaming.

It was a warm night, so he had worn only his jockey shorts to bed. He pulled the sheets to the bathroom, dragging them with him to take a warm, soapy shower. He left his jockey shorts on. He had learned long ago it was not smart to be found naked. He washed himself with scented soap until the smell of sewage was finally gone. He got out and dried himself, leaving the wet soapy sheets on the floor of the shower.

When the anger had surfaced before, he had always fought it—but he gave in to it with the ticket taker. Thinking about the ticket taker, he suddenly felt a sense of power he had never felt before. He took his wet shorts off and threw them in a corner.

The digital clock on the man's desk read 3:42 AM as he pulled a clean sheet of paper from the drawer. Sitting naked at his desk, he turned the lamp on and picked up his pen, letting his new feelings flow out with the ink as he wrote.

Out of the Abyss

I saw Ozzie and Harriet.
    What phony, unreal lives!
You're so stupid—you don't know
    children are a power base.
Hey, Ozzie! Real men drink!
    You're such a pantywaist!
Respect is earned through bruises & blood.
    Dave & Ricky have no respect.
A family gathered around the dinner table
    to discuss petty little problems.
BULLSHIT!!

Mother is a wimp—
    cook his dinner
    wash his clothes
    open his beer
    pick his toenails
    sacrifice your son to his moods.

He always thanks you—
    with a black eye
    with a broken nose
    with a loose tooth
    with a split lip
    but you never got cigarette burns like I did.

Where did I come from?
    Anahita wondered—others soon will too!
I came from Hell!
    and Hell is where I'm headed.
I came from
    army boots that bruise your legs,
    electric cords that cut your back,

> fists that snap your head,
> > cigarettes that burn holes in your skin.
> > See the circles in my armpits?
> —a reminder.
>
> I came from hanging by the wrists,
> > forgotten for hours in the dark.
> I came from a nightmare
> > Dave and Ricky couldn't begin to dream.
> What happened to me I did not choose,
> > but I learned one thing very well.
> It's better to be the father than the son.
> It's better to have all the power than none.
>
> Abaddon/Apollyon

The man smiled, put his pen down, and turned the light off. The clock blinked 4:17 AM. As he lay naked in the dark on the bare mattress, he was pleased and comfortable. "Others soon will too!" On that note he fell asleep.

* * *

DeMayo saw the envelope addressed to "tom hold-the-mayo—personal" on his desk. Although he was sure there would be no evidence on the envelope or the letter, he put on a pair of latex gloves before carefully examining them. He called the crime lab and made a copy of the poem.

After reading the poem, DeMayo pulled Richards's file. He had been physically abused by his father as a child. He also pulled Paskel's file. He had been abused as a child as well. The details of the abuse in the poem fit several things in Richards's file. According to Paskel's file, he had been beaten only with a belt. Neither file said anything about cigarette burns nor being hung in the dark. DeMayo took the poem and the files to Captain Harpor's office.

After reviewing the poem, Captain Harpor looked up. "So what do you think you've got?"

"I think we have a killer who plans to kill again, and I think we've got the goods to stop him." DeMayo remained standing.

"You still think it's Dale Richards?"

"Well, everything points to him."

"That's just the thing. Why would he do this? I mean, if he wants to confess, why not just come in and give us a statement?"

The conversation had a déjà vu feeling. "Well, I think he just wants to play a little cat and mouse. He doesn't have the guts to turn himself in. I think he'll kill again if we don't get him."

"I'll tell you what you've got … nothing. Someone writes you a couple of poems. Not illegal. You can't even prove who did this legal act. But let's just say you could prove Richards wrote the poems … then what?" Harpor handed the poem back to DeMayo.

"Look at this line." DeMayo leaned over Harpor's desk and pointed to the line that said, "Anahita wondered … others soon will too!"

Harpor read the line. "Yeah … so what?"

"Don't you get it … 'others will too!' He's going to kill others. They will wonder too … before they die. If we have this, and we don't do anything, and someone else is killed … well, what're we going to say then?"

"What if Richards is just doing this so we'll do something to allow him to get a harassment suit? Why else would he point the finger at himself if it isn't to get you all riled up. He addresses the thing to you and makes fun of your name to boot. I think he's just trying to get under your skin. There … is … no … body." Each word was stated as if it were a separate thought.

"You're willing to risk someone's life on that?"

Captain Harpor digested that for a few seconds. "What do you want to do?"

"Get a search warrant and pull the little bastard in."

Again Captain Harpor took a few seconds to mull it over. "Okay, this is what we'll do. No search warrant; you couldn't get one with this.

You talk to him and find out what you can. Take Detective Bonner. Go easy. You understand?"

"Perfectly."

* * *

DeMayo returned to his desk to follow up on the missing girls. Maria Gomez and Terrie Sanderson had both been found. Charlene Gonzales was still missing. As he finished checking on the girls, his phone rang. "Hello, DeMayo here."

"Hi," came the familiar voice.

"Shari, how're you doing?"

"Fine, I guess. Saundrea has been pushing me to take on a new assignment."

"So?"

"So the assignment was to do an article on Russell Blaine." Shari sounded a little defensive.

"Blaine? Is that the guy I put away for child molestation? You're not going to do it, are you?"

"Saundrea thinks it would be good therapy for me, and I agree."

"So you're going to take it then?"

"I guess I already did take it ... and it's sort of expanded to helping him write a book about his life."

"A book? He's just going to sugarcoat himself."

"Not with me. If it comes to that, I'm dropping out. I've already told Saundrea that, and she agrees."

"Well, no one is going to publish it ... you know that."

"Saundrea is going to have it published, but I don't care if it's published. In fact, I think I'll be happy if it isn't."

"Then why do it?"

"It will give me a chance to face Carl ... but vicariously, in a way I can feel safe, and I'll be the one in control."

"You think that'll help you move on?"

"I'm not sure, but I know I have to do something. I met with Russell last Tuesday."

"You waited three days to tell me?"

"It's because … this is hard to talk about over the phone, but Russell said some things … things I need to talk to you about. I have been tossing it around in my mind ever since I talked to him, and I can't seem to get a handle on it. Can we get together tonight? I know it's short notice again, but …"

"Look, you know you can call on me any time. How about dinner?"

"The Old Spaghetti Factory?"

"Sounds good. How about I pick you up at six?"

"Okay … and thanks."

"No problem. See ya then." Tom hung up the phone. Something bothered him, but he couldn't put his finger on it. Then it came to him; Shari had referred to Blaine as Russell—not Mr. Blaine or something like "that pervert." Russell—that seemed too personal.

★ ★ ★

Great Salt Lake was a puny remnant of the prehistoric Lake Bonneville, which had covered a great deal of Utah and Nevada. The surface of Lake Bonneville had remained stable long enough to establish a beach that stretched for hundreds of miles along the Wasatch Mountain Range in Northern Utah. After the lake dried, the beach remained as a flat bench that stuck out from the mountains and then dropped to the valley below. The Utah State Capitol was constructed on a section of that beach just north of downtown Salt Lake City. West of the capitol was a small residential area on the steep hill going down to the valley floor. It had one of the largest criminal populations in the city. The current address for Dale Richards was on Wall Street—almost in the middle of this area.

DeMayo and Detective Bonner drove there to talk to Dale Richards. Several little houses were at the bottom of the hill where Wall Street came down off the bench. They looked like two- or three-room houses with seven or eight hundred square feet inside at the most. It was the kind of neighborhood where people screaming at each other was normal background. Bonner knocked on the door. Richards opened it. "Whadda ya want?" He squinted at the bright light.

"We want to talk to you." Bonner flipped out his badge.

"I ain't done nuthun! Why don't ya jus' leave me alone?" He started to close the door, but DeMayo stepped forward and pushed the door open. "What the fuck? Ain't you guys ever heard of the Constitution? Get the fuck offa my porch." Richards pushed back on the door.

DeMayo pushed harder, almost knocking Richards over as he stepped into the house. "Thanks for inviting us in. Right neighborly of you. We won't be long … just have a couple of questions for you," DeMayo stated in a mockingly cordial voice.

"Fuck you!" Richards backed into the living room. He was five feet ten inches tall and weighed about 185 pounds. His face was angular, showing prominent cheek and jaw bones. He was wearing faded Levi's, no shirt or shoes. The Levi's had a large hole in the right knee. An old couch to the left of the door was covered with messed bedding. The floor was strewn with dirty clothes. On the coffee table were the remnants of a pizza still in its box. A nineteen-inch portable TV sat on the floor across from the couch. An old floor lamp with no lampshade stood in the corner. DeMayo surveyed the room, hoping to see some evidence. A computer with an inkjet printer would be nice. Next to the lamp was a small desk covered with unopened envelopes, but no computer.

DeMayo walked past Richards into the kitchen. It had a double sink with some stale water in one side and dirty dishes in both sides. Most of the cupboard doors were open. DeMayo turned back to Richards. "God, Richards, this is a pig sty. Don't you have any pride? And what the hell is that stink? You got a dead cat under the couch?" DeMayo looked around the room, paying attention to every detail.

"Fuck you!"

"You lose your meager ability to talk Richards?" DeMayo walked to the door on the right of the kitchen and opened it. It was the bathroom.

The mirror was speckled with dried water spots. The tub was a shade of yellow-gray. A partially torn shower curtain hung from a bar. On the counter was a tube with dried toothpaste hanging onto the countertop.

"You gotta warrant for this shit?" Richards said.

Looking at Detective Bonner, DeMayo commented, "Ah-ha, it does speak."

"Fuck you!" Richards said with a quiver in his voice that belied the bravado of his words.

DeMayo grabbed Richards by the shoulders and threw him against the wall. "This can be easy or we can take you downtown. What's it gonna be?"

Bonner pulled DeMayo to the side. "Listen man, we gotta be careful," he whispered.

DeMayo pushed past Bonner. "You know you can get hurt messing around like this." DeMayo said as he moved up to Richards face-to-face. Richards instinctively lifted his arms to protect himself. The tattoos on the outside of his upper arms wrapped around to the underside, but they did not hide the circular scars from old cigarette burns. "Your daddy burn your little armsies?"

"Your fuckin' breath stinks" Richards said as he dropped his arms.

DeMayo pulled copies of the poems from his pocket and put them in front of Richards to see his reaction. "Did you write these?"

"Fuck you." Richards hardly looked at the poems—as if he already knew what they said.

DeMayo wadded one paper up and pushed it in Richards's face. "You better start to talk or you're going to eat this!"

Richards turned his head away. "So what if I did write it, dickhead? Is there a law against writing ... 'cause if there is, it's news to me." Richards started laughing. "Dickhead ... get it ... dick ... head. I'll remember that one. Ha ha ha."

DeMayo jerked Richards nearly off his feet. "Don't get smart with me you shit, or I'll hang you in a dark hole till you rot." DeMayo carefully picked his wording to gauge Richards's reaction.

"You got no fuckin' business cumin in my fuckin' house like this. I know you, 'detective hold-the-mayo.' You fuck with me, and I'll have your fuckin' ass." Richards straightened up and thrust his chin out.

"Where did you get that name?" DeMayo took half a step backward, as if something unseen had hit him.

"Fuck you, asshole!" Richards moved forward with his chest and chin stuck out, following DeMayo's apparent retreat.

You let something out there, didn't you? DeMayo pushed Richards against the wall. "Whatsa matter? You don't like dark rooms? I'm watching you, you little prick. When Charlene's body shows up, you're mine."

"Fuck you!" Richards's brief bravado was squashed, but his mouth still spewed filth.

DeMayo pulled his fist back, but Bonner caught his arm. "Come on, Tom, we're not getting anywhere." He pulled DeMayo to the door.

"Fuck you, dickhead … and the bitch that bore you!" DeMayo broke loose and ran at Richards. He hit him, a glancing blow to the side of the head, before Bonner could recover and pull him off. Bonner pulled him to the door. Richards followed holding the side of his face. "Really enjoyed your visit dickhead … do come again."

"Jesus, Tom, you're really gonna get your ass in a sling if you keep that up," Bonner said when they were outside.

"He isn't going to do anything. I didn't actually hit him. He's not hurt, but he's scared shitless; I can feel it. The thing we gotta do is find Charlene. Did you see those cigarette scars? And he let that hold-the-mayo thing slip out. Now he knows we know. Now he's worried … that's what I wanted."

★ ★ ★

Shari Darling mailed her rewrite of the notes for the first chapter back to Russell. She hated everything about him, and yet some nagging feeling pulled her to him, kind of like Ralph and Carl. Shari met Ralph during her first year at Utah State University in Logan, Utah. Logan was located about ninety miles north of the house where she had grown up in Salt Lake City. That was the first time Shari had lived away from home. It was an exciting time for her. She and a couple of her friends lived in a basement apartment on Fifth East, just down the hill from the campus. Shari worked at the campus bookstore. Ralph was a handsome and popular junior in business. She met him when he came in winter quarter to buy books. He asked her out right there in the bookstore. He had recently returned from a mission for the Mormon Church. Young men in the Mormon Church were encouraged to go on a two-year mission shortly after they turned nineteen to teach and convert nonmembers. Among active Mormon girls, a returned missionary was considered a good catch.

After their first date in December, they began to go out together regularly. Soon they were engaged, and in April they were married. Four months—not much time to get to know each other. Shari thought she knew all about him by the time they were married. She knew his spiritual ideas, but she was soon to find he had earthly ideas she could not agree with.

Shari was a virgin on their wedding day, and she thought Ralph was too—at least he said he was. Shari had "saved" herself for her husband to be; this was not because it was forced upon her by overbearing parents or even by the strict doctrine of the church, but because she truly believed it was the right thing to do. Ralph tried to have sex with her on several occasions when they were dating, but Shari refused.

They were so happy those first few months that Shari was sure she had fallen into a fairy tale dream. In three months she was pregnant. It was the happiest day of her life until she told Ralph. He was not pleased. His plan was for Shari to support him until he got through school, had a steady job, and could afford a house.

Then came that fateful night when she had come home from work early. She was four months pregnant. She worked the four-to-ten shift at the local Hardee's, a fast food hamburger joint in Logan. She had gotten nauseated and left work just after seven. She was sick a lot, but

Ralph had convinced her to keep working so he could devote his time to studies.

When she got home, the living room of their apartment was dark. A dim light came from their bedroom. As she walked down the hall, she heard a low moaning. When she walked into the bedroom, she saw Ralph on his back with Marcia Potter on top. Up until that night, Marcia had been one of Shari's best friends. Shari's first impulse was to turn and run, but for a few seconds she was mesmerized by the sight of Marcia bouncing on Ralph. Then, as she was about to turn, she started to vomit. It came with no warning. What a surprise for Marcia and Ralph—right in the final moments of ecstasy, the wife comes in and starts throwing up all over everything.

Marcia grabbed her clothes and ran out of the house naked. Ralph was angry as hell. He got right in Shari's face and yelled, "How long have you been watching? Did you get some kind of thrill out of it?" Shari answered by throwing up more hamburger and fries, right in his face. Later—much later—she would smile about her response.

Ralph blamed Shari, saying she just was not sexy being pregnant and sick. He needed sex. "All men need it, and it's not natural or healthy to do without it." He claimed that was why the church had instituted polygamy in its early history. Shari pointed out that the church was against polygamy now, but he answered, "That's just a technicality, because the church obeys the law of the land. Polygamy shows that man is created to have more than one woman." However, when Shari suggested they talk that concept over with their bishop, Ralph promised to be faithful.

Although they stayed married several years, things were never the same. Shari could not get past the image of Marcia sliding up and down on Ralph. She lost interest in sex. She wanted to get therapy, but Ralph was against it. He said the mental pictures came because she had never forgiven him, so it was her fault. All she needed to do was to look into her heart and fully forgive him. He did not want strangers to know about their secrets—his secret, really.

In time, Ralph started seeing other women again. Once more he blamed Shari. She was just not warm enough for him. Sex with her was "uninspiring." Shari divorced him shortly after Tami turned five years old.

Shari met Carl Paskel eight months after the divorce. He was a car salesman at a dealership where she was shopping for a used car. It was to be the first car she would buy on her own. He was a big man, over six feet tall and over two hundred pounds. Although it appeared his body was lean and strong, his face was round and soft. He had a pleasant voice, and he was very helpful.

Tami was with Shari at the time, and Carl used his money to get Tami some candy from one of the candy machines. He went out of his way to befriend Tami. Shari was almost embarrassed at Tami's cold attitude toward him in spite of all his efforts. Tami was six and headstrong. Carl helped Shari make a good deal for the car, and seven months later they were married.

During the short courtship, he never tried to do anything sexual. He was a perfect gentleman. Shari was looking forward to an intimate, physical closeness after the wedding. They were married in Las Vegas and spent a week there on their honeymoon. Their wedding night was a disappointment to Shari. Carl was not able to have sex that night. In fact, he was not able to perform the entire honeymoon. It was nearly two weeks before he was able to consummate the marriage, and he was done in less than thirty seconds. During the entire time they were married, they had sex less than two dozen times. All of those times were like the first. Carl adamantly refused to get any kind of outside help for his problem.

Then came the terrible day Shari would never forget. After they had been married two years, once again Shari came home from work early. She heard strange noises coming from Tami's room. When she opened the door, she gasped when she saw Carl on the bed raping Tami. She was so little at the age of eight; it was too unreal to even fully register. When he heard her, Carl jumped up. There he was with a full, hard erection. He was a pedophile! No wonder he had refused to go to therapy.

In therapy with Tami, Shari found that Carl had started to have sexual encounters with Tami within months after they were married. He had threatened to kill her mother if Tami ever told anyone. It was a terrible burden for a child to carry. It would take years to undo that wrong, perhaps more years than are available in this lifetime. Shari wanted to kill Carl then, and she still dreamed of seeing him die—painfully.

Then there was Tom DeMayo. Here was a man who had dedicated his life to protecting society from the likes of Carl and Russell. There could be no doubt that his interest in Shari went beyond just a friendship. Why was she not able to feel romantic feelings for him? She wondered whether she would she ever have those kinds of feelings again.

★ ★ ★

Tom picked Shari up at six o'clock for their dinner date. He was dressed casually in slacks and a polo shirt. Shari was wearing pleated slacks and a light blouse. He drove to the parking lot on Fifth South across from Trolley Square Shopping Mall. A pedestrian bridge crossing over Fifth South connected the parking lot to the second story of the Trolley Square. It was a glass-enclosed structural-steel crossing offering a clear view up and down Fifth South. As they approached the Trolley Square side, the distinct smell of potpourri along with cool air from inside the air-conditioned mall welcomed them. Once inside, they found themselves looking over a balcony to the first floor. A young boy was playing with a toy flying saucer and a handheld launcher. Shari leaned on the rail in front of Fowl Weather Friends to watch the flying saucer glide up, turn sideways, and fall back to the boy. The Fowl Weather Friends was a little shop specializing in stuffed ducks and statues of various kinds of waterfowl. The smell of potpourri came from there.

"Whadda're you thinking?" Tom was standing beside her.

"I was just wondering what could change a boy like that into a monster when he grows up." She watched the boy pick up his flying saucer and load it back onto the launcher.

"Maybe the boy is already a monster."

Shari turned and looked at Tom. "Carl is a monster."

"Well, what he did to Tami was monstrous, but the therapists at the prison say he is not a danger anymore."

"Do you believe that, Tom?"

"Is that what you wanted to talk to me about?"

"Yeah ... in a way ... yeah."

Tom put his arm around her shoulder and turned her toward the Old Spaghetti Factory. "Well, let's get something to eat and talk it over." Something inside Shari winced as he put his arm around her. She walked with him, uncomfortable with his hand on her shoulder but afraid to offend him by telling him to remove it.

The Trolley Square Mall was constructed by converting the old bus barns of the Salt Lake City Lines Bus Company. The mall was full of quaint little shops, many of which dealt in antiques or crafts. Tom had no problem navigating the path to the Old Spaghetti Factory. Their table was not quite ready. Tom took Shari to a classy bar just inside of the entrance to the restaurant, where they waited to be seated. He had a Coke, and Shari sipped on a Diet Dr. Pepper. When they were called to their table, Tom poured the rest of his drink down his throat and set the glass on the bar. Shari took her drink to the table. They were seated in a secluded booth, where they engaged in small talk. After the main course was served, Shari started the conversation. "Russell thinks Carl is dangerous and has just been fooling people ... you know ... the police and the doctors."

"Well, I know that you're concerned. I'm also concerned, but not about the same thing. Over the years, I've seen a lot of Carls pass through the system. Most of them just go through the revolving door ... you know ... the system lets them out, and in a few months or years they are right back again. It's not just Carl ... I feel the same every time they let one of them out. Based on the statistics, Carl may be a repeater. If he does start again, we'll catch him. We'll be able to put him away for a long, long time. He'd be a three-time loser, and the courts are getting tougher. The thing that really pisses me off is that he would have one or more new victims before we catch him. But as far as him getting revenge on you or Tami … I just don't see that happening. These guys just aren't that way … they move on to new victims."

"You don't think he could have fooled everyone?"

Tom took a bite of spaghetti. "Well, I'm not saying he didn't fool the parole board. Obviously, they let him out; maybe he's going to be okay, but statistically, he'll have more victims. But what I'm saying is that these guys don't try to go back and hurt someone. What they're interested in is finding a new victim and staying away from those who know what they're capable of."

"I'm not concerned about those guys," Shari said. "I mean, I am, but I'm most concerned about one specific pervert."

"Well, of course, when you're considering just one person, you have to throw the others out. I'm aware of that, but still there are some generalizations to work from." He took another mouthful of spaghetti.

Shari was becoming aggravated with Tom. She couldn't tell whether it was because he seemed to be arguing with her or if it was the way he kept talking with his mouth full.

"I know you're concerned about Carl. I talked to his parole officer and let him know that you want Carl to stay completely away from you and Tami. Be assured, he will get that message in the strongest terms."

"Thanks, Tom. That's a relief. I just don't know what I would do if I had to see him again."

"I did some checking on him. He got in contact with the church shortly after going to prison." Shari understood that "the church" referred to the Mormon Church. "He has gone through the steps of repentance, and he has been active in his local ward since he got out. The bishop of the ward got him a job as a janitor, and he seems to be starting his life over. He's planning to start courses in computer drafting this fall quarter. His career goal is to be a draftsman in an engineering firm. As you know, he was a real estate salesman before.

He wants a more structured career … you know … nine-to-five sort of thing. It really looks like his intention is to completely revise his life."

"He was a car salesman when I met him, then he worked on construction, but he didn't like to work, so then he got his real estate license. So now he's thinking about being a draftsman while he happens to be working as a janitor. I'm sorry, but I don't see the change."

Tom was twirling some spaghetti, using his spoon to hold the spaghetti against his fork. He put them both down and looked Shari right in the eyes. "The fact is he doesn't even need to work anymore."

"What do you mean?"

"His parents died while he was in prison and left him several million dollars."

"You've got to be kidding; he didn't even like his parents! I bet we didn't go to their house more than three or four times the whole time we were married. And besides that, his parents were not rich."

"Well, it seems that they put a little nest egg in uranium stock back in the fifties. They made a bundle, and then they just kept reinvesting in stocks over the years. They built up a fortune by never taking any of their money out of the market … the all-American success story."

"Oh, that's just great! Now he's not only out, but he's rich. That's just disgusting."

Tom took another mouthful of spaghetti. "Well, how do you think he got paroled in the first place?"

"What do you mean?"

"I mean … slam bam and he's out. No fuss … he's just suddenly a free man."

"So how did that happen?"

"Best attorney money can buy. I can't prove it … but probably a few palms greased. Anyway …"

"I can't believe that! Money takes care of everything. Damn it! Goddamn it to hell!" Shari had thrown both her arms in the air.

"Anyone with money will use it to gain freedom. The system can be pretty shitty. There's nothing that can be done about that now. But I think it's a good sign that he's willing to hold down a job; I mean, well, in a sense it is voluntary, you know ... giving up his freedom, making it easier to keep track of him ... that sort of thing."

Shari did not feel relief. "I don't know if he can change. I think it's all an act. I just don't want him to hurt anyone else."

"Well, it's crappy that he got off so light. It's just too easy for him to spend three short years in prison, and then just go on with his life. But what I'm saying is that is one issue ... the need for you to fear him is a different issue."

Shari pushed her plate aside and leaned forward on her elbows. "Let me ask you this. How long did he have the millions before he got himself a high-priced lawyer, and how long after that did everyone decide he was safe to send back into society?"

Tom stopped chewing. "It wasn't very long, Shari. But the thing is, he isn't coming after you."

"Did I ever tell you about the rat, Tom?"

"What rat?"

"Once there was a rat in our yard. It got into our tomatoes. When we caught the rat, Carl tortured it for several hours. We're eating, so I won't go into the details. I asked him why he did that, and he said it was his duty to get the accounts balanced ... with a little rat for crying out loud. He treated his parents like crap. If I said anything about it, he would just say, 'I'm balancing the accounts.' He has a side that needs revenge."

"Well, it's one thing to kill a rat or mistreat your parents. It's quite another thing altogether to act out violently on a human being."

"But you do think that eventually he will molest someone else, don't you?"

"Unfortunately, that's the pattern, but I think he has a better than average chance to change because he's willing to make big changes in his life. He's seeing his therapist regularly, and his bishop and stake president know his history."

Shari sat back in her chair. "You hear about Catholic priests molesting children in their parishes all the time. They must be pretty good at fooling people. They had to go to some kind of priest school ...

they had to fool a lot of people. I just … you know … Carl is out there. Who's going to watch him?"

"Well, there's nothing in Carl's history to indicate that he's violent toward people."

"He fools people, but I know he's vengeful and violent, and I just get the willies when I think of what Russell said. He knew Carl when his guard was down. Russell thinks he has already started raping young girls again."

"It's just possible that your Russell is saying these things only to keep you interested in his book."

"He's not my Russell, but I suppose it's possible. I don't know … he's just so convincing."

"Well, Carl has been warned to stay away from you, and he knows we could be watching him."

"As long as he stays away from me and Tami … that's the main thing."

"I know you have had some bad experiences with marriages in the past, but if you were with the right person, you might worry less."

"I'm not ready for that, Tom. I don't know if I ever will be."

"I know. It took me a long time to get over JoLynn." JoLynn was Tom's first wife. She was raped and killed thirteen years before. The killer was never caught.

The rest of the evening was spent in pleasant conversation about Tami, who was spending the summer in girls' camp in the Uinta Mountains, where her father worked.

★ ★ ★

The next day, Shari had another meeting with Russell. She hadn't recorded their first meeting because she wasn't sure about the assignment. This time she took all her recording equipment and a notepad. She was ushered into the room before Russell arrived, giving her time to set the recorder up. As Russell walked in, the first thing Shari noticed was a black eye and a swollen lip that looked like it had been split. "I heard they beat your types up pretty regularly here. Is that your weekly beating?"

"No, it doesn't hurt much. And thanks for your concern." Russell took his seat.

"I'm sorry. How did you get it?" Shari was surprised that she really was sorry.

"Would you be disappointed awfully if I wasn't beaten?"

"I don't know. Were you beaten, or are you going to tell me you fell down the stairs?"

"Nothing so exotic as being beaten nor as mundane as falling down the stairs. I ran into an elbow playing basketball."

"They let you play basketball here?"

"The nonviolent prisoners are allowed to play some pickup ball a couple times a week."

"So, are you any good?"

"I'm not a great ball player. My main forte is getting rebounds."

"You don't look like you can jump that high."

"Rebounding is not jumping. I love to play against guys who think it is."

"So what is rebounding?" Shari was not really interested in the answer; she any background information about his life would give her information to fill out the book..

"It's a lot like life. To be successful, you have to have timing, position, strength, determination, and luck. When I'm playing, I focus on rebounds. As soon as someone lines up to shoot, I take a position where the ball is likely to go. People will try to push me out, but I won't be pushed. If the ball comes into my area, I'll have the best chance at it because I anticipated it and prepared. The ball doesn't always come my way, but every time it does, I get it. All the guys say, 'Damn, he sure is lucky.' But it's not luck at all.

"That's the way it is with most successful people. When luck sends an opportunity their way, they're prepared to take advantage. When people look at them, they don't see the times they prepared themselves, all the work and trouble they went to so they could take advantage when the opportunity came. They just say, 'Damn, what a lucky bastard. If I had that kind of luck, I could be successful too.' But the thing they never realize is that opportunities have come their way plenty of times; they weren't ready ... didn't have position ... didn't see it coming ... and so some lucky bastard, who was ready, succeeded.

"This book we're writing is not going to be a great book ... it will be good. But there are opportunities in this circumstance. Lady luck is looking our way. You watch the drama unfold and be ready to jump when the opportunity comes, and you will be one of the lucky ones," Russell concluded.

"What makes you think there is any luck in this situation?" Shari asked. "You say evil acts are being committed. I don't want that kind of luck."

"Some things you don't get to choose. You're going to play a vital role in stopping a murderer. You're going to play a part in saving the lives of people who do not have a clue their lives are in danger. Is that luck? Look at Bugliosi back in the seventies. And then here's this sick group of people ... the Manson gang. And Bugliosi gets the case. He was ready to deal with Manson, his attorney, the publicity ... you know ... all the players and circumstance that worked against him. But Bugliosi saw the lane, took his position, and then when the ball came his way he held his position and took advantage. Bugliosi becomes famous, and then he writes a book, and it's a good book, so he writes more, and he builds his reputation and his fortune. At the same time, he does it by removing a cold-blooded murderer from society.

"Some people will say Bugliosi was lucky to have the crime and trial of the century dropped in his lap. Maybe, but then there's Marsha Clark, who also has the crime and trial of the century put in her lap. She has a whole set of circumstances and difficulties to face that are different from Bugliosi. But the fact is, Marsha didn't take the lane ... didn't have the timing ... so in the end, Cochran got the rebound. Maybe he committed a foul with the race card ... so what? Everyone knew it was out there. It was up to Marsha to anticipate it and do something about it. She had enough evidence to win the case, and yet it slipped away. Who was prepared? You don't have to foul to be successful, and I'm not suggesting Marsha should have, but you have to play strong and take advantage of everything that comes your way … good or bad."

"You said rape and murder. Who's going to be raped and murdered?" It was difficult to even say the words.

"I think it has already come to that." Russell made eye contact as he spoke.

Shari wanted to turn away, but something about Russell's eyes held her. "Are those some more of your feelings?"

"They are very strong feelings … I wouldn't take them lightly."

"Maybe if they were my feelings I wouldn't. Do you feel he will try to rape and kill me?" Shari intended the question to sound sarcastic, but it came out serious.

"I said the ball is coming our way. It will be up to us to prepare."

"I don't like the term 'us' when you talk about you and me. We may or may not finish this book that even you admit is not going to be a great book, but that's all there is to us. We are not any kind of team, and so why don't we just keep it to the book."

"Okay. I looked at what you did with my first chapter, and you took all the good stuff out."

"You mean all that ego-serving stuff about how good you were?" Now her sarcasm came through strongly.

"What you are missing here is the point. There is a duality that should be pointed out. Look at Carl's public face. People who think they know him think he's a great guy. I think people should know that even those who seem to be good, or even may be good at some level, could have a secret problem. That is important."

"To some extent, but there's no need to go overboard." Shari had enjoyed cutting out all the incidents that showed Russell in a good light. He was a sick, perverted animal. All the flowery words in the world could not change the rot inside. They spent a half hour discussing the progress of the book, and then Shari left with the envelope for the next chapter.

Conquering the Ever-Widening Circle
Chapter Two: The Beginning

How does an evil compulsion start? Where does it come from? The process began in Ogden, Utah, on June 5, 1959. An eight-pound seven-ounce boy was born. How much of his personality did he bring from a previous existence? How much will be developed from birth onward? Things begin to happen to the boy, and he responds to life. Innocence is traded for mistakes and bad decisions.

I wet the bed until I was about twelve years old. When I was nine, my parents tried many different programs to help me stop. The consulted a professional who told them they could shame me better. She started by having me disrobe. As part of her examination, she fondled me until an erection developed in front of my parents; the shaming had begun. Many things were tried over a period of several weeks. Some that impacted me the most included; locking me outside in the front of my house naked, laying me naked on the bed and putting a diaper on me, forcing my older sister to watch as the chanted "Look at the little baby." I feared this would all get out to my friends and the kids at school. My solution was to avoid going home in the evenings and staying away from my friends. Finally, my parents fired the professional. By that time, I had pretty well developed the habit of staying out late at night and staying away from my friends. My life was changed to the extent from then on I allowed myself to only have a limited few number of friends.

For dinner in the late summer and early fall, I could get a good variety of fruits and vegetables by foraging through backyard gardens. Sometimes I would destroy something in the yard while I was there. In time, the occasional destruction took on a force of its own and turned into random, wanton destruction. This action was always associated with feelings of anger and self-justification.

Most of the time, I was respectful of other people's property, and I felt guilty about the destructive things I had done. That did not stop the behavior. One Saturday night when I was around twelve years old, my friend and I were out playing. It was just past dusk and getting dark fast. While running through an alley, we came upon a shed behind the local neighborhood IGA store. I threw a large rock through a window on the side. We crouched behind a lilac bush. When no one noticed the noise, we climbed through the window. There were several crates of empty soda bottles in the shed, which we began to break. We were throwing things around the shed in the dark when my friend found the light switch and turned it on.

Suddenly, we heard someone from across the alley yell that he was calling the police. We climbed out of the window and hid in a nearby field. I knew we could get away by any number of escape routes. My friend decided to go back and turn the lights off! He ran right into the arms of the man from across the alley!

"Who was with you?" the man demanded.

"No one. I was alone."

"Bullshit, I saw someone else!"

"I was alone."

"We'll see about that!"

I took a circuitous route through the fields and alleys until I got home where I sneaked through the basement window. It was almost bedtime, and I was beginning to feel relaxed when there was a knock at the door. I heard my mother say, "He's down in the basement. He's been home all night."

My dad called me. When I walked into the front room there were two intimidating policemen! The officers took me to the police station. I confessed to everything. I was a juvenile delinquent. I would never be worthy of good friends. I would never get a good job. I would never find a good girl to marry me. I would have to spend the rest of my life hanging out with criminals and taking menial jobs.

The next morning my folks insisted that I go to church. In the Mormon Church, the sacrament, consisting of bread and water, is passed to the membership each week. In order to prepare for the sacrament, the congregation sings an inspirational hymn. On this Sunday the hymn was "I Know that My Redeemer Lives." I tried not to hear the words of the song, because I felt I was unworthy of His love, but some part of me made me listen as the words accused me of my crimes. I cried the quiet, humbled, tearful cry of a sinner wanting to come home. I had never felt this bad. Even the thought of destroying anything was repulsive to me. I knew I would never be tempted to destroy another thing for as long as I lived.

Within two to three months, my friend and I were throwing rocks at streetlights. Why? The whole thing seemed so necessary when I did it, and the urge to do it was so strong, even though I knew the feelings of guilt and shame would return after.

About that time, I began shoplifting. The feelings I got were similar to those I had when I was destroying property. I gradually devoted more of my time to shoplifting. This ultimately ended the phase of destroying things. I didn't defeat the problem; I replaced it with something else.

One day as I walked out of a store with a pocket knife I had just slipped into my pocket, a store guard grabbed me by the arm. I was caught again! My record was growing, and I was only fourteen. Ninety percent of my time I had been involved in school, church, family, and wholesome activities, but I was a two-time loser.

The next Sunday I was back in church going through the shame and guilt of a sinner. That was the end of shoplifting in my life. I now had rid myself of two compulsive behaviors. However, slowly turning in the background was the major problem that would most control my life. When I stopped shoplifting, I was already engaged in an activity that could give me the thrill, the release of anger, the excitement, the sense of control, and the power that destructive behavior and shoplifting had given me.

I know the things that happened to me do not excuse the behaviors I developed. I don't bring them up to excuse myself, but to complete the picture of the path I followed to the ultimate defeat of my compulsions.

* * *

Two days after his visit to Richards's house, DeMayo was called into Captain Harpor's office. Lieutenant Randal Spencer, who was directly under Assistant Chief Jack Henderson, was there. "Take a seat," Harpor ordered.

"What's this all about?" DeMayo sat down. Harpor was seated behind the desk, and Spencer was sitting in a chair at the side of the desk.

Harpor leaned forward. "Assistant Chief Henderson got a call from the Honorable Daniel Jay Newton the Third, Esquire, this morning. What do you think it was about?" It was common for people in the department to use Newton's full name and title, usually in a sarcastic tone. Daniel Newton III was a defense attorney who specialized in high profile cases, generally involving misconduct by the police department. He was a pompous, overbearing opponent, and there were few detectives who had not been embarrassed by him at least once.

"Geez ... I don't know."

"If I told you his client is Dale Richards, would that help you?" Harpor asked.

"Jesus. How can he afford a Daniel Newton?"

"The Honorable Daniel Jay Newton the Third, Esquire, says you roughed up his client, Dale Richards. He also alleges you searched his apartment without a search warrant. Is that true?" It was obvious from Lieutenant Spencer's tone that he did not like having Daniel Newton III poking around in the Investigation Division's business.

"I had a talk with him. I think he may be a killer, based on some poems that were sent to me."

"Harpor showed them to me, and I don't think we have anything that justifies pushing a citizen around."

"Richards is a lowlife. He just got out of prison. How can he afford Newton? I don't get it." DeMayo said.

"Newton likes this kind of stuff. He may be doing it pro bono." Harpor leaned back in his chair. "At this point it's just a warning."

"So if we leave his man alone there's no problem?"

"You got it, DeMayo," Spencer said.

"Why does Richards want to keep me away if he doesn't have anything to hide?"

"You're going to have to back off him unless you have something more than these two poems. The fact is, we don't have proof that a crime has been committed. You have gotten way ahead of yourself."

"Richards is a violent sex offender. He has no right to be out where he can harm someone else."

"He has served his time, and now, right or wrong, he's a citizen, and he has rights." Spencer stood up, and DeMayo could tell the meeting was over. "Now, you are going to stay away from him … get my drift?"

"Yeah … but what happens if this creep kills someone?"

"It's a bitch, but then I guess if we could suspend the Constitution we could stop a lot of crime. I just don't think that's the way we want to do it." Spencer pointed at DeMayo. "You stay away from Richards." He held DeMayo's gaze for a couple of seconds and then walked out the door.

DeMayo turned to Harpor and shrugged his shoulders in a questioning manner.

"You know you went overboard with Richards. I warned you about it. What did you think would happen?"

"I know. I know."

DeMayo returned to his desk. *I really goofed that up. Thirteen years I have been after these guys, maybe that's enough.* It had been fifteen years since his wife, JoLynn, was murdered. They had been married six months when they got the exciting news she was pregnant. At only two months along, she started to hemorrhage. After two weeks in the hospital, she was released to go home, but she would have to stay in bed for the remainder of the pregnancy.

DeMayo was a private first class assigned to Fort Douglas with two years left on a four-year stint. When he got home on that fateful day, he found JoLynn in the hall with her hands and feet tied. A trail of blood led from the bed to the hall where she was lying in a pool of blood. She had been tied and raped. She'd had a miscarriage on the bed and started to bleed. DeMayo found her in the hall trying to get to the phone in the kitchen. She was barely able to tell him what had happened. Just a little over an hour later she died. They never found the man who killed her.

It was then DeMayo decided he wanted to become a policeman. He joined the force two years later and stayed in Sex Crimes, because each time he got a conviction, he imagined this was the one who had killed JoLynn. But he would never know for sure; he would always be chasing a shadow. Perhaps it was time to transfer to another division.

DeMayo had always gone by the book, but this thing with Richards was different. Maybe it was his strong feelings for Shari—feelings he thought he would never have again. If Paskel, or someone else, came after her, could he protect her? What if he lost her like he lost JoLynn? He decided to have a talk with Paskel.

Chapter Three

THE MURDER

The man dressed in his best clothes to deposit an important package in the natural beauty of God's creation. Trees and wildflowers crowded the shoulders of the road as it meandered up from the valley floor. Everything had been just as he had planned it. He named the girl, Barbelo, and for two days he taught her all about the sensual side of human bodies. It had been better than any of his wildest fantasies. The final climax, as he shared her final breaths, had been so draining and so completely fulfilling that it was beyond anything he could have fantasized. He had shared the very breath of life as she passed through the veil separating this existence from the next.

It was a beautiful summer morning. She died innocent, but not inexperienced in the carnal pleasures of the body. The flowers and the girl were perfect compliments of beauty and grace.

The man found the spot he had picked ahead of time. It was a pretty field of wildflowers near the road. He wanted her to be found so hold-the-mayo would see the man's power. He laid the girl out with her arms folded on her chest. The peacefulness of the celestial kingdom was on her face. He took one final picture of her lying in the flowers.

She was at peace now—a peace he had given her, dressed in the new clothes he had bought for her.

The poem he had dedicated to her was tucked in the front of her new white panties. *Let him find it. Let him know he's dealing with someone who can't be caught.* It was exhilarated to think about Detective DeMayo trying to understand his clue. He knew he had total power over DeMayo.

His spirits collapsed as he drove down the canyon. It was a strong letdown—not guilt. *Barbelo was perfect. She was the first. There will never be another like her.*

★ ★ ★

By the time the man got home, his mood was dark. The door of hell was open to him, and he wished he could undo what was done. *Damn you, Anahita!* Just a twist and what was to be a simple game of sexual discovery was magnified. But once that bridge was crossed, the door to Barbelo was opened. He had known the instant Anahita died that his life and future were changed forever.

The cool moisture in the air gave the man a sense of the thick walls as he stepped into the windowless room. The scent of a living body turned to death hung heavily in the air. He absorbed himself into the room and the sense of death. Then he turned the light on. He removed the sheets from the cot. They were soiled with traces of blood, urine, fecal material, and semen. He rolled them and Barbelo's old clothes in the disposable plastic sheet he had used to protect the mattress. He would throw the bundle of soiled sheets and clothes in a dumpster. He mopped the floor and washed the frame of the cot to freshen up the room. The stench of sweat, urine, and feces, had added a mortal sensuality that helped the man build up to the final act: that point when her life had merged with his for a fleeting, ejaculating second as she passed to her glory.

Finally the room was clean. In addition to the cot, the room held a chair, a bookcase, and a floor lamp. On the bookcase the man had a

Polaroid camera and a three-ring binder. The binder was a scrapbook of his angels and his original handwritten poems. *When I die they will collect these poems into a volume like Walt Whitman's* Leaves of Grass. *I'll call it* Dead Angels. *It will become world famous.*

He had four pictures of Barbelo—none of Anahita. One of the pictures was of Barbelo lying on the bed with the clothes she was wearing when he picked her up. She was still unconscious. Two were of her tied to the bed with no clothes on. She was awake and had an expression of obvious fear. The last was with her new clothes, at her resting place in the mountains.

The man burned incense and sat naked in the chair. He looked at the pictures of Barbelo and masturbated. That was the fifth climax in three days. He was drained and sore. He read the poems about Anahita and Barbelo and looked at the pictures. He cried. Things could never be the same for him again. He threw the book on the cot and left the room.

★ ★ ★

DeMayo got home at six fifteen looking forward to a quiet evening. One of the many streams flowing from the Wasatch Mountains had been dammed off to create a small duck pond in the condo where he lived. DeMayo could remember skinny dipping in this stream when he was ten years old. At that time it was in an undeveloped area south of Salt Lake City. A shopping area had long since replaced the open meadow, and DeMayo's condo was right on top of his favorite fishing hole. The natural channel of the creek was replaced with concrete and rocks to control the water during the high spring runoff. DeMayo and his friends used to hitchhike the seven miles from his house to this spot. No one thought much about hitchhiking in those days.

When the call came from the watch commander, DeMayo had just put some leftover Chinese food in the microwave. "Some kids on mountain bikes found a body in Immigration Canyon. Captain Harpor wanted me to give you the following information: It looks like it's Katie Sopkov. It's foul play. She has been dead only a few hours. She's not wearing the clothes she was reported missing in. He said you would want to know, and that you would probably want to check the scene personally."

DeMayo hung up the phone. *Holy she-it!* He took the food out of the microwave and put it back in the fridge. He gulped down the rest of the Diet Coke he was drinking, rinsed the glass, wiped it, and put it up.

Katrina Sopkov had been reported missing from her home in Kerns two days ago. Kerns was a bedroom community just west of South Salt Lake. She was eight years old. DeMayo arranged to have Richards's house staked out when they found he was not there. No one had shown up for the past two days. Now there was a body. Now that it was too late for Katie, things would start to happen!

It was a thirty-five minute drive from his house to the crime scene. The shadows were deepening in the canyon when Tom got there. Even though it was summer, the sun set early in the canyon. The crime scene was taped off, and Joe Alexander of Homicide had already taken charge. DeMayo knew Alexander briefly when he had been in Sex Crimes about four years ago on a rotation. He never got to know him well, but he knew Alexander transferred out because he didn't like to deal with young victims of sexual predators.

DeMayo walked over to Alexander. "What have we got?"

"It's Katie Sopkov, but she's wearing new clothes, and they don't fit her."

"You're sure it's Katie?"

"Uh … yeah. You can tell from the picture, but it isn't official yet."

"Any clues?"

"Nothing yet. We were damn lucky to find her so soon. I don't think she had been here more than a couple of hours. We'll know more when we get the autopsy report."

"Was her neck broken?" DeMayo asked.

"I don't think so. It's too soon to tell. They say you got some crazy poem that might connect."

"The poem talks about getting new clothes for the victim."

"I'd like to see it first thing in the morning."

"The poem talks about a girl he killed before this one, but we don't have a body yet. There's another poem in which this guy predicts there will be more killings. This is not the first victim, but I think it will be the last one."

"What makes you so sure?"

"I'm pretty sure I know who the killer is. The only problem will be to prove it. He's so cocky about this that I'm sure he'll make a mistake."

"Do you have enough for probable cause?" Obviously, Alexander wanted to get a warrant and make an arrest right away.

"I know it's him, but the evidence is minimal. I have talked to Captain Harpor. He was not impressed, but that was before we had a body. When I first heard Katie was missing, I checked the suspect out. He has disappeared. His place is being watched. If he shows up, we have enough to pull him in."

"What's his name?"

"Dale Richards. He served thirteen years of a twenty-year sentence for molesting young girls."

It was after ten thirty when DeMayo got home. He was tired, but he knew he would not sleep. He could not stop thinking about how Richards had slipped through after the first poem.

★ ★ ★

DeMayo called Shari first thing the next morning. He knew she would want to hear this news from him personally. She suspected Paskel. He made an appointment with her for dinner. By then he would have more information.

Even though DeMayo came in early, Alexander was already in his office when he arrived. "You're getting an early start, aren't you?" DeMayo asked as he walked up to Alexander's desk.

Alexander handed a sheet of paper to DeMayo. It was a copy of a poem. "This was in Katie's underwear … addressed to detective hold-the-mayo."

"Jesus! Well, I knew it." DeMayo took the poem and sat down to read it.

Barbelo

A perfect one is needed
    Baresches I go to see.
Dark-haired and perfect in glory,
    Barbelo he sends to me.

My consort for a time,
    many things for her to learn.
Each one I teach her lovingly.
    By my act she did earn
swift, sure passage to
    her Hev'ly Home on High.
Skipping the judgment and the pain
    by which the rest must cry.
Forty-eight hours to expand,
    to taste the carnal ways.
Time while still in innocence
    to fulfill her last days.
She could never understand
    my willing sacrifice.
How deeply into Hell I descend
    my knowledge will suffice.
It was only right I should
    my fantasies fulfill.
And use each part of her body
    with my consummate skill.

Her own life's breath
    I did mingle with mine.
After that gentle kiss,
    she with Angels will dine.
I clean her pure body
    and with soft tenderness

> I dress her in new clothes
>> to rest in wilderness.

Cosmocrater

DeMayo noticed this poem was done with rhyme, which the previous poems did not have. A lot about this poem was different, but the most notable thing was the name of the author.

Alexander turned on his chair to face DeMayo. "I've done some preliminary work. I got copies of the other poems. First, the poems were all printed on inkjet printers, but the paper is different, so I'm guessing he doesn't have a computer of his own. He probably rents a computer to write and print things out. You can do that at universities and your local library."

"Yeah, and he's using these strange names. Latin or something." DeMayo tossed the poem onto Alexander's desk.

"I've been thinking about those names." Alexander put a plain white paper on the desk. "The victims are Anahita and Barbelo." Alexander wrote the names in a column. "The perpetrators are Abaddon/Apollyon; Baresches, who sent the victim; and Cosmocrater, who killed Barbelo." He wrote those names in a column beside the first column.

"So the names are going through the alphabet. I don't know how that helps us." DeMayo slid his chair closer.

"What I wonder is how many perpetrators we have. There are two victim names, and there are three perpetrator names. At first blush, it seems like there are at least three perps involved. This may be some kind of occult religion making sacrifices. The poems are coming to you, so this group has some kind of grudge against you. Have you busted up any kind of devil worshiping group or maybe arrested an individual from a group that could be doing this?"

DeMayo pushed his chair back. "The key here has something to do with me, but the tone in the poems has to do with an individual. I don't see it as a group … this guy is just changing his name to meet some psychotic need he has to confuse the issue."

"There's no doubt that Abaddon or Cosmocrater, or whatever the hell, is the killer ... or killers. We can't rule out the possibility of more than one perp just yet. They've used the Abaddon name twice. So maybe Abaddon killed Anahita and is also the one who was abused as a child. Perhaps Baresches is some impotent member of this group who just isn't into sex. He agrees to kidnap the girls for the rest of the group. You know, like Abaddon wasn't competent because he accidently killed the first girl when he kidnapped her. He screwed up, so now Baresches does the kidnapping and then Cosmocrater makes the final sacrifice ... probably after Abaddon rapes her first."

"No. That doesn't wash. I'm pretty sure the poems are about one guy. He didn't use a different name in the second poem because no one was killed in the second poem. Maybe he only changes the name when he kills someone."

"That could be. I'm not saying it's more than one ... just brainstorming. He didn't just change the name. He also started to rhyme the poem ... like someone else wrote this one. I can't rule out more than one perp. But if there is more than one, we know they're working together."

DeMayo stood up and began pacing in front of Alexander's desk. "I think it's obvious that Anahita was killed accidentally when the Abaddon guy kidnapped her. He was going to rape her for his pleasure and then let her go. That's why he was disguised with a false beard and dark glasses. I don't know why he's changing all the names, but I'm pretty sure he's just one guy. He wasn't taking Anahita to a group meeting when he killed her."

"Maybe it's one guy who has more than one personality."

"Maybe." DeMayo stopped pacing.

"The preliminary report this morning states that Katie was raped. The poems seem to indicate that the primary motivation is sexual."

"When is the autopsy coming in?"

"I got Fred Corrigan in early this morning. He figures he'll have a preliminary autopsy report before noon. It looks like we've got a serial killer. Based on these poems, I'm getting an arrest warrant on Dale Richards. I'm getting a fugitive warrant to put him on the NCIC."

The NCIC was a National Crime Information Computer system used to alert agencies all over the country that a fugitive was wanted. "I'll also get a search warrant for his pad."

"Well, I would consider it a big favor if you would keep me informed as to what's going on."

"Are you kidding?" Alexander got up to walk out with DeMayo. "I'm putting a task force together, and you're on it. I'll be calling you as soon as we have anything from Fred."

"Thanks."

★ ★ ★

DeMayo got the call from Alexander at 9:20 a.m. "Fred will have some info for us at ten. He wants to see us in his office then."

"Was her neck broken?"

"I don't have any answers; you can get yours when we get ours. They've given us Dr. David Adam Piszczek. I will have all the available evidence to him this morning. Of course he isn't going to give us anything until after he reviews the autopsy report." Dr. Piszczek was a doctor of psychology. He had also gone to the FBI profiler's academy in Quantico, Virginia. Many cities used the services of the FBI to have criminals profiled by their experts in Quantico. Salt Lake City opted to have its own criminal profiler. A local expert would be able to deal with evidence faster and would have the added advantage of being able to visit the scene of the crime while the evidence was still fresh. The first time DeMayo had seen Piszczek's name, he thought the secretary must have gotten her fingers off the home keys when she typed it.

"You should get in touch with Detective Ralph Thompson in Provo," DeMayo said." He's working on the Charlene Gonzales case. She went missing just a few days before the first poem. I think that she's Anahita."

"We should get together before ten so you can get me up to speed on what you have."

"I'll bring my file right up ... but I don't have much yet."

"Bring it up. We need to get a central file. Carolyn Peterson is going to keep the records. It looks like this thing is going to break open pretty quickly, but you never can tell with something like this."

"Well, I'll just get my stuff together, and I'll be up in a few minutes."

★ ★ ★

After reviewing his ideas about the case and leaving the files with Alexander, DeMayo returned to his desk. He made a couple of calls on other cases he was turning over to Detective Bonner and then headed up to Corrigan's office. DeMayo ran into Alexander in the men's room down the hall from Corrigan's office. Alexander was using one of the two urinals. DeMayo stepped up to the other one. "Ready for the meeting?"

"Yeah. I asked my captain, Bob Unger, to sit in. You know him?" Alexander zipped up.

"I've run into him a couple of times at functions, but I can't say we have ever been formally introduced." DeMayo faced the wall and talked at it. "Is he good or will he be getting in our way?"

Alexander had rinsed his hands, and now he wiped them. "He's okay ... he likes to get results though."

"Who doesn't?" DeMayo undid his pants, and straightened his shirt tails. "Speaking of results, do we have the search warrant yet?"

Alexander tapped his breast pocket. "I figured we'd head out there as soon as this meeting's over. I have some lab guys already on alert to go with us."

"Good." DeMayo fastened his pants and rinsed his hands. Alexander had already gone through the door as DeMayo rushed out about fifteen feet behind him.

DeMayo caught up with him at the door to Corrigan's office. Captain Unger was already there chit-chatting with Fred Corrigan. "You know DeMayo, from Sex Crimes, don't you?" Alexander said by way of introductions.

Captain Unger stepped forward with his hand out. "I reckon we've run into each other a time or two." Unger was six feet tall and weighed about 190 pounds. His chin bone was prominent, and the skin seemed to be pulled tight from the end of his chin to his collar bone. It gave him an almost lizard-like appearance.

"I'm sure we have. Well, what have we got so far?" DeMayo directed the question to Corrigan.

"She was definitely raped before she was killed." Corrigan had an oval face. His eyes were so close together that he seemed to be cross-eyed. "She died of suffocation. After she died, she was douched and given an enema with a weak solution of drain cleaner ... I suppose in an attempt to destroy DNA. Besides the cleaner damage, we found torn tissue in her throat, vagina, and anus. There are some strange abrasions on both sides of her mouth ... as though he may have used something to pry her mouth open."

"We are considering the possibility there may have been more than one perpetrator. Is there any evidence to lean one way or the other on that?" Alexander asked.

"Not at this time. She was alive most of the two days she was missing. She was dehydrated. She didn't have food in her system. She may have been given a laxative. There is one small piece of good news. We found one pubic hair in between her check and her gums."

"Good work, Fred," Unger said.

"What condition is it in?" Alexander asked.

"It's in very good shape. We'll be able to make a pretty good match once we have a suspect. "The hair has a root, so we'll also send it out for DNA, but you know how backlogged that system is."

DeMayo turned to Alexander. "We've got to be sure to do everything right about getting evidence at Richards's. Daniel Jay Newton the Third, Esquire, will nit pic everything we do."

"No one ever told me I would be searching a man's room for pubic hairs when I was thinking about becoming a cop," Alexander said. "What about other trace evidence?" he asked Corrigan.

"The body was cleaned. The clothes are new. So far we haven't found a single other thing. There aren't even any fibers or anything like that in her mouth, nose, or throat to indicate how she was suffocated."

"So the cause of death was suffocation. What about her neck? Was it broken or damaged?" DeMayo asked.

"No. She was suffocated in some manner, but there was no damage to the neck itself."

"Could it have been during the oral thing?" Alexander asked.

"The tearing in her throat shows some signs that it had started to heal and no cleaning fluid was used there. I'm confident the oral thing happened the first day, and that's probably why the perp didn't bother with cleaner."

"Maybe he used a plastic bag to suffocate her. That would explain the lack of fibers," Unger suggested.

"That's possible, but there would have had to have been some holes in it. From the damage to the lung tissue, I would say this was a slow suffocation."

"What do you mean slow?" DeMayo asked.

"I mean she was getting some air, enough to prolong the death, but obviously not enough to sustain life."

"What else?" Unger asked.

Corrigan consulted his notes and crossed things off as he went through them. "She was tied too tightly around the wrists and ankles. The abrasions on her ankles go all the way around … so I would say she was probably tied the two days with her legs apart. Blood to her right foot was completely cut off by the ropes. Her foot was dead before she was. Her left foot was severely damaged from lack of blood and would probably have had to be amputated if the girl had survived. That's all for now. We're doing some toxicology work etcetera, but I would be surprised to find anything. Might be some drugs. At least I hope so."

"Why?" DeMayo asked.

"This would have been a terrible ordeal. I'm hoping there are some sedatives … something to have made it easier on her."

"Well, gentlemen," Unger said, "it looks like we better get back to work. I want this bastard, and I want him or them before another little girl disappears. Tom, would you come with me a minute."

DeMayo caught up with him in the hall. "You are important to the investigation because the poems were sent to you," Unger said. "That indicates some connection between you and the perpetrator that may make it possible for you to see something everyone else might miss."

"I'm pretty sure it's Dale Richards. I put him away when I first got on the force."

"Your connection is a two-edged sword."

"How so?"

"You have some personal connection to the perpetrator … at least from his point of view. Normally, I wouldn't let a detective work on a case where there is a personal connection. I hope you understand the sensitivity of the situation."

"I don't see that causing any problem."

"I hope not, because we definitely need you on this case. I understand Newton is representing Mr. Richards. Whatever you do has to stand up to that scrutiny."

"Understood."

"Good." Unger turned on his heel and walked down the hallway.

* * *

DeMayo got to Richards's house about five minutes before Alexander and his team arrived. There was no sign of Richards. Alexander unlocked the house. It was basically in the same condition it was in when DeMayo had been there. The pizza box was gone, but in its place were several partially filled take-out cups of dried Chinese food. "Look what was under the couch," said Don Cassidy, one of the lab boys, as he held up a small pair of panties.

"Better get in touch with Detective Thompson," DeMayo said. "Unless I'm in left field, those belonged to Charlene Gonzales." The panties had evidence of dried urine and fecal material. They were white with pink flowers, which matched the report DeMayo had gotten from Thompson. Katie Sopkov had been wearing light pink panties with a "K S" embroidered above the elastic on the front of the right leg.

Cassidy dropped the panties into a clear plastic evidence bag. John Page, the other lab technician, came out from the bathroom and said, "There's plenty of hair evidence in there."

"Good ... get all of it. I don't want to miss anything," Alexander responded.

They also dusted for fingerprints. None of the prints were of children. Cassidy vacuumed the floor and furniture for trace evidence. DeMayo pulled his gloves off as he stood with Alexander on the porch. "Well, what do you think? Have we got enough to convict?" DeMayo asked.

"Depends on the lab results. If the panties turn out to be Charlene's, then we've got enough to arrest the guy ... I would like more ... there never is enough to make me happy. Let's assume the panties turn out to be Charlene's. That will tie Richards to Charlene. If the hair matches the hair we got from Katie, then we have him tied to both girls. That's pretty good circumstantial evidence, but quite frankly, I was hoping to get more ... maybe a scrapbook ... more of the clothes."

"What more would that add? I mean, we have a pretty sure case as it is."

"I may be getting a jump on Piszczek, but the fact that we found the panties means he's a saver. He likes to keep souvenirs. All the clothes should have been together. How did these get separated from the rest? Where is his stash with all the other stuff?"

"What are you trying to say?" DeMayo asked.

"This couldn't be the place he used to rape and kill Katie. She was held someplace for two days, raped at least three times, and killed. She was tied to something flat with her legs apart."

"So he has another place somewhere."

"So he has a place we don't know about, and now he has disappeared to it ... probably somewhere rural where he can be sure he won't be bothered. The question is: how does Richards get a place like that fresh out of prison? That takes money."

"Dealing dope, burglary, not something legal, you can count on that."

"He must be saving his trophies at the other place. But if that's true, what're the panties doing here?" Alexander asked rhetorically.

"Well, suppose he likes to keep some of his souvenirs with him, and he accidentally left one behind. I think he may have spotted the stakeout, and then couldn't clean things up. Personal items like his shaver, toothbrush, and stuff are all gone. He must have been in the process of moving when he saw the stakeout."

Alexander started to walk to the car, talking as he went. "Makes sense. Maybe he made a mistake and rented the other place in his own name. That's not likely, but I'll have someone check into it; we don't want to miss anything."

DeMayo walked with him to the cars. "I think I'll review his files and talk to his parole officer. See if he has some favorite hangouts or friends."

Alexander opened the door and stepped into his car. "How about calling Thompson for me?"

"I'll take care of that."

★ ★ ★

Tom held Shari's chair as she sat down. "You're in Sex Crimes, so how come you're on this case?" Ever since Tom's phone call this morning, Shari had been waiting to hear what he knew. The news of the discovery of Katie Sopkov's body had been on the radio all day.

"I'm involved for two reasons: the girl was raped before she was killed, and that makes it a sex crime, and the perpetrator left a poem addressed to me."

"From Carl?" Shari noticed the scent of her Anaïs perfume. It was stronger than she had intended.

"I'm pretty sure it's from a guy named Dale Richards. He was released from prison about three months ago."

"God I hate that word."

"What word?"

"Released!" Shari shouted. "What was he in for?"

"Take it easy. Jesus, the whole place is looking at us."

Shari was thinking about when she caught Carl with Tami. She had not realized she was standing or that she was shouting. As she looked around, she saw that several people were staring at her. She sat back down. "What was he in prison for?"

"Promise me you aren't going to make a scene, and I'll tell you."

"You don't have to tell me; it was rape or child molestation, wasn't it?"

"Yes."

"Why do you think Richards did this?"

Tom reviewed the evidence and explained the clues in the poems.

The waitress brought their meals and put them on the table. Shari had ordered chicken and Tom had steak.

"So you have Richards in custody." Shari had completely lost her appetite.

"Not exactly."

"But you just said you ta ..."

"I talked to him after I got the first two poems. We haven't been able to find him since we found Katie's body. He's disappeared, but we have an APB out ... he won't get far."

"That first girl ... was she before the warning from Russell or after?"

"It was before, but this isn't Carl."

"How do you know?"

"I told you, the poems and evidence point to Richards. I knew he was a suspect before he kidnapped Katie."

Shari had experience with investigation for articles she had written. She was always skeptical of circumstantial evidence. "Someone sent you some poems describing Dale Richards as a murderer. You got a hair from a crime scene, and now you are getting hair from Richards's room, which you think will match. You don't suppose someone else could know enough about Richards to write the poems, or that someone else could get hairs from his room to plant on the body?"

"Someone, meaning Carl?"

"Look, we have had a warning from Russell. It's like he knew about all this, but we know Russell didn't do it; he has an alibi." Shari had not touched her food. Tom had been eating right along.

"Well, I'll look into this, and I will not rule Carl out. Would that make you feel better?"

"Come on, Tom ... the fact that you think you know it's Richards sort of rules Carl out in your mind. But at least check to see what he was doing when the girls were kidnapped."

"I'll do that, and I'll do it with an open mind ... okay?"

"I have a question that has been bothering me."

"What?"

"How did Carl's parents die?"

"They were killed in a botched burglary."

"Thanks. I'm just not hungry right now. I'm not mad at you, but I'm upset with the system you work for. I think I'd like to go home. Would you please take me home?" Shari did not wait for an answer, but got up and walked to the door.

Tom caught up with her. "Carl was in prison when his parents were killed."

"I know."

"Are you going to be all right?"

"I'm kind of afraid. It's not fair that Carl should be out there. You know, it probably is this Richards guy ... this time. But I don't know that, and I don't know what will ... I mean every time a girl is raped or someone is killed, I can't help but think of Carl. As long as he's free, I'm in this emotional prison. He put me there, and now he's the one who's free ... he's the one ... just take me home ... don't talk. I'll be better in the morning."

★ ★ ★

The next morning there was another meeting with the task force. DeMayo got a Styrofoam cup and poured it full of black coffee. He took a sip and walked to the homicide conference room. Carolyn Peterson was already there. "Everything ready?" he asked, taking a seat.

"Pretty much. Is this your first homicide investigation?"

"I guess it is."

"Big difference, you know ... with homicide you can't interview the victim."

"Fortunately, the perp in this case has as much as given us a confession."

"You mean with the poems?"

"Yeah." DeMayo took another sip of hot coffee.

"True, but clues, evidence, confessions ... it all gets twisted once the attorneys get involved. You need a strong case ... especially for murder."

"What? You trying to discourage the new man?" Alexander quipped as he walked in. "I like to keep these meetings informal and short. We have a little more data to go over, and then we can hash out some possible ideas."

"Sounds good to me." DeMayo leaned forward in his chair, somehow feeling like a sophomore in high school.

Bob Unger, Fred Corrigan, and Ron Lawrence, Corrigan's assistant, came in together. "Tom, I don't go to all these meetings, but I thought I would see how this one gets going," Unger said.

Alexander called the meeting to order. "It looks like we're all here. Why don't you all sit down, and we can get started. Doctor Piszczek is finishing up a courtesy profile for the Provo PD."

"What case in Provo?" DeMayo was interested in any police activity in Provo since Charlene's disappearance.

"That usher thing behind the theater."

"Very interesting. You know, that was around the time Charlene was reported missing," DeMayo commented.

"You don't think it was the same guy, do you?" Alexander asked.

"There just aren't that many murders in Provo ... then two practically the same day? Maybe this guy saw the kidnapping or knew something about the body. It seems like a strange coincidence."

"He was killed after work at about twelve thirty Monday morning. Charlene was kidnapped around ten Sunday morning ... almost fourteen hours earlier. We have to assume she was killed about the same time she was kidnapped. That usher deal was an angry, bloody, violent thing. The murderer reached in and rearranged the guy's insides as he was dying. He left his gloves in the body. Plus the usher was a grown man. The only coincidence is they were both about the same time. Let's not get sidetracked."

"When is Piszczek going to be done in Provo?" DeMayo asked.

"In a day or so. But that is not a hold up. He has the stuff on this case, and he's working on it. We'll call a special meeting when he's ready. Corrigan, did you have anything new?"

"Everything proved to be about as we had stated in the prelim. There's no sign of any drugs, but she was gagged."

"Maybe he had her in a populated area," Unger proposed.

"What if he's just careful?" DeMayo asked. "This could be in a cabin in the mountains where he might be concerned about hikers coming by."

"We can assume that if she could scream, it's possible someone could hear her," Alexander said.

"Or maybe he just didn't like to hear her himself," Lawrence put in.

"Okay, we know the girl was gagged. This indicates that she was held prisoner in a house in the middle of town or in a cabin in the mountains. The room was soundproof or not. That's a good start," DeMayo said.

"Sarcasm aside, this kind of investigation is always a puzzle. When we fit this piece with other evidence, it could be an important part," Unger explained. "Anything else, Fred?"

"There were teeth marks on the inside of her cheek that probably came as a result of the gag pushing her checks into her teeth. I still don't know about the marks on the outside of her cheeks except they happened close to the time of death."

"Could it be that they are teeth marks too?" DeMayo asked.

"It's pretty hard to bite yourself on the outside of the cheek."

"Oh God … you think he could have?" Alexander asked, looking at DeMayo.

"Could have what?" Unger asked.

"He might have suffocated her by putting his mouth over hers. Let me see the poems." Alexander took about twenty seconds after

Peterson handed him the poems to find what he was looking for. "Listen to this, 'Her own life's breath, I did mingle with mine. After that gentle kiss, she with angels will dine.'"

"That's it! That son of a bitch suffocated her with his mouth. Jesus." DeMayo slapped his pencil on the pad of paper.

"That would explain the slow death. Either he didn't make a tight seal, or worse, he breathed air into her on purpose to prolong the experience," Corrigan added.

"I'll bet he purposefully breathed air in and sucked air out. That's what he means by 'mingle.' I want him off the streets, Joe." Unger looked directly at Alexander, challenging him as he spoke.

"We'll get the guy." Alexander did not flinch under Unger's stare. "What've you got Lawrence?"

"Cassidy personally took the underwear to Thompson in Provo. It was positively identified as Charlene's. Several of the hair samples we pulled from the bathroom match Katie's hair."

"So we got Richards dead to rights," DeMayo said.

"The hair matches the hair on the victim, so we assume, since Richards lived in the house, he must be responsible for the hair," Lawrence said. "But maybe it was from someone who visited Richards. It's the kind of thing defense attorneys love to tear apart. It's not a problem though, because when we get Richards, we'll make a match directly to him."

"Look, we need to find the guy," DeMayo interjected. "Is there anything that could tell us where he is … for instance, the fast food … is it from his neighborhood?"

"So far everything is close to his house or to the place where he worked. We're still looking at trace stuff."

Alexander stood up. "Okay, we need to talk to everyone who lives in his neighborhood and all his coworkers. This is the shoe leather drudgery of the job. Let's get on with it. Anything else?"

No one had anything to add, so they all started milling to the door.

* * *

Shari opened her eyes to the sound of birds chirping outside her window. Sunlight had rolled across her bedroom floor and splashed up the wall opposite her bed. Another Sunday morning. With Tami gone, she felt no need to get up. She lay back and closed her eyes. *One thing about church … it sure gave structure to Sundays.* Before Ralph, the church and family meant nearly everything to her. Now, the only meaning to her life revolved around Tami. Shari sat up in her bed and looked around the room. Her clothes from the past week were scattered at random on the floor. She was sure some analyst would consider it all meaningful. To Shari the meaning was clear, *Time to get out of bed and clean this mess up.*

Shari rolled out of bed. Stepping over yesterday's blouse, she walked out of the room, across the hall, to the bathroom. Shari and Tami shared the only bathroom. There was a tub, but no shower. Ralph had promised to remodel the bathroom and convert the tub into a tub and shower. Another of the heap of promises Ralph had made merely to hear the sound they generated as they spilled from his mouth.

Shari longed to take a hot shower and then decided to skip the bath. She brushed her teeth thoroughly—front, back, top, and bottom. Then she brushed her hair, not nearly so thoroughly. Still wearing the cotton jumbo nightshirt she had slept in, she walked down the hall to the kitchen. Saturday's dishes stared accusingly from the sink. A scrambled egg would be nice. The small frying pan was soaking in soapy water that had long since lost its bubbles. Bloated particles of yesterday's scrambled eggs clung insecurely to the bottom and sides of the pan. As she regarded the pan and its contents, she decided on a can of peaches and toast. She put one slice of bread in the toaster. The peaches were in the storage room in the basement. She put on her house slippers and went down the stairs.

The rafters of the ceiling were little more than six feet above the bare concrete floor. Even though the house had a full basement, with no headroom, it would not be worth the cost to finish it. She had friends who had done it to similar houses. Cozy was not the word Shari would pick to describe the result.

An old coal-burning furnace stood in the center of the basement, its six large, round ducts reaching out to each of the rooms upstairs. Ralph had compared it to the heart of the house, reaching arteries out to warm all who lived in it. To her, it looked like some genetically aberrant octopus reaching tentacles out to the house. The furnace had been converted to a gas heater years before they had bought the house. The relic firebox remained as a reminder of the way things used to be. The heavy cast-iron door to the firebox gaped open. Frozen there by time and rust, it looked like the mouth of someone who had died slowly and painfully. It seemed to breathe out old, stale air—the breath of a phantom ghost.

To the left of the open firebox was the coal room. The coal delivery chute was closed off and sealed, but not removed. Someone had cleaned the room of coal dust and installed shelves for food storage. The Mormon Church encouraged its members to store at least one year's supply of food and water. Shari stopped in front of the firebox. A shiver passed through her. The house, the furnace, the storage room—all remnants of a life unfulfilled—of promises broken—of hopes and dreams shattered. She suddenly realized everywhere she looked in the house she saw only failed purposes and empty dreams.

Shari stepped into the dark, and waving her arms in the air found the light bulb hanging from the ceiling. Holding the smooth bulb with her left hand, she felt for and found the switch near its base. It was a cold, flat plastic knob. She gave it a clockwise turn, and the room flooded with light. When she released the bulb shadows swayed. In the far corner, the shadow of a dust-laden spiderweb danced. The spider had abandoned it long ago. Shari found a can of peaches, and using one hand, she turned the light off and then walked back up the stairs.

The smell of toasting bread was refreshing. The phone rang as the toast popped up. Shari put the phone to her left ear, pushing up with her shoulder to hold it in place as she put the toast on a saucer and reached for the margarine.

"Hello?"

"Hello. Sister Darling?" Shari heard the vaguely familiar male voice—definitely from the church.

"Can I help you?"

"This is Bishop Lundgren."

"Tami is with her father all summer. I thought you knew." Shari went to church with Tami, but she let everyone know she was there for Tami and had no personal interest in participating in church functions.

"Yeah ... I know. I would like to meet with you ... today if possible."

Shari's ward (like a Catholic parish) had the early block of time for Sunday meetings. Two other wards used the same building. "You know how I feel about the church. I don't think there's anything to talk about." Shari had no specific bone to pick with the church; it just did not mean anything to her anymore.

"It's not exactly about the church. I would much rather discuss this with you in person. It's important, or I wouldn't bother you."

"Something about Tami?"

"Sort of, but not exactly. I would really like to talk to you in person."

"What do you mean, 'not exactly'?"

"I can explain it all if we could just have some time to talk ... but not over the phone."

"What time?"

"How about two this afternoon?"

"How about one?" Shari had a perverse need to exert control over the bishop's day.

"Okay ... see ya at one." Shari hung the phone up. It was rude, but she could not think of a good closing remark.

The bishop arrived right at one o'clock. His first councilor, Brother Pritchard, was with him. Church leaders were discouraged from meeting with members alone—especially single women. Shari let the two men in. She dressed casually in slacks and a blouse. She invited them to sit down. "What did you want to talk to me about?"

"I know ... I guess we all know ... what a hard time you and Tami have had because of what Carl Paskel did."

"You do?" Shari wanted to sound sarcastic. The bishop's face showed she had succeeded.

"It was a very hard thing, and I know Tami is still in therapy. You know the Church Social Services provides counseling for members who need it. You can be sure all the treatments will be done in accordance with the principals of the Gospel."

"I'm very happy with the counseling we're getting now. Are you out drumming up business for the Church Social Services?" It was strange that the bishop would be showing concern now—over three years after the molestation had been disclosed.

"No ... of course not." The bishop sounded nervous. "The thing is, we feel that by working through the church you would stay closer to the Gospel, and you would know the work is being done through prayer and under priesthood direction."

"The damage was done by a priesthood holder."

"That's true, but you can't judge the whole church by the failings of one member."

"I'm not judging the church over what Carl did, but just because someone holds the priesthood doesn't mean he can do me any good either."

"I ... uh ... we didn't come to try to get you to change therapists. It was just a thought ... but if you already have someone you're happy with, then by all means stay with him."

"Her."

"Huh? Oh ... yeah ... well then, stick with her. You know ... whatever does you the most good."

Brother Pritchard sat dutifully on the couch with his mouth closed.

"So if you didn't come to get me to change therapists, why did you come?"

"Last night Bishop Alfred Fairley called me. He's Brother Paskel's bishop."

Shari was momentarily stunned. *Brother* Paskel! A mental picture of the rat came to her; she could almost smell the burning hair and flesh. "I've made it clear that I do not want to hear from him." She was surprised that she was afraid instead of angry. She had not expected Carl to use the church to get to her.

"I don't know if you knew this, but Brother Paskel has come into some money."

"I heard." Her response was cold.

"He realizes you and Tami have both been hurt by the things he did, and he wants to help make it right. He's offered to pay all of the therapy bills including a reimbursement for past costs."

As the reality of what was happening surfaced, the seeds of anger began to germinate in her. It felt good. "What does he want in return for this giant good deed?"

"No strings whatsoever. You tell him how much, and he'll send you a check."

"No."

The two men waited for an explanation. None came. "No?" the bishop finally ventured.

"No." Shari held the bishop's eyes and enjoyed it. It was almost as if he were afraid to ask why. "Well … if that's all." Shari stood up.

The bishop finally found his tongue. "Why wouldn't you accept assistance? He owes you and Tami, and he has a responsibility to help set things right."

Shari sat down. "My concern is to help Tami. It is not my concern to participate in Carl's charade of pretend remorse."

"I have not met the man, but after talking to his bishop, I'm confident he is sincerely remorseful. You realize that part of the repentance cycle is to make every effort to make amends to the person who was hurt."

"So what you're saying is that by accepting this money I would be helping him with his repentance."

"To an extent, but it would also help you."

"I'll be the judge of what helps me."

"Would it be so bad to accept his help?"

"You ever been raped?"

"You can't carry hate in your heart. People were killing and deriding Jesus, and he forgave them."

"He did? How do you know?"

"He said 'Father, forgive them, for they know not what they do.'"

"Not the same as saying, 'I forgive them.' Did his Father forgive them? Were they never held accountable for their sins? The rest of the quote says 'for they know not what they do.' Did Carl tell his bishop he didn't know what he was doing when he stuck his penis inside of an eight-year-old girl! Did he tell his bishop he didn't know what he was doing when he told the little girl he would kill her mother if she ever told anyone what he was doing! Did he tell his bishop that ..."

"Sister Darling ... please!" the bishop interrupted. "I don't think we need to go into that much detail."

"I'm glad to see you're shocked. But, you seem more shocked that I would tell you what happened than by the fact that *Broootheeer* Paskel actually did these things. I think if people would actually see in their mind what he did, they wouldn't be so quick to forgive."

"But he has repented of the things he did. There's no need to get sarcastic about it."

"God, I love this. *Broootheeer* Paskel molested my daughter from six years old till she was eight. Now he says he's sorry, and he's okay with the church, while I describe with words what he did, and you're warning me to be careful?"

"I am sorry. I certainly had no intention of upsetting you. I thought I was bringing good news, but I see I was mistaken."

"I'm never going to accept money he *chooses* to give me. He took the sense of power and control from both of us. He owes us big-time. If I were to sue him and force him to give me something he didn't want to give me, then I could feel power over him. If he gives me something voluntarily, then he still has the power."

"I'm not sure I understand. He's willing to make amends ... to provide the best help possible. Are you threatening to sue him because of that?"

"He's willing to spend some money he doesn't need on me so he can fool his bishop. He is, was, always will be a pervert. I'm making no threats, but you can tell his bishop to tell him to stay the hell away from me and Tami, and that we do not want him in our lives in any fashion. The reason I don't sue him is because I want him totally out of my life. If he's going to keep meddling in it, I might as well go ahead and sue him for all of his newfound riches. You know what I mean?"

"I don't know how to see that as anything but a threat."

"I want him out of my life!"

"Okay, I'll pass that on. But …"

"Thank you, Bishop. I think that's all I want to hear about Broootheeer Paskel." Shari walked the men to her door and closed it behind them. She was shaking … from fear or anger, she was not sure.

★ ★ ★

Shari was late for her meeting with Russell. When she walked in, he stood up from the table to greet her, but he did not make the mistake of offering his hand. Shari felt a twinge of excitement instead of revulsion. Warning bells went off in her head.

"I got your rewrite of the second chapter. At least you left in that I felt bad about what I did." Russell took his seat.

"I didn't do much really. This is your book." Shari knew she had chopped it up, but she wasn't about to admit it.

"Does that mean you're going to quit on me?"

"If I quit, I will be quitting Saundrea's assignment … not you. I'm not here for you. I'm here only because she wants me here. I don't give a damn about you or your book."

"You're still pretty hostile." Russell pushed a folder to her. "Here's chapter three."

"Why don't you just mail these to me, and I can mail my comments back? It would save me a lot of time. I don't like coming here." Even as she said the words, she hoped he would not agree. *What is it about this man? Why should I care?*

Russell ignored her suggestion. "I have some questions about the changes you made and the approach to the work I'm doing now." They talked about several points, and Shari made some suggestions. She was surprised when she checked her watch as they discussed the final point. Forty-five minutes had gone by, and it seemed like only ten. She was even more surprised to find she had enjoyed it. Russell's questions were well thought out, and he was responsive to her suggestions. "Have you had any more feelings about Carl?" *Oh damn! The last thing I wanted was to start that up again!*

"I don't want to scare you ... but ... I do want to make you be very careful."

"Did you know he's going to church regularly, and he's working as a janitor in spite of the fact that he's a millionaire?"

"I know all that. And I know he donated about fifteen percent of his newfound fortune to the church for tithes and other offerings. Big deal ... he can afford it. I'm keeping track of him ... you can be sure of that."

"How? You're stuck in here."

"I have contacts on the outside."

"I just don't see how Carl can be doing anything like you're suggesting. It looks like he's making an effort to change. And he's putting his money where his mouth is."

"Come on, Shari. It's all so easy to make a show of spirituality. First you fool the preacher. The congregation thinks their leader is somehow more spiritual, closer to God, and so they think the guy must be okay if the preacher thinks he's okay. If you can fool the preacher, you get real credibility to whatever lie you put out. The funny thing is that the preacher wants to feel he's doing God's work, so he's predisposed to look for the best. And then he gets all caught up in the thing and wants to think he's making a difference. So the preacher is the easiest to fool. He gets a vested interest in the outcome. A preacher is the last person I would trust when it comes to knowing if a sinner has really turned over a new leaf. It's even worse than a shrink ... who, by the way, has the same vested interest in seeing success. Carl's bishop has absolutely no training in human behavior, but he believes he has some supernatural inspiration by virtue of his priesthood that lets him know these things. And the congregation believes he has that inspiration too."

"You think you know Carl better than his bishop?"

"Oh, no question about that. Carl was very open with me, but there is another tie I have to him … something … I don't know what it is, but it's getting stronger."

"The bishop says he's inspired by the Holy Ghost, and you say you have some psychic power; it's all magic to me. I stopped believing in magic when Santa Claus turned out to be a lie."

"The mind is the most powerful tool in the world. Do you believe that?"

The power of the mind to heal had been a topic more than once in Shari's therapy. "It may be powerful … a lot of people say so, but it doesn't work that way for me."

"It's not easy to tap into that power. It's often buried in layers of doubts and fears. Anyone can break through those things, but it takes effort and time. You have to relax and believe. There may be a time when you will need to tap into that power. If that day comes, remember to relax and believe. You will be surprised at how powerful you are.

"I have a lot of free time in here. I spend a great deal of that time in meditation. I've studied and thought about a great deal in my life, but I've never taken time to really practice it. Now I have nothing but time to relax and get in touch with my mental powers. You hear there's a purpose to everything. So maybe the whole purpose for me to be here was to meet Carl and find a way to stop him. If that's the case, then all that has happened to me makes sense. Some of this is new to me, but I'm still sure Carl is putting on a show. Something life changing has happened to him … I'm sure of it."

"You know Detective Tom DeMayo, don't you?" Shari watched for his reaction. Her knowledge was a surprise, as she had expected.

"Yeah."

"He arrested you, didn't he?"

"You knew that before you brought his name up. What has he got to do with this?"

"He arrested Carl too."

"I knew that, so what?"

"Tom happens to be a friend of mine."

"Just a friend?"

"Yeah ... something wrong with that?" Shari was enjoying this.

"No ... in fact I'd say that's good."

Good? "I've talked to Tom, and he's going to keep an eye on things. He has also talked to Carl's parole officer, and they've made it clear to him that I don't want any contact with him."

"I'm glad you're taking precautions. You can't be too careful, but Carl's ignoring the warnings. He's looking for a back door ... someway to bypass the order and make contact."

A hot flash went through Shari's face and neck. Was Russell referring to Carl's attempt to make contact through the church, and if so, how did he know? Shari told Russell about the visit from her bishop.

"You did the right thing. He's not going to like that you have shown strength. That will confuse him. He thinks of you as a weak person. He's quite wrong there."

Something in Russell's voice nearly choked Shari up. She managed to answer him with a clear voice. "I don't feel strong ... I feel afraid and talking to you makes it worse."

"Trust me ... refusing Carl was a strong action, and it was strong for the right reasons."

Shari was grateful for Russell's immediate and unreserved support, attracted to him for some reason she could not explain, and resentful about having those feelings. It was confusing, and she wanted to get away from this personal discussion. Almost without thinking she blurted, "You heard about the girl who was killed?" *Oops! That's another subject I didn't want to bring up with him.*

"Only that she was found in the canyon, and that she was raped. Carl did it. I think that first feeling I had was that he had killed someone."

"This just happened last week."

"I know that. I think this is the second ... or maybe even the third or fourth. There's something he's working toward, and when he gets to it, he'll come for you. We've got to catch him first."

The picture of the rat came back. Shari began to shake. She hoped Russell would not notice. Suddenly, Shari had to get out! "I've got to be going now." She quickly packed up her recorder.

"Okay, but be careful."

As she drove away from the prison, a cold envelope of evil seemed to be reaching to engulf her and Tami.

Conquering the Ever-Widening Circle
Chapter Three: The Circle Expands

When I was about eleven years old and heavily involved with my friend in destructive behavior, there were nights when he couldn't come out. On those nights I would spend hours creeping around alleys and backyards looking through windows. Sometimes I would see a woman getting ready for bed. I kept a record of the times and places so I could return. Soon I had a list of places to go. I looked for girls and women from puberty up to about thirty years old. I developed a fantasy in which a girl would see me watching and invite me in. In my fantasy the girl would do a striptease, and then we would have sex. She would invite me back, and I would return often for a private show.

Some of the women I watched seemed to parade around in front of the window, as if they were intentionally putting on a show. If there was ever a chance of having my fantasy come true, it would be with one of these women. Occasionally, I would move around in front of the window of a woman like that to reveal I was watching. Generally, the woman would scream and cover up.

When I was fifteen, after I had given up destructive behavior and shoplifting, I had been watching a particular woman for a couple of weeks. She always went through a sexy little dance routine as she undressed in front of her open window. Finally, one night I moved up to her open window and leaned in with my elbows on the windowsill. When she noticed me, she gave a startled little scream and then smiled. I said, "Hi," and I prepared to make a run for it.

"Hi," she answered. "You like my show?"

"Yeah, you're a good dancer."

"You really think so? Why don't you come in where you can see better?"

"Uh ... I don't know," I answered. I was afraid, but I did not know why.

"Aw, come on. I'll give you a real good show. Then maybe we can give each other a good time." She winked as she talked and crooked her finger at me in a "come on" jester. This was my fantasy come true; but instead of climbing through the window, I ran away as fast as I could, and I never went back to that house again. I don't know why I did not pursue my fantasy when it was right there for me. Over the years I retained the fantasy that my voyeurism would lead to something more intimate, and on a few occasions similar opportunities presented themselves. In spite of those opportunities, in no case did I ever go beyond looking through windows.

At the age of fifteen, I was spending two or three nights per month prowling around the neighborhoods of Ogden looking for windows where I could get a show. Between episodes I felt guilt and shame. At varying intervals, I would fall into a depression and make promises and commitments to myself to quit. I could never understand why this thing had such power over me. At the times when I made the attempts to stop, I really felt I could just stop. I was always surprised and disappointed in myself when I started the behavior again.

On the night of graduation from high school, my life was in front of me. I had gone to the honor banquet and graduated in the top of my class. I had taken the most advanced courses in math and business. I planned to go on to get a degree in college. My life was planned and progressing in order. I was preparing to go on a mission for the Mormon Church before starting college. I was aware of my problem with voyeurism, but I perceived it as being serious only if caught, and I believed I could stop when I was ready. I was headed into the challenge of my future. I had no idea how powerful the tiger was whose tail I held.

★ ★ ★

After Shari finished working on the last chapter from Russell, she put the manuscript up, walked to the bathroom, and turned on the water in the tub. She walked to her bedroom and took her clothes off. In spite of a good build and a pretty face, she was home alone because of her fear of choosing another loser.

Her therapist had talked to her many times about living in the present. She said Shari spent too much time resenting the past and worrying about the future. Shari turned the water off in the tub and prepared to get in. Ralph and Carl had both soaked in that same tub. Shari let the water out of the tub and went back to her room. *This is stupid. Are you going to stop bathing just because of these crazy feelings?* She sat on the bed in her robe.

During her younger years she looked to the church as her anchor point. Back then she would go to her bishop for advice, believing he could tell her how to solve her problems. The bishop told her to take Carl's money, forgive him, and go back to church. Russell would tell her to prepare to fight Carl. Tom would tell her to marry him and let him do the worrying.

"What do *you* say?" Shari asked herself out loud. The sound of her voice startled her. The answer startled her even more. "To start with, I'm selling this house." That would not solve her problems or resolve the question of what to do about Carl, but it would be a present-time action and would do for starters. Shari went back to the bathroom and filled the tub with warm water again. It was the best bath she had enjoyed in months. She did not see the man in the shadows outside her window.

Chapter Four

THE GAUNTLET

The man sat in the room looking at the pictures of Barbelo. He stroked his penis, but it was still sore. A week had passed since he had sent Barbelo to heaven. He left the room and drove to a neighborhood he had been scouting near Liberty Park. The houses had garages at the back of their lots, which opened to alleys. He parked his car and walked a block and a half to the alley he had selected. Several garbage cans lined the sides of the alley; one of which was turned over. The faint smell of rotting meat permeated the air. The man felt at home in this shadowy world of late evening.

Four houses down, he silently climbed on the roof of a detached garage. From the garage to the house was about thirty feet. The house had a window about two and a half feet high by six feet wide. From his vantage point, high on the peak of the garage and relatively close to the window, the man could look down into the room.

It was about time for the girl to go to bed. He had his binoculars, but this time he also had the new video camera he had purchased yesterday. The most important features were clarity of the picture and power of the zoom lens. He wanted to get every eyelash, every wrinkle and fold of skin. He would watch the movies of this girl until he was ready to get her. Then he would make her watch the movies while he did her.

He crawled under the branches of the apricot tree that hung over the garage. He sat up a small tripod for the camera. He had put a piece of tape over the red light on the front. He could see the single bed on the opposite wall from the window. Above it was a Disney poster of Cinderella with her mice and bird friends. When he zoomed in, he could see every line and detail of the poster through the viewfinder. *This will be perfect on a big screen TV.*

When he first found her three days ago, the girl had undressed and playfully romped around naked as her mother tried to get her pajamas on her. There was something about her black skin that really turned him on. One day he would get her to his room and completely explore her. He would make movies of her bedtime rituals until it was time to take her.

The man pulled his shorts off—he wore no underwear. It felt good to have the cool evening breezes blowing on his sore penis. He picked an almost ripe apricot and ate it, savoring the tartness in his mouth. The light in the bedroom of the house next door went on. *Hello, old witch. I wondered where you were. Okay, flop 'em out.* He raised his binoculars but did not move the camera. A woman in her mi fifties was in the bedroom undressing. He had seen her before. He was not interested in making a movie of her. She could not excite him.

She took her blouse off. Underneath was a white bra. She had short dark hair, probably died. With his binoculars, he could see the skin on her face had begun to show the leathery signs of too much sun. He looked down her neck to her chest. The skin above and below her bra was smooth and white. He could not see her lower body from the garage. He could get a perfect view by climbing the cherry tree in her yard, but he was not interested in her.

When she removed the bra, her large breasts hung from her chest. The man was not interested in breasts, but he felt powerful watching her without her knowing it. She stood in front of the window. After a couple of minutes, she left the room; he suspected to take a shower. He knew she would be back in about fifteen minutes all flushed. *Do you diddle yourself in there?*

As predicted, she returned drying herself with a pink towel. When she was through, she stood looking out the window—almost as if she knew someone was watching. Then she put on a nightgown and left the room.

From his perch on the garage he looked back to the girl's bed. Her mother usually left a night-light on, which made it possible to watch the girl sleeping. Where was she? It was getting past her bedtime. He had been on the roof for almost an hour. Finally, the girl and her mother came in. The girl was talking loudly. "Please mom ... it's so hot."

"You can use our fan. You heard the news. There's a bad man somewhere in the city. We have to be careful. We're going to keep your window closed from now on. I mean it Asura, don't you open it after I leave." The woman walked over to the window, closed it, set the latch, and closed the curtain.

You fucking bitch; open the curtain! Fuck! Fuck! Fuck! The man almost screamed out loud. It was not fair! He had the camera this time! A whole night was wasted! Why had the bitch done that now? *And she's closing it from now on? Bitch! Bitch! Bitch!* He put his pants back on, and packed his camera and binoculars.

"Goddamn fuck!" he shouted, pounding on the steering wheel of his car as he drove away. He got home in time for the ten o'clock news. A police news release came on saying there may be a serial killer in the area and warning parents to close and lock their children's windows. The man spoke out loud to the TV, "DeMayo, you fucking bastard son of a bitch! So this is how you want to play? You're going to be so fucking sorry! You can't stop me. I'll get even with you, you fuck face."

The man got up, kicked the couch—too hard—and limped to his desk. "Fucking, meddling bastard." He picked up his pen and a clean sheet of paper.

* * *

Shari slept fitfully the night after her decision to sell the house. Visions of Carl came and went. He laughed at her, as though his inability to have sex with a woman was a sign of strength. Then she saw him on the bed with Tami. His perversion gave him power over the weak and innocent. Shari lay awake trying to drive the vision away. Evil, heartless cruelty—that was it! God help anyone who fell in his control. He chose little girls and small animals to dominate, but could he direct his cruelty to adults? Then she got up and called Tom.

"Hi, Shari. How're things going?"

"Tom, I had another meeting with Russell. I need to talk to you about it."

"He still telling you the killer is Carl?"

"He said a lot of things that make a lot of sense. I don't know for sure if this killer is Carl, but I would like to talk about it."

"Well, what did he say?" His tone showed interest, which Shari appreciated.

"I don't want to talk about it over the phone. Could we do dinner tonight?"

"What time and where?"

"My place at six thirty? And could you bring the poems?" This was the first time she had invited Tom to her house for dinner.

"Sure."

* * *

DeMayo found Piszczek's profile on his desk when he got to work. The task force had a meeting scheduled for nine thirty.

KATRINA SOPKOV CASE
SUSPECT PROFILE

Sex: Male
Race: White
Age: Thirties
Marital Status: Single or divorced — problems w/women
Military: Possibly
Occupation: People job w/o structure — salesman
IQ: 120 or more
Childhood: Abused — probably tortured animals
Criminal Record: Has served time in prison or an institution
Personality: Pedophile — Domineering — Egotistical
Religion: Mormon — probably active
Car: Large, dark color — Crown Victoria or similar
Accomplices: Loner, very doubtful more than one UNSUB
Victims: Girls & maybe boys under eight years old
Comments: He is getting more organized and better at what he does. He will kill until we catch him. He may leave the area when he senses we are getting close.

by Dr. David Adam Piszczek, PhD

Piszczek would not have been given any information about any suspects in the case so it would not color his evaluation of the evidence. Most of the attributes fit Richards to a T. DeMayo could have predicted that much, but nothing in the report would help them find him. At nine fifteen, a messenger brought DeMayo another envelope addressed to detective hold-the-mayo. DeMayo put on a pair of gloves and carefully opened the envelope. Inside he found another poem.

The Impotent Stalker

Take care Tom!
    Consider what it is you have taken from me,
        what you try to steal from me now.
Freedom soaring Falcon!
    I have it inherent in my nature from God.
        I hold it by my great power.
Anahita, first Angel
    brought majestic vocation from Divinity.
        I found the power to fulfill it.
Pancia, born Pure.
    A stare and magic evoked the sword from Heaven
        but I pushed it through to conquest.
Raun, your Riddle.
    Destroyer, insurgent—but not from creation,
        proudly displays dark black feathers.
Barbelo, perfect Beauty.
    Together we mapped that human knowledge from flesh
        and shared the blazing light of death.

See the world of color, taste, sound, touch, smell.
    Experience it to the fullest.
But Bat Qol has forfeited power to experience
    the abundant Glory of Earth.
I dream the perfect restoration—bringing
    full embrace with the source of pleasure.
But know this—that the Celestial Kingdom
    is not there for everyone.
Anahita and Barbelo flew to those heights.
    Others must sink to my abyss.
Hold-the-mayo—sandwich man—intermediate man,
    not the top or the bottom bread.

An easy toy for me to taunt and tease.
    You like your power?
A marionette dancing and jerking on my strings,
    powerless to stop my hallowed work!

My plans include my just revenge
    made for you.
My payback is infinite
    recompense for all.
Worms and rot disintegrate the prize.
    Satisfaction is for God.
You and all your legions
    come for me.

Come! Be Disappointed!

Abaddon/Apollyon

DeMayo could feel Richards getting right in his face. This poem mentioned three other possible victims—Pancia, Raun, and Bat Qol. The new names blew the theory that Abaddon was going through the alphabet. He made copies to distribute to all the members of the task force, and then called the lab to pick the poem up.

    At 9:25, DeMayo grabbed a cup of coffee and headed to the conference room. Alexander and Peterson were both sitting at the table going over the latest poem. "Jesus, DeMayo, what the hell did you do to piss him off so much?" Alexander tapped the poem with the middle finger of his right hand.

    "Looks like he wants to make a fool of me."

    "More like he wants to kill you," Piszczek said as he walked in. He was just a little overweight and in his late forties. He had a soft face with very hard eyes. The contrast was intriguing. He shook hands with everyone in the room and then put his files at the head of the table. He carefully took hold of the crease on each of his pant legs just above the knees and pulled them up about an inch as he sat down.

"I'd like to see him try," DeMayo said.

"I don't think you really want that." Piszczek opened his file and spread three sheets of paper in front of him. "The unsub is toying with us now, but if he senses we're closing in, he'll strike out at DeMayo. He's probably already figured exactly how he'll do it. It won't be in a way you would expect. I suppose everyone has had a chance to go over the profile. Why don't we go through that before we get into this new poem?"

"Okay," DeMayo said. "I'm new at this, so maybe I'll ask some dumb questions. To start with, how do you know it's a male?"

"This whole business of profiling criminals is as much an art as it is a science. Now, the object is to try to get into the criminal's head to see the crime from his point of view. I do that based upon the evidence, past experience, acquired skill, and sometimes intuition. In the end, all these things are probabilities. Now, most of them will be right on, but some could be wrong. So you can never take just one thing by itself. You have to take the package and see who fits most of the description. That can point to an unsub, but the evidence has to prove the case."

"Excuse me … what's an unsub?" DeMayo asked.

"In profiling we call the suspect an unknown subject or unsub for short. The main clues that the unsub is male come from 'Out of the Abyss.' The unsub makes a statement about his mother sacrificing her son to the father. Then after describing how his father abused him, he tells us it's better to be the father than the son. Now, in this poem, he mentions a father, a mother, and himself … no siblings. That leads me to believe he's an only child.

"Race is one of those things you'll have to trust me on. The majority of serial killers are white males. I put his age at somewhere in his thirties. Now, he kept the girl for two days and raped her several times and in several ways, indicating he is acting out a well-developed fantasy; generally that level of development is not seen before the age of about thirty.

"I judge him to be single because of his complete lack of empathy for the girl. This attitude would carry over to his intimate relationships and make it highly unlikely that he would have a stable relationship with a woman. He has either never been married, or he is divorced or separated.

"Now, most serial killers don't do well in the military. Either they never join or they don't last too long. However, this unsub is highly organized, so it's possible he could have gotten through the military, but he would not have excelled in it. He would have an occupation that allowed him a lot of freedom. Something like a door-to-door salesman. Now, in public he would be pleasant, glib, and outgoing. However, in his private life, he would be domineering. He would especially have problems in intimate relationships with women.

"He is much higher than average in intelligence. This will make it difficult to catch him. And for your edification," Piszczek looked at DeMayo, "I wouldn't want to have him after me."

"Maybe so, but if we could get him to come after me, we might trap him."

"Sometimes we do get proactive. We'll look at that as the case progresses. Now, in 'Anahita' he talks about being sent back. I believe that refers to prison. However, we can't rule out the possibility he's talking about a mental institution."

"Why is prison a more likely possibility?" Alexander asked.

"He's a pedophile, so it's likely he has been arrested for child molestation. He would go to prison for that. However, murder is a new expansion of his fantasy."

"How do you know that?" DeMayo asked.

"The first killing was an accident. He was trying to control the girl, not kill her. In 'Anahita,' he talks about a disguise, which indicates he planned to let the girl go when he was through. Now, after the killing he recognizes that his soul is damned. Until the first killing, he was holding back on the full expression of his fantasy. We see in the 'Out of the Abyss' line 'others soon will too' that he has realized Anahita's death has actually freed him to go after others."

"If this was a well-developed fantasy, why didn't he act it out on Anahita?" DeMayo asked.

"The fantasy is there for years, but the unsub does not act it out until something in his environment pushes him over a boundary. It could be the loss of a job, the loss of a relationship through break-up or death ... anything like that. We call that a stressor. Now, in this case it seems the unsub was holding back over fear of damnation. The death of Anahita made that fear irrelevant."

"What happens if there never is a stressor?" DeMayo asked.

"Without a stressor the fantasy is not fulfilled."

"So you're saying that if there is no stressor, a potential killer will be okay?" Alexander asked.

"A potential killer may fail to fully develop into a killer if he's lucky. But once the decision is made to kill the victims, the sexual acts will extend to the full level of the fantasy. The unsub probably has a past history of pedophilia, but it didn't rise to the level of violence that we see with Katie. The victims in this case have been girls, but it's not uncommon for pedophiles to seek out both sexes.

"Now, his knowledge of Mormon doctrine regarding children and the celestial kingdom indicates he's probably a Mormon, and he'll be active as part of his cover. He'll drive a dark car similar to the cars used by the police department. I say this because most serial killers operate from a need to control others. Many of them have tried to be policemen, or they hang out with policemen. I doubt he would have accomplices, in spite of the clear reference to a possible accomplice in the Barbelo poem. My gut feeling is he's a loner.

"As a pedophile, he would be attracted to children up to puberty. His poems indicate he views himself as doing his victims a favor by killing them before they turn eight. So he will prefer kids under eight.

"Well, gentlemen, that was my report before getting this last poem. How about we take a short break, and then we can get into the new poem and questions."

"I'm for that," Alexander agreed. "We'll meet back here in fifteen minutes."

★ ★ ★

"So what does this new poem add?" Alexander asked after everyone had returned to their seats.

"Quite a lot" Piszczek said. "There are three distinct parts. Now, in the first part, the first line of each stanza contains three words. The first and last word are capitalized and begin with the same letter. The second line always ends with a prepositional phrase using the preposition from; from God ... from divinity ... from heaven and so on. It begins with a salutation to DeMayo where he refers to something DeMayo stole from him and something he wants to steal from him now. In the next stanza, he talks of freedom ... something he got from God and holds by superhuman power. I believe freedom is the thing DeMayo stole, and it is what he is trying to steal now."

"Someone I arrested in the past," DeMayo commented. "Someone I am trying to arrest again."

"That makes sense. Now, in the rest of the first part he talks of four victims: Anahita, Pancia, Raun, and Barbelo. I believe these are people he has killed, and they are given in the order he killed them. I agree with DeMayo that Charlene Gonzales is most likely Anahita. We know Barbelo is Katie Sopkov."

"What about the other two?" Alexander asked. "We don't have any other young girls reported missing."

"We get a clue about that in the second part of the poem where it states that Anahita and Barbelo flew to the heights of the Celestial Kingdom and implies there are others that must sink to his abyss. What does that mean about Pancia and Raun?"

"They must have been over eight years old because they don't automatically go to the Celestial Kingdom," DeMayo said.

"I'm pretty sure you're right; they're probably over eight. Now, the poem says Pancia evoked the sword with a stare and magic. I think pushing the sword through to conquest describes a rape. The stare and magic probably refer to his thinking she was flirting with him. He's a pedophile, which implies that because she excited him, she had not yet gone all the way through puberty. I think Pancia is a girl, or possibly a boy, around nine to twelve because so many children that age go missing and many have not gone through puberty. This act happened on impulse, because he was not acting on his fantasy."

"How so?" DeMayo asked.

"Part of the fantasy is to write a detailed poem about the act. In these two cases, they are just mentioned in a poem about the big picture."

"I don't think a twelve-year-old kid flirts with a thirty-something-year-old man." Peterson said.

"Neither do I, but it's not a question of what we think. Pedophiles often think children find them sexy. Almost any look from a child could be interpreted by the unsub as flirting.

"Now, that brings us to Raun. Raun is a destroyer, but not from creation, the poem says. It's as if she was created for one thing and acted against her creation to destroy something. Now, this could be any number of things, but the first thing that comes to my mind would be an abortion. Black feathers could refer to more than one act of destruction. Now, if my guess is correct, Raun would be someone he knew well enough to know she'd had more than one abortion. I say we look at missing person reports for someone in late teens to early twenties who has had multiple abortions. There is no indication of anything sexual about Raun."

"That might not even be information we can find. A lot of people have abortions without advertising it to their friends and families," Peterson said.

"No one said this was going to be easy. So summarizing: Anahita was killed by accident, we know this. Pancia most likely was an impulse killing. It appears Raun was killed out of the unsub's sense of justice. I don't believe any of these three killings fulfilled his fantasy."

"How can you know that?" DeMayo asked.

"The Barbelo poem starts out with the statement, 'a perfect one is needed.' Now, I think that indicates that although he has had three victims, none of them was perfect; none of them fulfilled his fantasy completely. He talks about teaching Barbelo many things. We see from the evidence on her body what those things were. He also states she fulfilled all his fantasies. He killed Barbelo by putting his mouth over her mouth and slowly suffocating her ... probably masturbating while he did it. He allowed her enough air to live until he finished his orgasm. That's what he meant by mingling his breath with hers. The ritualistic raping and killing of the victim is his signature. The other three victims lack the signature actions."

"What do you mean by signature?" DeMayo asked.

"In reviewing the specific actions of a crime, some are modi operandi or MOs. The MO actions are things that have to be done in order to commit the crime. An MO might change as the criminal gets more sophisticated or as circumstances dictate. Signature actions are those parts of the crime that form the reason for the crime. For instance, with this unsub, the age of the victim, the idea that he is teaching the victim through the ritualistic rape, mingling his breath with the victim as he suffocates her, cleaning her, buying new clothes, and leaving her body in the mountains are the reasons he commits the crime. Though the MO may change, the signature will remain the same fundamental series of actions.

"Suppose Abaddon's reason for killing his victims was so they could never identify him. That would be a modus operandi action. It wouldn't make much difference how it was done. He might suffocate the victim, or shoot her, or whatever was most handy. It could change from crime to crime. Now, if killing the victim was part of the thrill of the crime, it would be ritualized in some way and not change. Abaddon tells us he is mingling his breath with that of the victim ... a ritual. That's his fantasy ... the reason he committed the crime. I expect from now until he is caught, his killings will have the signature rituals he performed on Barbelo.

"Now, the second part of the poem is directed at DeMayo personally. That leads us to the possibility that Bat Qol might be another name for DeMayo, but the peculiar use of the letter Q could indicate it's an acronym for something about DeMayo."

"What else?" Alexander asked.

"The third section of the poem consists of four, two-line stanzas. The last two words of each stanza are prepositional phrases having an increasing hierarchy of the object. First it's 'for you,' referring to DeMayo. Then it goes up to 'for all.' Then up to 'for God.' But he doesn't end there. He adds one more line with 'for me,' referring to himself. Now, I don't think that's accidental. In his mind, he puts himself above God.

"Now, this last poem is angry. He's threatening DeMayo directly. He has taken the gloves off, and that makes me wonder … what has happened since the last poem?"

"Well, we have put together the task force," DeMayo observed.

"He would have expected that. He would have also expected the news would report on the death of Katie when her body was found, but there may be something unexpected in the news release. Could we get a copy of that?"

"I have a copy right here," Peterson said as she shuffled through her files. "Yes, here it is." She handed it to Piszczek.

Piszczek studied the news release. It stated that Dale Richards was wanted for questioning regarding the murder of Katrina Sopkov. The article included a picture of Richards. Piszczek had known the department had a suspect, but he did not know anything about Dale Richards.

"Okay," Piszczek began when he had finished the news release, "he hasn't sent any of his poems to the news media. He doesn't want to taunt the public. Now, assuming this Richards guy is our man, I think he may be angry that we put his picture in the paper, and he may be angry that we have already discovered he's the unsub."

"Okay," Alexander interjected, "Richards is a very good suspect. He disappeared the same time Katie was reported missing. We need to find this guy before he gets another victim." Alexander looked directly at Piszczek. "Have you got anything that will tell us where he's located?"

"I understand Katie's funeral and burial were watched closely. I suggest a twenty-four hour watch be put on the grave. Chances are pretty good he will visit it sometime. He feels a connection to her … like he had something to do with her salvation. Also put a watch around her house. Also, since we have a definite suspect, we should try to find out if anyone he knows or is related to has had abortions and is missing."

"Well, what else have you got to help us?" DeMayo asked.

"I would like some time to look at Richards's background and history. Perhaps there's something specific there. Give me a day or two."

"Someone may die in a day or two." DeMayo stood up, looking down at Piszczek.

"I'll have something tomorrow morning. Now if you'll excuse me, gentlemen, I have work to do." Piszczek stood up, picked up his notes, and walked past DeMayo on his way out.

★ ★ ★

Tom knocked on Shari's door right at six thirty. He was dressed casually with olive-green pleated pants and a baby-blue polo shirt. Shari could not help noticing how handsome he was. She served the dinner of pork chops, corn of the cob, tossed green salad, and homemade dinner rolls while Tom opened and poured two glasses of the wine he had brought. There was some ritual to it Shari did not quite understand because of her Mormon background. "Thanks for the invite. The food really smells good," Tom said. "I guess you know how ... I mean, well, I've wanted to tell you for some time how much I have come to like you. You know ..."

"Don't, Tom. Uhm ... this is kind of hard, but ... right now there's no room in my life for anything romantic."

"Why not? You're still young. You have a great deal of life ahead of you. You can't just spend it alone."

"Tom, I've had some real bad luck with men in the past."

"I know, but you can't just curl up and hide from life because of a couple of mistakes. You are the most important thing in my life, and well, I hate to see you just living so ... alone."

"I'm not alone; that's just it. I have Tami, and everything I do affects her. These mistakes are more than just minor goofs that have hurt me. They have hurt Tami too. Nothing I do is done in a vacuum."

"That's right. But deciding to live alone is a decision too. It's deciding on the kind of example Tami will see as far as relationships are concerned. It's not showing her how to make a relationship work."

"I'm beginning to think I don't know how to do that. I'm afraid anything I could teach her would just be a worse example."

"Then what are you going to do? You can't put both your lives on hold indefinitely; sometime you have to decide, or the lack of a decision will decide for you."

"I know that, but right now is just not the time."

"I know where you're coming from. After JoLynn was killed, I put my life on hold. Partly because I was afraid I might lose again if I ever took a chance. But even more, it was like I would be untrue to her if I ever let myself have feelings for anyone else. It has taken me a long time, but as I look back, I wish I had dug myself out sooner. The only plus is that by waiting I found you, but you don't have to take as long as I did."

"Thank you ... maybe someday you might be surprised. Anyway, let's eat while the food is hot."

"I'll go for that." Tom started on a pork chop. "So what's new?"

"Did you know Carl is trying to contact me through the church?"

"You're kidding!"

"Nope. I had a visit from my bishop Sunday. Carl wants to give me money for Tami's therapy."

"Carl contacted your bishop?"

"Nope, it seems Carl's bishop called my bishop. Carl is trying to go through the steps of repentance, and one of the steps is to try to undo all the wrong he did ... as if that's even possible. So now he wants me to participate in his little deception."

"You told the bishop no, didn't you?"

"In no uncertain terms. Did you talk to Carl about Katie?"

"Yes. He has an alibi."

"What is it?"

"Well, we know that the killer had Katie Saturday, Sunday, and then killed her Monday morning. He took the body up the canyon on

Monday around noon. Carl has no alibi for Saturday. He says he was home most of day, and he did a little shopping, but no one can verify that. Sunday he was in church meetings all day."

"The church doesn't have meetings all day."

"Yeah, I know, but he had Sunday services, meetings with the stake president and the bishop, and he took the bishop and his family out to dinner. That doesn't account for every second, but it does cover most of the time. But most important, on Monday he was at work from eight thirty till six thirty, according to his boss and the time clock he has to punch."

"So you think there's no way he could do it?"

"Everything just points in another direction."

"And you don't think Carl could be leading you on?"

"Well, if it is him, he's the best actor I've ever seen. He didn't have any resentment about me checking up on him and his alibi. He was straightforward. He said he realizes that he will be a suspect for sex-related crimes until he can prove himself. He took it as a matter of fact ... not loaded down with emotion about it."

"So basically you're saying he's either innocent or he's a good actor. Is that about it?"

"I've seen a lot of criminals in my day ... some very good ones. This would be the best. According to the poems, this perp is very hostile to me personally. I would have sensed some of that from Carl if he was the one."

Shari walked to the sink. "Did you bring the poems?"

"You still want to look at them?"

"I talked with Russell again yesterday. He's still sure it's Carl."

"You mean he still has those feelings about Carl?"

"Isn't that what you just said about yourself?"

"What do you mean?"

"You just said you would have sensed it if Carl was lying. That's like having a feeling about it ... isn't it?"

"Feeling based on experience and evidence, and I talked to his boss and saw the time card."

"Let me just give you some of the experience and evidence Russell is talking about." Shari walked back to the table and put her hands palm down leaning forward. "Number one, he knew something terrible had happened before there was any news out about the first girl. Number two, he says Carl killed Katie and some others you don't know about yet. Number three, before Katie was killed, he told me …"

"He told you Carl had already killed some others or that he would kill more?"

"He said there are more already, and that there will be even more if we don't catch him. Have you found more bodies?"

Tom was sitting straight in his chair and had stopped eating. "Not exactly, but we did get another poem that implies he has killed two others. We can't confirm that because there are no bodies."

Once again the cold underlying fear moved to Shari's consciousness. "He also knew Carl was trying to make contact with me through unconventional methods before I said anything about the bishop. Another thing … he said people like Carl are very good at fooling people."

"I know, but it's much harder for them to fool someone with experience. I won't say that I can't be fooled, but it's pretty hard to do. This Russell guy says that Carl has done something, and he's going to do something. That isn't much help." Tom began to eat some of the corn.

"What about the other victims he knew about?" Shari sat down.

"Maybe there is a psychic connection after all, but he's missing the boat about who it is?"

"Russell seems pretty sure it's Carl."

"I know, but he hasn't produced any information that we didn't already have."

"That's true, but he got it independently … and he says the pictures are getting stronger."

"Okay, let's just go through the profile." Tom put his briefcase on the table and gave Shari a copy of the profile summary.

"Oh my God! This is Carl. This is almost a perfect fit."

"Well, it misses on a couple of important points. It says he would have a job without structure, but he has purposefully taken a job that is very structured. He has a small red car rather than a big black one. And then there's the poetry. Carl doesn't have much of a background in literature."

"He doesn't? How would you know?"

"Well, we checked his high school records. He didn't do well in literature."

"That's interesting, because he has several books on poetry, which he used to read to me. How does this fit the other man?"

"Well, English literature was Richards's best subject in high school ... though you would never guess it listening to the way he talks now. We know he has used violence on young girls before. On the other hand, he's not an active Mormon, and from all appearances he isn't organized ... at least his apartment was a mess."

"I think it's Carl, Tom."

"Do you know if Carl has scars from cigarette burns under his arms?"

"No, not unless they have faded. Why do you ask?"

"That's all in the poems." Tom put the copies of the poems on the table in front of Shari. She read each of them. At times her eyes watered as she was reading. "Tom this is terrible. I had no idea. As I read these, I keep getting a picture of Carl torturing that rat. He really enjoyed it."

"These murders were terrible, but there's nothing to indicate the killer tortured them ... not for the pleasure of seeing pain at least. He raped Katie, and I know that was torture for her, but torture wasn't the motive. There is nothing to indicate that he got pleasure from the pain he inflicted."

"I still can't get the picture out of my mind that Carl is doing this, but the second poem about Ozzie and Harriet doesn't match him. I know he was abused and hung in a dark room, but the abuse didn't involve all the other stuff in the poem. He didn't have cigarette burns ... I'm pretty sure of that, and I don't think his dad beat his mother. Maybe you're right. Russell may be mistaken about who the killer is. What do these names mean?"

Tom explained the various speculations they had regarding each of the names.

"Do you mind if I copy the names and see what I can find out about them?" Shari had only picked at her dinner. Now, she completely forgot about the food.

"Are you trying to play detective?"

"I've done some detective work for my articles. In fact, I bet I can find what they mean in two days max."

"Okay, you're on."

Shari copied all the names. "Apollyon ... I think I've heard that name before ... maybe from mythology. I think I'm going to solve this part of the case by tomorrow. But the bet is still two days."

"If this isn't Carl, why are you so interested in the case?"

"I feel helpless and afraid all the time. I'm thinking maybe if I do something that will help catch this animal ... I can't explain it, but something inside me will not rest if I don't do something. And besides, I'm still not sure it isn't Carl ... not yet."

"I can understand that." Tom had finished eating and pushed his plate back. "That was really great. You didn't tell me you were such a good cook."

"Thanks for coming over and giving me a chance to contribute."

"Just don't let this get back to my captain," Tom kidded as he packed up his briefcase. "I guess it's getting time for me to leave. You want some help cleaning up the dishes?"

Shari did not want to be left alone just yet. "Would I be a poor hostess if I had you help?"

"No, I really would like to help." Tom helped with the dishes while they discussed the complexities of getting a book published. Shari had a faint longing to have Tom kiss her good-bye when he left, though he didn't try. This was the closest she had been to having a date in years. It had been fun, in spite of the shadow hanging over it.

* * *

The next morning, Shari went to the library at the University of Utah. It was a large, square building constructed in the side of a hill. The first level opened to a flat area that was cut into the hill for the foundation of the building. The main entrance was on the second level. A bridge connected the top of the hill to the entrance. It was sort of like crossing a dry mote to a castle. Shari had used the library many times to do research. During the night, Shari remembered where she had heard the name Apollyon. She knew exactly what she was looking for. After two hours of research she had all the information she needed. She couldn't wait, so she called Tom from a pay phone at the library. Tom answered on the second ring.

"Detective DeMayo. Can I help you?"

"Detective Darling here. I think I can help you."

"Shari? What's up?"

"I found out what the names mean." It was hard to keep her voice from shaking.

"You're kidding! How did you find them so fast?" The interest and excitement in his voice could not be hidden by the electronic distortions in the phone line. "Where are you?"

"Tom, I'm at the university library. The names are all angels."

"Angels? Come on. Angels? Are you sure?"

"Yeah, I'm sure all right. Even Abaddon slash Apollyon."

"He thinks of himself as an angel? I guess that shouldn't surprise me."

"Listen to this, 'Abaddon is the angel with the key to the abyss.' That's from a picture done by a German artist. He's also called death's dark angel ... the destroyer ... the angel of the bottomless pit." Just saying those words caused the familiar sense of fear to surface in her.

"Jesus! Where did you get all that?"

"Research. I make a pretty good detective, don't I?"

"Well, I won't argue with that."

"There's more. I got them all ... and Tom, if this is right, you guys are way off on some of your assumptions."

"Could you bring that information to my office?"

"Sure. Now?"

"Two days ago, if you could."

"Sure. It'll take about twenty minutes."

"Fine, I'll see you in about twenty."

When Shari arrived at the station, Tom was waiting for her. She had not been to his office the whole time she had known him. In a way, she was nearly as excited about seeing where he worked as she was about the information she had gathered.

DeMayo took her to a conference room, where two men and a woman were already waiting. "Hello, everyone. This is Shari Darling." DeMayo pulled a chair out for Shari and introduced her to the members of the task force. "Shari has been interested in this case for personal reasons. This morning she took the names from the poems to the library. She has gotten some interesting information. So I'll just let her explain."

"When Tom asked me to come down here, I thought I was just going to be talking to him. This is kind of a surprise for me." Shari's mouth was dry as she fumbled for her notes. "Here … I uh … I copied some notes." She handed DeMayo a sheet of lined yellow paper.

DeMayo handed the paper to Peterson. "Would you make copies of this for everyone?" Then he addressed the group. "I might mention that Shari has been meeting with a Russell Blaine at the Point of the Mountain for a book she is working on. He knew Carl Paskel when he was there, and he thinks Paskel is the killer. Shari was married to Paskel, and she is the one who sent him to prison."

"What information does Blaine have?" Alexander asked.

"Well, he says that Paskel told him he was going to change his MO, and that he was fooling the psychologists at the prison."

Peterson returned and passed out the copies she had made, returning the original to Shari. They took a few seconds to review the notes.

The Angels

Abaddon/Apollyon — male; "death's dark angel," holder of the key to the abyss, destroyer
Anahita — female; "the immaculate one"
Barbelo — female; "perfect in glory, superior angel," consort of Cosmocrater

Cosmocrater — male; "ruler of the material cosmos," disguised as the devil, sings praises to powers of light with Barbelo

Baresches — male; "beginning," evoked to procure women
Pancia — male; "most pure angel," invoked magic to summon the sword
Raun — male; fallen from the order of the throne, great earl in hell in the form of a crow, his mission is to destroy

Bat Qol — female; "heavenly voice — daughter of voice," symbolized as a dove. Voice that accused Cain by calling out, "Where is thy brother, Abel?"

"Where did you get this?" Alexander asked Shari.
"At the library."
"What I mean is, did it come from one source or several?"
"Several sources." This seemed like the third degree.
"He's just trying to figure how Richards gets the information for his poems," DeMayo interrupted. "Could he have one book with all these names in it, or does he have to go to the library to do research?"
"Oh. I used three books, but there could be a dictionary of angels."
"Well, we're going to have to revise our first analysis," DeMayo said. "We had the sex wrong on Pancia and Raun, and Bat Qol is a female, not an acronym for me."
"That's right," Alexander said. "I don't think that creates a great problem with Pancia and Raun, though the idea of abortion as a motive doesn't work. We suspected he might go after boys too. The argument that they were older because they couldn't go to the celestial kingdom still holds. The idea that Bat Qol was DeMayo doesn't fit with a female—unless DeMayo has been keeping something from us."
"Not funny," DeMayo responded.
"Right," Alexander continued. "From the poem, we get that Bat Qol is someone who's not fit for this world ... in Richards's mind

anyway. I think that's his next victim. And I think he has already picked her out. It looks like he scouts his victims and prepares to take them."

"Maybe so," Unger interrupted. "But I think the distance between the first two victims … one in Provo and the other here in the Salt Lake Valley, would make it difficult for the unsub to know a lot about them."

"Well, I don't think Charlene belongs in the group," DeMayo said. "He had something else in mind with her. I think that, with the decision to kill his victims, the method of selection changed."

"DeMayo has a point," Alexander agreed. "But who could Bat Qol be? Richards just got out after over ten years in the pen. If he is going after girls younger than eight, this has to be someone he met since he got out."

"Or someone he knew before he was sent up," Unger said. "Someone who did something to forfeit heaven, so age doesn't matter. We should check on all the witnesses who testified against him. It also may have been a victim he was planning to assault before he was caught. Bat Qol could be somewhere in that original case file. I'm going to get someone working on that. You guys finish this up." Unger got up from his chair. "Miss Darling, this information may be just the thing we needed to break the case. Thanks for your help."

"You're welcome."

After Unger left, Alexander continued with the meeting. "Okay, Baresches, Cosmocrater, and Abaddon are role players."

"I still think they are different roles played by just one man," DeMayo interrupted. "He looked to himself to procure Barbelo in his role of Baresches. She was the first perfect victim, so he wanted to see her as his consort, so he found the perfect match in the relationship of Barbelo and Cosmocrater singing praises. If it suits his message, he will use different names, but I think it's just one man."

"Maybe," Alexander said. "We'll have Piszczek look at this latest data. I think we have all we need, so let's get started. Thanks again, Shari." Alexander and Peterson both got up and left the room.

Shari grabbed DeMayo's arm. "I know this is weird, but I can't quite shake the feeling Russell is somehow connected to the killer.

I want to talk to Russell, and see if maybe directing his energy at Richards he might be able to point the way to him faster. I think you ought to see him too."

"Well, I'm going to be pretty busy following up on this new info."

"I understand, but I want to talk to Russell about this angel idea. It's pretty hard for me to get an appointment to see him without making arrangements several days ahead of time. I was wondering if you would call the prison. Maybe a call from you could get me in today."

"I'll see what I can do."

★ ★ ★

Shari took her seat in the visiting room at the prison just five hours after the meeting with the task force. Russell came in right behind her. When she was with Tom and his physical evidence, she believed Richards was the killer, but now, with Russell and his psychic connections, she believed it was Carl again. "You must have pulled some kind of strings to get this meeting on such short notice," Russell said as he sat down.

Shari could tell that Russell sensed something was up. "Tom DeMayo has another suspect."

"Really? Anyone we know?"

"His name is Dale Richards."

"I know Dale. He's bad. He could do something like this, but it's not him."

"You know Dale Richards? How?"

"He just got out of here a few months ago. Dale, Carl, and I were all in the same therapy group."

"God, what is this, some kind of pervert fraternity?"

Russell smiled. "We don't exactly choose whom we associate with. And there are some here by mistake. But you didn't come so I could reminisce about the good old days."

"Tom has let me do some research on this case."

"What research?"

Shari told Russell about the poems and explained the names. She told him two of the names were males. She explained the task force thought they must be in their early teens.

"Why teenagers? Why not grown men?"

"Because they know the guy's a pedophile, and there are so many reports of missing teenagers that it's impossible to know who are just runaways."

"He's a pedophile all right, but he's only interested in girls. These other victims are probably men who knew something or saw something."

"Is that your feeling?"

"Carl doesn't like little boys. He could have married other women before you, but they had sons, and he didn't want to be bothered with trying to pretend to be a father to them when there would be nothing in it for him."

"But what if the killer is Richards? You said you know him. Don't you think it could be possible that you are tapping into him instead of Carl?"

"It's not Dale. It's Carl. Why would I have feelings you were in danger if it was Dale? He doesn't even know you."

"He could know about me if Carl talked about me. Did my name come up in any of the group sessions you guys had?"

"Yes, but that …"

"Oh God! That just makes me feel all the more violated. I hate this. How did I ever get mixed up in this?"

"I'm sorry. It's shitty."

"Carl has an alibi for the time Katie was kidnapped and killed."

"Check into it … it's phony."

"The police have already checked into it. It's good."

"I thought DeMayo was smarter than that. You're a reporter, you check into it."

"How do you know it's not good?"

"He did the killings … so he can't have an alibi."

"That's not even logical."

"That is perfectly logical. Check it out ... you'll see."

"There's also good evidence pointing to Richards. Charlene's underwear was found in his apartment. Also Katie had a pubic hair from Richards on her body," Shari argued.

"Those could be planted."

"You're a hard one to please."

"What does Dale have to say about this?"

"He disappeared."

"That's pretty convenient, don't you think? Maybe he's one of the male angels."

"Before he disappeared, he called Tom by the name hold-the-mayo. That's how the poems were addressed to Tom."

"Hell almighty, Shari! DeMayo put a lot of guys in here. We all refer to him as detective hold-the-mayo. That includes Carl. He probably used it more than anyone. That isn't evidence."

"In one of the poems, the killer indicated that his father had burned him in the armpits with cigarettes."

"That's Dale's dad all right. Dale was proud of those marks. We all saw them plenty of times. Anyone could write that in a poem to point the finger at him."

The sickening fear shot cold rays throughout Shari's body. "Every time I think I have a handle on this it gets all confused."

"I have no confusion. It's Carl, and you need to take precautions."

"Like what?"

"The first thing is to check out the alibi."

"How?"

"Shari, you're the reporter ... figure it out."

A sudden flood of anger pushed the fear out. Shari stood up and started to pace. "Okay, I found the angels ... I'll check the goddamned alibi too. You're no goddamned help ... that's for sure!"

"While you're at it, here's the next installment on the book."

"The hell with you and your book!" Shari picked up the envelope.

Conquering the Ever-Widening Circle
Chapter Four: Caught!

One night shortly after I was graduated from high school, I was babysitting for a divorced woman near my house. She was in her late twenties and had two sons, three and five years old. After the boys were in bed, I went into the woman's bedroom and opened the curtains just a crack. I went outside the window and back several times until I had adjusted the opening just enough to allow me to see in clearly, and not make it obvious from the inside that the curtains were open. After she came home, I went straight to my perch to wait for the show to begin. She was already in the room by the time I got there. She started to unbutton her blouse, and then she left the room. A little later she came in with a sandwich, which she put on the table near her bed, and then she left again.

Suddenly, someone grabbed me by the shoulder! I turned to see my bishop. In the Mormon Church, the leader of the local congregation is the bishop. Apparently, the lady could see me through her window. She had called the bishop and fixed the sandwich to stall me until he could get there. There was no point in running; he knew me. He took me home, and I had the unpleasant duty of waking my parents to be confronted by the bishop and what I had done. The bishop set up a meeting with me and my parents in his office for the next morning. I wished I could die.

The next day, the bishop gave us a long discussion about repentance. He had already set up an appointment with a church psychologist. "He's not a licensed therapist, but he has had very good luck dealing with the problem you have."

My parents and I had our first meeting with the psychologist in his home. He talked about the love of Christ, and how the sins of the repentant would be taken away as if they had never happened. All Jesus wanted from me was a broken heart and a contrite spirit. I definitely had those along with a sincere desire to do better with my life. I felt Christ was going to take away all of my problems, because I was truly repentant.

In the fall I was called to go on a mission for the Mormon Church. I enjoyed the work and was fully enmeshed in it. I had every reason to think I had totally overcome my problem. A little over two years later, having completed my mission, I registered for school at Weber State College. I started to date the girl whom I was to marry eight months later. By that Christmas, I was going to school, had a job, and was newly married. A year later, my wife was pregnant. Over three years had passed without a repeat of my voyeurism.

Then, once again, the old fantasies and thoughts returned. Before our son was born I was acting out again. I thought I had conquered the problem, but I was leading a double life again. I was totally sincere in my church assignments and the life I lived in public, and I was doing well in school. I hated what I was doing those other times. However, there was something very different about me when I was engaged in voyeurism, and I didn't care about all of the other considerations. If I could feel about the behavior at those times in the same way as I felt about it at church, I would not have had a problem.

One day in the summer between my sophomore and senior years at Weber State, I received a call from a detective in the Ogden Police Department. He wanted to talk to me, so I made an appointment for that afternoon. When I got to the station, I was ushered into the man's office. After the introductions he said, "Do you know why I asked you to come in?"

"No."

"We have reports that your car has been seen in several areas where a peeping tom has been active."

"Your reports must be mistaken. With school and work, I don't have time to do that even if I was so inclined—which I am not." He described my car, gave me the license number, and asked if that was my car. "I have a car like that, but I'm not sure what the license plate number is."

"Trust me, that's your license plate."

"Did someone report that license plate number to you?" I was stalling for time to think. I was quite surprised at his response.

"We've had several reports of a car fitting the description of your car, and we have a partial plate number that matches your plate."

"There must be a mistake." Sweat was beginning to run down my back.

"Look, all I want to do is help you get the help you need."

"I don't need any help; you have the wrong guy."

"You think you're pretty smart, but let me tell you this: I know it was you, and I know if you don't get help, I'll be seeing you again, and I'll have the proof, and I'll see to it that you do time! I know your kind of perversion, and I know as sure as I'm sitting here tat you will not be able to control it. You think you will, but in a month or a year you will be at it again, and you'll make a mistake. I'll see you then. Now get out of my office!"

I should have felt elated or at least relieved, but what I felt was sick. This wasn't a childish prank. I was a grown man with a family and responsibilities. The man's comment, "I'll see you again," was eating at me. I just couldn't understand why I was stuck with this. Why me? I drove to Salt Lake and went up to the top of one of the tall buildings downtown. Silent tears turned to cries of pain when I was alone. As I looked out, I could see the Salt Lake Temple, the Eagle Gate, and the Beehive House. These were the symbols of my faith. I pondered my life. I was a worthless hypocrite. I was an embarrassment to myself, my family, the church, and my God. All of my attempts at holiness and righteous living were meaningless, because my basic nature was wicked and unsalvageable. In deep sorrow and through tears I tried to jump from the building, but I couldn't bring myself to do it. I couldn't even kill myself!

It's a Mormon doctrine that God will never allow any of His children to be tempted beyond their capacity to resist. I thought about that and decided with His help I would overcome! This was no game, this was life, and my happiness and those who depended upon me were at stake. It would be hard, but from that day foreword I would change my life. I went home that day with the light feeling of one who has cast aside an overpowering burden.

* * *

Shari put the manuscript up. It was hard to understand why Russell would continue to do something knowing he risked everything if he got caught again? Was he really as religious as his book said he had been? She checked the records of his mission; he had been honorably released as he claimed.

Shari slept only fitfully during the night. Carl was at work when the body was deposited in Immigration Canyon. How could that alibi be broken? Maybe something had been done to foul up the determination of the time of death. Carl had to punch a time card, but was it possible for him to leave the job without anyone knowing? Shari would have to go to the apartment complex where he worked. She decided to talk to the manager under the pretext of looking for an apartment.

The next day she went to the apartment complex, which consisted of three different buildings originally built at different times by different owners, so they didn't look at all alike. Two of the buildings were on the same block, and one was on the other side of the street. The business office was in the biggest of the three buildings. She arrived at the complex at eleven thirty. A receptionist in the outer office greeted her. "Hi, my name is Dorothy Singleton. I'm looking for an apartment in this area. Could I talk to the manager?"

"He's not in right now. Could I help you?"

"It's my understanding that all three of the buildings are under the same management. Is that correct?"

"Yes, we run them all from this office."

"I'm interested in a three-bedroom apartment with a view of the mountains. I'm not sure which of the three buildings I would be most interested in."

"They're all very nice inside. The newest building is the one behind this one. But all of them are in good shape."

"Which one has the best janitorial staff?"

"They are all taken care of by one full-time janitor. We have a contract with a very good maintenance company that comes in twice a month and is on call to do the major cleaning and maintenance."

"That must be a lot of work for just one man."

"Not really. Our full-time man keeps the carpets vacuumed, picks up the garbage twice a week, and takes care of odds and ends. Other than that, he calls in the maintenance service."

"Then you're saying he doesn't have specific scheduled work to do each day?"

"He's on his own to patrol the buildings and make sure everything is kept in good order."

"How do you get him if you need him for something?"

"He generally stops by my office every couple of hours to see if anything has come up. Why all the questions about the janitor?"

"It's just that I've been in some places that have gotten really messy. It seems it could be pretty hard to find him if something came up. I don't know your guy, but I suppose some guys might take advantage of a situation like this … you know … disappear for a few hours every once in a while."

"Not this guy … he's an eccentric millionaire. He doesn't even need the job. If he wanted to take off, he wouldn't need to be sneaky about it." The receptionist frowned and her eyes narrowed.

"I have an appointment in a few minutes near here. I'll call to set something up with the manager in the next week or two. Thanks for your time." Shari offered her hand to the receptionist. Outside the office, she saw Carl coming down the hall! She quickly walked out the main door. She felt the pulsing of her arteries in her neck. *What if he saw me? What dumb luck that he should happen along just then.* She wanted to look back at the door as she hurried down the street, but what if he was in the doorway looking at her? She turned the corner and ran to her car a half block away.

* * *

Shari called Tom as soon as she got home. "I just came from the apartment where Carl works."

"What in the hell were you doing there?"

"I was checking on this ironclad alibi. It's not so good, you know."

"In what way?"

Shari explained what she had learned from the receptionist.

"That kind of playing detective could be dangerous if Carl is the killer," Tom said.

"If he is the killer, it doesn't make much difference, because he's going to be coming after me anyway."

"Well, I would prefer that you leave the detective work to the detectives."

"I did." Shari regretted saying that even as the words left her mouth.

"I know this case is getting inside you, but we have very strong evidence that the killer is Richards."

"What if one of the unexplained angels is Richards? What if he's dead and buried someplace? That would explain why you haven't been able to find him. What if someone is framing him? The guys in the prison therapy group all call you by the name 'hold-the-mayo.' They all know Richards's history ... I mean about the cigarette burns and all that." When Shari stopped talking there was silence on the line. "Are you there, Tom?"

"Uhm ... yeah. You got that information from Russell?" Tom's voice was different—a little subdued.

"Yeah ... I mean, all except for what I found out from the receptionist."

"I'm going to do some checking on this. I want you to stay away from Carl."

"You don't have to tell me that. He's the last person I want to be around."

"You know what I mean. Stay away from anything that has to do with him. Will you do that?"

"Does that mean he's a suspect now?"

"It just means that I want to check up on some things. Will you please stay out of this until I check it all out?"

"I don't want to be involved. It was just that ... I don't know. No one was checking, and I wanted to know for sure."

"Well, don't do anything like that again. It could be dangerous."

"Okay."

"Good. I got some things to do ... thanks to you. Bye."

"Let me know what turns up, okay?"

"I will."

"All right then. Bye." Shari hung up the phone. *What if Carl saw me? I should have told Tom.* Shari checked all the doors and windows. She was alone with her fear—again.

★ ★ ★

It was late afternoon when DeMayo got to the prison. He was ushered to a private room to talk with Blaine. Shari's involvement in the case was disturbing, but she was providing information DeMayo knew he should be chasing down.

"Detective DeMayo, I've been expecting you." Blaine took a chair across the table from DeMayo.

"I'll bet."

"You here about Carl or Shari?"

"Both."

"Why am I not surprised?"

"What's all this crap about psychic connections to Carl?"

"Carl's your killer, but he's got you out chasing down that asshole Dale. Tell you what," Blaine leaned over the table, looking DeMayo in the eye, "you ain't ever going to find Dale. He's dead."

"How do you know that? Some more of your phony feelings?" DeMayo stared back.

Blaine leaned back in his chair and relaxed. "Katie was suffocated."

"That was in all the news reports ... so what?"

"Carl tied her up, pinched her nose with his left hand, put his mouth over her mouth, and shared her final breaths. Do you want to know what he was doing with his right hand?"

"Shut the fuck up!" DeMayo stood up and walked to the wall. He paused for a few seconds then turned to face the table—Blaine had not moved. "How did you know that? And don't give me that bullshit about psychic connections."

"Besides killing Charlene, Katie, and Dale, he killed another man who he thought saw something the day Charlene was killed. He stuck a knife clear through him."

"That murder was in the news too."

"Carl killed him."

"You think every murder committed since he got released was done by Paskel. What've you got against him?"

"Wish I knew."

"You got no psychic connection to that?" DeMayo asked sarcastically.

Blaine sat in his chair regarding DeMayo. "You don't like me much, do you?"

"Well, now your psychic ability is getting believable. You're just a sick little man." DeMayo walked to the side of the table and bent over to lean on it with both palms flat down. "Now answer my question!"

"More like an oxymoron," Blaine mumbled.

"What?" DeMayo leaned closer.

"You know my answer to that question, and you told me not to give it to you." Blaine remained calm. "You know there's a killer out there, and we both know it's not me. Why don't you sit down, and let's see what we can do about it."

DeMayo turned his back and walked around the table to his chair. He looked back at Blaine. He was still leaning back in his chair. DeMayo sat down. "Okay, you've told me what we already know. What have you got that's new?"

Blaine pulled himself up to the table. "I don't have anything except I know it's Carl. We shared the same cell for five months. I learned a lot. Just forget the psychic stuff, and let's look at the evidence."

"I'm doing this only for Shari's sake. I don't work with self-proclaimed psychic criminals. That's just too *Silence of the Lambs*, don't you think?"

"Let me tell you something ... Carl was only sorry he was caught and put in jail. He wants little girls, and he's of the opinion he's entitled to them. He planned to make a conscious change in his MO. He accidentally killed the first girl. Carl has always been a killer in his heart. He has dreams of cutting a hole in some girl's chest, inserting himself, and letting her last heartbeats ... you get the picture," he stated rather than asked. "That's the kind of dreams he had before Charlene. Whatever thread of humanity had held him back was broken with her. God help Shari if he gets her."

"He told you about those dreams?"

"That and more. You know why he hates you so much?"

"Yeah ... I arrested him."

"You think that's his reason?"

"I don't actually know that Paskel hates me. He seemed friendly enough the last time I talked to him. But Richards ... now that's different ... he hates me."

"'Cause you arrested him thirteen years ago?"

"Well, you can never tell when some pervert is going to take something like that personal."

"You arrested Carl, but only because Shari pressed charges. He hates her passionately. But he has always thought of her as his property ... something he would deal with when he got out ... teach her a lesson. Then about six weeks before he was released, he got word through the grapevine that Shari was seeing Tom DeMayo. He went completely ballistic. He wants you because you took Shari. He wants to embarrass you ... make you regret you ever saw her."

"He said all that to you? Shari wasn't seeing me. We were just friends."

"Maybe, but you were seen hanging out together. He didn't mention anything about killing you or Shari ... but since Charlene ... I think now killing is a pretty good conclusion. So can we look at the evidence?" DeMayo opened his briefcase and pulled out his folders. Blaine twisted each piece of evidence to show Paskel framing Richards. Paskel could have planted the panties in Richards's room after he killed him. He could have picked up the hair evidence at that time and planted it on Katie. He could have written the poems purely to incriminate Richards. His alibi had a hole in it. After examining the poems, Blaine said, "In the first part of 'The Impotent Stalker' he is saying you took his freedom. But what you're stealing now is Shari. He is plenty pissed about that. Pancia's stare must mean he saw something. This would be the usher, and the sword pushed through has to be the knife. He says, 'Raun your riddle' because Raun is yours. That's Dale ... you arrested him ... that makes him your riddle. He dealt drugs, and that's what Carl means when he calls him a destroyer."

"When we catch Richards, I just hope he doesn't get you for a defense attorney," DeMayo commented when they were through. "You haven't proven anything, but if creating doubt was your intent ... you've done that. This has been interesting. I'll look into these other things about Paskel, and I'll watch out for Shari."

"I wish you the best of luck with Shari, and I mean that."

"Sure you do," DeMayo mustered as much sarcasm as he could.

As DeMayo reached the door Blaine said, "One last thing ... Bat Qol must be Shari." It was like a cold shower. DeMayo spun on his heel and stared at Blaine, but Blaine didn't flinch.

As DeMayo drove back to Salt Lake, he found it difficult to resolve his disbelief in psychic connections with the knowledge Blaine had. He had expected to dislike him, but on the contrary, he had a positive feeling about him. That was the weirdest thing of all.

Chapter Five

THE PREDATOR

The man woke feeling powerful and invincible. He closed his eyes and lay in bed replaying his dream in his mind.

The big cat loped along the edge of the clearing, paying no attention to the herd of impalas nearby with their flicking tails. His feigned disinterest relieved the impalas, as they warily watched the cat move away. The Serengeti was hot and dusty. The rainy season had ended long ago, and it was time for the herds to move. Several of the young impalas were dancing and frolicking in the sun.

The lion liked to hunt and kill his prey alone. Fighting and scrapping for pieces of others' kill did not suit him. He was a rogue. As he moved away, the impalas watched. At just the right moment, he wandered into the brush and started to double back. He was downwind and hidden. A hundred yards away a group of young impalas was playing near the brush. Slowly, quietly, the big lion drew closer.

Several of the young impalas split off and ran close to the brush. The lion singled one out. He tensed as the tip of his tail began to twitch, and saliva dripped from the corner of his mouth. At just the right moment, he sprang. He saw surprise and fear in the eyes of the young impala as he rapidly closed the distance. The young animal's fear meant nothing to him. In less than twenty yards the lion overtook the impala, and with a powerful paw, he swiped the *hind legs from under her. She fell, but in one fluid motion she rolled, twisted to her feet, and sprinted out of the lion's grasp. In a heartbeat the lion took another swipe, knocking the impala off her feet again. This time he caught the impala by the neck before she could spring to her feet. She struggled as the lion closed massive jaws, crushing her throat. A few more kicks and it was over. She died of suffocation before she had a chance to bleed to death.*

The lion loped easily to the brush with the limp body of the impala dangling from his mouth. For a moment he laid the body in front of him and surveyed his kingdom. He was the king of predators. The jackal, the hyena, and the vulture would all stay back. No one dared attempt to take his prey.

* * *

The man parked his car in the lot at the University of Utah. He walked to an adjoining lot he had watched for several days. He had picked a car that was parked every day in the same spot from 8:00 a.m. to 5:30 p.m. He could borrow this car and return it before anyone would miss it. He broke into the car and drove to his car. He got his duffel bag from his car and drove to Sugarhouse Park in the stolen car. In a secluded area, he put on his disguise.

After he didn't find what he wanted there, he drove to Fairmont Park. The park had a couple of areas that would be suitable to pick up a young girl, but he had no luck. The man drove to a side street near Jordan Park. Time was running out; if he didn't get someone here, he would have to wait for another day. Several picnic tables were set up. It was obvious there was going to be a large party. He walked into the park disguised as a bum. Three girls of the right age were playing near the tables. He could not grab one of them with all the family around.

As he started to leave, he heard one of the girls ask if they could play in the Peace Garden. That was more like it. The Peace Garden was in the northwest area of Jordan Park. It was a collection of international displays from many countries around the world. The western border of the gardens was formed by the Jordan River—a wide, slow-running river with many dangerous undercurrents.

It would be difficult to separate one girl from the group of three, but if he was lucky he might be able to pull it off. He drove the car about a half block north to a small park called the Eighth South Park. It had a small parking lot where he parked the car. He got out of the car with his old canvas duffel bag and walked south to a railroad track that crossed a dirt path leading into the back of the Peace Garden. He entered the Peace Garden behind the Great Britain display and followed a dirt path along the Jordan River. Next to the Great Britain display was the display for Switzerland, with a sixty-foot high scale model of the Matterhorn. The dirt path went behind the Matterhorn. The man hid his duffel bag in some undergrowth.

No one paid any attention to the old bum as he limped slowly from behind the Matterhorn along the edge of the grass. His hair and beard were long, dirty, oily looking. He wore a long loose coat even though it was a hot day. The coat may have been a raincoat or an old overcoat. He walked past the three little girls who were dodging in and out of the brush and trees around the edge of the grass. The man had passed from the Switzerland display, through the Norway display, and was in the Holland display when he observed the three girls coming through the Switzerland display behind him.

He disappeared into some brush and trees about fifty yards away from the girls. Once in the trees he moved quickly through the brush along the riverbank back toward the Matterhorn. He was alert as his eyes continually scanned his path to make sure there was no one there. Finally, he was just out of sight near where the girls were playing. He reached in his pocket and took out the surgical gloves and put them on. Then he got the pad of gauze and the bottle of ether. He opened the bottle, took one more look around, and crouched in the underbrush, waiting, ready to pour ether onto the pad.

The three girls run around the path, which encircled the Bauta Stone in the Norwegian display. Suddenly, one of the girls ran toward the end of the hill located near the border between the Holland display and the Norway display. Her long hair swayed from side to side as she ran. Her two friends remained behind.

The man was hidden behind a natural hill separating the wild area along the river from the well-kept gardens in the park. He drifted along the river path behind the hill, keeping even with the girl as she drew closer. Finally, the girl circled behind the hill and the man stepped out blocking her path. The girl gave a startled scream as she stopped in her tracks. She was temporarily frozen as the man took a quick look around. He poured ether on the gauze pad. As he took a step toward her, the girl turned to run. He grabbed her under the arms with his left arm; simultaneously, he cupped the gauze pad over her mouth and nose.

She kicked both feet up in the air. He ducked deeper into the brush behind the hill as she kicked a couple more times, and then, with a slight tremble, her body went flaccid. The man stood up to make sure no one had seen. The other two girls were laughing and playing nearby. The little body hung from his left hand like a rag doll.

He tossed the limp girl almost causally under the brush and hurried back up the path. She landed on her face, filling her nose and mouth with dirt and decaying leaves. He checked the path back to the Matterhorn. He came back, found the ether bottle, and grabbed the girl by her upper left arm dragging her behind the Matterhorn, where he stuffed her into the duffel bag and put the bag in some bushes. He walked back along the path with a tree branch and brushed away the trail. One of her shoes had fallen off. He put it in his pocket.

When he got back, he picked up the bag, and, swinging it over his shoulder, he headed back along the path at the river's edge. He came to a perfect spot for his diversion. The ground all around was dry, but just at the edge of the river, the ground was wet. A tree trunk grew at an angle over the pathway. He dropped the bag and got on his knees. He took the girl's shoe from his pocket and reached in the bag for the other one. Using the shoes he made several footprints in the mud, which made it look like someone had struggled to avoid falling in the river. He obliterated all the other signs. He put the shoes in his pocket, picked up the bag, and walked north.

The railroad tracks crossed the Jordan River on an old wooden bridge near the point where the man left the park. Some tree branches, an old tire, and other debris had been snagged on one of the bridge pillars near the bank of the river. The man carefully placed one of the girl's shoes in this debris at the waterline so it could easily be seen from the bank. He picked the bag up and started back to the car. As he crossed the tracks, he heard in the distance, "Marty, come out. This is not even funny anymore. If you don't come out now, we're telling your mother!"

The man headed east on Fourth South, driving by the Newhouse Building. Less than a minute later he drove within a half block of the police station as he continued east on Fourth South. "Catch me if you can," he said out loud, thinking of DeMayo.

There was no one around his car as he moved the duffel bag into the trunk and locked it. Then he drove the borrowed car to the parking lot where he had picked it up a couple of hours ago, left it in its spot, returned to his car, and drove off.

The man pulled his car into the garage and closed the door. He took the duffel bag to his special room. There he removed the girl from the bag. She was a pretty girl. He laid her on the cot and straightened her yellow skirt. It was crumpled and a little dirty. She was unconscious. He brushed the dirt and leaves from her mouth and face. The smudge of dirt on her cheek looked pretty. He left it that way. She looked angelic. He took a picture—the latest addition to his collection. He took her clothes off and took another picture before he tied her up and gagged her. He had to leave her for a few hours, and then the fun would begin again.

* * *

Detective DeMayo arrived at Jordan Park shortly after 1:20 p.m. When he got the report that Marty Sawyer was missing, he knew he still had time to save the little girl and catch Abaddon. He called the Salt Lake City Mobile Neighborhood Watch Program to put them on alert in the Jordan Park area. The Salt Lake City Mobile Neighborhood Watch Program was officially organized in July 1993. It was based on the concept that effective law enforcement is a partnership between the police force and the community. The program consisted of private volunteers who patrolled the streets of their neighborhoods. The volunteers were trained to patrol, observe, and call the PD when suspicious behavior was observed. They had magnetic door panels to mark their cars when they were on patrol. Their high visibility was a crime deterrent. About six hundred volunteers patrolled the streets, armed with mobile phones, video cameras, and police scanners. The city was divided into eleven different patrol areas. Jordan Park was located in the West Salt Lake Area, but just at the north border of the park was the Poplar Grove area. A couple of blocks to the east of Jordan Park was the People's Freeway area. The word that there had been a possible kidnapping in Jordan Park was put out on the scanners in all three areas before DeMayo reached the park.

If the pattern for Katrina Sopkov was repeated, DeMayo would have two days to find Marty before she was killed, but the raping would start sometime today. Several policemen were already at the park when Detective DeMayo arrived. Alexander pulled in behind him. "I'll follow up on physical evidence." Alexander said to DeMayo. "You can get background from the family."

Just then an officer arrived with a wet shoe. It was identified by the father as belonging to Marty. "Where did you find it?" Alexander asked.

"In the river, at the railroad bridge ... not far from where the kids were playing."

"Show me!" Alexander followed the officer.

DeMayo started interviewing the father. Marty's family was in the park as part of a big family reunion. Marty had been playing in the Peace Garden with two of her cousins. She disappeared from the game without saying anything to them. DeMayo tried to talk to the mother, but she was too upset to be coherent. DeMayo talked to the two girls who had been playing with Marty before she disappeared. She was playing hide and seek from them most of the time. They were visiting from Colorado and said Marty was showing off how well she knew the Peace Garden by disappearing in one area and reappearing at a different area. As DeMayo finished interviewing the girls, Alexander returned.

"It looks like she got too close to the river and fell in. I had one of the officers with a handheld call in for search and rescue."

DeMayo didn't want to believe this was just an accident, so he checked the site. It appeared the girl had fallen in the river from a dirt path running along the bank about five feet from the water's edge. The bank dropped steeply from the path to the water. Three distinct footprints could be seen in the mud near the edge of the river—obvious signs of someone sliding into the water. The trunk of a tree came out over the path at an angle of about thirty degrees from the ground. The trunk was too high for her to have actually run into, but it could have startled her if she was running along the path. Something was wrong, but DeMayo couldn't quite put his finger on it. "Tape this off and don't let anyone touch this area." DeMayo ordered one of the uniformed officers. DeMayo paced back and forth a few minutes. Then it dawned on him! He ran to the picnic ground as fast as he could. Alexander was just getting into his car. "Wait!" DeMayo called. "This is Abaddon's work."

"This is an accidental drowning. I wish it were Abaddon. Then at least there would be a chance we could get her in time."

"Just come with me a minute. I want to show you something."

When they got to the river, DeMayo pointed to the tracks. "See there, where she was supposed to have slipped. See what's missing?"

"No. What?"

"There are footprints, and it looks like someone slid into the water."

"Right," Alexander agreed. "The shoeprints match the shoe we found."

"I'm not a tracker, but if she struggled, how come there are no marks of her fingers digging into the bank?"

Alexander stepped closer. "If she fell out away from the bank, there wouldn't be any other marks."

"Look at how the prints are made," DeMayo said. "The three prints look like she is struggling. Look how the toe of the foot nearest the river is pointed away from the river, and the toe is digging into the mud. She couldn't have been falling back with her toe digging in like that. She would have fallen forward, away from the water, as she slipped. There should be some scraping marks from her hands in the soft dirt as she slid into the water."

Alexander took a closer look. "We'll go ahead with the search and rescue, just in case she did fall into the water. If Abaddon went to all this trouble to fake the drowning, we ought to let him think it worked. Behind the scenes, we'll treat it like an abduction."

DeMayo explained all the latest information he had gotten from Russell and Shari about Paskel and his alibi as they walked back to the parking lot. "I think that if Paskel is our man, we might be able to catch him red-handed with a search warrant."

"That would be a real break for us. I'll get Kilpatric started on the warrant. In the meantime, we need to locate Paskel."

"Let's put a watch on his house, and we can check his work."

"Paskel is a long shot, but I'll make the calls," Alexander said.

* * *

After returning to his car, DeMayo checked in with the radio dispatcher. She informed him there had been a call about suspicious activity in the Eighth Street Park from a member of the Neighborhood Patrol. The call came in at about one thirty, but he was reporting something he had seen about an hour before. The member who had made the report was not on patrol, but was with his family in the park. The dispatcher called the member on his mobile phone—he was still in the park. "Call this guy and tell him I'll be in the park in a couple of minutes."

DeMayo turned left on Genesee Street. It went about a block and dead-ended in the small parking lot for the Eighth Street Park. As he pulled into the lot, he saw a man in his early fifties walking from a family group having a picnic under some trees near the banks of the Jordan River. The man approached DeMayo. "Are you Detective DeMayo?"

"Yeah, are you the guy who called in the report about a suspicious man?"

"That would be me all right. My name is Lynn Straub. It was strange, 'cause the man looked like a homeless bum, but then he gets into a new Volvo. He was carrying a duffel bag with something heavy in it. I figured him for a burglar."

"What time was it?"

"Here … just a sec … I took notes." Straub reached in his pocket and pulled out a small wire-bound notebook and thumbed through the pages. "Okay, here it is. It was 12:36 when he got in the car and left."

"It was some time later before you called it in."

"Yeah, my mistake. I wasn't officially on patrol, so I didn't have my mobile phone with me. I sent my daughter to get it."

"What did this homeless guy look like?"

"One thing I learned pretty fast is to take good notes. I been doing this for about three years now 'n my notes have helped before."

"Excuse me … Lynn, this is not a suspected burglary. An eight-year-old girl was kidnapped from the Peace Garden. We think the kidnapper left the gardens with the girl from right over there." DeMayo pointed toward the railroad crossing about two hundred yards from where they were standing. "I need to get an APB out on the car right away. Could we just skip all the other stuff until we get that done?"

"I gave all the information when I called it in. But this guy didn't have no girl with him."

"Wait here." DeMayo called police dispatch about Mr. Straub's call. The dispatcher told him they had put an APB out and had given the name and address of the owner to Alexander.

When he got back, he asked Mr. Straub to continue.

"Like I said, the guy was alone. All he had was this bag, and he was dressed like a bum."

"Was the bag big enough to put an eight-year-old girl in?"

"It looked big enough from here, but there was nothing moving in it. If there was a girl in it, she was already dead or knocked out."

"This guy doesn't kill the girls right away."

"You mean you think it's the guy that killed that girl in Immigration Canyon?" Straub looked awestruck by this cognition.

"The same. Did you get a look at his face?"

"Geez, no. I actually saw that freak?"

"I don't know yet."

"Okay ... let me see." He turned the page. "I never got no closer than about a hundred feet from him. I seen him walking across the grass, and I seen he was a bum. Dirty old torn clothes, wearing a dingy raincoat or overcoat, I couldn't tell fer sure. The bag didn't look heavy till he tried to put it in the car. That's when he was having some trouble with it. I wasn't paying much attention to him till he got to the Volvo. I would put him at over six foot. It's hard making a judgment on the body size 'cause of the loose coat. He wasn't fat ... I'm sure about that. Not much more though.

"Anyways, he walks up to the car on the passenger side and opens the door without using a key and puts the bag in. He worked the bag in and adjusted it on the seat. Then he opened the bag and reached in to adjust something in the bag. Anyways, while I was watching all of this I sent my wife, Clara, to get my binoculars from the picnic basket. By the time she brought 'em, he was already in the driver's seat. He didn't use no key for the driver's door neither. I used the binoculars to get the license plate numbers, but by the time I had 'em, the car was driving away, so basically I couldn't get no better description."

"You did a good job, Mr. Straub. I think we have a chance to catch this guy now. If we do, you can give yourself a great deal of the credit."

"I'm just glad to be able to help out. There's so much going on that ... well you know ... it's more than the police can keep up with."

"Well, thanks again. I got to get going." DeMayo shook hands with Straub and left.

★ ★ ★

The car belonged to Zak Kressel, a physical ed teacher at the University of Utah. He worked in the Einar Nielson Fieldhouse. A patrol unit had found the car parked in the lot east of the building. When DeMayo arrived, Alexander was examining the car. DeMayo asked, "Did you see Paskel at his work?"

"He wasn't readily available. According to the time card, he was somewhere in one of the buildings. I left Detective Ibey there to find and question him. I wanted to be here to check the car out. We're pretty sure this is the one. The license plate and description are a perfect match. Two detectives have already gone in to get the owner. Here comes Detective Sandoval now."

A detective, dressed in a suit and tie, walked up to the car, leading another man who looked extremely confused. "Hey, Alexander, nice to see you."

"Where's Detective Martin?" Alexander asked.

"This is the owner of the car. He says the car has been in the parking lot since a little after eight this morning. Says he's been here all that time too, and that he has plenty of witnesses. Martin is checking with them now."

"Well, we're interested in the time period from noon to about twelve forty-five. That would be your lunchtime, wouldn't it?" DeMayo asked.

"Will someone tell me what this is all about?" the man standing with the detective asked.

"Are you Zak Kressel?" Alexander asked.

"I am."

"And is this your car?"

"It is."

"We have reason to believe this car was used in a kidnaping around noon today," Alexander stated.

"Not possible. The car has been here all day."

"The car was seen near Jordan Park at precisely 12:36."

"No it was not. I've been here all day, and I can prove it."

"He says he was playing chess at lunch, and there are several people who can vouch for it," Sandoval volunteered.

"You mind if we just look in the car?" Alexander asked.

"I don't know, maybe I should have an attorney here."

"Look, Kressel," DeMayo stepped up to him, "we have very good reason to believe that a serial killer kidnapped an eight-year-old girl at Jordan Park. We also have reason to believe that he used this car. The trail is still warm. You can get an attorney, and if you are the kidnapper, I would recommend that you do that. But if you didn't do this, and your alibi is as good as you say, any delays now could allow the kidnapper to get away and might result in the death of the little girl. What do you say?"

Kressel gave a sigh and handed the key to DeMayo. DeMayo put on a pair of latex gloves. "You got the lab boys on the way?" DeMayo asked Alexander.

"They should be here any minute."

"Good. I'm going to just take a look." DeMayo took the key and opened the trunk. "Mr. Kressel, would you take a look at this."

Kressel walked over to the car and looked into the trunk. In an exasperated I-told-you-so tone he said, "Everything in there is exactly the way I left it. Sorry there's no girl in there, but as I told you already, the car has been here all day."

DeMayo walked to the passenger door and opened it. Some dried leaves lay on the edge of the passenger seat; a few more were on the floor on the same side of the car. There was also a trace of mud on the brake pedal. Under the dashboard some wires had been cut. "Come and take a look at this. Should those leaves and debris be there?"

"Uh … why no. I just washed the car two days ago."

"Up under the dash … you see the cut wires?"

"I don't know how that happened."

"It appears someone hot-wired your car and used it to commit a crime." Alexander took the keys from DeMayo. "I'm sorry, but we're going to have to borrow your car for a few hours. We'll be happy to provide you transportation in the meantime."

"Sure, get whatever you need."

DeMayo pulled Alexander to the side. "The lab boys will take care of things here, so I think I'll run down to the apartment building and see if Paskel showed up. Um, it just occurred to me that if Paskel is the killer, Shari could very easily be Bat Qol."

"Good thinking ... where is she?"

"At her office."

"I'll have a couple of officers sent there to protect her. Call her and let her know they are on the way. I have a couple of patrolmen at Paskel's house, and the paperwork for the search warrant is in process. I'm going over to Paskel's house."

"I'll call Shari and check out Paskel's work. If I don't find him there, I'll meet you at his house."

* * *

Shari finished some minor touch-ups of chapter five of *Conquering the Ever-Widening Circle* before packing her things to leave for the day. As she was getting up to leave, the phone rang.

"Hello."

"Hello, yourself."

"Is that you, Tom?"

"Yeah."

"You sound like you're in a tunnel."

"It's this mobile phone. Can you hear me okay?"

"Sure. It's just a little hollow."

"Good. The reason I called is that an eight-year-old girl is missing. You'll be hearing it on the news."

"You mean she was kidnaped?"

"The evidence points to a kidnapping, but the scene was doctored to make it look like she fell into the Jordan River. Search and Rescue was called in just in case, but we are pursuing it as if it is Abaddon."

"What about Carl?"

"We have an officer at the apartment complex. Last I heard, they hadn't been able to locate him on the premises. We have already sent a unit to his house."

"Why don't you just break in? If he has the girl there, he may be raping her right now!"

"The officers are aware of the situation and will act accordingly. If he's our man, I think we've got him bottled up."

"He's got her, so it's up to you to get in and save her."

"We'll get in, but I sincerely doubt that he will have the girl at his house. According to the first poem, Charlene soiled the seat of his car. We'll have the lab check the seat for stains. If Carl's our man, we'll find souvenirs of his conquests in the house. But you know we can't overlook any possibility, so we're also increasing our efforts to find Richards."

"I'm sure you'll find everything you need at Carl's house. Be sure to call me as soon as you can."

"Listen, with Carl being a suspect again, I'm going to put you under police protection. There'll be a couple of cops keeping an eye out at your place and following you around until we settle this with Carl. So you'll wait at your office until they get there?"

"Uh ... yeah, tell them to hurry. Call me when you're done." Shari could almost feel the hot breath of a burning rat.

"It could be quite late before we're done with everything."

"I don't care what time it is. I'm not going to be sleeping until I know."

"Okay, I'll call."

"Thanks, I'll be waiting."

* * *

As DeMayo hung up the phone, he monitored a radio call between Kurt Ibey and Joe Alexander. Kurt reported that he had found Paskel at the apartments, talked to him, and that Paskel was on his way to his house. Ibey was following him to make sure he went home. DeMayo turned his car around to go to Paskel's house. When DeMayo arrived, the crime squad had already begun to search the house. Paskel was sitting in Alexander's car, and it appeared Alexander was interviewing him.

The house was a small brick building with a porch across the front. DeMayo walked around the porch to see whether there was any way to get under it. The concrete foundation of the house went all around, so the only way under the porch would have to be from inside. He walked in the front room. Two detectives had turned the couch over and were checking for hiding places in the bottom. The living room was a rectangular room with widows on the front and side wall. To the left as he entered the house, a large archway opened into the dining room; it was also a plain rectangular room with widows to the front and side of the house. To his right as he entered the dining room was a door into the kitchen. A detective was checking the cupboards and appliances. At the back of the kitchen, a door went out the side of the house. DeMayo had to go down four stairs to a landing before he could exit the door. From the landing on his left, stairs went down to the basement. DeMayo opened the outside door, which went into the attached garage. It was added after the house was built. The brick on the exterior of the house formed one wall, and the window that had looked out from the kitchen now looked into the garage. Some large cabinets were at the back. A lawn mower and other garden tools were stored in them. Beside the cabinet was a door from the back of the garage to the backyard.

DeMayo went out the back door. A grassy area in the middle was mostly dirt and weeds. Around the edges were gardens with fruit trees. They were full of weeds and the trees were in bad need of pruning. Near the back fence was an old shed with a rusted, jammed door. DeMayo forced the door open. It was stocked with some rusted tools and a lot of spiderwebs. At the side of the shed was a pile of old, rotten firewood. Along the back of the yard was an alley. The yard had been fenced in, but much of the old wooden fence had deteriorated and fallen down.

DeMayo walked around the side of the house and the garage, back to the front door. He could not see anything out of place. He went back in through the front door, and this time he walked down a hallway that led from the dining room. At the end the hallway were three doors, one right, one left, and one straight ahead. Left and right were bedrooms and straight ahead was the bathroom. The tub was on the opposite wall from the door. A toilet and sink were to his left. Another door out of the bathroom led directly into the bedroom on the right. DeMayo checked all three rooms thoroughly.

DeMayo walked back through the house and down into the basement. It had a low ceiling. There had been a coal burning furnace at one time, but it had been replaced by a modern gas furnace. A gas water heater sat next to the furnace. The rest of the basement was one large open space, except for an old coal room. The coal chute had been replaced by a window. The back wall of the coal room had cheap wood paneling. In front of the paneling was a light hanging from the ceiling over a broken down pool table. He could barely tell the felt cover was green because of the accumulated dust. He looked under the table to see if there was space to hide a girl. The bottom was broken up, but there were only dust and cobwebs. Under the stairs were shelves with dusty home-bottled fruit and jams.

Remembering the porch, DeMayo went to the front of the basement. The walls and floor of the basement were solid concrete. There was no entrance to a crawl space under the porch from the basement.

DeMayo had started out with high hopes they would find Marty and incriminating evidence. Gradually those hopes were replaced by an internal I-told-you-so. It was obvious the killer had to be Richards. When he got back upstairs, Alexander was on the front porch talking to Ibey. "What did Paskel have to say?" DeMayo asked.

"Says he's been at work all day," Ibey answered.

"Anybody there who can vouch for that?"

"No one can vouch for the whole time," Ibey said, "but he was seen off and on. I checked his car to see if it had been driven. The block and radiator were cold. It hadn't been driven since morning. Besides, he parks it right by the back door to the main building. If he had used the car, someone would notice. There was no sign of any stains on the front seat."

"Damn! I hoped we would catch a break! What else did Paskel say?"

"He's upset," Alexander answered. "He feels we went too far coming to his work. He thinks the department has singled him out because of your involvement with his ex-wife."

"So what's the bottom line?"

"Says he's changed his life … going to church … trying to cooperate with the police. But now he's pissed that we went to his work, searched his house, and made this commotion for his neighbors to see. Says we better leave him alone, or else."

"We need to pull all the stops to find Richards."

Alexander pulled DeMayo by his upper arm as he walked down the four steps from the porch and down the driveway. "This guy is a millionaire. He isn't going to have anything in his house. I got a gut feeling this guy is hiding something."

"Now you're sounding like Blaine. Didn't you hear Ibey … his car hadn't even been used. Wadda ya think … he took a bus?"

"It's just one block from the apartment complex to North Temple. The bus goes straight up North Temple to the university."

"This is some kind of conspiracy between you, Shari, and that Blaine."

"We've got to follow every lead until it leads us to the killer or completely dead-ends. This one hasn't dead-ended yet."

"What do we do then?"

"You're going to leave … and with any luck Paskel will not have noticed you were here at all. In a few minutes I'm going in there with the most humble and apologetic face I can muster, and I'm going to beg his pardon and tell him I'm sorry all to hell. I'm going to admit we were totally mistaken in our suspicions of him. I'm going to kiss ass until he's placated. Then I'm going to have him followed twenty-four hours a day until we find Marty."

* * *

The news reported Marty Sawyer had fallen into the Jordan River near the Peace Garden. Shari turned the TV off. The mental picture of Carl on the bed with Tami kept coming to her mind. It was unbearable for her to think Marty was in Carl's power. She tried to force that picture out of her mind, but in doing so, the picture of Carl and the rat replaced it. Finally, Tom arrived. He said he was not hungry, which was good because Shari had not even thought about food.

"How's the case going?"

"It's getting frustrating. It just seems that all the leads go nowhere."

"I take it you didn't find anything at Carl's."

Tom looked beaten. "Carl is a red herring. I'm concentrating all my effort on Richards. He must be our man, but there's less than two days left to find Marty."

"Are you just going to ignore Carl then?"

"I'm through with chasing that false lead. We got him totally by surprise, but there was nothing there. I checked the place out myself."

"But you can't just let him go. Maybe he has another place. It would be stupid to have the girl and the evidence right there in his house."

"Not a problem, Shari. Alexander's going to make sure he can't take a leak without someone watching ... at least for the next couple of days. Carl's in his house right now. His empty house, I might add. The front and back doors and all the windows are being watched. He thinks we realized we were wrong and have backed off. He's totally covered, including a planted transmitter in the car. If he makes any attempt to go to a hiding place, we'll be right on him. Alexander has called the guys that were watching your house to help with the surveillance. I guess as long as they're watching Carl, there's no need to waste men watching you."

"What if he catches on, or is just careful and doesn't go to her? She could starve or die of thirst. Isn't there some other way to get to the bottom of this?"

"I'm telling you that he's just not the man. The one we have to find is Richards. However, if we don't find Richards or Marty by Monday morning and Carl hasn't made a move, Alexander'll bring him in and start to put the screws to him."

"Are you totally sure that Carl couldn't be the man? I just get the willies thinking about how cruel he can be." Shari couldn't shake her fear.

"Carl is a distraction. It isn't interfering with the investigation right now because, unfortunately, we don't have many leads to follow up on Richards. All this interest comes from Russell. I can't quite figure out what his motive is, but as soon as we get Richards put away, I plan to give that some attention."

"Do you think you have a chance to get Richards in time?"

"I don't know. We need a big break about now." The faint sounds of defeat were in Tom's voice. It was probably be too late to save Marty from molestation. "I'm going to the station to look over some of Richards's files and see if I can find something to lead us to him."

Shari saw the vulnerability in Tom and felt it in his voice. "You need some sleep." She wanted to invite him to spend the night. Were her feelings born out of her fear of Carl? She could not tell. "You should go home and rest first."

"I couldn't sleep now. There's a cot at the office. I'm not going to hype myself up with coffee. I'll go to sleep there if I can. I have to do everything possible to find Marty in time. Sleep can come after that." Shari walked Tom to the door. She watched Tom's car until it turned at the corner two blocks down.

★ ★ ★

DeMayo got out of bed at nine thirty Saturday morning. Yesterday had been a day of near misses. Now Marty was stashed away. She would certainly have been raped by now and would probably be killed tomorrow if he did not find her. He had worked at the station until two thirty this morning, but he did not find anything in Richards's files to lead to where he could be. He had come home but still could not sleep. It was after four in the morning before he dozed off.

He put toothpaste on his toothbrush and stepped into the shower. The cold water was a shock. He brushed his teeth as the water warmed up. Ten minutes later he stepped out to a steam-filled bathroom. He picked the phone up on the fourth ring and sat down on the edge of the bed. "DeMayo, we may have gotten a break. We found John Danton. They're bringing him in now."

DeMayo recognized Alexander's voice. He remembered Danton's name from Richards's file. "I'll be right down." DeMayo quickly dressed, combed his hair, and drove to the station. Twenty-five minutes after the call, he was walking through the door.

Alexander was in his office. "He said anything yet?"

"Good morning to you too."

"Come on, what've we got?"

"He's down in detention." Alexander stood up. "I think he's ready for us."

"What's the charge?"

"We got him with a pocket full of marijuana. He's on parole, so this is a ticket back for him. He should be willing to deal."

"Danton went to high school with Richards, and they were in prison together. What's their connection now?"

"Danton got out four months before Richards. He helped Richards get his job. We got all the cards, so I think we just put 'em on the table. And let's not mention anything about Marty. If he knows where Richards is, I don't want him to pass on that we know the drowning was a set up."

"What about Paskel?"

Alexander stopped at the door to the interrogation room. "Nothing last night. Everything was covered ... he didn't make a move. Hasn't left the house this morning. We'll keep him under surveillance till we find Marty."

When they walked in, Danton looked up from the table. He wore slacks and a polo shirt. He looked like he was on his way to a golf course. "You're looking pretty prosperous. I'm Detective Alexander, and this is Detective DeMayo."

Danton looked up and nodded. He had a worried look on his face.

"You're in a lot of trouble. Maybe we can help. We're looking for an old buddy of yours."

"Who?"

"Dale Richards ... you know where he is?"

"He's got a pad up on Wall Street. What do you want him for?"

"He left that place and dropped out of sight. We want to know where he is now."

"What do you want him for?"

"We want to talk to him. Can you help us or not?" Alexander's voice was almost matter-of-fact.

Danton turned to DeMayo. "You're that hold-the-mayo guy, aren't you?"

"Where did you get that name?"

"That's what Richards uses all the time. Last time I talked to him, he said you had shook him down. Said you went too far, and he had a friend with some influence. Said he was going to teach you a lesson."

"When was that?" Alexander asked.

"Richards told me that the day after you rousted him."

"Who was the friend?" DeMayo asked.

"Somebody with money and power is all I know. He never told me his name."

"What, exactly, did he tell you about him?" Alexander asked.

"It's someone with money and connections that money can buy. Richards said he was going to ruin DeMayo's career."

"What is this guy ... a politician maybe?"

"I don't think a politician ... he mostly talked about money and buying people off."

"And that was the last time you saw him?" Alexander asked.

"Yeah."

"Did he say anything about plans to disappear?"

"Hell no ... just the opposite. He was going to start putting the screws to DeMayo. I got the idea he was going to be very visible."

"He didn't say anything about moving or laying low?" Alexander pressed.

"Look, I'm no dummy! You can't find him, so I guess he disappeared. From what he said, that's pretty convenient for DeMayo."

"Don't get smart. You're not helping much here." DeMayo held back an urge to slap his face.

"Maybe I can help you best by just keeping my mouth shut." Danton seemed to have gotten over his fear as he continued to imply that DeMayo may have had something to do with Richards's disappearance.

"You got nothing to deal with on that count." Alexander was calm but forceful. "We have already dealt with his powerful attorney. So far you haven't helped us."

Danton sank noticeably in his chair. "Look, he didn't say anything to me about dropping out of sight. We weren't really that close. He was a loner. Not many people hang out with a child molester."

"But you did," DeMayo said.

"I knew him from before that came out. We were old friends, but I don't consider us to be friends now. He looked me up when he got out of prison, but we haven't talked more than five or six times since he got out. You say he's missing. I wouldn't have missed him. Just the fact that you're here asking these questions means he probably raped another kid. No way I would protect someone that does that."

Alexander blew the air from his chest through his lips, almost a whistle. "Okay, you don't know where he is. Where do you think he would go if he wanted to hide out?"

"He would head for the mountains now. He hates the cold though. He'll come out in the winter."

"Do you think he may have access to a cabin?" DeMayo asked.

"I don't know of anything like that. Maybe his rich friend. But in the summer a tent would be fine for him."

"What about a car?"

"Didn't have one, but he could steal one easy enough. That's probably what he would do if he wanted a car."

Alexander stood up. "I need to see you for a minute," he said to DeMayo. The two men walked out leaving Danton alone. "This guy's not going to be much more help. He's telling us all he knows," Alexander said.

"I'm afraid you're right. He might know something he's not aware of. I'll question him some more about mutual acquaintances and Richards's personal habits."

"Go ahead, take as much time as you need. When you're done, kick him loose. I'll have him followed, just in case he does know where Richards is and tries to contact him."

"Well, I won't keep him long. The sooner we find Marty the better it's going to be for her." DeMayo questioned Danton for another hour with no luck.

* * *

Shari hit her breaks as the Taurus in front of her braked. Someone had cut him off. She had not slept well last night after Tom left. However, as the day had worn on, her depression over Marty had turned to anticipation about seeing Russell. She hoped he might have more information about Carl and how to find Marty. Going through prison security was second nature to her now.

"You look tired." Russell took his seat. Shari tried to focus on the fact that he was a convicted child molester, but she realized she was beginning to believe he had been framed. *What are you falling for?* "Knock knock. Is anybody in there?"

Shari snapped out of her reverie. "What? Oh. It's just that, with another girl missing, I haven't slept very well."

"Another girl kidnapped?" Russell seemed surprised.

"Geez. I thought you had a psychic link?"

"I get general ideas but no details. When did it happen?"

"Yesterday. It's been in the news."

"I've been spending my time writing and meditating."

"I wish your meditations would get better, but it seems they're getting worse."

"I've hit a wall. Maybe he has sensed me and is cutting me off. So tell me what happened."

"A little girl named Marty Sawyer disappeared from the Peace Garden at Jordan Park. The news is reporting a possible drowning, but the police are sure it's Abaddon."

"Oh shit!" Russell's eyes widened. "Carl has her!"

"How do you know that?"

"It's like a dam broke when you were talking."

"Where is she?"

"Tell Tom to search his house. She's very close to the house. The key is in the house."

"She isn't in the house?"

"It's close. It's a room, but no windows. It's cold ... maybe in a basement."

"They searched the house yesterday."

"They didn't find anything?"

"No. Tom went there himself, and he was very down after. He personally went through the entire house."

"The basement too?"

"Yeah. Tom said it was just an open room with no place to hide anything."

"She's close. They missed something."

"What?"

"I don't know ... something ... something that leads to the room."

"Could you find it if you were to go to the house?"

"I think I could ... I don't know." Russell's voice lacked conviction.

"How do you know she's close to his house? Couldn't he have her near where he works?"

Russell got up and began to pace as he talked. "Carl thinks of himself as a lion at the top of the food chain. He talked about how he would hunt children as if he were a lion. To him it was like being out on the plains of Africa. The victim was there only to satisfy his needs.

He'll keep his prey close until his hunger is satisfied. He has her close to where he lives, and eats, and sleeps. Tell Tom to concentrate close to the house." Russell paced back and forth like a cat in a cage.

"How can he be so evil to a little girl?"

"For Carl, people are things. The crying and pleading of a child has no more meaning to him than the bleating of a baby wildebeest has to the lion that has started to eat it before it's dead."

Shari took a deep breath. She wanted her voice to be steady as she asked the next question. "When you peeked at people, did you think of your victims as things?"

"I was suicidal at times over my behavior, but that feeling came from the fear that God was going to punish me. I didn't think about how the victims felt. They didn't even know I was there."

"But you wrote that sometimes you tried to be seen to make your fantasy come true."

"Right, but it would be someone I had watched several times. I picked a woman based upon my feeling she was putting on a show ... hoping someone was watching. When I showed myself, the reaction I wanted was for the woman to be interested. If a woman showed fear, that was a turn off. Why was my fantasy one in which the woman enjoyed it? Why is Carl's fantasy one in which the victim dies? Maybe there is empathy in my fantasy."

"And yet you were not thinking of them."

"I was looking for a victim who appeared to be rebellious. For instance, the Mormon Church teaches it's a sin to smoke, so I looked for women who smoked. There were other more subtle things. All predators learn to find the victim that is most likely to fulfill their fantasy. I was thinking of my victims in the sense that I was looking for women who would be pleased to know someone was watching."

"I'm not sure that shows any real empathy."

"I'm just saying the character of my fantasy showed a level of concern for the victim. Maybe that played a role in my ultimate victory over the behavior."

"What about Carl? Is there any hope he'll stop like you say you did?"

"All barriers have collapsed for him. We have to catch him and make sure he never gets another opportunity."

"So how do we catch him?"

"Catching him won't be enough. He'll be able to work the system with his money so that eventually he'll be out again."

"So then, what are we supposed to do?"

"He'll have to be killed."

"You're crazy. That would go against everything the law stands for."

"Who stands for the innocent girls?"

"The law."

"The law stands for the rights of the accused. For instance, if you have evidence that proves a man guilty beyond any shadow of doubt, but there was some nit-picking thing wrong with the way the evidence was collected, then see whom the law protects."

"So what are you proposing? Vigilantes?"

"If Carl gets sent to this prison, I'll find a way to kill him. I don't know how or when, but I'll be the one to finally stop him. That may be the entire purpose of my life."

"We need to find Marty today. Couldn't you just meditate and get a fix on her?"

"I don't know. It doesn't seem to work that way. I have feelings about how Carl feels. He feels powerful now. Tom has to make sure he's followed. They can't lose him for a moment. He'll lead them to her. He has an uncontrollable need to complete his perversion with her. Just remember, she's close to the house."

"They are following him. He's not going to be able to take a leak without being watched … that's what Tom said."

"Then there is hope." Russell produced an envelope and handed it to Shari. "Here's the next chapter."

"Already? You're moving pretty fast."

"I may not have time to finish it."

"What do you mean by that?"

"You and I will stop Carl, but it's going to be costly … maybe too costly." A picture of a rat tied to a board came to Shari's mind.

"In the last chapter, you talked about your wife and son. That's not the wife with the daughter."

"No. I don't think she ever got over my first arrest. We had another son, but ultimately she divorced me. It was several years after I had overcome my problem, but she had fallen for another man. She got custody of the boys and married him. They moved to northern Idaho, where he is a forest ranger. I see the boys three or four times a year, but I haven't heard from them since this last arrest. Well, I think they are better off … up in the mountains … fishing, horseback riding … that sort of thing. They seem very happy. Are we done?"

"Yes … I think that will be all for today."

Shari tried to call Tom as soon as she got home. She was not able to get him at home or at his office. Finally, she managed to contact Detective Alexander. "This is Shari Darling, Tom's friend. I met with you a few days ago about the angels."

"Yes, I remember. You were a big help. What can I do for you?"

"I was trying to get in touch with Tom."

"He's in the field trying to locate Dale Richards. Is it an emergency?"

"Russell says Marty is someplace near Carl's house and there's a clue about where she is in the house. You should check his house out again."

"There isn't much chance that we will get another search warrant without more evidence. But you can rest assured we are watching Mr. Paskel very closely. If he tries to get to the girl, we'll be there."

Shari hung the phone up and opened the envelope Russell had given her.

Conquering the Ever-Widening Circle
Chapter Five: The Darkest Hour

What is the nature of compulsive behavior? Part of me was personally committed to the depths of my soul to overcome this need to peek through windows. Another part of me could not give it up. Within three months of my experience with the police officer, I was peeking at women more than ever. In the beginning, I usually went out in the late evenings. I would tell my wife I had homework to do in the library at school. However, I found early mornings were a better time. I would tell my wife I was jogging.

I kept a coded listing of all the places where I could see what I wanted. About 70 percent of the time was spent looking for new women to watch, and the other 30 percent of the time was going back on my list of favorites.

My life was a mess. I had passed through the crisis of nearly committing suicide, and not only was I unable to curtail my behavior, but it was getting worse. This was the classical war between good and evil. The ever-widening circle was engulfing my life. When I wasn't acting out, I was either planning to do it more or regretting what I had done. During all this time, I remained active in the church.

One morning, as I was coming from behind a house, a police squad car pulled up alongside me. The officer in the car rolled the window down and said, "Hey, you! Get in the car!"

I stepped onto the parkway and prepared to make a dash for it. "What do you want?"

"Just get in the car, right now."

"I will, but I just want to know what for." I was hoping he was there for something else.

"I'll tell you what I want as soon as you get in the car. Don't make any unnecessary trouble for yourself. Get in!" Passing up an opportunity to make a run for it, I got into the car, and he started his interrogation, "What's your name?"

"John." It was the first thing that came to my mind.

"What's your last name?"

"Smith." I could not believe I said that!

"Really? Where do you live?"

"Just up the street."

"What's the address?"

"We just moved into an apartment. I don't know the address right off, and I'm not sure I can even find it right away." Can you believe this? My brain must have decided that if my body was not going to run away at least it would get itself out of there.

The officer picked up the microphone of his radio and made a call. "I have the suspect here in the car with me."

"*Squawk, squawk, squ*—there now. *Crackle*—him—*squawk?*"

"In a minute." Then to me, "You just came from behind that house, didn't you?"

"No. I was coming down the street."

"The lady in that house just called to report a peeping tom. What do you say to that?"

"It wasn't me."

"I saw you coming from behind the house." Then on the radio again, "I'm going to have to have him identified."

"Car—*squawk*—waiti—*crackle*. Call back—*squawk crackle*—there."

"Ten-four."

"What—*squawk crackle*—wenty?"

The officer then gave our location.

"Ten-four. *Crackle crackle*—minutes."

Then he said to me, "Okay, I am going to have you ID'd." He stood me by the car and then put a pair of handcuffs on me—very tight and uncomfortable. Another police car showed up, and the first officer went up to the house. A lady came out on the porch. I heard her say, "That's him," as she pointed to me. I had plans for that day! I had classes to go to! I did not have time to be arrested! I did not have money for bail! I could not face my family with this!

At the police station, I was taken to a detective. He told me the case was ironclad. He said if I would cooperate with him, it could go easy on me. He had a whole list of reported incidents of voyeurism in the area where I had been arrested. I soon understood that cooperation for him meant he wanted to clear up as many of these cases as possible. As he went through them I admitted to most of them, even though the only lady I had looked at in that area was the one where I was caught. I was very cooperative.

When we were done, he made a phone call. On his end of the conversation he used adjectives like very sorry, cooperative, remorseful, and so on. After the call, he told me that if I was willing, the judge would see me right now, and we could clear everything up today.

After consideration of my status as a student and an active member of the Mormon Church, the judge told me he would let me off with no fine or jail time. After a period of some preaching and explanation about his responsibility to protect the community, he sentenced me to six months' probation with a warning that if there was a repeat I would do jail time.

What had my life come to? I had just barely missed going to prison. I had a wife and a son who were depending upon me. One more slipup and I would go to prison. So many times I had tried to stop, and just as many times I had failed. Well, it was over now. I had no more say in the matter. When I was caught it did not matter what I had planned for my life, I was suddenly in someone else's power. That was unacceptable to me. The chapter of my life that involved voyeurism was over. I had too many other things with my family, church, and career to mess around with it anymore. This wasn't a tearful, suicidal thing. It was just the way it had to be, and I would do whatever was required to make sure that it never happened again.

★ ★ ★

DeMayo spent Saturday afternoon and most of the night on the streets checking Richards's known haunts and friends. At three in the morning on Sunday, he went home to try to sleep.

Sunday he got up at six and took a cold shower followed by downing several cups of coffee. He was still groggy. His mind felt like the tingle he got in his leg when it went to sleep. He took another shower—no help. He drove to the office to look at John Danton's file. It was a shot in the dark, but he knew he had to do something. Once in the office, his head began to clear. He had picked up Danton's file and started to look in it when the phone rang. "DeMayo here."

"Yeah ... this is Reynolds at Dispatch. Just got a call for you. I taped it. I think it's that poet killer."

DeMayo sat up in the chair. "Play it!"

After some static and various other noises, the metallic sound of a heavily disguised voice came over the phone. "Tell that prick, hold-the-mayo, to look behind the swimming pool at Fairmont Park for the thing they thought was lost in the Jordan River."

"That was it?"

"That was all, and then he hung up."

"I'm heading out there right now. Call Alexander and let him know we may have found Marty." DeMayo ran to his car and squealed the tires as he left the station. He drove up Fourth South to Seventh East, where he turned right heading south. Seventh East was a main arterial where he was able to reach speeds up to seventy miles per hour. At Twenty-First South he made a left turn and sped up the two blocks to Ninth East, where he turned right. After a couple of blocks, he was pulling into the parking lot closest to the Fairmont Park swimming pool.

He jumped from the car and ran the sixty yards to the back of the pool. The I-80 Freeway ran east and west behind the pool. A four-foot walkway went between the fence around the pool and the fence along the freeway right-of-way. The walkway was empty. The freeway was about thirty fee above the park. The slope up to the freeway was landscaped with trees and bushes. DeMayo climbed over the fence and started to look in the bushes and trees near the pool. There was nothing directly behind the pool, so he started following the slope east, away from the pool. He was about to give up when he saw something red about a hundred feet east of the pool. He found the body of a very small girl sitting cross-legged with her back to a tree, facing up the slope to the freeway. She was wearing a new red skirt with a white blouse. Just under the hem of the skirt DeMayo could see she was wearing white panties. A folded piece of paper was tucked in the right leg of the panties. She was small for her age. DeMayo pulled the paper and sat on the slope above her. Just days ago she was alive and happy. Frustration flowed down DeMayo's checks with his tears as he read the new poem.

DeMayo heard Alexander calling his name. He did not respond. Alexander ran along the fence until he was even with DeMayo. "Hey, buddy! What's up?" DeMayo still did not answer. He sat on the hill looking at the tree on the slope in front of him. "Hey! Come on, man. It's Alexander here! You find the girl?"

DeMayo did not make any kind of acknowledgment that he had heard Alexander. Alexander climbed over the fence and walked up the hill to DeMayo. As Alexander approached, DeMayo looked up. He handed the poem to him. "He did it again, Joe ... right under our nose. We knew it was coming, and we couldn't do a thing about it." Alexander sat down beside DeMayo with the poem.

The Lion and the Angel

Muscles rippling under tawny skin
    the lion stocks his prey.
In majesty he moves upon the herd;
    no one can tell him nay.
He takes just what he wants and needs;
    that's what the herd is for.
He is the king of all the plain;
    who dares to keep the score?

I am a king and stand above
    the noble in the street.
My needs become most paramount;
    before me all retreat.
The herd in silly impertinence,
    would seek me to destroy.
But I am above their little games,
    and play them like a toy.

Angel of purity, sweet Tahariel;
    you fit my wants so well.
I taught you life and you went on;
    how lonely now, Michelle
sits on her chair up in your room.
    You move on to heaven;
sent there by the true lion king
    four years before eleven.

A higher call than your friends;
    the lion king you feed.
Your freshness, youth, and innocence
    where just what I did need.
While those who belong among the herd
    predator would call me,
I'm proud to go by that noble name.
    It is the top, you see.

And silly members of the herd
    would catch me in my game.
Forgetting all the laws of nature,
    they hunt me just the same.
I lead them here, I lead them there.
    The clues I just alter.
They think that dear Tahariel was
    drowned beneath the water.

One of the seventy amulets
    Tahariel must be.
But seventy times seventy
    is not enough for me.
I come I go where I please.
    My name—invincible.
Follow all the clues I give, but
    catch me—impossible.

Abaddon/Apollyon

"Come on, DeMayo, this isn't the first child to die, and it won't be the last."

"She's not an *it*, Joe. She's a little girl who was depending on us to save her. We had two days, and we didn't even get close. I can't be on this case anymore." DeMayo had stopped crying.

"Why are you dropping out now?"

"This is too personal. He's an arrogant son of a bitch, and if I get to him first ... I'll kill him."

"Look, DeMayo, this is the worst kind of setback, but Abaddon is making mistakes. Mistakes he doesn't know about. You've been able to spot them. We need you to stick with this."

DeMayo stood up and took a step down the hill beside Alexander. He stared at him eye to eye for a moment, and then without saying a word, he walked past him down the hill and climbed over the fence. As he walked past the pool, the lab van pulled into the parking lot.

Chapter Six

THE THREAT

The man made the phone call, and then returned to the park and waited in a stand of pine trees. He had not waited long when he saw someone run behind the pool as though he were looking for something. His heart raced as he put the binoculars to his eyes. It was Detective DeMayo searching behind the pool! The man watched as DeMayo looked around and then climbed the fence and started looking along the hill below the freeway. The man had placed the body where he could get a clear view of DeMayo's reaction when he found her. DeMayo found the body and sat on the hill in front of it. The binoculars were not powerful enough to see the expression on his face. DeMayo got up, reached his hand to the girl, and sat back down with the poem. In a short time, he dropped his hand to his side and sat motionless. The man thought he could see the sheen of wetness on DeMayo's cheek. *He's crying! God Damn! He's crying!* The man wanted to get closer to see the pain. There was no other cover closer, but he had to see the pain. He started to walk toward the pool. He had taken only a couple of steps when he saw someone come from the parking lot. He could faintly hear him call DeMayo's name. Reluctantly he stepped back into the cover of the pine trees.

He watched as the second man climbed over the fence and approached DeMayo. He knew that soon the park would be filled with police officers. He left to clean the room.

This had been even better than Barbelo. This time he had seen DeMayo suffer. Soon he would get that bitch Bat Qol and make DeMayo suffer the ultimate humiliation. Then he could leave. But before Bat Qol, he wanted to get the little black girl. Then he would spend the rest of the summer in Chicago. He would send poems to DeMayo from there. Then he would move on to Los Angeles for the winter and send more poems to DeMayo. Each poem would signal a new section to his growing scrapbook of angels.

Azura? That was the name her mother had used to call her. In a week or ten days he would be ready to make his move. He had been patient and thorough in his preparation for her. She would be special, and he needed to know as much about Azura and her family as possible in order to make the snatch as he had planned it.

* * *

It was dark when the man parked his car near Liberty Park. He quickly walked two blocks then into the alley. His heart beat faster as he took his place under the apricot tree. The girl's window was open, and the light was on, but there was no sign of Azura. He hoped her mother had started to the leave the window open again. He had been there only a couple of minutes when the girl and her mother came into the room. He brought the binoculars to his eyes. He could see her pretty face. Soon she would be his.

Suddenly, the view was obscured by a blue veil. He took the glasses from his eyes. *Son of a bitch!* The mother had closed the window and the curtains. He waited a few minutes and then quietly climbed off the roof. As he got to the ground, he took a look around. Across the alley, in the shadows, he saw a faint glow—like a red eye watching him. "Who's there?" he whispered. As he walked gingerly across the alley, he could smell the faint odor of pot. He wanted to run, but he knew he had to find out who was there. As he got closer to the shadows, a teenage girl stepped into the dim light. The sides of her head were shaved, and the top seemed to have been arranged by a mad scientist. It reminded him of the way Cyndi Lauper did her hair about ten years ago. The girl wore a short, dark skirt that barely covered her crotch. "What're you doin' on that garage? You some kind of sicko peeping tom?" Her voice was defiant, and her words were a little slurred. She looked directly at the binoculars as she spoke.

"I wouldn't worry about that. I can smell what you're doing. Whadda ya say we make a truce?"

The girl took a deliberate puff of her joint and blew the smoke from the corner of her mouth. "I know how Mrs. Gillis shows herself at the window. She's jus' beggin' to be seen, but I wouldn't tell her … she'd jus be all flattered. Besides, my boyfriend and I look at her from the cherry tree. She ain't such a much."

"You think you're any better?"

"You'll never know."

"Okay, but have we got a deal … about keeping quiet?"

"Waddaya mean?"

The man took a small step toward the girl. "I mean, I don't say anything about the marijuana, and you don't say anything about Mrs. Gillis."

"You know me … I never get involved in other people's business."

The man did not know her, and he was not sure whether she would say anything or not. When Azura turned up missing, she might have a lot to say. He took another small step. "Good. I'm the same way myself. Hey, you got any of that you could spare?"

"Not likely," she took a step back into the shadows.

The man took another step. "How about just a puff for the road?"

"No. Take a hike, pervert." Those were the last words she would speak. The man took one more step and swung his binoculars with all his strength. There was a crack, followed a sigh, and the sound of broken glass hitting the concrete pad they were standing on. The girl fell into the back of the shed and slumped to the ground. The man quickly pulled her blouse around her head to catch the blood. She was unconscious. He couldn't leave her alone to go get his car in case she woke up, so he put his hands around her throat and squeezed as hard as he could. The girl began to struggle, but only for a few seconds. When he was sure she was dead, he pulled her skirt off and wrapped her head in it.

He walked rapidly to his car and drove it into the alley, parking it about five feet past the girl's body. He popped the trunk from the inside of the car and, leaving the lights on, quickly dropped the girl in the trunk. He got in the car and slowly drove away. By the time he reached the end of the alley his heart was racing. Now he would have the unexpected problem of disposing of this body.

★ ★ ★

The man took the body to his room. There was almost no blood. He undressed her and washed her. She was a pretty girl; too bad he'd had to kill her before he got her to the room. She had small breasts. The man shaved her pubic hair. She looked small and angelic when he was done. She would have been fun to play with, but she was not going to heaven. She was a drug user—a whore and a slut. He checked; she was not a virgin. He took a picture of her for his scrapbook. He would have a special section for those he sent to hell.

He left her so he could watch the report of the discovery of a body in Fairmont Park on the ten o'clock news. In the report, the smug police PR prick was making stupid claims that they knew Tahariel didn't drown before he gave them the last poem and saying that an arrest was eminent. The man threw a half-empty can of beer toward the TV, hitting a table beside it. *Those fucking bastards have no idea who they're dealing with!* He had planned to hide this latest body where no one could find it. She would have just been another of those druggy teenagers who disappear. But now his plans changed.

He needed to find a name and write a poem. This poem would hold a hidden warning to DeMayo about Bat Qol. He would never figure it out in time to save her. Then, when he did figure it out, he would blame himself for being so stupid. The plans for her were made. The location of those final moments was set. It would not be in his special room. He had something else in mind for her.

Lying naked on the cot beside his latest victim, he mentally worked out the plans to get Azura. She would be the last in this room. He would dispose of this latest victim so it would be found quickly, and then he would make his move.

★ ★ ★

Ring-ring. DeMayo turned in his bed and knocked the alarm clock off the table. *Ring-ring.* Confused, he shook his head. *Ring-ring.* Sitting up, he rubbed his burning eyes, trying to clear the heavy clouds of a bad night's sleep. *Ring-ring.* He reached for the phone. "Hello."

"DeMayo, this is Alexander. We got a task force meeting at ten thirty this morning."

DeMayo reached to the floor and picked up the alarm clock. The face was broken—it had stopped at nine fifteen. "DeMayo, are you there?"

"I told you yesterday … I'm off the case. I'm taking myself off." His head hurt and talking only made it worse.

"You're the killer's target. You can't back out."

"You have no idea what a bad time this is. I didn't sleep last night … my guts are burning up … we already know it's Richards, and if I get to him, I'm gonna kill the bastard."

"I know about JoLynn, DeMayo. We all got our pasts and the things that drive us. We're depending on you. This is something you wanted."

"How'd you find out about JoLynn?"

"I make it a point to know these things."

"That's crap. Why did you take the time to research that out?"

"You're paranoid."

"You checked me out as a suspect … didn't you?"

"This kind of thing … you know … where someone gets this kind of poem. We got to check out all the possibilities."

"You thought I sent the poems to myself?"

"We just have to check everything out. It isn't good police work to let something go undone."

"Shit!"

"Come on, DeMayo. You don't think we should have checked that out?"

"Screw you!"

"Think about it … you'll see I'm right."

"I'll see you at ten thirty." DeMayo slammed the phone down. He knew Alexander had done the right thing, but he hated it just the same. He would finish this case, but then it would be time to reevaluate his life. Catching all the criminals in the world was impossible. It was time to concentrate more on Shari.

At 10:20 a.m., DeMayo walked into the police building. Alexander was there to greet him. "You look like shit."

"Feel like it too." DeMayo took his blazer off and hung it over the back of his chair.

"This was a terrible setback. Everyone on the team is in the dumps."

"Paskel?"

"He ran some errands Saturday, but most of the day he spent at home. He did several hours of work in the backyard organizing and stacking the firewood behind the shed. He went in for the night at," Alexander consulted the report he had in his hand, "exactly 6:27 p.m. A pizza was delivered at 8:14 p.m. He stayed in the house all the rest of the night and hadn't shown his face when I called off the tail after we found Marty. He was covered the whole time."

"Anything new?"

"I think that fellow Danton knows more than he's saying. After we kicked him loose, he made a call from a phone booth."

"You think he contacted Richards?"

"Don't know, but I got with Piszczek yesterday, and he's been looking this all over. He has some more ideas to go over in the meeting this morning."

"It really ticks me off that Richards is still running around loose. He just never struck me as being smart enough to pull this off."

"It's time for the meeting to start."

"Go ahead, I'll be right along."

At ten thirty DeMayo walked into the meeting room. Piszczek, Peterson, Unger, Alexander, and a man DeMayo didn't know were already there. Corrigan came in behind him.

When they had taken their seats, Alexander stood up. "I guess we're all here. I know it was hard to lose Marty, but we have to learn what we can from this and move forward. Piszczek has a guest from Provo PD. I'll let him introduce him."

Piszczek stood up and said, "I've given some thought to DeMayo's suggestion that the murder of the usher in Provo may be tied to our unsub. I have invited Detective Ralph Thompson of the Provo PD to meet with us." Piszczek pointed to the new man. "I think it would be wise to compare notes on these two cases. Now, in the Provo case the unsub used a knife. After the victim was stabbed, the unsub put his gloved hands inside the victim and scrambled his insides as he died. Now, the physical action was different, but on an emotional level there is a similarity in the sense that the unsub is actively sharing in the death of the victim. Detective Thompson will give you more info."

Detective Thompson gave all the details they had on the Provo murder. There wasn't much.

"Sometimes you can get fingerprints and DNA in the powder on the inside of a glove," Alexander commented.

"The gloves were turned inside out, so any finger prints were smudged by the victim's blood," Thompson explained. "We have sent the gloves to get DNA testing, but that's a long shot."

"Could the girl in the theater identify the man?" DeMayo asked.

"She did notice a strange man the usher told her about, but she wasn't paying any attention. We have tried hypnotism, but it didn't help."

"Is there anything else?" Alexander asked.

"That's all we have so far," Thompson replied.

"Corrigan. What have you got for us on Marty?" Alexander asked.

"This was exactly the same as Katie. Raped multiple times ... hands and legs tied too tight ... washed inside and out ... new clothes ... teeth marks on the outside of the cheeks ... death caused by suffocation. It'll all be in the report."

"Could you match the teeth marks to a suspect?" Thompson asked.

"No, the skin wasn't broken, so what we have is unclear bruising."

"You got anything new to add?" Alexander asked Piszczek.

DeMayo was thinking of JoLynn—trying not to think of Marty in the grasp of Abaddon. "... call was placed in from a phone booth in Sugarhouse."

"What? What about Sugarhouse?"

"DeMayo? Where the hell've you been? Piszczek was just talking about the phone message leading to the discovery of Marty's body."

"Sorry ... I was thinking about something else. What's this about Sugarhouse?"

"The phone call was made from a phone booth in Sugarhouse." Sugarhouse was a shopping area located near Fairmont Park.

"Then he was probably waiting there to see my reaction when I found the body."

"I would say that's exactly right," Piszczek said.

"Son of a bitch!" DeMayo was livid. He looked at Alexander. Alexander looked back—neither said a word.

"What?" Unger questioned.

"Nothing! Not a goddamned thing!" Resentment and anger were seething in DeMayo's response. Richards had watched him find the body and had seen him crying.

Piszczek paused a second, then continued. "We should try to find out if anyone around the park noticed someone with a pair of binoculars. Now, that means a lot of footwork and door knocking in the neighborhood around the park, but we may just get lucky."

"There's only one party to this case who's lucky, and it ain't us," DeMayo said.

"What's your problem, Tom? You want to get yourself kicked off this task force?" Unger asked.

"Bingo!"

"DeMayo's just a bit frustrated," Alexander interjected. "He'll be all right."

Unger stared at DeMayo, and DeMayo smiled back. "Go on," Unger said to Piszczek, still looking at DeMayo.

Piszczek shuffled the papers in front of him. "Now in the phone message he refers to the girl as 'that thing.' He doesn't see his victim as human. This is sociopathic thinking. Another thing, the voice is computer generated."

"So how did he come to have a computer set up in a phone booth?" DeMayo asked.

"He probably made a recording off of the computer," Corrigan responded.

"But that means he's pretty handy with a computer," Alexander commented.

"The software is not that hard to operate, but the unsub would need more than just basic computer knowledge," Piszczek said.

"That sort of leads us away from Richards as a suspect," Alexander offered. "There's no record of him having any interest in computers while he was in prison."

"He could have learned since he got out." DeMayo was less sarcastic this time.

"I suppose so, but we didn't find anything in his apartment that even remotely connected him to computers," Unger volunteered.

"Are we saying we should drop him because of a damn phone call?" DeMayo's interest in the case was rekindling.

"No. Of course not. There's still a lot of strong evidence, but we need to keep our minds open to the possibility that it could be someone else," Alexander said.

"I know what you mean about checking all the possibilities." DeMayo looked directly at Alexander. "If it's not Richards, that puts us back to zero."

Alexander met his stare without a flinch. "We'll look for Richards until we find him or until all the leads come to a dead end. We're a long way from dropping him, but we can't put our heads in a tunnel and ignore evidence that points in a different direction."

"So where else do we look? Paskel?" DeMayo could not stop the new sarcasm in his voice.

"Okay," Piszczek impatiently began again, "let's move on to the poem. This one rhymes, but unlike the last poem, the second line of each couplet is exactly six syllables, giving it a singsong cadence. Reading it out loud feels kind of like kids playing jump rope. He seems to be adding his own rules each time ... always making it more difficult to write the poem. He brags about leading us here and there with clues he makes up. He's proud of the fact that he fooled us into believing Marty was drowned. In the poem he introduces a new name ... Michelle. Turns out that's the name of Marty's favorite doll."

"So does that mean he knew Marty before he kidnapped her?" Peterson asked.

"He wouldn't know Marty would be the one of the three girls to run off alone. Now, he had to knock her out and carry her to the car in a bag. He had to steal the car. He took a big chance someone would notice him. If he knew her, he could have arranged something much less elaborate and chancy. No, I think he must have gotten the name of the doll from Marty directly.

"Let's look at the amulets. Now, an amulet is supposed to be a charm or token to protect against evil spirits." Piszczek shuffled the papers in front of him. "Here it says, 'One of the seventy amulets Tahariel must be. But seventy times seventy is not enough for me. I come I go where I please.' I think he sees himself as omnipotent and omnipresent ... he can do and go where he wants. He implies it's not only impossible to catch him, but it would even be against the laws of nature to try."

"Anything else," Alexander asked as Piszczek paused.

"This unsub puts himself on a par with God. He's going to get more reckless as a result. That's why we have taken a proactive approach."

"What do you mean?" DeMayo asked.

"You mean you didn't see last night's news release?" Alexander inquired.

"I was a little out of it yesterday."

"Peterson, you got a copy handy?" Alexander asked.

"Yeah, I'll get DeMayo a copy right away."

Piszczek explained, "We put out a news release in which we talked about how Abaddon tried to fake the drowning and how it failed. The story stressed he's making mistakes, and they're stupid mistakes. It says he was seen in the park at the time of the discovery of the body. We almost caught him at the university when we found the car. The story made him appear stupid and that we are closing in on him."

"What if we just scared him off with all that?" DeMayo asked.

"This guy thinks he's more powerful than God," Piszczek said. "He knows he stirred up a hornet's nest. Now, I believe he will leave the area soon, but he won't run from a threat. Besides, he's certain to make some kind of attack on DeMayo before he goes. We have to watch DeMayo closely, but at the same time we have to make sure the unsub is not aware of it."

"This is something that could just make him mad and cause someone else to be killed," DeMayo quipped.

"I know it's a dangerous game. But I'm sure he'll respond to the threat by attacking DeMayo. Once he strikes back, he'll believe he can leave on his own terms."

"You know it's dangerous, but would you be willing to bet your life it will work?" Alexander asked.

DeMayo stood up. "I'd be willing to bet mine! I say we stay proactive. Let the little bastard come for me. He'll find something more than an eight-year-old girl waiting for him."

"He could just snipe you out of the picture," said Peterson.

"No, he won't do that," Piszczek said. "It would go against his ego. He'll invent something that will put all the cards in his hands. He'll want DeMayo to see who is killing him and know he had lost before he dies. Now, I can't stress this too much ... he'll come in some way we haven't thought of, so we have to think of everything, and then be prepared for the unexpected."

"I don't give a shit about any of that." DeMayo stood up. "This is the guy my career has been about. He's coming after me anyway, I say let's set the terms."

"Glad to see you back on the team," Alexander commented.

DeMayo sat back in his chair. *That little prick saw me crying over Marty's body, but the next time he sees me he won't be happy with what he sees. The next time—he goes down.*

"Okay then, the next thing we have to do is set up the protection for DeMayo," Alexander said.

"No cover." DeMayo was adamant. "We can't take a chance of anything tipping him off. He's too cagey. This may be our only chance to get to him. If we blow it, more girls are going to die."

"He may kill you, and then where would we be?"

"Right where we are now. But he won't get me. He and I are going at it 'mano a mano,' and he's going to lose. I know he's coming ... that's my advantage."

* * *

Shari had set up a meeting with Russell this morning. She cried when the news broke yesterday that Marty had been found dead. She called Tom several times, but there was no answer. She had still not heard from him when she got to her appointment with Russell.

Russell was sitting at the table when Shari arrived. "He killed another little girl."

"You saw the news this time."

"Yeah. What've you heard?"

"Mostly just what's on the news. I haven't been able to talk to Tom about it yet."

"Why not?" Russell asked.

Shari was not offended by his abrupt question. "I haven't been able to reach him. I talked to Detective Alexander, and he said Tom took this last killing very hard. He told Alexander he was quitting, but I think that was just a first reaction. He really wanted to save the little girl. He's taking this case hard because the killer is making it personal."

"What about Carl?"

"They had him under surveillance the whole time. I think the department is pretty sure he's not a viable suspect."

"It was Carl all right. He's a sick man, but he's also smart."

"I can't understand why God created sex. We should be like hydras ... reproduce asexually. That would get rid of most of the problems in the world."

"Sex is the highest level of physical creativity. It's the act that creates new life. If we were asexual beings, we would live lives like hydras ... boring, uncreative, and uninspired. At its best, sex is a highly creative act. Unfortunately, it gets perverted, and then it becomes destructive. There are two sides to that coin ... they are both very strong."

"But I'm not so sure the good side is worth having the bad side."

"What are you passionate about?"

"I don't know. I guess I'm passionate about Tami."

"No, that doesn't count. That's just instinct. What about you as an individual person?"

"Nothing. I feel like life is not real."

"Like a hydra? In a sense you may have become asexual."

"You think I need a lover to waken my life?"

"Not necessarily. It's possible to have a creative passion. Something apart from a lover, but something that could be inspired by a lover."

"I don't have a passion like that, and I don't have a lover either. What's your passion?"

"Ah ... you want to turn this around."

"The point is to write a book about you ... isn't it?"

"Right." Russell leaned back in his chair and stared at the ceiling. "I suppose my life has been gray too. I think at the time I set out to finally overcome my compulsive behavior, I was passionate about succeeding." He looked at Shari, and she stared back. "I'm passionate about stopping Carl."

"And yet he has killed another girl. It seems that no one can stop him." Shari wanted to keep the subject away from her feelings.

"The hardest part is having the patience to succeed. And I know too well that means more innocent victims. But the time is close."

"How? I don't see anyone is at all closer. He picked Marty right out of the park in broad daylight. And if it was Carl, the police were on him right from the first couple of hours. He was watched every minute."

"I don't know what the answer is. But I do know the answer is in the house. That's where you have to go to find the key."

"What am I looking for in the house?"

"The key to the mystery, the answer to everything, is in that house. You've got to get Tom to go back and look closer. Look for something that's not obvious."

"Tom's not going to do that. He's convinced Dale Richards is the killer."

Russell sighed. "I just wish I could get out of here for one day. I would end the whole thing."

"How would you end it?"

"I'd kill Carl."

"Just like that? You'd be judge, jury, and executioner?"

"The thought of him with a little girl is so … I don't know how to put it in words … it's almost as if I have seen it, and it's so revolting, so evil, that even to see it would drag me down. Stopping him is my passion, and I don't have a clue why it's so all consuming. It drives me crazy that the answer is just out of focus."

"Do you think you are close enough to stop him before he gets another victim?"

"The only thing I am absolutely sure of is that somehow you and I will stop him."

"What do you mean, you and me? What am I supposed to do?"

"I don't know. He's angry. I think I can tie into his anger better than any other emotion. If he gets angry enough, he'll make a mistake … and I'll know about it."

"Am I supposed to make him angry?"

"He is angry about the cops being in his house, because he realizes they were close. You have to get Tom back there, if for no other reason than to make him angrier. I'm going to tie into that anger."

"I'll talk to Tom." The conversation about passion and sex had awakened sexual feelings she had not experienced in years, but she was not thinking of Russell.

* * *

Shari left the prison and pulled onto I-15 northbound. Her mind was drawn back to thoughts of passion. She realized the intensity of her life had been suppressed. Suddenly, the red lights on the cars in front of her warned her that she was coming up on a traffic jam. "Oh damn!" she said out loud as she put her foot on the brake. She was not familiar with the surface streets this far south, so she didn't want to exit the freeway. She turned the radio on and started flipping stations to get a traffic report. Finally, she turned the radio to KFAM, a station that played soothing instrumental renditions of popular songs from the '50s and '60s. She liked those songs that were already classics when she was growing up. She thought of her younger days, when life was full of excitement and promise. A girl was trying to kiss a boy on the ear as he drove a Buick in front of her. He was playfully pushing her away. They looked like college kids. Shari moved one lane to the right. If she didn't get back to the office at all today, what difference would it make? The stories she worked on were just something to make a living. Even this book held little interest for her. Before Ralph, her life was full of excitement, and she had enthusiasm. *Was it Ralph's cheating? Carl's impotence? Carl's rape of Tami? All of those things—none of those things? Is this just the way life takes energy and fills the void with apathy and old age?* "But I'm not old," Shari said out loud as she braked to a stop. The cars in front were stopped. They inched forward, and Shari inched one car length forward with the pack. Cars slowly passed her on the left. A harried businessman talking animatedly on a large mobile phone crept by in a small Pontiac. A mobile phone would be useful now. Share had looked into getting one but the minute charges were expensive, the reception was unreliable, and she had heard horror stories of people having their numbers hacked into and finding thousands of minutes charged to their accounts. The music was relaxing. Traffic stopped again. *Thank God for air conditioning.*

Shari rummaged through her purse to find her appointment book. It confirmed there was nothing really important today—she might as well relax. *Honk! Honk! Honk!* Startled, Shari dropped her appointment book between her feet on the floor. She looked up to see she had let the cars move up two car lengths. She pulled forward to fill up the space and stopped. She reached between her legs to pick up the book. Her elbow and forearm brushed against the inside of her thigh as she brought the book up. She felt a tingling sensation in her stomach and a chill in her leg from the light touch of skin on skin. Sensual feelings spread through her body. Shari immediately suppressed them.

Shari moved forward again. "Chantilly Lace" was playing on the radio. She realized she had suppressed her body and her feelings for years. Dr. Langley had suggested she was suppressing a tigress within. She put her hand on the inside of her right knee so that her fingertips and fingernails touched her skin at the same time. She slowly moved her hand up the inside of her thigh, sensing both the softness of her fingertips and the light scratch of her nails. Her body seemed on fire. The rhythm of "Wake up, Little Susie" filled the car.

Shari put both hands on the steering wheel. The tigress ached to be awakened. What would Tom think if he knew she was fantasizing about him? Shari pulled off the freeway at Forty-Ninth South. She had something important to do now, and this snail's pace was not part of her plan.

* * *

DeMayo left the task force briefing in a bad mood. The desire to quit was replaced with a desire to get to Richards and kill him if need be. The phone rang as he sat at his desk daydreaming of getting Richards. "DeMayo here."

"Tom, I had to call you. I tried to get you several times yesterday. How are you?"

"Well, I guess you saw the news."

"Yeah. It's terrible isn't it?"

"Terrible is not the word. I just got out of a task force meeting. They purposely put the story in the news last night to make the killer angry. They think he'll make a mistake if he's angry enough."

"Angry is good. I just got back from a meeting with Russell. He senses that Carl is getting angry. The angrier he gets, the better Russell can read him."

"Shari, there's no possible way it could be Carl."

"Tom, let's not argue about this today. How would you like to come over for a home-cooked meal?"

Tom hesitated. He noticed new warmth in her voice, but now that they had made him Abaddon's target, he knew it would be dangerous for Shari to be near him. He didn't want to do anything to put Shari in danger, but he didn't want to tell her he was a target either.

"Tom?"

"Uhm, you know there's nothing I would rather do, but tonight is just not a good night."

"Why? Is there someone else?"

DeMayo recognized the disappointment in her voice. "No, no, Shari. It's just that this case is ... well, I'm really in the middle of something, and my time is not my own until I get it worked out."

"Does work always come first with you?" Shari sounded a bit peeved.

"No. Please, just give me a couple of days. We're close to a solution."

"Not if you still think it's Dale."

"I don't know who it is ... but I know he's making mistakes. He's starting to crack, and we're ready for him."

"Thank God for that. Call me when you get some free time." Shari hung the phone up.

DeMayo looked at the phone for a couple of minutes. He could not believe he had just brushed off the woman he most wanted in his life.

The phone rang. He hoped it was Shari. There was something unsaid in the phone conversation. He picked up the phone, anticipating her voice.

"DeMayo, it's Alexander."

"What's up?"

"We got another body."

"Already?"

"Found her in a restroom in Fairmont Park."

"Abaddon?"

"Complete with a new poem."

"Holy shee-it! When did they find her?"

"Come on over to my office, and I'll update you."

DeMayo hung up the phone. It was incredible that Abaddon would kidnap another girl this soon. That meant he had not held her his normal two days. Was this retaliation for the news release? DeMayo walked straight to Alexander's office. "Okay, what's the story?"

"This is a teenage girl. Looked to be fourteen or fifteen. Still haven't identified the body."

"When did they find her?"

"About two hours ago. She was naked, but she is too old to be a preferred victim. They didn't suspect it was related to our case until Corrigan found the poem. It was rolled into a tampon applicator and pushed up inside her."

"You see it yet?"

"Yeah. Here." Alexander handed DeMayo a copy of the poem.

The Sacrifice

Derdekea came to save but fell into my power,
    exiting this life at my bidding.
Moved by love, I teach my angels the laws of flesh
    and then send them from this hell.
You puny humans attempt to outwit me.
    Oh how stupid to try.

Love like mine is beyond mere human thought.
> Only God can know its depth.

Venus could not comprehend the fullness of my sacrifice,
> even Jesus did not rise that high.

Sacrifice like mine sails in clouds of exaltation

> stopped only by my death.

How much greater my sacrifice of physical death
> and then eternal damnation.

Rivers of grief flow through my mortal veins
> in eternity, greater grief for me.

Try your best to stop me—you will fail.
> Only age can find me.

Oblivious to your puny attempts to catch me,

> by my superior cunning

and intelligence, I push beyond your levels,
> driven by love and true sacrifice.

Finding the still innocent and pure, I send them
> on to Celestial Glory,

Rejoicing in the power I have to save.

> Happiness eternal is their lot.

Eternal hell fire is the totality of my
> Reward.

Abaddon/Apollyon

"Well, he's consistent as far as his growing ego," DeMayo commented. "Now he's calling his sacrifice greater than Christ's. Instead of getting more complicated the poem is simpler ... rushed."

"That's my thought too. However, the spacing for the stanzas doesn't make sense. In some cases it breaks up couplets. I wonder if there is a message in that. First there are six lines, then five, and then five again, and then four with just three lines each. Does the number 6-5-5-3-3-3-3 mean anything to you?"

"No, but he must have spaced the poem like that for some reason."

"I have a task force meeting set for three this afternoon."

"Three! What the hell! Are we just going sit on our hands till three?"

"That's when we'll have all the information on this latest killing. It'll take some time to finish the autopsy, and Piszczek is checking the poem and the scene."

"Screw that! We need to be kicking ass!"

"Settle down, DeMayo. Now is not the time to run off half-cocked. Let's give the lab boys and Piszczek some time to collect and organize the evidence."

"I can't just sit around, for Christ sake."

"You better find something to do. Why don't you check the files and see if you can find something related that number?"

"That's a chump assignment." DeMayo walked toward the door.

"What're you going to do?" Alexander asked.

"Sit at my damn desk and look at those damned files that I've already memorized to see if can find something related to a number in them."

Dan Bonner was walking by DeMayo's desk when he got back. "What's new?"

"That bastard, Abaddon, has killed another girl. The news release last night was supposed to make him mad enough to come after me, but no ... he went out and killed a teenage girl instead. Piszczek thought he would come in a way that no one expected, but this was ... unexpected."

"And he sent you another poem?"

"Yeah ... here." DeMayo shoved the poem to Bonner.

Bonner read the poem. "You think he killed this girl because of the news release?"

"Yeah. That's pretty obvious. Outsmarted again." DeMayo was livid.

"I'm not so sure. I mean, he says Derdekea came to save something and fell into his power. I think the girl got killed because of something she did. Then he starts going on about what a great guy he is and how stupid you are to try to outsmart him. Maybe that part is about the news, but the girl looks like something separate."

"You're right. And another thing … the poems were getting more organized, but this one seems more like the first one. No rhymes, no complicated rhythms. And now he's talking about celestial glory instead of celestial kingdom … a condition instead of a place."

"He's getting wild. Maybe he's about the make a mistake."

"Just a sec." DeMayo opened his newly acquired dictionary of angels. "Look, Derdekea is in here. It's a female angel who descended from heaven to save mankind. You're right; he killed her to stop her from saving something, but what? Maybe she saw him do something … like she might have seen him in the park."

"Makes sense."

"I think it's about time for me to do something proactive," DeMayo said.

"What do you suggest?"

"Well, suppose he's watching me. I think maybe I'll just make myself a target. What do you say I go up to the shooting range? That's out of town. Gunfire is not uncommon there. If it's not too busy, and if he's following me that would be a good place for him to make his play."

"You paint a target on yourself like that, and the next thing you know you're dead."

"Piszczek is pretty sure he'll want to face me and make sure I see it coming. That'll give me a second or two to make a play. If I'm ready and expecting him, there's a good chance I can get him first. This is my trap; that's going to give me the advantage."

"I guess that's better than just sitting around here. How about I go with you?"

"No. Too many people might scare him off."

"You going off by yourself might be suspicious. Besides, this prick thinks he's more powerful than God. One person more or less isn't going to deter him."

"You're right. Besides, I'll need someone to make sure Jerry and the customers are kept out of danger."

★ ★ ★

After Shari hung the phone up from inviting Tom to dinner she paced around the room. How could he pretend to be interested in her, and then just when she opened the door, he pulled back? She was hurt and confused, so she called him back, but no one answered. Maybe it was better this way; maybe she was not ready for another man after all. She decided to work through the latest chapter from Russell to kill some time. She did not want to go into the office, so she called Jane and told her she was working in her house for the rest of the day.

Conquering the Ever-Widening Circle
Chapter Six: The Deal

My first talk with the probation officer lasted about twenty minutes and covered the following points:

1. I could not leave the Ogden area without prior permission from him.
2. I would have to make a report to him each month.
3. I had gotten off easy, but if it happened again, he would throw the book at me.

After being caught, I made up my mind to tell my wife. If I was really going to give this behavior up, there was a cost. I would have to let her know and have her support. I explained to her that I had the problem long before I ever met her. After we talked, she went to our room and would not let me come in. She would not talk to me for several days. I had opened a wound in the relationship that, with time, scabbed over but never healed. After a couple of months things were back to normal, at least on the surface. I was not bothered with the old desire, I was paying more attention to school, and I felt good about myself. I do not know how or why, but the fantasies came back within three months after my arrest. By the final two months of my probation, I was fully involved with voyeurism again!

After graduation, we decided I would take a job in Denver. It would be an opportunity for me to get a fresh start in a fresh city. I went ahead to find a place to live, and then my family was planning to follow. I got started in my new job and began looking for an apartment. In a few days, I began to think about voyeurism again. I felt I owed myself one last time. Soon my family would be there and I would settle down to a daily routine, which would not give me the time to do it anymore. I knew I had promised myself I would not do it in Colorado, but I told myself that doing it just a couple of times until my family got there wouldn't hurt.

I started prowling the neighborhoods at night and during the predawn hours. By the time my family came, I had already found several "regulars." Early morning "jogging" became a part of my regular routine. Soon I began to take stock of the life I was living. I was continually going up and down that roller coaster from emotional highs about my family and career to deep depression about my bad behavior. I came to the conclusion there was no way for me to overcome this problem—not by myself—not with the help of the church—not with the help of my family—not by the power of sincere prayer—not out of fear of jail—not out of fear of losing everything I held dear—not through therapy—not by any means I could imagine or devise. I made a deal with myself. Instead of trying to beat it, I would exert control over it. I would carefully determine when I did it. I could defeat the temptations to take risks as long as I knew I would eventually give in when I found a safer situation.

Because I believed it was beyond my power to stop, I lost all sense of guilt and shame over the behavior, and the emotional roller coaster ride was over. I settled into this new lifestyle, wishing it could be different, but accepting myself as flawed and determined to make the very best I could out of it. I worked hard in my career. I provided good support for my family and was able to make a down payment on our first house. My wife was able to stay home to take care of the house and children, as that was her dream. I continued to be called to leadership positions in the church, which I enjoyed. Since all of these callings were supposedly made based upon inspiration, I concluded I was okay with God and the deal I had made with myself was also okay. I was rarely confronted with a direct question about where I was or what I was doing, so it was not necessary for me to lie. I was living a lie though, and I knew it.

It had been our original plan to move back to Utah as soon as I got my career well under way. Five years had passed since we had moved to the Denver area. Over that period, my antisocial behavior patterns had not changed appreciably except that the deal I had made with myself made life easier for me. I had established myself in my career, and it was time to leave Colorado. I was actively looking for a job in Utah and anticipating another change in my life.

★ ★ ★

The Hendric shooting range had two police ranges, one of fifty yards and one of twenty-five yards, along with a public shooting range and a public skeet range. When detectives Bonner and DeMayo arrived at the range, Jerry was on the twenty-five yard police range collecting brass. DeMayo was relieved that there were no other customers on the range. "Hi, Jerry! How're things going?" Bonner said, announcing their presence.

Jerry pulled the ear plug from his right ear and said, "What?"

"I said hello!"

"You guys here for the twenty-five or the fifty?"

"I think we'll shoot the twenty-five today," DeMayo answered.

"Hey, aren't you on the serial killer case … you know, the one who kills the little girls?" Jerry knew all the police officers who used the range.

"Yeah, I'm on the task force. Homicide is heading it up."

"I hope you get him soon. I would have never believed anything like this could happen in Salt Lake. All those people moving up from California. Mark my words … it's going to be one of them."

DeMayo took his gun out and checked it over. "This is a tough one, Jerry. I wish I could say we're close. We do have a pretty good suspect, but he disappeared."

"Californian I'll bet."

"No, born and raised in Salt Lake." DeMayo slammed his clip into his pistol.

Jerry put his ear plugs in and yelled, "Clear," before DeMayo and Bonner emptied their pistols into the targets.

Jerry pulled the plugs from his ears. "Leonard says this guy is sending poetry to the department."

"That's right. Sends 'em to DeMayo here. Shall I tell you how he addresses them?"

"That's all I need is for that damn handle to take hold in the department." DeMayo dumped several bullets from a box onto the table and started to refill his clip.

"I'd like to look at the poems … if you wouldn't mind that is," Jerry said.

"What for?" DeMayo asked.

"I have an interest in things like that. You know I was an English literature professor up at the U until I retired and moved up here. Sometimes you can tell something about a guy by looking at his writing. How much education he has, what kind of books he reads, stuff like that."

DeMayo slammed the loaded clip back into his gun. "We got a professional profiler to do that."

"It wouldn't hurt to let him have a look." Bonner gave DeMayo a knowing nod.

"Clear," DeMayo shouted, and they both emptied their clips.

"How about it?" Jerry asked when they finished.

"Yeah, how about it DeMayo? You've got that latest one in the car. He could take it down to his house and look it over while we shoot."

DeMayo put the full clip in his gun and walked past Bonner mumbling, "Maybe he'll break the case ... stranger things have happened." Less than two minutes later, DeMayo returned with the poem. "Check it out, Jerry ... we'll be here for about a half hour."

Jerry took the poem down to his house. He returned about fifteen minutes later.

"Jerry, you break the case already?" Bonner asked.

"I don't think this is very good stuff myself. It's okay though. Who's Shari?"

"Shari?" DeMayo asked.

"Yeah ... in the poem ... the one he's threatening. Your girlfriend, I would presume."

DeMayo snatched the paper from Jerry. "I don't see Shari here," he said, thrusting the paper back to Jerry. "Show me how you came up with Shari."

"You mean you didn't see it? She doesn't have police protection? My God! This is an acrostic, DeMayo!" Jerry handed the paper back.

"What in the hell is an acrostic?"

"It's a poem where the ... look, just read down the first letter of each line."

DeMayo studied the poem for about a minute. "Holy shee-it! Get your gun, Bonner. We're out of here!" DeMayo ran for the car.

DeMayo was on the radio when Bonner caught up, "... and get the closest squad car there bells and lights as fast as you can." DeMayo gunned the car and threw dirt and rocks up the side of the mountain as he tore down the narrow dirt road from the range to the highway.

Bonner managed to get his seat belt fastened by the time they reached the paved road. Only when they were darting between cars on the freeway did Bonner pick the poem from the floor.

D-e-M-a-Y-O L-O-V-e-S s-H-a-R-I T-O-O b-a-d F-o-R H-E-R

* * *

The call came on the radio as DeMayo and Bonner raced past the Seventh East Expressway exit. A patrol car in the area of the Boston Building had called in to dispatch. The secretary said Shari had taken the day off to work at home. DeMayo had driven past her exit less than two minutes ago. He pushed the car faster, running down the shoulder. As he approached the State Street off-ramp, he cut across three lanes of traffic. He slid nearly to a stop at the bottom of the ramp and then peeled into traffic as he crossed State Street, turned under the freeway, and then returned to the freeway going back the way they had just come. The speedometer was pegged out at the highest number on the gauge, and the engine was screaming as they nearly flew up I-80. DeMayo figured they were well beyond one hundred miles per hour, as the steering began to get mushy. He started to slow down as he approached the 2300 South off-ramp. He just barely made the right turn onto 2300 South and then floored it going south. Less than two minutes after exiting the freeway he skidded to a stop in front of Shari's house. Her car was in the driveway by itself.

DeMayo jumped from the car leaving it in gear. As the car began to roll forward, DeMayo ran behind it and up to the door. Bonner was left to stop the car and put it in park. DeMayo knocked and called Shari's name furiously. In seconds he lost patience and kicked the door down. As he walked into the living room with his gun out, Shari stepped out of the bathroom with a towel wrapped around her. Although she seemed frightened, she managed to ask nonchalantly, "So ... you changed your mind about dinner?"

"Jesus Christ! Jeesuus Christ! I was afraid we'd gotten here too late." DeMayo sat heavily on the couch, put his gun on the seat beside him, and put his head in his hands.

"Tom, what's going on?"

Bonner came through the door. "DeMayo here just about killed everyone on Interstate 80 from Mountain Dell to State Street and back again."

"How about going out to the car and calling this in ... and bring the poem back."

"Yeah ... sure." Bonner went back to the car.

"You look like you just raced the devil. What's this all about?"

"Not the devil ... Abaddon. It's a good thing that your schedule was different today, or it's a race I might have lost."

"What in the world is going on?"

DeMayo explained about the latest body. As he was finishing, Bonner came in with the poem. DeMayo gave it to Shari. "You see the threat to you?" he asked when she finished reading it.

"To me? Just a second." She studied it some more.

"Here, let me show you." DeMayo reached for the poem.

"Wait a minute ... this is an acrostic."

"Jesus Christ. Was I the last person in the world to learn the meaning of that word?"

"You know guns ... I know language ... tools of the trade."

"Well, there's more." Tom explained how the team had gone proactive and how they figured Abaddon would take it out on him. "That's why I couldn't come to dinner tonight. I thought Abaddon would be after me. Now it looks like he's already trying to get to me through you."

"But this proves Russell was right all along. He knew Carl would be coming after me." Shari sat next to the gun beside DeMayo.

"It shows that the killer knows a lot about me. This guy isn't after you because he has something against you. He wants to hurt me by hurting you. Don't you see, it has nothing to do with you personally. If anything, this proves Russell was wrong. The killer decided to come after you only after we put the article in the paper."

"No, he only made it public after you made him mad. I think he would have gotten me if I had followed my normal schedule. I changed it after I talked to Russell. He said he would save me, and maybe he already has by the disruption to my schedule. What do we do now?"

"We have to put you under police protection starting now," Bonner said.

DeMayo stood up. "I think we should move her to a safe house, maybe even put her under protective custody."

Shari stood up and walked toward the kitchen. When she was about ten feet away, she turned to face the two men. DeMayo noticed how sexy she looked wrapped in a towel with her wet hair curling on her shoulders. "I'm not leaving this house. If he is after me, then let's set a trap."

"With all this commotion he's going to know it's a trap," Bonner said.

"Maybe he doesn't know. I mean if he were around the house, he would have already tried to get me. This is a perfect time to trap him. If we let this opportunity go by and he kills even one more child, I won't be able to live with myself."

DeMayo could hear the determination in her voice; it would be useless to argue with her. "Maybe you're right."

"You know I'm right."

"Okay, Bonner, you take my car and get out of here. Let's get a tight watch on the place. In the meantime, I'll hide out in the house in case he makes his move before we're ready."

"I don't like this." Bonner did not make a move for the door.

"You don't exactly have to like it, Bonner. This is the only way to draw him out. I was supposed to be the target. It can't be helped that he chose a different way of attacking me. We're just going to have to deal with it. We all knew it was a dangerous plan. I knew it when I bought into it. The plan is working, just not the way we thought, but it is working. We just have to deal with it. Now get out of here!"

"I guess you're right, but I don't like it. Not a bit." Bonner walked out.

DeMayo got on the phone. He was able to contact Alexander to set up a surveillance plan to protect the house. "Look, DeMayo, I need to have you at the task force meeting this afternoon."

"Holy shit! I forgot about that!"

"You got about thirty minutes to make the meeting."

"Okay, we'll be coming in Shari's car."

"See you in about thirty minutes," Alexander said and then hung up.

"Is it too late to have dinner with you … later, I mean?" DeMayo asked Shari.

"Of course not," Shari answered. "Excuse me, but I'm going to have to change into something a little less comfortable."

"Well, if you have to. But I'm not supposed to let you out of my sight."

"Why don't you check the room for me, and then you can wait outside the door."

"Kill-joy." DeMayo checked the bedroom.

★ ★ ★

Tom closed the door as he left the room. Shari laid out a white long-sleeve spandex T-shirt along with a dark-blue crochet vest. She found a pair of white-and-blue plaid shorts with a Hollywood waist and pleats. She opened her underwear drawer and took out a pair of satin briefs. Then she hesitated. *Not tonight.* She put the briefs back and found a pair of hi-cut, lace panties. She pulled them on. All of her bras were slightly padded. She was a large A or a small B, depending upon the manufacturer. Tonight she chose not to wear a bra. The clothes on the bed were not right. Shari left them there and went back to the closet. She did not buy a lot of sexy clothes, but she found a light, airy polyester flare skirt. She found a white blouse with faux pearl buttons on the sleeve and down the front. *Not exactly a fashion statement, but I'll bet it gets his attention.*

After she was dressed she walked back and forth in front of the mirror watching how her bright red skirt bounced and flipped. Her legs were smooth and lightly tanned. She would not need to wear stockings. She put on her normal makeup, and with a few strokes of her hair brush, she was ready.

Tom was sitting on a chair in the living room. Shari did a fast 360 turn as she came out of her bedroom. She wanted to throw the hem of her skirt high enough to show off her lace panties. From the look in Tom's eyes, she knew she had succeeded. "Holly cow! You look great!"

"You like?"

"I love!"

"I guess we better get you to your boring old meeting then."

"It won't take long." Tom stood up and playfully put his arm out to Shari. All the way to the police station Shari noticed Tom stealing glances at her legs, which she displayed prominently. She felt surprisingly good having him give her so much attention. When they got to the station, DeMayo escorted her to his desk. The men in the building were doing double takes as she walked by. In the past she would have been bothered by those kinds of looks, but walking beside Tom she felt very good about herself. "I'll be back in a few minutes," Tom said once she was comfortably seated at his desk.

* * *

"I called this meeting for two reasons." Alexander stood up to take charge as soon as Corrigan had taken his seat. "Number one, we need to get updated on the latest victim, and number two, we need to evaluate the proactive approach we're taking."

"This was not his normal victim type. He may have been sending us a message," Peterson said.

"I think we can assume that." Alexander nodded to Corrigan. "Let's start with you."

"It's difficult to pin down an exact time of death, but I'm fairly certain it was between eight and ten o'clock last night."

"The first reports of our news release were on the ten o'clock news on the network stations. So if he saw it on the news, and he got angry, he would have had to leave his house and go on the prowl to find a victim. I don't think he could have possibly made the kill before eleven thirty," Alexander said.

"Well, I disagree," DeMayo said. "I think the soonest he could find a victim after the news report would be later. He wouldn't pick anyone close to his hideout."

"He was angry ... let's not forget that," Corrigan rejoined. "He may not have been as careful as he normally is."

"I still say a response to our release could not have happened before midnight and possibly much later. The chances of finding a young girl alone that late are slim. I think he got her earlier," DeMayo insisted.

"I won't argue that," Corrigan said. "The girl was struck violently to the side of the head. However, the cause of death was strangulation."

"Not suffocation?"

"No, her windpipe was crushed. Her pubic area was shaved. Apparently, he tried to make her appear younger, but she was not raped."

"So his motive was not to rape a girl and send her to the celestial kingdom," Alexander said. "Could the news release have leaked out early?"

"You would have to check with the media on that," Corrigan continued. "There were some shards of glass in her hair and in the wound in her scalp."

"Could you tell anything about the glass?" DeMayo asked.

"I feel safe in saying the glass came from some kind of lens like a flashlight."

"How about binoculars?"

"Could be. We'll be able to tell better when we determine the quality of the glass."

"Well, I don't think the killing had anything to do with our news release," DeMayo stated.

"How so?" Alexander asked.

"Several reasons. One, the time of death is not right. Another thing is the poem. It doesn't make any allusion to getting at us as a reason for the killing. The angel in the poem is an angel who came to save mankind. From what? Maybe Abaddon."

"And how is a teenage girl going to save mankind from Abaddon?" Peterson asked.

"Well, suppose she saw something and intended to report it?"

"She could have seen him at the park when he was watching me, but I don't think that's too likely. The time of death is hours later."

DeMayo looked at Piszczek. "Suppose our man was scoping out his next victim with binoculars … the ones you think he had at the park."

"You ought to get into profiling," Piszczek replied. "Now, if he was watching his next victim, and this girl came up on him … he may have hit her with the binoculars."

"If that's the case, when we identify her, we'll have a good idea where the next victim lives," Alexander said.

"We have identified the girl as Jennifer Moffett. She lives just south of Liberty Park," Corrigan said.

"When was she last seen alive?" DeMayo asked.

"We have talked to her parents. She was watching TV with them till after seven. After that she could have been in her room or at a friend's house," Alexander responded.

"She had been smoking marijuana near the time of death," Corrigan said. "So I doubt she was in her room."

"The neighborhoods around Liberty Park have alleys between the blocks," DeMayo said. "If he was scoping out a new victim, it would most likely be from the alley where he could watch through a window. Jennifer could have been smoking back there. We need to sweep through the alley behind her home for matching glass and possibly blood stains."

"You want to look for broken glass in an alley?" Corrigan asked. "You might as well look for grass in a golf course."

"If we start near her house, we might be lucky," Alexander said.

"I'm going to get as much manpower on this as possible. But we don't want to make a circus out of it. In the meantime, let's get a map and mark all the houses that have girls in the age group of five to ten years old within three blocks of Jennifer's house."

"I'll get going on the demographics," Peterson said.

"Well, there's one thing," DeMayo quipped, "we went out on a limb with the news release and Abaddon sawed it off."

"We're getting closer, and he's making mistakes," Alexander said.

"One other thing," Piszczek interjected, "for the time being, we should back away from the news releases. Now that we have something to work from, we don't want to push him into action until we can narrow down the field of possible victims."

"Right," Alexander agreed. "We cool the news releases, cover DeMayo and Shari, and put every available resource to narrow down the next victim."

★ ★ ★

Shari sat at Tom's desk while he was in his meeting. Bored, she picked up his stapler and checked to see how many staples it had in it. As she reached to put the stapler down, she noticed a blue paper dot on the desk where the stapler had been. When she tried to brush it away, she found it was stuck down. She picked up the staple remover—another blue dot. Everything he had on his desk was marked by a blue dot. Using her fingernail, she carefully removed each dot and moved it one or two inches. She replaced each item over its dot and sat back to admire her handiwork. The desk looked about the same to her. She made a mental note to get Tom a more flattering picture of her to put on his desk.

Finally, Tom returned from his meeting. "How'd it go?"

Tom gave her a brief rundown on the meeting. "If we're right about the reason he killed her, we have a pretty good idea where his next victim lives. This time, we'll be waiting for him."

"You know who the next victim is?"

"Not exactly, but we know the neighborhood. We'll have someone in the area for each potential victim."

"Won't that make him suspicious?"

"They'll be disguised. It's the best lead we've had so far."

"Second best." Shari wished she had not said that. The last thing she wanted was to start an argument with Tom tonight.

"Russell?"

"Never mind. I'm sure you'll catch him this time. You getting hungry?"

"Yeah, I just need to make a call." Tom picked up the phone. For a second he hesitated, looking at his desk. Then he dialed a number from memory. "Jerry? DeMayo here." As he talked, Tom picked up his staple remover and absently looked at the dot on his desk. "Yeah, she's okay. She didn't go in to work today, so my guess is he couldn't find her." Tom put the staple remover down and picked up the stapler. "Well, she's here now, and we'll have her covered from now on until we get the guy. Thanks again for your help. Okay. See ya later." Shari was smiling and trying desperately to keep from laughing as Tom looked up from his desk. "Cute, Shari, real cute."

"Dots, DeMayo?" She had never called him DeMayo before, but somehow as she said it, it felt more familiar and even more intimate than Tom.

Tom looked back at his desk, leaned back in his chair regarding it, then looked back at Shari. "This is good, Darling. Yeah, I like this; I'll leave it this way. We still on for dinner?"

Shari was momentarily taken aback by his use of her last name. She decided she liked it. "Yeah, but I sort of got sidetracked and didn't get anything fixed. I promise I was going to fix something very special, but could we just go out somewhere to eat, and then you could take me home for a nightcap."

"Sure."

"Who was that on the phone?" Shari asked as they walked out of the office.

"Jerry Olsen. He runs the shooting range where we go to practice. I'll take you out to meet him sometime. He figured out the acrostic, and so he just might have saved your life."

"Really?"

In spite of all the tension over the Abaddon case and the fact that two plainclothesmen were following them for protection, Shari had an enjoyable dinner with Tom. He was in a lighthearted mood, and they spent the time kidding around and making small innuendos about how their relationship seemed to be headed toward a more intimate level. Shari realized Tom was relaxed and being himself, and she was relaxed and open with him. It was a level of emotional intimacy she had never experienced before. On the way home, Tom got serious. "Look, Shari, we're going to have four cops outside your house, but I think there should be a couple more inside. I'm thinking of having a couple of female cops sent over."

"I don't know about sending over two more cops. Don't you think you can handle this yourself?"

"You're absolutely right. This is definitely something I can handle myself." Tom got on the radio and made arrangements for the guards outside and let them know he would be in the house outside her bedroom door. At Shari's house, Tom checked every room and closet with his gun drawn.

Shari turned her CD player on. It held five CDs programmed with enough romantic music to last the evening. She sat on a chair in the kitchen, showing as much of her leg as modesty would allow, while Tom poured them each a drink from a bottle of wine he had purchased. Shari stood as he approached with the wine glasses, and she took one with her right hand. She took one small sip, put her glass on the table, and then put both arms around Tom's neck and kissed him on the lips. She could taste the wine from his mouth, and she knew this would always be her favorite brand.

Shari pulled Tom's shirttails from his pants and ran her fingers up the taunt skin along his ribs, pulling his shirt up as she did. She allowed her fingers to pause as they kissed again—this time deeper and longer. It had been only a sip of wine, but something was going to her head. Their mouths parted, and she moved her hands under his shirt from his sides to his chest. With her palms spread flat against his chest, she focused on the sensual sensation his chest hair and hard nipples made on the sensitive area in the center of her palms.

Tom pulled his shirt off, looked down at her, and then physically swept her off her feet. She nuzzled her head under his chin as he carried her to her bedroom. Inside he put her down and reached behind to close the door. *Cute*, Shari thought. The light was still on. Tom was no Apollo, but his shoulders were wide and strong. His stomach was flat, though the muscles bodybuilders are so proud of were not evident. A promise of love handles made a slight swelling above his belt. Tom stepped forward and slowly unbuttoned her blouse. He cupped her breasts and gently squeezed them. She felt her nipples come erect. "You're very sexy without a bra," he said.

"You always know the right thing to say." Shari fumbled a few seconds with his belt before getting it loose. Her heart was beating faster, and an almost painful hunger began in the pit of her stomach. For a brief second she was about to push Tom away. She had never considered doing anything like this without being married first. Then she released his body and reached into his pants—no pedophile here.

Tom pushed his pants past his hips and pulled her close. In almost a panic of desire to please him, Shari pushed her pelvic bone hard against him and thrilled in the strong pulsations of his response. After a few seconds, Tom pushed her gently away, knelt in front of her, and pulled her skirt past her hips letting it drop to the floor. Then he removed her panties. Shari dropped to her knees to kiss his eyes, cheeks, nose, and then his mouth. She could not get enough of him.

They walked to the bed together, where they lay tenderly exploring each other. Tom was on his back, and Shari was on her side. She drew circles on Tom's chest and then nipped playfully at his hard nipples. He rolled her over on her back and began to trace circles around her belly with a feathery touch, sending chills through her body. She could not hold back the waves of ecstasy that rolled through her like thunder down a canyon. Finally, Tom rolled on top. Shari knew she was as high as she could go. Her legs were bent so she could move with him. Then she was caught up in a conflagration of emotions, which carried her to a place she had never been. The world collapsed into her body, and there was nothing in the world except her and her man.

In the afterglow, lying beside Tom, she realized he was the first man to really make love to her. Ralph had used her for nothing more than a living masturbation device. And Carl was pathetic. Never had she experienced anything to compare to this. With Tom it had been exquisite baritone waves of excitement, tension, and release that emanated from deep inside and flowed out through her whole being. The music she had programmed continued to play as they lay in each other's arms.

"Shari."

"Uh huh."

"Would you believe me if I told you I have never experienced anything like this before?"

"I guess so ... I'm in the same boat. I don't think it happens with many people ... if it did, there would be words to describe it."

"Shari."

"Yeah."

"Would you marry me?"

Tears filled her eyes but did not spill over. She had given up on the idea that life could be so good for her. "Yes."

Tom sat up in bed. "You would?" He sounded like a little boy who had just heard he was going to Disneyland.

"Let's do it after Abaddon is caught and Tami's back. She'll be pleased. You know she has already suggested we get married."

"Well, she's a smart girl."

Shari started making plans in her mind. The last song she had programmed was "Darlin'" from her *Sling Blade* sound track. As it finished Tom dreamily said, "I love you darlin'." Then she heard Tom's heavy breathing beside her, and she finally fell asleep.

Chapter Seven

THE DETECTIVE

The man stepped out of the shower, but he did not feel clean. It had been great to see DeMayo suffer. He had planned to deal with DeMayo and Bat Qol and then leave the area, but now he was worried about the pot-smoking girl. There was a chance the police would be watching her neighborhood. It would be dangerous to get Azura now. That was something he hadn't planned on. It would be best to leave now and come back in a year or so to surprise DeMayo. By then Azura would be too old for the celestial kingdom, but there would be plenty of others—there was no reason to take a chance now.

The man packed the few things he wanted to take with him. He put his albums and the special souvenirs he wanted to save in his small suitcase—he would travel light. When he finished packing, he checked the mail. Along with a couple of pieces of junk mail was an envelope with no name, stamp, or cancellation mark. The man took the envelope to the kitchen table and opened it. Inside was a poem.

Abaddon—Your Time Is Up

"I have been young, and now am old,
    yet have I not seen the righteous forsaken,
        nor his seed begging bread."
I am many things, I am chancellor of heaven.
    The tears of those whom I teach
        demand my righteous vengeance.
In power I challenge thee, death's dark angel.
    Blinded by my authority and glory,
        you must deliver thy key to me
to lock thee away, demon of the abyss.
    I, aged of the covenant,
        come to fulfill my calling.
Abaddon, you must succumb to thy brother.
    Meet now the rod of Moses,
        endowed with power for life and death.

Metatron (a pillar of fire to burn out thy heart)

The man put the poem on the table and sat back letting the anger simmer. *Who the hell is Metatron?* He read the poem again. He got his book and looked for Metatron. The book said Metatron was more powerful than Abaddon. The more he read, the angrier he got. *There can be no Metatron! This must be from that fuck, hold-the-mayo. How could he know? But if he knows, why doesn't he arrest me? He's playing games. I'll show that bastard! He was going to get an extra year before the final payment, but that's all changed now. I was going to skip Azura, but not now. I'll find a way to get her, and I'll let the family know I was going to spare her, but hold-the-mayo changed my mind. He thinks he can trap me? I'll show him who has the power!*

* * *

Shari woke with her head on Tom's chest, hearing his heartbeat. She hated to disturb him, but it was getting late. "Tom, dearest."

"Huh?" He seemed confused.

"Better get up."

"Oh! Morning, darlin' … I could sure get used to waking up like this."

"Me too."

"That was the best night's sleep I've had since I got the first poem."

"Me too."

Tom sat up in the bed. "You know this case is so much more personal than any of the others I've handled over the years. And now, just when a dream seems about to come true, he's threatened that too. I couldn't stand another failure."

"You thinking of JoLynn?"

"I guess I am, but not in terms of what we had. It's just that feeling of failure."

"It's not going to happen like that again."

"I don't want to leave you."

"You've got to go after him. I'll be all right."

"Sure?"

Shari was not sure, but she would not let him know. "Keep your mind clear … really, I'll have your people with me. I'll be just fine." Shari got out of bed. "Come on! I want to see you shave and brush your teeth."

"You're a loony." Tom got out of bed. "Besides I don't have a toothbrush or my shaving things."

Shari walked out of the bedroom to the bathroom. "Come on, you can use my stuff."

"You're kidding." He followed her to the bathroom.

Shari sat on the toilet seat watching Tom prepare for the day. She talked about the weather and her plans for Tami.

"Tom?"

"What?" Tom mumbled around the toothbrush.

"I want to show this acrostic to Russell."

"Russell? Why? He's still stuck on Carl. I don't know what he's tied into, but Carl's not our killer."

"I know … but come on … a favor for me. Could you arrange it?"

"Yeah, I suppose so, but I'm a busy man you know. This isn't something I would do for just anyone."

"I'd really like to see him this morning, and then we could get together for lunch."

"Well, for a lunch with you I'd move a mountain. I'll make it for this morning. Just one question … am I going to be henpecked from now on?"

Shari recognized the playfulness of his tone. "Maybe."

★ ★ ★

When DeMayo arrived at work, he could sense Alexander was tense. "What's up?"

"We got another poem."

"Another body?"

"Nope. Another poet."

"What?"

"Look, there's a meeting starting right now."

DeMayo followed Alexander to the meeting room. "Where did they find the poem?" he called after him.

"It was on the dispatch desk. My name was on the envelope, and the author's name was Metatron."

"Maybe it's not connected," DeMayo offered as they walked into the meeting room.

Alexander ignored the comment and addressed the group. "Okay, just so you all know, we have another poem. I got Piszczek in early to look at it. There are copies here for everyone. This poem throws a complete new wrinkle on the case. In the first place, it's addressed to Abaddon."

"What?" DeMayo grabbed his copy.

"In it someone calling himself Metatron is telling Abaddon he is about to put a stop to him."

"More power to Metatron," Peterson said.

"Yeah, I guess it would be nice to find someone to do our job for us." Unger had not been to the last couple of meetings, but he had showed up for this one, and he did not look pleased.

Piszczek broke the uncomfortable silence. "I've done some research, and there is an angel named Metatron. Now, this guy is a very interesting character. He has many names and titles. Some of them are used in the poem and others are alluded to. For instance, he is known as the chancellor of heaven. He is the liberating angel. Now, the first three lines of the poem are actually a quote from Psalm 37:24. In angel lore, Metatron was supposed to be the author of that verse. He's the most powerful angel of heaven, even more powerful than Michael or Gabriel."

"Wait a minute," DeMayo interrupted. "He's an angel in heaven, so that makes him a good angel doesn't it?"

"This angel is complicated. He has several different names representative of his callings. He has a female aspect to him called Shekinah. He is one of the leaders of the good angels, and yet, he is sometimes identified as being Samael, who is the chief of the Satans and the angel of death."

"He's the best and the worst?" Peterson asked.

"It gets even better," Piszczek continued. "Abaddon himself is sometimes identified as being Samael."

The room was silent as the meaning of that last statement sank in. Unger finally asked the question on everyone's mind. "Do we have a split personality?"

"I think we have to accept that as a possibility."

"Bullshit!" DeMayo interrupted. "Abaddon doesn't have a split personality; he may be trying to lay a foundation for an insanity claim in case he's ever caught."

"DeMayo has a point there," Piszczek said. "He's clever, no doubt about it. Abaddon also has a giant ego. Now, my take on this is that he would not even consider the idea that he could be caught. I don't want to completely discount preparations for an insanity plea, but my guess is this is something else."

"What?" Unger asked.

"Perhaps this guy's no expert on angels and started picking the names alphabetically. Then as he studied them more, he started using names that fit his mood. The first name he came up with for himself was Abaddon. Now he's been studying, and he comes across this Metatron ... the most powerful, so he takes on that identity."

"Yeah," Peterson jumped in, "and now he's getting rid of the name Abaddon, and letting us know there's a new angel in town."

"It makes sense that he would take on the identity of the most powerful angel." Piszczek took control of the conversation again. "In this poem the good aspects of Metatron are pointed out along with the fact that he is more powerful than Abaddon. Now, Abaddon likes to think he's doing his victims a favor, so in that sense he thinks of himself as good."

"What if this is a group of some sort?" Alexander said. "I know we've been going on the assumption of one perp all along, but we have Abaddon, Baresches, Cosmocrater, and now Metatron. We could have a group, and perhaps there is some in-fighting going on."

"I don't think so," Piszczek said. "I don't see why we would be getting a poem like this from a group. Now, if this Metatron wanted to duke it out with Abaddon, he would send his poem to him, not to us."

"I don't think this poem is from Abaddon," DeMayo insisted. "It's not just the name at the bottom. He's quoting from the Bible in this one, and notice he is not capitalizing Celestial Kingdom, in fact he is not using any unnecessary capitalization."

Piszczek continued, "I would expect that kind of thing in a multiple personality. Multiple personality is one way of dealing with the kind of abuse described in the poem about the abyss. Now, Metatron may be a good part of Richards that's fed up with what's going on. Metatron may have even sent a copy of this poem to the Abaddon personality, and

Abaddon might not even know where it came from. Metatron could have sent us a copy to let us know he is going to take care of things."

"And how would he take care of things?" DeMayo asked.

"There have been suspected cases where one personality in a multiple situation has actually killed the other personality by killing the body."

"You mean committing suicide?" Peterson asked.

"Not exactly. Now, it looks like that, but the personality doing the killing thinks of it as killing someone else, not himself."

"You think this guy is going to kill himself?" Unger asked.

"I think DeMayo is right when he says this last poem was not written by the same person who wrote the others. But it could have been written by the same guy but through a different personality that may have surfaced as a result of the news release. Now, would Metatron go so far as to kill Abaddon? I don't know. He may leave clues to trap Abaddon, and that may be the reason he sent us a copy."

"He may?" DeMayo questioned. "Are we getting any closer, or is this whole thing just getting more confused? What if this poem is just made up to divert us?"

"More pieces of the puzzle," Alexander responded.

"Well, when are we going to know we have enough pieces to make a picture?" DeMayo asked.

"We'll know when we see the picture," Unger answered. "Have we got anything more on Jennifer?"

Corrigan opened the folder in front of him. "We have narrowed the time of death to sometime around nine. She was killed before the news release was out."

"Given that, I'm confident Jennifer saw something she shouldn't have seen and died for it," Piszczek said.

"I think he was scoping another victim," DeMayo said. "How are the demographics coming?" he asked Peterson.

"I have a good map, and I'm marking all the homes that have children in the age group. Boys are blue, and girls are red." Peterson laid a map out on the table. "This green dot with the circle is Jennifer's house, and the other green dots are her known friends. I'm still going through the school records and marking houses. So far, there are none real close to Jennifer's house."

"I see that there is an alley behind her house. Have you checked it out for broken glass and blood?" DeMayo directed the question to Corrigan.

"We have a crew out there working that area right now. There's a lot evidence to sift through."

"We're close to a potential victim here. If we need more men out there, let's get them," Unger said.

"What I need is more trained men in the lab to sift through everything that's being brought in," Corrigan said.

"Well, I'd think possible fingerprints on the last poem and the glass and other stuff from around Jennifer's house would be top priority," DeMayo said.

Corrigan picked his papers up, dropped them on their edge to make a neat stack, and put them in his folder. "I can damn well determine what the priorities for my lab are," he said to DeMayo as he stood up. "I haven't got anything more to add to this meeting, so if you don't mind, I'll get back to work."

DeMayo stood up. "Jesus, man! I'm sorry, it's just this is getting very frustrating to me and … well … I know you're doing your job."

"Right." Corrigan walked out the door.

"Shit!" DeMayo sat down and put his head in his hands.

"Okay, Tom," Unger said, "let's lighten up here. Let's keep the focus on the killer."

"DeMayo and his girlfriend are targets. Let's not forget that," Alexander added.

"Okay then," Peterson said, "what about a news release on Jennifer and this latest poem."

"I say we go ahead on a news release about Jennifer. He knows we know about her. If anyone asks about Abaddon, we say we're looking into it. We don't give any information about our suspicions as to motive," Unger said.

"But shouldn't we warn the parents in that area to watch their children closer?" Peterson asked.

"I don't think we should say anything that could go public. This is the best chance we have had to get this guy. If he finds out we're watching, he'll just go somewhere else and kill a different girl."

"DeMayo's right," Piszczek concurred. "Even if he has no plans to get a girl right away, it would be too big of a temptation for him to get another girl just to throw it in our face. Now, letting something like that out could actually result in his killing a girl he wouldn't kill otherwise."

"Even if there is a risk here," DeMayo jumped in, "letting him get away is a bigger risk."

"Okay, the plan is to put undercover police to watch every child located in the area," Alexander said.

"You've got to be kidding!" Peterson said. "I already have four kids marked in the area. There'll be more by the time I'm finished. The whole area would be flooded with strange men. You can't pull that off."

"I'll get the manpower," Unger said. "And I want them to start to be placed this afternoon. We'll work out the logistics, but I want these children covered, and it better be done without raising suspicions."

DeMayo knew the logistics would be near impossible. There are just so many repair men, ice cream trucks, phone and cable men, vans, and so forth that can be put into a neighborhood without causing suspicion. There was no telling how many days would be required, but it felt good to be doing something—to feel they were now ahead of Abaddon.

★ ★ ★

DeMayo got a copy of the map Peterson had been working on. He began to look at the records of the girls to see if one or two stood out more than any of the others. He was not even sure what he was looking for, but he hoped something helpful would pop out. DeMayo jumped as the phone rang. "DeMayo here."

"We got a problem. I need to see you in my office right now." DeMayo recognized Alexander's voice.

"What is it?"

"Tell you when you get here." He sounded angry.

DeMayo walked to Alexander's office. "What's up?"

"We got problems with Paskel. His attorney has requested a meeting with me and you."

"When?"

"He's on his way ... should be here any minute."

"So what's his beef?"

"Word is he's talking about a possible harassment suit if we don't leave Paskel alone. We had good probable cause for the search ... but ... at a level it may have been a little early. Anyway, I think we're okay up to now, but we didn't find anything, and the girl was killed while Paskel was under surveillance. From this point on we're going to have to back off."

"Who's his attorney?"

"The Honorable Daniel Jay Newton the Third, Esquire."

"He's the one who got Paskel his early parole."

"Yeah, that's what I heard."

"Well, he's also Richards's attorney."

"He may be using Paskel to create an impression that we're in the business of harassing people to help him lay a foundation for the Richard's case."

DeMayo stood up and paced back and forth. "I don't know what his game is, but I'm seeing too much of the Honorable Daniel Jay Newton the Third, Esquire."

"The Honorable Daniel Jay Newton the Third, Esquire, says he can't find Richards, and he's making sounds that you might have something to do with his disappearance. I would give a month's wages to know what the Honorable Daniel Jay Newton the Third, Esquire, is up to and how he plays in this mess." Alexander stood up and walked to the door. "Paskel is out of this case at this point. We know he didn't have anything to do with Marty, and outside of Blaine's so-called psychic connection, there's nothing to tie him in to any of this."

"Well, I never really liked him as a suspect anyway. I don't know if Blaine is just jerking me around or if he has some plan in mind, but he does have my attention."

"In any case, we're back to Richards as the main suspect," Alexander said.

"Well, so far it seems that every move we make is wrong."

"Sometimes these things take time."

"Yeah ... sure ... in the meantime people are dying." DeMayo said. "And so far as I can see, we aren't any closer to finding Richards than we were when Katie was killed. I should have had him followed after my first interview."

"You know the Honorable Daniel Jay Newton the Third, Esquire, would have had you pulled off."

"Yeah ... well as far as I'm concerned, he's a sleaze."

Alexander opened the door. "Wait, I'll see if the Honorable etcetera, etcetera, is here."

DeMayo sat down. He wondered what motivated a high-priced attorney like Daniel Jay Newton.

Alexander returned with Newton and Unger. Newton was six feet one inch and weighed 245 pounds. In spite of his weight, he did not look fat—portly perhaps. He was wearing a dark-blue, three-piece suit with a white shirt and a burgundy silk tie. His hair curled over his ears and was parted on the right side. It looked as if someone had carefully placed each hair in the exact right spot. His nails were professionally manicured. The introductions were formal. "You seem to really get off on representing the dregs of society," DeMayo commented.

"That will be enough of that," Unger interjected.

"No offense taken," Newton responded. "It's just that the detective does not have the proper perspective on the calling of the defense attorney."

"The calling of the defense attorney is to use every trick, in and out of the book, to keep the criminal on the street." DeMayo was looking for a place to vent.

"That erroneous perspective, which is held by many, makes my job all the more laborious."

"Erroneous?" DeMayo questioned sarcastically.

"My calling, and that of my peers, is to stand at the front lines in defense of the Constitution."

"God, can you believe the arrogance?"

"The Constitution says a man must be presumed innocent until proven guilty ... something people don't generally understand. Presumption of innocence has no place in what you do. You do your job with vigor, using all the resources the State can muster, and you are respected. The judge and the jury presume the defendant is innocent until proven guilty. Their presumption is passive. The defense attorney must presume his client is innocent but not passively. He has to actively defend his client.

"He does this by forcing the State to do its job ... to prove its case beyond a doubt. He attacks every piece of evidence, every witness, and every allegation in every conceivable way. He looks for cracks and weaknesses in the case and spotlights each and every one.

"When it's all over, if everyone does their job, the guilty will go to jail and the innocent will be set free. If an innocent man goes to jail, the defense attorney didn't do his job. If a guilty man gets off, the prosecution didn't do its job.

"If I start a case believing my client is guilty and, as a result, I don't try as hard as I can, and he ends up being convicted, the Constitution would be violated. The man would not have been convicted by a jury of his peers ... he would have been convicted by one man ... by a defense attorney who failed to do his job of providing his wholehearted, best defense. He has to do his best ... not to get the guilty off, but to force the State to do its job to prove the case beyond a reasonable doubt."

"How do you feel knowing that you get guilty men off who then go out and victimize others?" DeMayo asked.

"I get very angry ... angry at the State for failing to do its job. And when I hear of an innocent man's life being ruined by being sent to prison," Newton stood up, "I get angry at the defense attorney for failing to do his job. Now getting back to my client," Newton paced in the confined space of Alexander's office, "he was a guilty, scumbag pile of shit ... and he went to prison for that, but he served his time. My client is extremely upset by the way you have harassed him."

"You mean you have been in contact with Dale Richards?" DeMayo wanted to make the point again that Newton represented and might be helping hide the most promising suspect in this case.

"I'm here on another matter," Newton answered in a sticky, patient voice. "It seems this department has decided to inflict itself on an upstanding citizen who has been put under a canopy of suspicion because of past peccadilloes for which he has already paid a debt to society.

"You've been harassing one Carl Paskel, an upstanding, tax-paying, church-going member of society, who is trying to rebuild his life after having made some regrettable mistakes in the past."

"What do you think you're talking about? Come on, he's a sick little pervert." DeMayo was angry.

"Tom, that will be enough," Unger said.

Newton ignored DeMayo again. "You and a bunch of your henchmen, in a tall state of excitement, waded unceremoniously through my client's house, causing a neighborhood-wide perturbation, which was an embarrassment of Brobdingnagian size to my client."

Unger jumped in, "We searched his house with a legal search warrant ... one which was granted because there was probable cause."

"Well, you had a fine frolic at his expense, but in the process you shown a light of unwarranted brightness on a past he is mending at great effort and personal expense. You embarrassed him at his work and at his home. In spite of your heroic efforts to pin this crime on Mr. Paskel, the real killer continued in his onerous activities completely unabated."

Alexander responded, "In the investigative process, we normally start with many suspects. The solution of the crime comes, in part, as we work through the process of eliminating suspects."

"Can we assume you have now provided my client with an alibi that will satisfy each of you?"

"You can make that assumption," Unger answered.

"Can I now assure my client that such uncalled for embarrassments will not be repeated in the future?"

"There will be no uncalled for embarrassments to your client," Unger said. "However, his past was not created by this department. He is still on probation. Having money and a high-priced attorney is not going to give him carte blanche to repeat his former actions."

"Captain Unger, let me assure you that my client is devoting himself to a life intended to repay society for the mistakes of his past. He has served his time, after all."

DeMayo, frustrated at being put down or ignored every time he said something, took a deep breath. "Not exactly. Some high-blown, self-important defender of the Constitution, using influence purchased with money and past reputation, got him an early release from the just sentence passed upon him by the rightly empowered magistrate, who acted in the interest of the real past victims and possible future victims of this misguided pervert whom you choose to represent for God knows what fee."

Newton stopped pacing and turned to DeMayo. He looked as though he intended to say something, but didn't.

"Look, Tom," Unger raised his voice, "why don't you save your opinions for a while?"

"No problem," Newton continued. "I operated fully within the limits of the law. If you are not satisfied with the time Mr. Paskel served, once again your side failed."

"It was purely a play of power and influence purchased with Pastel's newfound for …"

"Tom!" Unger's face was red, and he had stood up.

DeMayo put both of his hands up, palms out. "Okay, okay, I'll be a good boy."

Unger looked at him eye to eye as he sat back down.

"We can sit here and argue philosophy all afternoon, but first let me make this point … if you have any more questions you want to ask my client, or any more searches, or if you want to follow him around anymore, you better do it through me. If the tracking device has not been removed from his car, do it today. If any similar harassment happens again, or if his rights are violated again, you are going to be spending valuable time in deposition and court proceedings. Right now, I'm trying to create an amiable solution to this problem, so that my client can quietly proceed to rebuild his life without the embarrassment of constant police harassment."

"First off, this department and its representatives acted fully within proper procedure," Unger said. "No constitutional rights have been violated. Carl Paskel was a viable suspect when the search warrants were acquired. At the present time, he is no longer a suspect in this case. If he should ever become a suspect in this or any other case in the future, we will deal with him in a manner that is consistent with department policy and that will protect his rights."

"I'm sure you will." Newton walked to the door. "Now if that's understood, I'm sure we all have work to do." Newton opened the door, walked out.

"I hope that guy never runs for office," DeMayo said.

"He has a way with words. A very nice summation, I'd say," Alexander answered. "But we better stay away from Paskel."

"There's no need to mess with Paskel, but if the Honorable Daniel Jay Newton the Third, Esquire, thinks this little charade is going to make me back away from Richards, he can just forget it!" DeMayo left the room.

* * *

Shari pulled into the now familiar parking lot at the Point of the Mountain prison. Tom had made arrangements for her to meet with Russell. She got through the normal security checks to the visitor's area. Russell came in almost immediately. "So what's going on now?"

"You up with the news?"

"It's Jennifer Moffett, isn't it?"

"Abaddon killed her. They know it was Abaddon because he left another poem."

"This girl was not his normal victim. He felt he had to kill her on the spot because of something she saw him doing."

Shari was not surprised that Russell knew, but she was surprised at herself for not being surprised. "Are the pictures getting clearer? Do you know where the room is?"

"His anger is building. The feelings are stronger now. He took this girl to his room, but she was already dead. He laid naked beside her all night. I've taken steps to make him angrier. He's beginning to focus on you more."

"That's part of why I came to see you. In the poem that came with Jennifer there was a message, an acrostic that said the killer was going to get me to make Tom suffer."

"He actually made a threat?"

"The whole police force came rushing to my house yesterday. They had a guard at my house all last night."

"I don't think he thought they would see the acrostic. You've got police protection all the time now?"

"Oh yeah … well, I do get to go to the bathroom without an escort."

"Tell them to get you a female cop to go with you."

"I came to talk about some new stuff. The police are more convinced than ever that Carl is not a viable suspect."

"You've got to convince them otherwise." Russell was adamant.

"I don't see how that can happen."

"I know what the connection between him and me is now."

"What is it?"

"The answer came in a long, detailed dream last night. It's like a butterfly trying to write his autobiography. Is the memory of being a caterpillar clear? Can he even relate to what it was like to have been a caterpillar?"

"I'd be surprised if a butterfly has a memory. It's a bug."

"Just suspend your disbelief and hear my story out."

"Okay, go on."

"The dream starts with a young man living somewhere in the South in the 1830s. His parents died and left him with a small plantation. He wanted to improve his education, so he left the plantation in the care of his uncle and went to New England. While he was there, he met and fell in love with the daughter of a rich, aristocratic family. The girl's parents were abolitionists and would not give her permission to marry a southern slave owner. In a desperate plan, they intentionally got pregnant so the girl's parents would have to permit the marriage. When the parents found out, they disowned her. He took the girl to his plantation, where they were married.

"The young man kept his uncle on in the position of overseer. The uncle had no property and no prospects for another job.

"When the wife went into labor, she had a very difficult time. Twin boys were born, but the mother died. The father was devastated. He wanted nothing to do with the boys, and so he left their upbringing to his uncle and overseer, Ben. Ben named them Beau and William. Two months before the birth of the twins, one of the slave women gave birth to a daughter named Stella. Ben brought the mother into the house so she could wet-nurse the two boys.

"Ben beat the boys often. Beau grew to be as cruel as his father's uncle. When they were twelve, Beau and William forced Stella to have sex with them. William felt guilty about it afterwards and tried to make amends by using a *McGuffey's Eclectic Reader* to teach Stella to read. At that time it was against the law to teach a slave to read. Over the years Beau forced Stella to have sex with him often.

"One afternoon, when they were fourteen, the boys were forcing another slave girl to have sex when she threatened to tell Ben. Beau began to beat her. At first William held her, but as Beau got more violent, William let her go. She fell, and Beau continued to kick her and beat her with a stick. Finally, William pulled him off, but the girl had long since stopped fighting. She was dead. The boys threw the body in the river. William felt extreme guilt, but he was afraid to tell anyone what happened. He knew Beau could be hung for killing a slave. William stopped raping slave girls after the girl died. He knew Beau was still doing it, but he kept Beau's secret.

"After a failed marriage, Beau became obsessed with children and began having sex with the slaves as young as six years old. In the meantime, Stella fell in love with Leo, a male slave about two years older than she. Stella and Leo asked permission to be married. Beau was adamantly opposed to a wedding. William tried to intercede, but Beau would not relent. That night Beau had Leo tied in a barn. He came later with Stella and raped and beat her in front of Leo. Then he allowed Ben to do the same. Beau had already sold Leo. The next morning he was taken away. This happened just weeks before the outbreak of the Civil War.

"At the end of the war, Leo came back seeking Stella. The plantation was in shambles. Most of the former slaves had left. Stella had remained, hoping Leo would come for her. The price for staying was that Beau raped and beat her whenever he wanted. Beau believed Stella stayed because she was in love with him. Beau was losing everything to carpetbaggers, and William had moved to town to take a job in a dry goods store.

"Leo ran into William in town on his way to get Stella. William warned him that Beau had become an alcoholic and could not be reasoned with. He suggested Leo wait a day so that he could go with him. Leo couldn't wait. When Leo got to the plantation, he went to Stella's room in the barn. As they were planning their getaway, Beau came in and hit Leo in the head with the butt of his rifle, knocking him unconscious. He overpowered Stella and tied her and Leo up. When Leo woke, Beau tried to rape Stella, but he was so drunk he was impotent. This so enraged him that he shot Leo in the face.

"Meanwhile, William had found out Leo had gone to the plantation alone, so he rushed to the plantation. He heard the shot and ran to the barn. He found Beau holding Stella with a knife to her throat. William pointed his gun at Beau and ordered him to let Stella go. Just then Stella tried to pull free. Beau pulled the knife into her throat and at the same instant William fired his gun hitting Beau in the head. William rushed to Stella, but he could not stop the bleeding, and she died in his arms.

"William lived to see the turn of the century. He never got over that violent night and the fact that he was too late to save Leo and Stella. He never married, and he died a lonely old man. I know in my soul that I am William."

"How does all that relate to what's going on now?"

"I know I helped Beau kill that first slave girl. I loved him in spite of his dark side. You think this is pretty strange don't you? I mean reincarnation and all?"

"You think you and Carl are William and Beau reincarnated?"

"Yes. When William finally made the right choice he was too late to save Stella. He raped her when they were twelve, and then he allowed Beau to use her the rest of her life. He could be sorry, and he could do a lot of good, but he could never make it up to her. He picked up bad Karma ... something he would do anything to repair. Maybe what he did was so evil he shouldn't have had a chance to fix it in that life. But for me ... more than the suffering ... more than avoiding suffering, I want to undo that wrong."

Shari knew the answer to the question, but she asked it anyway. "Who is Stella?"

He looked her in the eyes. Words were not required. Tears sprang up in his eyes and seemed to defy gravity as they bulged over his lower eyelids before falling. "I have let you down so many times. Now it's all so clear to me. I know Carl is Beau. All those years ago, we started entwined together in the warm comfort provided by a woman who died to provide it. Our paths were twisted in evil actions, until our paths finally separated. Now they have come together again. We both have a chance to make amends, but he will not.

"In that life you were weak and powerless because of the place society put you. But now you are what you make of yourself. You will have to fight just as I will ... that's your Karma ... your chance to learn and grow."

"How? How can I fight this evil?"

"The evidence and the solution are in Carl's house. You have to get the police back in there."

"DeMayo, he's Leo, right?"

"I think so."

Shari left the prison frightened but resolved to take charge of her fear of Carl. Reincarnation was a belief that was foreign to her, but it was a concept that could put form to what she faced.

★ ★ ★

When he entered the Royal Eatery, Tom was still agitated from the meeting with Newton. The muscles of his neck relaxed as he saw Shari sitting at the table. She was wearing a sleeveless yellow button-front dress. The bottom button was a foot up from the hem. Her skin was lightly tanned, and she wore no stockings. He had to consciously pull his gaze from her leg to her eyes. The two plainclothesmen assigned to protect her were two tables away. He knew this was not a purely social meeting, but memories of last night filled his head. As Shari stood to greet him, she nudged herself into his arms. He hugged her and gave her a short, self-conscious kiss. "How did the meeting with Russell go?"

"Pretty strange. How was your morning?"

"Tough ... waddaya say we order and then talk." Tom put his arm around her shoulders as they walked to the counter.

Shari ordered a salad, and Tom ordered French fries and a drink. When they returned to the table, Shari began, "So what happened this morning?"

"Well, for one thing, we got another poem this morning."

"You're kidding! Not another victim?"

"Nope. The new poem is by a new angel ... Metatron."

"He's using a new name?"

"Not exactly. This poem actually says that Metatron is going to put an end to Abaddon." Tom showed Shari a copy of the poem and pointed out some of the information they had about Abaddon and Metatron and how they both tied to Samael. "Of course, the most obvious conclusion is that the killer has multiple personalities and that one of them is fighting to stop the other."

Shari leaned forward. "There's another explanation."

"Well, I'd be interested to hear it. I don't like the split personality thing."

"You're not going to like this one either, but …"

"Number forty-three."

"I'll get it." Tom got up.

Tom returned with the food. "Okay … just hear me out before you start objecting," Shari said as he sat down.

Tom put a French fry in his mouth. "Um kay … go ahey."

"What if Carl has a twin?"

"He doesn't. He was an only child."

"What if Carl and Russell were twins?"

"Jesus, Shari, look at the age difference! That's impossible."

"I know, I know. But what if … look, I don't know what to think of this myself. It's something Russell said this morning … it's so strange, but it does explain a lot."

"Well, if Russell said it, it's bound to be strange, but go ahead."

"Promise you won't laugh or get upset?"

"I promise to be completely emotionless."

"Okay … just let me go through the whole thing."

"All right already."

Shari told Tom the story of William and Beau in abbreviated form—leaving out the reference to Tom being Leo.

"That's a good story, and it would make a hell of a good movie," DeMayo said. "But reincarnation doesn't make it in the real world. Besides, if what you're saying is true, that would imply that Russell is Metatron. How would he get the poem out of prison?"

"He would just need a friend on the outside to deliver the poem."

"Did he say he wrote a poem?"

"No, but he said something about having done something to make Carl mad. I was going to ask him about that, but we got onto another subject. One thing he did say was the key to this case is in Carl's house."

"There was more this morning than Metatron. I just got out of a meeting with Carl's attorney."

"Carl's attorney? What did he want?"

"He wants us to leave Carl alone. Seems that all the attention he got has made him the talk of his neighborhood."

"Tough ... if I had my way, all those perverts would have to be publicly identified so everyone would know where they are."

"They're all registered now."

"They need to be tattooed so you know them any time you see one. Is the department going to let that attorney push you all around?"

"Nobody pushes us around." Tom had a French fry in his hand, which he put down. "Carl has ceased to be a viable suspect on his own."

"You mean he's in the clear just like that?"

"Look Shari, we had a tail on him from the afternoon Marty was kidnapped until the body was found."

"So maybe he ditched the tail sometime."

"I know when you do research on a story you go into it with an open mind. Why are you so closed minded about this? Do you believe in reincarnation?" The question sounded more like an accusation than a question.

"If you had asked me yesterday, I would have said no without even giving it a thought."

Tom jumped in the pause that followed. "It's not yesterday. What about today?"

Shari sucked her tongue to the top of her mouth producing a quiet sucking sound as the vacuum was broken. "I don't know Tom. I think I don't believe in it ... and yet, it makes a lot of sense."

"Well, I don't believe in reincarnation or psychic powers or any of that supernatural stuff. I believe in what I can see ... what's real." Shari silently regarded him. "What are you thinking?" Tom asked.

"I was just thinking that here we are having an argument, and it doesn't affect my feelings for you."

"And what are those feelings?"

"I really do love you, Tom."

"In spite of all this craziness?"

"In spite of anything. But getting back to the current problem ... Russell is sure the key to this whole mess is in Carl's house. I'm sure that if you search it again, you'll be able to find something real that will solve this mystery."

"Jesus, Shari ... haven't you been listening? Carl couldn't have done it."

"You ever watch *Matlock* on TV?"

"A couple of times ... so what?"

"If you watched it enough you would see there is only one plot. It's always the same. The killer has an ironclad alibi. Near the end, Matlock gets a clue ... something the audience doesn't get to see, but you always know when he got it. For instance, someone might hand him a piece of paper or something. He looks at it, and then he looks at the camera with an 'I-got-it' look in his eyes. Then in court he springs the clue and ... voilà ... the alibi is broken."

"Jesus, Shari ... it would be so great if real life would be as easy as TV. This is not a *Matlock* plot."

Shari half laughed. "I'm not 'Jesus Shari' ... just plain Shari will do. Couldn't you just check again for me?"

"Okay, you got Matlock. I'll see your Matlock and raise you one Daniel Jay Newton ... the Honorable Daniel Jay Newton the Third, Esquire. You ever hear of him?"

"Yeah, he's that big-time defense attorney, isn't he?"

"Big-time is right, and he just happens to be Carl's attorney. He's talking harassment suit. You couple that with the complete lack of a single piece of evidence against Carl along with the alibi we gave him, and I think you can figure what the chances are of getting another search warrant."

"Not good?"

"Does 'a snowball's chance in hell' mean anything to you?"

"Why would Carl do that ... get an attorney, I mean?"

"Why is not the point here. There's no evidence ... there's no way I could get another warrant."

"Russell is sure the key to the case is in Carl's house."

"We already searched his house, and there was no special room in there and no evidence. We searched every room and closet when Marty was missing, and she wasn't there."

"It must be a secret room. One you didn't know was there."

"A secret room? You are stubborn."

"I've thought about it a lot, and I'm sure Carl told me he was put in a room with no windows when his parents wanted to punish him."

"He was probably talking about a closet. We checked all the closets and the attic. There was nothing."

"No, it wasn't a closet. I'm sure from the way he talked about it that it was a room."

"Well, we checked all the rooms, and there was no room without a window … and there was no room with a little girl in it, or any evidence, or any key."

"That's because it's a secret room. He's hidden the door."

"There was no secret room. You don't think we know our job?"

"What about the basement?"

"Big open space with outside windows."

"What about a coal room? Those old houses always had dark coal rooms."

"There was a coal room with a dusty, broken pool table that hadn't been used for years. That's probably the room he talked about, but it sure as hell is not the room Marty was taken to."

"Maybe Marty was hidden in a secret compartment in the pool table."

"I looked underneath … the bottom was broken out. There was no place to hide a small girl."

"What about a room in the center of the house?"

"Shari, give it up! You were in the house when you were married to Carl. Did you see any kind of secret room?"

"I was there only a couple of times to visit his parents. No one ever took me on a tour. What about behind the staircase?"

"That would be smaller than the closet."

"Tom, Russell says there's a room. All we have to do is measure everything. Once we have measured all around the outside and all the rooms inside, we can have a draftsman draw it, and the room will show up on the drawing. It's that simple."

"The way things are now, even if I had a witness, it would be impossible to get another search warrant."

"Maybe we could just sneak in sometime when we know he isn't there."

"That's breaking and entering. Even if we found something, we couldn't use it."

"People are dying."

"People have always died to uphold civilization."

"Children?"

"I'm not the one killing children."

"Fine … just fine … then I guess Carl will just go on killing. Look, Tom, I'm just a bit uptight about this. Did you get anything else from the meeting this morning?"

"Piszczek and I both believe that Abaddon was probably scoping out his next victim, and Jennifer saw him doing it. That's why he killed her. If that's true, then there's a chance he's already picked his next victim from Jennifer's neighborhood. We're locating all the possible victims in that area and we'll be watching them closely."

"Shouldn't you just warn everyone?"

"That would just cause him to go somewhere else. The best thing is to keep this under control and watch the kids in this area. At least this way we have an idea where he'll strike."

Sheri was frustrated, but then another idea came to her. It would be dangerous. She could not mention it to Tom—not yet. "I guess you're right. It's just that I get caught up in this thing. Maybe at some level I'm hoping Carl is the killer … that way he could be put away forever, and that would solve my problems." Shari hurried through her lunch, making small talk about Tami. "You coming over to the house tonight?" Shari asked as she finished the last bite of her lunch.

"If that's all right with you."

"I think I should have a pretty close guard." Shari winked as she spoke.

"I think so too ... the closer the better."

"Okay then, I'll see you later." Shari got up and leaned over to kiss him on the cheek. At the last second, she kissed him on the lips.

★ ★ ★

As Shari left the Royal Eatery and walked to the parking structure on Exchange Place and State Street, her guards stayed a respectable fifteen paces behind her. She drove her car up State Street to the parking structure for the Crossroads Mall in downtown Salt Lake. Her two guards followed her into the mall. Shari left the mall and crossed State Street to the ZCMI store. She took some clothes into the fitting room in the women's department. While the guards entertained themselves, Shari slipped out the employee's door. It was easy, because they did not expect her to try to get away from them. Once she was past them, she ran to her car.

Shari drove as fast as she could to her goal. She parked in the alley a couple of houses from Carl's house. She ducked through a break in the fence between the parking area next door and an old shed in Carl's backyard. She tried to open the back door, but it was locked. Near the back door was a basement window. The window was about two feet high by four feet long. The bottom was eighteen inches below the level of the ground. A concrete window well was constructed to keep the dirt away and allow light to get in; it was an open box about two feet wide in front of the window. *I should have gone home to change,* she thought as she hiked up her dress so she could climb down into the window well. She found a piece of brick, which she used to smash the window and break the shards of glass from around the frame. Looking in, she could tell this was the old coal room. She carefully climbed through the window into the basement. The wall on the side she had climbed in was partially paneled, and the floor was bare concrete. It felt cold and had a musty smell. The pool table was exactly as Tom had described it. Outside the coal room, the basement was just a large open space.

Shari walked up the wooden steps to a landing four steps below the level of the kitchen floor. She stopped to take a breath. Her heart was pounding against her ribs. As she stood there, she could think of a thousand excuses Carl might have for coming home. Shari walked up to the kitchen and measured the length and width with a cloth tape she carried in her purse. The tape was only six feet long. She had to leave her comb on the floor to move the tape. It was not very accurate, but she was sure it would be close enough to find a hidden room. After carefully marking the dimensions, she walked into the dining room.

BRDRING … BRDRING … INTRUSION INTRUSION!

BRDRING … BRDRING … INTRUSION INTRUSION!

Shari screamed and threw her clipboard and tape measure in the air as she was surrounded by the blaring alarm!

BRDRING … BRDRING … INTRUSION INTRUSION! The alarm screamed back. Shari ran a couple of steps toward the front door, then stopped—ran back to pick up her clip board and tape.

BRDRING … BRDRING … INTRUSION INTRUSION!

BRDRING … BRDRING … INTRUSION INTRUSION!

Shari's knees suddenly felt weak. She turned back to the kitchen.

BRDRRRING … BRDRRRING … INTRUSION INTRUSION!

BRDRRRING … BRDRRRING … INTRUSION INTRUSION!

Shari started down the back stairs.

BRDRRRING … BRDRRRING … INTRUSION INTRUSION!

BRDRRRING … BRDRRRING … INTRUSION INTRUSION!

She realized it would be impossible to get out the basement window.

BRDRRRING … BRDRRRING … INTRUSION INTRUSION!

BRDRRRING … BRDRRRING … INTRUSION INTRUSION!

"Shut up!" Shari screamed as she fumbled with the back-door lock.

BRDRRRING … BRDRRRING … INTRUSION INTRUSION!

BRDRRRING … BRDRRRING … INTRUSION INTRUSION!

The door flew open and she stumbled out, falling down the stairs into the garage. She got up and ran out the door at the back of the garage. She tripped and fell over something as she crashed through the fence from Carl's yard into the parking lot next door. She stumbled to her feet and ran to her car. Fumbling for her keys, she dropped the clipboard. Finally, she got the door open and piled headlong in, slamming the door behind her, and then she opened it to pick up the clipboard. She closed the door again, took a deep breath, put the key in, started the car, put it in gear, and drove off. At least she had gotten away before the police arrived. She got a napkin from the door to clean the blood from her knee.

Shari drove to the university library and parked near the road, hoping the police would spot her car. She was sure Tom would put an APB out on her as soon as he discovered she was missing. It would be better if he found her at the library. She would tell him she had just wanted to be alone to review the next chapter of *Conquering the Ever-Widening Circle*.

Conquering the Ever-Widening Circle
Chapter Seven: Spiraling In

Take a ride with me as I drive to a neighborhood just outside Denver. It's still dark, but I can see my breath in the glow of a streetlight. It is mid-September. I'm wearing a dark-blue jogging suit. I begin walking up a street I have not been on before. As I walk, I see a light near the back of a two-story home. The light is on the second level of the house, but there is a large tree in the yard next door. I quietly move along the side of the house listening for dogs. I climb the tree. The leaves have started to fall, but there are still enough to give me cover. I push a small branch aside, giving me a clear view into the room.

A red-haired woman is standing in front of an ironing board, ironing a skirt. She is standing sideways to the widow facing to my left. She is wearing a short bathrobe, which is fully open in the front exposing her breasts. In profile I can see the slightly convex curve of her left breast projecting down to her nipple, with the full curve below. Her breast sways as she twists back and forth in time with her arm as she irons. Using my theater binoculars, I can clearly see the freckles on her face and upper chest. As her hips twist to counterbalance the sway of her arm, I can see glimpses of red pubic hair through the open robe.

When she is done, she shakes the cloth that she put over the skirt as she ironed it and then rubs it between her legs. She puts the ironing board up and lets the robe fall from her shoulders. She gets something from one of her drawers. With my binoculars I can see her lay a small vibrator and a magazine on the foot of her bed. She opens the magazine and turns the vibrator on facing toward the window with her legs wide apart. She begins to use the vibrator on the insides of her thighs. She slides it lengthwise back and forth along her crotch and pushes it inside. She rocks her hips as she works the vibrator in and out.

Even without the binoculars, I can see the definition of the muscles of her legs and stomach as the excitement builds. I begin to stroke myself in time with her. I allow my tension to build with her. Suddenly, she tenses. Even though I can't hear her, I can see the groans of pleasure in her face. I push hard and finish with her. In all my years, I have never seen anything like this. I get back to my car as daylight begins to emerge from the gray of dawn. I drive to a park, where I jog for forty-five minutes, and then I drive home, sweaty and physically drained. Already I am fantasizing about returning.

In the following days I began to consider the deal I had made with myself. Though I was acting out less, I was still appeasing the evil part of me. I remembered how hard I had fought against this perversion in the past and how devastated I was each time I failed. I remembered the near suicide, the tears in the night, and the frustration of always losing. I realized, even though I was prowling the neighborhoods of Salt Lake almost nightly and almost totally out of control back in those days, in a real sense, I was a better person then—at least I was trying. Now I was in agreement with evil. This last time I had vicariously shared a climax with the red-haired woman. I had crossed a line.

Perhaps it was my desire to quit that subconsciously caused me to get caught before. If I were to go back to those futile attempts at stopping, I might subconsciously cause myself to be caught again. It was peculiar that now a decision to try to stop this behavior might bring the dangers I experienced before. But I decided I would try to overcome it one more time.

For several days, I thought about how I could stop. It came like a bolt of lightning! "As a man thinketh, so shall he be." I had to control how I thought. How does one control the mind? Have you ever had a song repeat itself over and over? My new program was to not allow myself to think about or fantasize about voyeurism. To occupy my mind during times of temptation, I needed to think of something that would require my complete concentration. I came up with the idea of memorizing a scripture. In the first months, the frequency of needing to rely on this distraction went from several days between incidents to several times a day. The harder I tried, the more difficult it was, and the more frequently I was beset by the fantasies requiring me to memorize scriptures. It was as if the evil in me were fighting back.

Finally, a year had gone by. The frequency had decreased, and I was battling thoughts only two to three times per month. Five years went by. The part of my life involving voyeurism was out of my mind. I had developed a whole new thought pattern. I was cleared of compulsive behavior.

During the dark years of my addiction, I had a dual personality. I was a conscientious religious participant in my church and successful in my career. On the other hand, there were the times I acted out a degrading perversion. At the time of acting out the compulsion, some subtle change in personality had occurred, and there was no desire to resist. What was repugnant to my normal personality had become pleasurable, and the desire to resist was somewhat quaint and unrelated to the situation. I was able to finally overcome this when I decided to fight the problem at a point in the cycle where it was only a thought—before the temptation became an issue.

All of the days of my life are yesterdays except just one. All of the yesterdays, act as a rudder, which attempts to set the course for that single day. It is only by means of conscious choice and personal will that I control that rudder. If I could undo my past and rewrite my history, I would take from it all the compulsive behavior that has embarrassed me, my family, and hurt countless others. I did finally take responsibility for my actions, as each of us must in the end. I eliminated that bitter sugar from my life.

Each day I live is my creation of another yesterday. I have had to struggle to make the pattern of my yesterdays into a path that leads to personal development and happiness. With the completion of this book, I have pumped out the bilge, and I am now at the helm of my own ship. I wish the same success to anyone who struggles with similar problems.

★ ★ ★

Shari looked up as the shadow fell across the table where she was working. She had been in the library over three hours. Tom looked down at her—she could not tell if it was relief or anger in his face. "Hi, Tom. Sorry I slipped away from the guards, but I just needed a little time to think and work on this book. The Bobbsey twins were fencing me in."

"Don't, Shari." Tom sat down, "Let's not have this between us."

"I'm sorry, Tom. I needed to know."

"Well, you came damn close to being arrested."

"Arrested? By whom? What for?"

"You set the motion alarm off." Tom seemed exhausted.

"But I got away long before anyone got there."

"You were seen running from the back of the house. Someone got your license. How's your knee?"

Her knee was under the table. That was Tom's way of letting her know someone had seen her fall as she ran away. "I guess I really blew it. What happens now?"

"Nothing."

"Nothing? How come?"

"Carl refused to press charges ... even said he gave you permission to be in the house ... couldn't figure why you ran. He was really something to watch. But he could have had you arrested ... so whether you wanted it or not, you are in his debt."

"Tom, I don't know what to say. I'm sure he's out to get me. All I can say is that I was acting in self-defense."

"If he had wanted to get even with you, he could have had you arrested just like you did to him. Revenge in-kind ... isn't that the best ... tit for tat?"

"Let's just say, for the sake of argument, that Carl wants to get even with me in a big-time way ... say he has it all planned out. Wouldn't throwing me in jail put a crimp in it?"

"You sure are stubborn. But I'm asking you to please stay away from Carl and his house."

"I didn't get all the information I needed. I didn't get to take any measurements except in the kitchen."

Tom put his head on the table. When he sat up again, he took Shari's hand. "You can't go back. The alarm will just go off again, and you'll end up in jail."

"Not if you help me."

"I can't help you break the law, Shari. You're going to have to back off. Besides, there's nothing in the house. We were thorough ... we didn't miss a thing. My hands are tied."

"I know Carl was put in a dark room in that house."

"Maybe it was the coal room."

"I don't think so."

"Maybe it was a darkroom."

"That's what I said."

"I mean did he call it a darkroom?"

"Yeah."

"What if it was a photographic darkroom?"

"So what?"

"Just for the sake of conversation, let's just say that house had a darkroom that was used for developing pictures and for punishing Carl, and let's say he found a way to hide the entrance to the room."

"Yeah?"

"Well, a darkroom would have plumbing and electrical wiring."

"Yeah ... I suppose. So what?"

"So, chances are there would be a building permit for the room. Why don't you check that out? If you can find a permit for a darkroom, I'll try to get another search warrant."

"Do you think I'll find something?"

"Truth?"

"Yeah."

"I don't think there is a room, but I'd rather you check the public records than have you breaking the law again."

"Thanks. I'll check it out first thing tomorrow."

"One other thing … promise me you won't ditch your guards again. Whether Abaddon is Carl or someone else, it's obvious he is after you."

"Truth?"

"Truth."

"I don't know if I can promise that. You know this may only buy time. At some point the house has to be checked out. You mad?"

"Disappointed, but I guess I can see where you're coming from. My men won't be nearly so easy to get away from now."

Shari stood up. "You going to take me to dinner?"

"Sure. Where do you want to go?"

Chapter Eight

THE ROOM

The man began his preparations for Azura. This had to be the most complicated pickup, just in case the police were watching the area where Derdekea had lived. He would rub hold-the-mayo's nose in it this time. *DeMayo—hold-the-mayo—Metatron, it makes no difference what he calls himself. A DeMayo by any other name is still an asshole—still in my power. Metatron! What a stupid prick!*

The man got in the black car. Azura would be at the swimming pool in Liberty Park, where she had swimming lessons on Fridays. He had gone to the pool several times to watch her brown body in her yellow swimming suit. The man drove slowly past the pool and parked on the side of the road near the Tracey Aviary, a small zoo in the park specializing in exotic birds. Tall pine trees lined the road. Azura went along the path looking through the fence at the animals as she walked. This time he would talk her into going with him. He got out of the car and sat on the front fender. As the girl walked by, he said, "Hi, Azura, how're ya doin'?"

The girl stopped. "How do you know my name?"

"I've been a friend of your father and mother since before you were born."

"I don't know you."

"I know ... I've been living in New York since you were two years old. Your sister, Razel knows me. I used to babysit her."

"Are you coming over to the house?"

"I just came from your house. Danielle, your mom, I mean, left to get Razel. Your dad is taking off from work early to meet us all at my house for a picnic to celebrate my moving back from New York. We're all going to have a lot of fun times. You're seven, aren't you?"

"Almost eight."

"Yep ... that's right. Your birthday is ... don't tell me ... let's see ... it's September, right?"

"Yeah."

"Wait ... it's the sixth ... right?"

"How did you know that?"

"My little girl, Virginia, was born two days before you. I'll bet you'll be great friends."

"Is she in the second grade?"

"She just finished the second. She'll be in the third this year. You'll be in the third too, won't you?"

"Yep." She was very proud of this fact.

"Your mom said you're doing real well in your swimming class."

"I can swim all the way across the pool by myself."

"That's really great. Virginia doesn't know how to swim. Maybe sometime you could show her what you can do. That would be real neat."

"Well, I'm not a teacher, you know." She walked from the sidewalk, across the grass to the man's car.

"Of course, you aren't. I think it would be neat if she could just see you swim ... you know ... so she can see someone her age can learn to swim."

"I don't mind showing her."

"Come on. Let's go, and you can meet her."

"I can't go with a stranger."

"You're exactly right. Your mom will be you proud of you. But I'm not a stranger. I know your sister, Razel. I know your mom, Danielle, and your dad, Dean Curdwell. I even know your address and phone number." He had researched those few facts from the phone book, from watching the house, and from picking through their garbage. He had followed Dean and could have told Azura where her father worked. After giving the right address and phone number, he slid from the front fender and opened the door of the car. "Come on, we're going to be late."

Azura took a step back. "I don't know."

The man calmly took his wallet out and removed his driver's license. Holding it out to her he said, "Here's my driver's license. It's got my name and picture on it. It's positive identification. Here, you can take it."

Azura moved closer. He held it close to himself so when she reached for it, she was close enough to grab. He looked around—no witnesses. He was tempted, but he wanted to talk her into the car. Azura looked at the license, and then she looked back at the man. "You can keep it until we get to my house." The man motioned to the girl to get into the car.

"I'm not sure."

"Look, Azura ... I'm not a stranger. I know all about your family. You know my name and you've got my driver's license. Now come on; your parents are waiting at my house. We need to get going." The man used a quiet tone of authority as he spoke. The girl seemed a little unsure, but she got into the car.

"We're going to have a great day. Be sure and buckle your seat belt." The man put his seat belt on and started the car. She was going with him willingly. Nothing could stop him from getting all the angels he wanted.

The man got her in the house before she began to resist. Then he put his hand over her mouth and carried her kicking to the room, where he forced her on the cot, tied her up, and put on a gag. His license had fallen to the floor. He picked it up, showed it to Azura, and then put it in his wallet, leaving her tied to the cot with her swimming suit still on. He returned with the suitcase he had packed and removed the albums to get his camera. He took a picture and then carefully cut her clothes off. When she was naked, he took several more pictures from different angles. The shock and fear in her eyes grew with each second. *No one can touch me now. I'll get that bitch, Bat Qol, and take them both to the cabin. She can watch me do Azura before I kill her. I'll make a real nice video for hold-the-mayo, and then I'll be out of here by tomorrow night. I'll mail him the video before I leave.*

He found a name in his book and worked a short time on a new poem. Now it was time to get Bat Qol. "Sorry, girl ... I got some things to take care of before the party starts. We'll have some real fun when I get back." He noticed the tears falling from the corners of her eyes, but they had no meaning to him. He turned the light off and left.

★ ★ ★

Tom had spent the night with Shari, and they had made love again. At first there had been some tension between them, but they talked it out over dinner. Tom had brought a clean change of clothes for the morning. He left his clothes from yesterday folded on the floor in Shari's walk-in closet. Shari put on a pair of cotton denim pull-on pants and a blue seersucker shirt.

Tom left first, but Shari was not far behind. Myron and Alec, the two guards assigned to watch her today, were waiting to follow her. Shari went straight to the building department in the City and County Building. A large woman was sitting behind an old oak desk in the records department. She had long gray hair and appeared to be in her late fifties or early sixties. She wore a bright-green dress that did not go with her complexion. Her makeup was too dark, especially around the eyes. It was apparent from the way she acted that she thought she looked good, but she looked like a caricature from a bad cartoon. "Hi. My name is Shari Darling. I'm doing an article about some old houses in Salt Lake. I have a house in particular that I've been researching. I thought maybe I could get some information about building permits on the house. I'm looking for room additions and that sort of thing. Do you think you could help me?"

The woman looked up from her desk and smiled. "Don't know. How old is the house, and where's it located?" The woman looked quizzically at Myron and Alec.

"These are my research assistants. I understand the people who owned this house came into some money sometime in the late fifties. They might have made some additions to the house either in the fifties or possibly in the early sixties." Shari wrote Carl's address on a piece of scratch paper and gave it to the woman.

"Don't know." The woman took the paper and looked at the address. "We got some old records ... might have something in that time period."

"The other reporters told me not to even bother because that was so long ago, but I told them sometimes you can luck out and find someone who knows how to find just about anything."

"I don't mind saying, I've been here for over twenty-five years. Seen a lot of people come and go in this city ... I could tell you stories. But I haven't been in records that long. Don't know anything about the fifties. Just know there are some really old records back in the back, but what the heck ... let's see what we can find."

"I'd really be obliged if you could help me with this. I bet a lunch with one of the guys ... and, well ... he's one of those guys who doesn't think a woman can do anything. I'd sure love to rub this in his nose."

"You might as well come back and help. This ain't gonna be no picnic, you know."

"Sure ... uh, what's your name?"

"I'm Mrs. Cordon ... at your service." Shari and her bodyguards followed the woman back through stacks of file boxes on specially designed racks that allowed one to get access to whichever box was needed. "Don't say much, do they?" Mrs. Cordon said, nodding toward Myron and Alec.

"Not much, but they're very good." Shari hoped they were extremely good.

When they got back past the organized racks, a hallway led to a room with rows of metal shelves, each stacked high with boxes. It was filled with the smell of dust and old paper. "This is not organized as good as the more recent records. All the permits were moved into this building back in the late sixties. I remember it was back around the time of Woodstock. I don't even know if they filed them by address or by the year the work was done."

The permits were filed by the year, and within each year, they were filed by street name. "We should start at 1960. Mrs. Cordon and I'll work backward, and you and Alec can work up," Shari said to Myron.

They could not find records for 1960, so Mrs. Cordon started looking through 1959, and Shari started with 1956. "I'm sorry the files are so messy and so many are missing. The move was not very well organized." Mrs. Cordon explained. After about fifteen minutes Mrs. Cordon said she had to get back up to the front desk, but she left Shari and her two bodyguards to continue their search. With so many missing records, Shari realized it would take a miracle to find what she was looking for. The entire missing year for 1960 continued to bother her. Then, as they were almost done, an idea came to her. She walked to Mrs. Cordon's desk. "I noticed that the building permits cover not just the houses, but stuff in the yards, such as fences and storage buildings."

"That's right. They cover everything on the homeowners' property."

"That's what I was thinking. But what if they wanted to put something like a tree or walkway across the parkway in front of their house? Isn't that city property?"

"In most cases it is. If they want to do that, they have to get an encroachment permit instead of a building permit."

"Where are those filed?"

"Well, those are kept in the engineering department."

"I wonder if it's possible that the building permits for 1960 were accidentally moved to the engineering department during that move."

"It was such a mess. Let me just make a call."

Shari went back help to finish up with the files. About ten minutes later, Mrs. Cordon came back. "You were right. They have the 1960 files over there. The clerk there did a quick check, and she found a file for that address."

"She did!" Shari exclaimed.

"Yeah. She made a copy, and an aide is bringing it down right now."

"Thank you so much. You have been more help than you can imagine."

Shari was shaking as she opened the folder. It held a permit for an addition, but not for a darkroom. It was for an addition that would never have crossed her mind.

The City and County Building was just across the street from the police station. Shari did not even bother to get her car, preferring to run directly across Second East to the back door of the police building with Myron and Alec right behind.

★ ★ ★

Shari was breathless when she reached the receptionist's desk. It took less than a minute for Tom to come out after the call went back. "What's the matter?" Tom's face and tone registered concern.

"I was wrong about a darkroom." Shari tried to catch her breath. "But you were right about the building permit."

"What do you mean?"

"Just wait till you see what we found!" Shari took another breath. "It's like a one in a thousand chance I would find this in the mess they have over there."

"Well, come on back, and let's see it." Tom put his hand on her shoulder.

"I don't want to meet with the whole task force this time, if that's okay."

"Sure ... no problem." Tom led her back to his desk. "You look like you've been running from a ghost."

Shari sat down. "I didn't find a photographic darkroom."

"Well, obviously you did find something."

"Yeah ... I did." She could not keep the smile from her face. "Back in the fifties, what was the big fad as far as additions to houses was concerned?"

"I don't know ... that's a little before my time."

"You know ... that was the cold war ... the atomic bomb."

"What's your point?"

"In that time of the big bomb scare, what were people building?"

"Bomb shelters? Carl's folks built a bomb shelter!" Tom's voice rose from questioning to a near shout of excitement.

Shari's hands were shaking as she pulled the papers from the envelope. "Look at the sketch." She handed the paper to Tom. The plan showed a reinforced concrete room, twelve feet by ten feet, buried about five feet from the back of the house with a passageway from the basement of the house going down four steps and into the room, which was six and a half feet tall. From the back of the room, a ventilation pipe went to the side of the shed near the woodpile.

"Did they actually build this?"

"Look here," Shari pointed to the permit, "the final inspection was signed off."

"But I didn't see this passageway from the basement."

"Neither did I, but it comes from the coal room where the paneling was ... remember? And the opening from the basement is only about three feet tall. You have to go down these steps before you can stand up," Shari said, pointing at the plans. "There must be an easy way to move the panel. But I'll tell you what intrigues me. Look where this air vent comes out. This plan doesn't show how big the vent is, but if it's big enough for Carl to crawl through, that would explain how he got Marty out without being seen."

"Carl spent the Saturday Marty was missing organizing and stacking the wood. He must have suspected he was being watched. He was clearing the vent. We'll definitely get another warrant with this. You'll pardon me if I don't invite you to lunch."

"So then, now do you believe it was Carl all along?"

"Well, let's just say he has moved to the top of the list. With any luck, we'll be celebrating tonight."

"I'm sure this is going to put an end to Abaddon. I've got a few things to do at the *Easy Life*, and then I think I'll take the afternoon off."

"You're not going to do anything stupid?"

"Like try to get away from Twiddle Dee and Twiddle Dumb?"

"Exactly."

"Not a chance. I'll be right with them so you can call them on their radios to let me know as soon as something happens."

Tom stood up and pointed to the permit. "You don't mind if I keep this."

"Sure, keep it."

Tom walked Shari back to the rear exit of the building. They picked up Myron and Alec on the way out. "Well, I hope you don't mind if I don't walk you to your car, but I've got a lot to do."

"I don't mind. I only wonder what you're doing standing around here."

"Right, I'll get in touch with you as soon as we find anything."

* * *

DeMayo went directly to Alexander's office. "We may have just gotten the ultimate break on the case." DeMayo put the plans on his desk and described their implications. When he was done, Alexander got Neil Kilpatrick on a speaker phone.

"Hello ... Kilpatrick, this is Alexander in Homicide. Something has come up on the Abaddon case, and we're going to need another search warrant."

A hollow voice came through the speaker. "I got burned pretty bad on the last one. You better have some pretty convincing evidence for this one. I mean real tangible stuff, not just a hunch."

"This is real, touchable stuff."

"Okay ... who's the lucky guy this time?"

"Carl Paskel."

"Bullshit!" The speaker crackled. "No way!"

"Look, we got plans showing a bomb shelter in the backyard. We don't need the house ... just entrance into the bomb shelter."

"You're fucking serious, aren't you?"

"I'm sitting here looking at plans of a bomb shelter, complete with secret passages to the house and to the shed behind the house. I got enough here to completely break Pastel's alibi."

"I don't give a shit what you got. He's using fucking Daniel Jay Newton the Third! I can hear him laughing now. My ass is still sore from the last reaming he gave me."

"You want to wait until the creep gets another girl?"

"That you, DeMayo?"

"Yeah, I'm here."

"Who else?"

"Just me and DeMayo," Alexander responded.

"You in your office?"

"Yeah."

"Okay ... just hang on. I'll be right over."

"Sounds like he doesn't want to do it," DeMayo said in a mocking voice.

"I'm not surprised, but he'll go along. Problem is if we'll be able to convince a judge."

"We got this guy dead to rights."

"Listen to yourself. You woke up this morning certain the killer was Dale Richards and completely prepared to go after him. Now you got an ancient building permit, and all the sudden you're out to get someone else?"

"I've been giving this some thought. Paskel was a good suspect. Not only did I arrest him, but I had made friends with his ex-wife. Then the hair and the underwear in Richards's room threw me off. But it's like Shari said, anyone could have put Charlene's panties in his room. And anyone could have picked up a pubic hair from his room and planted it on Katie. The thing that really threw me was that Paskel always seemed to have an alibi. But if you take the alibis away and rethink the case, a totally different conclusion is unavoidable. So, let's rethink this. First, Paskel knows enough about Richards to set him up. Richards raped and beat young girls, but over puberty, so they aren't going to the Celestial Kingdom. That could make Richards qualified as the destroyer in Abaddon's poem. Paskel's alibi at work is no good, and now his alibi at home is no good."

"Richards is Raun?" Alexander asked.

"Exactly. Paskel kills Richards, hides the body, and plants the evidence. Result ... we spin our wheels looking for someone we'll never find. Second, Paskel gets a job that makes it look like he has an alibi but allows him plenty of time to do whatever he wants. Third, this thing about Bat Qol; she was the voice that asked Cain where his brother, Able, was, wasn't she?"

"Something like that."

"Yeah, an accusing voice, and Shari was the one who sent Paskel to prison with her voice. We thought he decided to go after Shari because he was angry at me, but he has had her in his plans from the beginning. The whole thing has been a setup from the beginning."

"I think there could still be a problem getting around Newton for a search warrant. We're going to need all the backup we can get."

"This can't wait, because if it's Paskel, he has enough money to disappear at the drop of a hat."

"You're right there. You know that woman who turned Shari in."

"Yeah, Sarah ... whatsit? The one with the big telescope who says she isn't nosy."

"That's the one. She also called the station last Saturday night to report a suspicious character in the alley. Turned out to be our man watching Paskel's house. I was ..."

"You were thinking old lady whatsit might have seen something she didn't report."

"If we're right, Paskel would have had to take the body out in plain sight of our woman."

"But the lady didn't report anything else that night."

"I know, but if Paskel looked like a homeless man rummaging trash bins, she might not have thought it strange enough to report."

"It's a real long shot. It would probably have been late, or even early morning ... before light."

"We're going to need everything we can get to break through the Honorable Daniel Jay Newton the Third, Esquire."

"I'll go talk to the lady while you wait for Kilpatrick. Don't take no on the warrant. We can't take a chance that he'll skip on us."

* * *

DeMayo parked in front of the house with Sarah Hayes's address. It was a wooden two-story house with a big covered porch across the front. The wood siding was cracked and in bad need of a paint job. A three-foot high fence circled the front yard. Through the gate, a cracked concrete sidewalk with dirt on both sides led to the porch. DeMayo opened the gate and walked to the front door. A hole was where the doorbell should have been. He knocked on the door and waited. After a short time, a teenage boy in faded Levi's and a white tank top opened the door. "Whadda ya want?"

"Does Sarah Hayes live here?"

"Who wants to know?"

"She reported some strange activity in the alley behind the house." DeMayo flashed his badge. "There are just a couple of more questions that we need to clear up. Would you tell her I'm here?"

"Yeah ... sure. She's my grandma." The boy opened the door wide and stepped back. "She lives upstairs. She don't come down much ... bein' old 'n all. Come on up. I'll get her."

DeMayo followed him up the stairs. An open door on the right side of the hallway at the top of the stairs led into a bathroom. Everything in it was neat and in place. It smelled of roses. The boy knocked on the next door. "Granny ... there's a cop here to see ya about the other night. You wanna talk to him?"

DeMayo heard a shuffling noise. The door opened, and a little old lady stood in the opening. She wore a plain blue dress with no waist. She had a pronounced roll to her back. DeMayo could see her scalp through her straggly gray hair.

"Who is it?" She looked up at DeMayo.

"Hello, missus Hayes. My name is Detective DeMayo of the Salt Lake Police Department. I just had a few questions I would like to ask you about what you saw last Saturday night. Do you remember calling the police that night?"

"Of course, I remember, sonny. I'm old … I'm sure not senile." She stressed the last line and looked at the boy as she spoke. "What is it you wanted to know?"

"Well, you reported that you saw a man loitering in the alley behind your house that night. You remember that, right?"

"Sure, I remember … I reported it, didn't I? And the police said he was one of theirs."

"That's right. Well, I was wondering if you noticed anything else about that house on that night."

"I'm not nosy, mister. I look at the stars at night sometime, but I'm not nosy about the neighborhood. I keep to myself. Only reason I called the police that night was because I was kind of scared with a man just hanging around the back of my house like that."

"I have a telescope myself. I don't know much about the stars, but mostly I like to look at the craters on the moon. I've noticed that when I'm out looking at the moon, I can't help but see some of the things going on in the neighborhood … like who's walking their dog or when someone is in the area who doesn't belong … sort of like you. I mean you noticed our man there Saturday night, and then just yesterday you noticed a woman in the area who didn't belong. It's alert people like yourself who help us keep the neighborhoods safe."

"Oh, that girl. She was running so fast, and then she fell. Bet she hurt her knee bad, but she was going like the devil hisself was after her. Did you ever find out who she was?"

"Yes, we did. She knew someone who lived in the house."

"Was she a drug dealer?"

"Why do you ask that?"

"Tell 'em, George. Tell 'em what I've been telling you and your mom all along."

"Come on, Granny, that isn't a crack house. I seen the guy at church."

"Seen? Seen? It's I saw or I have seen. I swear, I don't know why they bother sending kids to school these days. They don't even teach 'em English."

"Why did you think it was a crack house?"

"What do you think? All this police attention going on there ... police all over the place, but I guess you knew that. So, what did you want from me?"

"Well, I was just wondering if you have seen anything strange going on over there."

"Look, I don't want to get involved with any of this, and I don't want to testify in court."

"I can promise that you won't have to testify, and that no one will ever know what you tell me. I just need the information to point me in the right direction, so I can develop my case. Why do you think it's a crack house?"

"The man who lives there keeps a secret car. I think it's his drug car. Why else would he keep it secret?"

"How do you know it's a secret?"

"'Cause of the way he keeps it. He parks it in the lot next door. He's got plenty of room, but he keeps it parked right by his fence, but in the other yard. He has a red car that he keeps in the garage and uses in the daytime. The black car in the other yard he uses at night and sometimes on the weekend."

"What kind of car?"

"It's a Ford." George walked to a small balcony at the end of the hallway. "Look, it's out there right now. He took it someplace this morning. Had to park it out front while he took the red car out of the garage, and then he pulled the black one in the garafe for about an hour. I was at Ron's house ... across the street from that house. We slept outside last night. After a while he put the black one back here and left in the red one."

DeMayo walked onto the balcony and looked out as the boy talked. A large black Ford sedan was parked in the lot next to Paskel's house—right next to the fence near the shed and the woodpile. "You're sure he's not there now?"

"Don't know that. I seen him leave in the red car, but you can't tell from here if he came back. The entrance is in the front."

Sarah mumbled, "Seen again."

"What?" DeMayo asked.

"Nuthin."

"He's got a dark-green car too," George added. "I don't know where he keeps it, but I've seen him pull it into his backyard to unload groceries and stuff."

"What kind of stuff?"

"I don't know, just bags."

"How big?"

"Just grocery size."

"Not big enough to put a small child in for instance?"

"No, not that big. What're you getting at?"

"Nothing, I was just wondering about the size."

"The one he took out last Sunday morning was big enough," Sarah said.

DeMayo felt his heart jump. He took a breath to make sure his voice did not break as he asked the next question. "You say you saw him take a larger bag out last Sunday morning? Our man didn't see that. Are you sure?"

"Come in, and let's sit down. I'm getting tired standing here."

"Sure." DeMayo followed her back into her room. It was small and neat. It was furnished with a bed and one chair in front of a dressing table.

The woman sat on the bed and pointed to the chair. "Go ahead, sit yerself down. You can stand," she said to the boy. "Now, where were we?" she asked, dangling her legs from the bed.

"You were just saying that the man took a large bag out of the house last Sunday, and I was wondering how he did that without being seen by our man."

The woman rolled her shoulders from back to front as though she were trying to crack her back. "I was nervous about your man back there ... even after I called the police. I didn't know what he was waiting for. They didn't tell me that. There could have been a gunfight ... anything like that. I tried to go to sleep, but I just kept getting up to see what was happening. So, one time when I got up ... it was about three in the morning ... I looked out and saw the man from the house come from behind the shed. I didn't see him come from the house, but I wasn't looking. Like I said, I was trying to go to sleep. Maybe your man wasn't looking all the time either, 'cause the man from the house was there. He had a large bag ... it seemed to be pretty heavy too. He put it in the trunk, and then he drove away. He didn't bring the car back until after eleven in the morning."

DeMayo excused himself to make a beeline to his car.

* * *

Shari got to her office, but she was too excited to do any work. She had some editing to do on the *Ever-Widening Circle*, but she could not seem to get into it. Suddenly, the phone rang. "Hello, Shari Darling's desk."

"Shari, this is Russell. I called because it just became clear to me that Carl has another girl in the room right now. Someone he picked up this morning. You've got to get Tom to get in house. There's no time."

"How do you know this?"

"Just do it! This will be his last girl around here. I'm sure he's preparing to leave. But before he goes, he's going to try to kill you. Do you still have your guards with you?"

"Yeah, they're both right here." The fear and the vision of the rat came back.

"Okay, get Tom in the house, and make sure you have both of your guards with you at all times."

"Look, I'm just a couple of blocks from the police station. I'm going over there right now to meet with Tom. I'll be safe there."

"Good, be careful."

"All right, bye." Shari explained what the call was about to Myron.

Myron called the station and asked for Alexander. There was pause. "Yeah ... she's here and okay. She just got a call from that Russell character, and she says that he says Abaddon has picked up another girl and ... *no shit*! When?... DeMayo know?... Yeah ... sure, she wanted to come over right now anyway." Myron hung up the phone. "Alexander just got a report of a missing girl ... disappeared sometime this morning."

"Oh my God! Was Tom there?"

"No. He's out interviewing a possible witness. Let's get over there and see how things are going."

Shari walked and jogged with Myron and Alec to the parking shelter. It was the longest walk she could remember. Her parking space was on the second level. Shari took the steps up to the second level two at a time. Her heels made a hollow clopping sound as she ran from the stairwell toward her car with Myron and Alec right behind. Neither of them noticed the shadow closing in from between the cars next to the stairwell.

* * *

Sarah had provided enough information to get another warrant in spite of anything the Honorable Daniel Jay Newton the Third, Esquire, could do. As soon as DeMayo got to his car, he made the call to Alexander. "I got the goods on Paskel. The old lady actually saw him take the bag with Marty in it out of the house. He had a car parked in the lot next door. This is enough to get the warrant. Is Kilpatrick around?"

"No, he's already started on the warrant. We've had another girl reported missing from the house right across the alley from Jennifer's house."

"We didn't have that girl on Peterson's list. Didn't we have everyone covered?"

"Unfortunately, we used the public-school roles to locate everyone. This girl goes to a private school."

"Holy shee-it. When did she go missing?"

"Don't know for sure. Last time she was seen was at a swimming lesson at nine this morning. Report came in about twenty minutes ago, but she was supposed to be home alone, so there's no real accurate time."

"The old lady's grandson saw Paskel take the car next door out this morning. Jesus … she must be in the room right now!"

"Don't do anything stupid."

"Stupid! Waddaya mean stupid? The only stupid thing would be to sit on my ass. She could be in there getting raped, or maybe she has a hand that is dying from lack of blood. I got probable cause to go in."

"I'm sending backup right now. Be careful till it gets there."

"Yeah … right. Over and out." DeMayo dropped the radio on the seat, grabbed his flashlight, and ran through Sarah's yard to the alley. He checked under the engine of the black Ford. It was warm. Through the window he could see a distinct stain on the middle of the front seat. He quietly went to the side of the attached garage and looked through the window. The red car was gone. He went back out to the shed. He found a grated cover under a couple of small logs. DeMayo shined his flashlight in the grate. The vent was not very big, but Carl had lost a lot of weight while in prison. DeMayo couldn't get the cover off, because it was latched from the inside.

He called Azura's name through the vent. He thought he heard a muffled reply, but it was not loud enough to be sure. The only option was to break in through the basement. DeMayo went to the back of the house. The window Shari had broken was boarded up. DeMayo kicked the back-door in.

BRDRNG … BRDRNG … INTRUSION INTRUSION! The alarm squealed out frantically. DeMayo ran through the garage to the kitchen door and down the basement stairs.

BRDRNG ... BRDRNG ... INTRUSION INTRUSION!

BRDRNG ... BRDRNG ... INTRUSION INTRUSION!

One of the panels was hanging from hidden hooks at the top. He pulled it off and found the passage. He had to practically crawl to get into it.

BRDRNG ... BRDRNG ... INTRUSION INTRUSION!

BRDRNG ... BRDRNG ... INTRUSION INTRUSION!

He at the bottom of the stairs he could stand with his head bent over. The passage went about five feet to a heavy metal door. He pushed on the door and it swung open into the room.

Brdrng ... brdrng ... Intrusion intrusion!

Brdrng ... brdrng ... Intrusion intrusion!

DeMayo drew his gun and stepped down another step into the room. It was too dark to see, but he sensed someone in the room with him. It was just tall enough for him to stand up straight. He slid to his right with his back flat against the wall. The room was cool. Holding his flashlight in his left hand, and as far away from his body as possible, he began to shine it around the room. The walls were bare concrete. DeMayo could see the grain of the wood that was used to form it. Against the wall there was a cot. On the cot was a small black girl tied on the bed with a gag around her mouth. Her body was shaking, and her eyes shown wide with fear. DeMayo did not want to say anything until he was sure there was no one else in the room. Near the top of the back wall was the opening to the vent. Along one wall was a small bookcase with some books on the lower shelves and a camera on the top shelf. A lamp with a cord going to a plug on the wall was next the bookcase.

"Don't be afraid, Azura. I'm a police officer. Everything is going to be all right." He moved gingerly to the lamp. He moved the beam of his flashlight around the room as he went, just to make sure he had not missed anything. He could see heavy iron hooks cast in the concrete on each side of the door, which could support a large wooden beam to lock the door shut from the inside. He turned the lamp on. He and the girl were alone. DeMayo couldn't find the girl's clothes or a blanket. He took his shirt off and laid it over the girl's naked body. Then he removed the gag.

"Please, mister, don't hurt me."

"I really am a policeman. I'm not going to hurt you. I'm going to untie you, and then we're going to call your parents. They're very worried about you."

"I'm sorry I went with the man. I thought he was my dad's friend. Is my mommy mad at me?"

"What for?"

"For going with the man."

"No, she isn't mad at you." DeMayo got her hands free. "How do your hands feel?"

"I'm so cold."

"What about your hands?"

"They tingle."

"Good." DeMayo got her ankles loose and rubbed her feet. "How do your feet feel?"

"They tingle … and they hurt."

"Can you walk on them?"

"Yeah … sure."

"Why don't you stand up and give them a try?" The girl sat up on the cot and swung her legs over the side. "I'm going to turn my back so you can put the shirt on … all right?"

"Uh huh."

DeMayo walked to the bookcase. An album was on one of the shelves. He picked it up carefully with the corner, put it on the top shelf and opened it. On the first page were the pictures of Katie Sopkov. On the next page were some handwritten notes.

"Okay, I'm ready."

DeMayo left the album open and turned around. There stood Azura. DeMayo's shirt hung loosely from her frail shoulders. The tails reached the floor. Her small black hands protruded from the sleeves. She bent her arms at the elbow to keep the arms of the shirt from sliding over her hands. She was smiling from ear to ear. DeMayo never had seen, and probably never would see, anything so beautiful. Tears almost fell from his eyes as he realized he had pulled her from the brink of a hell she could not even imagine. "Let's go call your parents. They're going to be so happy." DeMayo put his hand around her shoulder and guided her out of the passage into the basement.

BRDRNG ... BRDRNG ... INTRUSION INTRUSION!
BRDRNG ... BRDRNG ... INTRUSION INTRUSION!
"Are we going to get in trouble?"
"What for?"
BRDRNG ... BRDRNG ... INTRUSION INTRUSION!
BRDRNG ... BRDRNG ... INTRUSION INTRUSION!
"The alarm ... did you break in?"
BRDRNG ... BRDRNG ... INTRUSION INTRUSION!
BRDRNG ... BRDRNG ... INTRUSION INTRUSION!
"Don't worry ... it was an emergency, and I'm a policeman."
BRDRNG ... BRDRNG ... INTRUSION INTRUSION!
BRDRNG ... BRDRNG ... INTRUSION INTRUSION!
"You wait right here. I'm going to check the house."
BRDRNG ... BRDRNG ... INTRUSION INTRUSION!
BRDRNG ... BRDRNG ... INTRUSION INTRUSION!
"But I'm afraid."

DeMayo had her walk up the stairs behind him. He found a blanket to wrap her in, and then they went out to the front yard to wait for the backup. They were on the lawn only a couple of minutes when backup arrived. The paramedics came right behind them.

Before the paramedics left with Azura, she insisted on giving DeMayo a hug. *This is one pay period they could just keep my check.* By the time DeMayo got back in the house, the alarm had been turned off. In the room were pictures of Marty and Katie, the originals of all the poems, and a new poem DeMayo had not read. It was handwritten and had no title:

Baby powder and spring lilacs are the smells of promise.
    Round; face-slobbering drops of dew
        greet the dawn,
        create the dawn of my hope.

Sour beer and stale cigarettes are the smells of despair.
    Round; face-clobbering fists of bone
        shape the demon,
        create the demon of my sorrow.

Metatron challenges—his false pride exposed.
    I will defeat him through Shekinah,
        formerly disguised as Bat Qol.
Sithriel protects—his false power exposed.
    I will defeat him through Manah,
        formerly disguised as Azura.

In the bookcase he found a dictionary of angels. Many of the names were highlighted, and there were notes in the margins throughout the book. DeMayo looked up Shekinah. Of the many definitions, one was that Shekinah was the female manifestation of Metatron. He looked up Sithriel. This was still another name for Metatron. Under this name, or title, Metatron protects the children of the world from the angels of destruction. It appeared that Paskel had planned to kill Azura to prove to Metatron that Abaddon could defy his will. DeMayo looked up Manah, the angel name for Azura in the poem. She was a goddess-angel of fertility. Her idol was destroyed by order of Mohammed. Paskel had already claimed his sacrifice was greater than Jesus' sacrifice. Now he was getting one-up on Mohammed by killing Azura. DeMayo put the album and the dictionary up. A small suitcase on the floor contained some of the girls' clothes and a description of the location of Charlene's body. Other notes indicated Paskel had killed the ticket taker in Provo. He also found evidence showing that Paskel had promised Richards half of his parents' fortune if he would kill them. Paskel framed Richards, and then he killed him and buried his body somewhere in the mountains.

    DeMayo went upstairs. Alexander was just arriving when he got to the front door. "Well, it was Paskel all along. There's nothing the

Honorable Daniel Jay Newton the Third, Esquire, is going to be able to do with this. Have they picked Paskel up yet?"

"He didn't show up for work this morning and didn't call in. I think he's about to blow. We have an APB out on him right now."

"What about Shari?"

"I talked to Myron right after we found out about Azura. He told me Blaine had called Shari to tell her Paskel had another girl. He knew it about the time we found out ... maybe sooner. Shari was headed from her office over to the station. She's going to wait there to see you."

"I better give her a call. She's probably better off there until we get Paskel in custody."

"Go ahead. I'll just look around a little till the mobile lab gets here."

DeMayo dialed the phone. "Hello, this is DeMayo. Is Shari Darling there?"

"DeMayo, we were just going to call you. Is Alexander there?"

"Sure, you want to talk to him?"

"To both of you. We just found Shari's guards in the parking structure where she parks. They're dead, and Shari's missing." DeMayo sat on a chair staring blankly ahead.

Alexander took the phone, spoke with the policeman, and then hung it up. "Don't worry. We're going to find him and Shari." Alexander's assurances were empty. It would take an incredible amount of luck to find Shari in time. She was in the devil's hands with no clue where she could be.

"I've never been a big believer in the occult, or magic, or miracles," DeMayo said, "but that Blaine guy knows things that he could know only if he were working with Paskel or somehow he is connected."

"You want to go talk to Blaine?"

"We're against a wall here. I can't think of anything else to do."

"I'll call the prison and have him waiting for you."

★ ★ ★

Russell was waiting when DeMayo arrived. "He's got her, but he hasn't done anything yet," Russell said as DeMayo walked in the room.

"How do you know?"

"I can't explain that, but he had something planned, but now it won't work. He has to make changes, so we have some time, but not much."

"You sure know a hell of a lot. Where is he?"

"He's left the city, but he's still in the area."

DeMayo was skeptical, but more than anything he wanted to believe Russell could find Shari. "Where? North? South? East? West?"

"He's headed someplace … not populated … out of the city. You found the room, right?"

"Yeah, and we saved the last girl."

"Good. I think he planned to use the girl with Shari. He had been planning on this girl more than any of the others. She was black. This was symbolic of his past."

"You mean that past life thing?"

"Is there any chance I could get to that room?"

DeMayo called Alexander and found that he had anticipated this possibility and had started the paperwork. When DeMayo got back to the visitor's room he said, "Looks like you're going on a trip."

"I know your men will have already searched the room and probably taken stuff out. Could you call ahead and have them close the room off? Don't let them move anything else till we get there."

"They won't have removed anything yet. The lab will check it all out before anything is moved."

"Good, just leave it like it is now."

DeMayo made the call. On the drive from the prison, Russell sat quietly meditating. When they got to the house, four officers were waiting. DeMayo, Russell, and two of the officers went into the room together. Russell lay on the cot and closed his eyes. "He's definitely not in a city or a populated area. Too much in this room has been disturbed. How about we try his bedroom?"

"Sure." This charade felt stupid, but DeMayo had to take a chance Russell could get a lead. At this point, it was his only hope.

Russell got nothing in the bedroom. He asked that everyone except DeMayo leave the room. After they left, Russell determined Paskel was headed east. He could not pinpoint a highway. "Isn't one of his cars here?" Russell asked.

"Yeah ... a black one that was registered under a false name. You want to try that?"

"Yeah, let's give it a shot." The other officers had found the key hanging near the door going out of the garage. DeMayo recalled that Russell told Shari the key to solving the mystery was in the house. Russell got in the car. "How about taking these cuffs off so I can put my hands on the wheel and the gearshift?"

DeMayo took the cuffs off. "You try anything funny, and you'll be back in prison before you know it."

"This car has been to the place where he took Shari."

"Where?"

"I can't tell, but it's a place ... a house ... an apartment."

"You said it was out of the city. How could it be an apartment?"

"Out of the big city. Could be in a town ... something like that. Let's check the room again. He's gone to a place that he set up just to torture and kill Shari." They went back to the room. Russell lay on the cot. "How about you tie me to the cot. Maybe I can get something from the point of view of his victim."

One of the other officers brought some rope, and DeMayo tied Russell to the bed. Russell said there was too much conflicting energy and requested that the guards wait outside the door. He closed his eyes. "Close the door a second," Russell requested. DeMayo closed the door and Russell meditated. "Untie me and let me move around a bit. I think I'm getting something else. He writes his poems in the nude." DeMayo untied him, and Russell walked over to the bookcase. "Pick the rope up and put it on the bed," Russell said. DeMayo turned his back to Russell and bent over to pick the rope up. Suddenly, there was a blazing light, and then everything went black.

Chapter Nine

THE PENITENCE

The man was on his way to pick up Azura, but when he saw the police cars in front of the house, he turned his car and drove away. *Goddamn DeMayo!* The man had such plans, but that asshole, hold-the-mayo, had screwed them up. He knew they were closing in, but he was surprised to see the ambulance in front of the house. Now they had his album and his souvenirs. As he drove, he mentally reviewed what was still left in the house. *Not everything. They aren't going to know where to find me. They got a couple of identities, but as long as I have the money, I can get all I need.* He looked at the woman slumped unconscious on the seat next to him. *Time to balance accounts.* She had turned him in and then had gone to be with another man. He would teach her the value of loyalty … and the penalty of betrayal.

★ ★ ★

Shari woke up in the front seat of a car. When she tried to move, she found her hands were cuffed behind her back. Stealing a peek, she saw Carl in the driver's seat. Pretending to be unconscious, she waited for an opportunity to escape. She was slumped against the window where she could open her right eye without Carl seeing her. They were driving down a freeway in a barren, hilly area she did not recognize. She saw a sign saying *Jordanelle Lookout*.

Shari vaguely remembered Carl had used a knife to cut Myron's throat. Then he had stabbed Alec in the chest. Next she remembered his face, distorted in anger, as he swung a fist at her. She could not remember being hit, but now her lip felt like a balloon. The sun was low, and it was behind them. After a time, Carl turned right and drove off the highway. He got out and opened a gate. They continued across a bridge and up a dirt road. She could see several mountain cabins spread among the pine trees. Carl parked the car in front of one of the cabins. "Like it?" Shari made no attempt to answer. Carl slapped her with the back of his hand. "You think I don't know you're awake. When I ask a question, I expect an answer. You'll learn that before you die."

Shari sat up. "Okay, okay." She looked around her. They were in front of a cabin that had been built to fit in the existing landscape. Through the trees, she could make out another cabin about a hundred yards away. "It's very nice, Carl." She hated that her voice was shaky. Carl slid next to her, reached across, and opened the passenger door. The fresh smell of pine trees was almost like Christmas.

"Get out," he commanded, pushing her out the door. He slid the rest of the way across the seat and got out behind her. Shari had fallen out of the car on her right side. She stumbled to her feet to avoid giving him an excuse to touch her. Carl pushed her to the front door. He fumbled for the keys. "Look around, Shari. This will be the last time you see the outside world."

The cabin was located on the edge of a meadow at the foot of a steep mountain covered by a forest of pine trees. In the front of the cabin, the meadow stretched about two hundred yards. On the other side of the meadow was a highway and a general store with two cars parked in front. A pickup pulling a trailer labored up the highway. A stream flowed down the meadow. Birds were singing. Shari could see another cabin about seventy-five yards away. *If I scream, someone might hear me before he could stop me.*

Carl got the door open and pushed her so hard she stumbled and fell. She managed to roll on her shoulder to break the fall, but she jerked painfully on the cuffs. She cried out. The man kicked her in the ribs on the right side. "What did I tell you about being quiet?"

Shari could not remember being told to be quiet. She rolled to her stomach and then, using her forehead to push up, she managed to pull herself to her knees. The effort produced so much pain in her ribs that she nearly passed out. "Now what?"

"Now we wait. The real fun begins tomorrow at ten thirty. In the meantime, we're going to have to get you ready, aren't we?" Carl put his foot in the middle of her chest and roughly pushed her backward. Her legs bent back at her knees with her ankles under her buttocks. The pain in her ribs, knees, and wrists caused her to lose focus. She could vaguely see him walking away, but he seemed more a shadow than a person.

"Don't move. If I come back and find you've moved, there'll be hell to pay. Do you understand?"

"Yes."

He disappeared through a door into another room. Her knees hurt viciously. She took a chance and straightened her legs out. As her vision cleared, she realized she was in a cabin similar to ones she and Carl had looked at when they were married. All the interior walls were pealed logs. She was on the floor of the living room. There was a kitchen with a mezzanine over it. The door Carl had gone through was next to the kitchen. A skylight above her had been removed, leaving an open hole.

★ ★ ★

DeMayo regained consciousness and stumbled to his feet. Was that pounding noise in the room or was it his head pounding? He shook his head—pain shot from the left side down his neck into his shoulder. He lurched to the door. A wooden beam was resting in the brackets, and the door was bouncing against it. He could hear the muffled sounds of someone shouting, "Open up."

DeMayo blinked his eyes and took a breath. He put his hand on the back of his head; it was wet and sticky. "Son of a bitch." He looked around and saw the bookcase was broken and the grill to the air vent was removed. He lifted the bar, and the door swung open. Two officers were standing in the passageway and two more were back in the basement. "Hurry! Have someone check outside! He escaped through a vent on the side of the shed in the backyard!" DeMayo shouted. Two officers rushed to the backyard. DeMayo edged to the cot and sat down, feeling light-headed.

"You all right?" Officer Jensen asked.

"Hell no! The son of a bitch bashed my head in with a bookcase! How long have I been out?" He put his head down to his knees to fight the faint feeling, but the instant he did, the pain was so excruciating that he immediately sat up.

"I don't know. You closed the door about ten minutes ago. We've been waiting. We just now tried to open it, and it was locked."

DeMayo took a breath. The room was cool, but he felt beads of sweat forming on his forehead and in the middle of his back. The paramedics arrived about five minutes later. DeMayo was still sitting on the bed, fighting nausea and a light head. "You're going to need some stitches." The paramedic was a lanky young man.

DeMayo stood on shaky legs. "Haven't got time for that right now." He reached in his pocket for his keys as he started for the door. "What the ...! Where's my car?" DeMayo walked shakily through the passageway. Alexander was standing in the middle of the basement with two other men. "Where's my car?"

"I didn't see it out front," Alexander answered.

"Shit! Looks like Blaine borrowed it."

"We'll get an APB out ... he won't get far."

"Wanna bet? Russell really snookered me. I'll have his ass for that."

"Yeah ... well that's one you'll be living down for some time to come."

"Not if I catch the bastard." DeMayo grimaced as a bolt of pain shot down his neck. "Shari taped her conversations with him. I believe the tapes are in her office. I need to listen to them."

"You need to get your head sewn up, and you've probably got a concussion."

"Yeah, I know. How about you make arrangements for me to get into her office while I get my head fixed?"

"Get your head examined on the inside while you're at it. You need the rest."

"The hell with rest! I need to find Shari!" His head did not hurt as he shouted his response. "You take care of the arrangements. I'll look out for me. We don't have a lot of time. God only knows what's happened to her already."

"Okay, I'll make some calls. I need to clean up around here. I'm having the lab boys work overtime on the stuff we got."

"Thanks." DeMayo turned to the young paramedic, "Well?"

"Huh?"

"Let's go get my head fixed."

"Oh … yeah, right."

"Alexander, send a car for me to the hospital, will ya?"

"Will do."

* * *

Shari could not focus on the time. She lay on her back in pain waiting to see what Carl had in mind. Then he walked back in. "We have to wait until the light is right tomorrow morning. There isn't a whole lot to do till then, but we must be completely ready by ten thirty, sharp. I figure about a half hour to forty-five minutes is all I will have to balance the accounts on you. I'll have that prick hold-the-mayo in a puzzle by then with my latest clue. I don't know how he got to my secret room so fast. This time he won't be able to crack the clue … not without my help, and I won't give it to him until it's too late."

"Too late for what?" Shari was afraid what the answer would be.

"I guess I can tell you … you won't be telling anyone, will you?" Shari just looked at him. "I've spread my money into accounts all over the country in fictitious names … plus a big portion has been moved to Swiss accounts. Carl Paskel will cease to exist tomorrow night. I'll live comfortably with new identities all over the world. No one will be able to stop me then. I'll be sending DeMayo pictures and poems. Each poem will be another girl sent to the Celestial Kingdom. He'll have the best stamp collection around. That will be part of his penitence."

"Penitence for what?"

"For putting me in prison and taking my wife."

"I put you in jail, and I divorced you before Tom and I ever became friends."

"I know what you did. Your so-called divorce doesn't mean shit. You're still my wife until I say you're not. There's an account to be balanced between you and me. You didn't ask what I meant when I said the poems would be part of DeMayo's penitence. Aren't you curious about the rest?"

"I'm sure you're going to tell me."

Carl walked into the kitchen. "You noticed the hole in the roof?" Shari did not answer. Carl walked back into the living room with his hands behind his back. "But did you notice these?" He kicked a large eyebolt, which was screwed into the floor. Three others were located in the same general area. "Can you picture yourself tied naked and spread eagled on this spot? Can you imagine what will be shining through the hole in the roof on this spot at ten thirty tomorrow morning?" He produced a large magnifying glass he had held behind his back. Shari tried to scream, but her throat constricted.

Paskel put the magnifying glass on the bar. "That damn DeMayo got my scrapbooks, so now I'll have to start over. There'll be hundreds of angels in my new books. But I'll really miss the pictures of Barbelo ... she was the first. I learned my true calling with her. I'm going to video your last minutes and make sure DeMayo watches it."

"Can I sit up, please?" Shari hoped to break through his cold detachment.

"Yeah ... sure; sit up. What do I care?"

Shari sat up, pulling on the handcuffs and hurting her wrists again. "What is your true calling, Carl?" Shari feigned interest.

"I'm going to send girls to heaven."

"How are you going to do that?"

"By killing them before they can commit any sins."

"Aren't you taking away their free agency?" The Mormon Church taught that God's plan was to give people free agency. Before Satan was driven from heaven, he proposed a plan whereby free agency would be taken away and salvation would be forced on everyone.

Carl walked over to Shari and, squatting in front of her, slapped her face so hard he knocked her over. Her ribs sent fingers of pain throughout her upper body as she twisted, falling to the floor. "Don't ask smart-ass questions!" Carl stood up, kicked her in the hip, and walked over to the bar. He sat on a stool and poured himself a beer. For a few seconds the room seemed to fade. Shari began to sob from the pain. She hated to give Carl the satisfaction. "Don't be such a goddamned cry-baby, Shari. You aren't hurt ... not yet anyway. Have you ever wondered what it would be like to smell your flesh burning? Save your tears for that." Shari shivered at the cold, detached tone of his voice. She fought through the pain and rolled into a sitting position.

Carl reached behind the bar and pulled out a large knife. "I guess we better start to get you ready for the party." Shari said nothing. When he got to her, he laid the blade of the knife on the side of her cheek. The cold steel snapped her to full consciousness. "You see now ... don't you?" Carl pulled the flat of the blade down her cheek and across her neck. "Don't you?" he shouted.

"Yes." Shari could smell the beer on his breath.

Carl cut the sleeve of her shirt up to her shoulder. He repeated the procedure with the right arm. "You always had terrible taste in clothes. Didn't you?" Shari heard the question, but it seemed rhetorical. Carl slapped her again. "Answer me, bitch!"

Shari nodded.

"That's better. See how easy it is to please me?" He went to the bar and came back with a pair of scissors, which he used to cut through the shoulder and neck of her shirt on both sides. He cut each of the buttons off and pulled the shirt from her body. Shari began to fade out again as Carl used the scissors to cut through the shoulder straps of her bra. He pulled the elastic under her arm and let it snap back. "Come on, angel ... don't drift off." The sharp pain in her ribs and the sting of the elastic slapping against her side brought her back. Carl pulled the elastic out again and cut it with the knife pulling the remains of the bra from her. He moved in close and pushed the flat side of the knife blade against the underside of her left breast. "What are we going to do with these ... huh, cow?"

Afraid not to give an answer, Shari weakly said, "I don't know."

"But you do agree they're ugly ... don't you?" His voice was patronizing.

Shari nodded.

"Yes ... of course they are. Shall I cut them off for you?" The tone was cold and serious.

"No! No! Carl, please." The fear was overwhelming, as she realized he would do what he wanted.

Carl turned the sharp edge of the knife up to her breast and pulled it slightly making a small cut. "I'm disappointed in you ... pleading like a child."

Shari realized he was teasing her and nothing she could do would change his mind. "Screw you, Carl. If you're gonna cut it off, just do it!"

Carl removed the knife. "That's more like it. Not now, bitch. We don't want to ruin the fun for tomorrow. Besides, who needs all the blood?" Carl knocked her down on her back again and pulled her pants off. She did not struggle. When he began to pull her panties off, she pulled her knees up. Carl laughed, "So you're going to make it hard after all. Good." He picked up the scissors and, pulling the elastic on the leg, cut through the side of her panties. As he did, Shari twisted, which jabbed the point of the scissors into her waist about a half-inch deep. Cal laughed harder as he pulled the scissors out and cut through the other side of her panties. Shari stopped fighting and relaxed. "So, the bitch doesn't want to fight anymore!" He grabbed the crotch of her panties and pulled them off. "Look at this," he exclaimed, "what shall we do with this ugly hair?" Shari was now lying on the floor completely naked. Carl stood up. "Okay, we got to go upstairs now." He gripped her under her left armpit and pulled her to her feet. The pain in her ribs was so intense she blacked out.

★ ★ ★

The security guard met DeMayo at the door and ushered him to the office of the *Easy Life*. He had wasted precious time at the hospital, where he'd gotten four stitches. Fortunately, there were no signs of a concussion, but the doctor had warned him to take things easy for day or two.

He went straight to Shari's desk and started looking through her notes. It felt strange going through her things, not knowing whether she was still even alive. *This can't be like JoLynn*. He could not waste his time reviewing morbid history. Almost everything on the desk had to do with *Conquering the Ever-Widening Circle*. DeMayo was not interested in reading that book. He opened her drawers and found the tapes of her interviews with Russell. They were labeled with the date they were taped.

The recorder was on a table beside Shari's desk. He plugged it in and put the first tape in. In it, Shari was having a conversation with Russell in which he was telling her she would be helping him stop Paskel from killing more children. As DeMayo listened, he began to go through the notes on her desk.

In the second tape, Russell talked about basketball and being prepared to take advantage of the opportunities that present themselves. DeMayo stopped the tape and rewound it, then started playing it again. Russell was explaining how he watches for opportunities, and then he takes advantage of whatever comes up. That was exactly what Russell had done with him—set him up to bash him in the head. *A smart son of a bitch*. Had he also played Shari?

In the third tape, Russell talked about how criminals fool people, especially people who had a vested interest in believing. He wondered if all Russell had been doing with Shari was creating a vested interest in her to believe whatever he told her. He realized he had also had a vested interest in believing Russell.

It was while he was listening to the fourth tape that he sat straight up in his chair. The tape was made on the Saturday when Marty was still missing. The startling thing about the conversation was his remark that Paskel thought of himself as a lion. That was before they found Marty and the poem about the lion. It was likely Paskel was working on that poem at the time Russell made the observation. *Jesus, he must have had some connection. But then why would he want to run away from me? The best chance to find Shari would be to work as a team. Maybe he used the connection only to create an opportunity to escape. Maybe he and Paskel were working together in some sick way. That son of a bitch!*

* * *

Warm water lapped on Shari's legs and up her sides. She blinked and tried to focus. Through the blur she could see she was in a small bathroom. Someone was there. Carl! Then she remembered.

The water was still flowing in the tub where she was half laying, half sitting. Carl was sitting in a chair beside the tub. "You're very dirty, but good old Carl is going to clean you good." He turned the water off and soaped up a wet washcloth. He rubbed the cloth vigorously in her face. She closed her eyes but still could not prevent him from getting soap in them. Her lip was split and had been bleeding. Carl scrubbed around her mouth extra hard. He scrubbed her breasts even though they were under water. He was especially rough on the spot he had cut. Shari's eyes were watering from the soap, and she could not see clearly. Her hands were free, so she splashed water in her eyes as Carl sat up on his chair to rub more soap on the washcloth. The water in the tub was soapy, but she was able to get relief using it to rinse the strong soap from her eyes. "Why don't I just drown you now, Shari?"

"I don't know. Go ahead ... do it. You're going to kill me anyway ... aren't you?"

"Maybe ... maybe not." Carl leaned forward and pushed the soapy cloth between Shari's legs and began to scrub. He pushed part of the cloth into her vagina and left it there. "Admit it. You like that ... don't you?"

"Bastard!"

Carl pushed her head under water for a few seconds and then pulled her up by her hair. "It's not going to be that easy." Shari coughed and choked as she came out of the water. Carl left the bathroom. The pain in Shari's chest was worse than ever. She gently pulled the washcloth from between her legs. She could see her pubic hair was shaved off. Carl came in with a rag in his hand. "Gotta run an errand, and you need a nap," he said as he pushed the rag over her mouth and nose. Shari struggled, and then everything went dark.

* * *

DeMayo ejected the tape and replaced it with the next tape. In this tape, Russell claimed his passion in life was to stop Paskel. Russell suggested to Shari that he could solve the whole case if he could get out for a day. "I think there may have been one that was black, or maybe he's looking for a black girl ... I just don't know." DeMayo stopped the tape as he heard Russell talk about a black girl. That tape was well before anyone knew about Azura, but Paskel had been watching Azura and making his plans to kidnap her. "The son of a bitch has the connection! Jesus ... he could find her. Goddamn him for running!" DeMayo said out loud.

There was nothing to do now but keep looking for a clue in the tapes. DeMayo pushed the play button again. When it finished, he put in the last tape. In this tape Russell made a comment that he had taken actions to make Paskel angry. DeMayo stopped the tape again. "So, the son of a bitch is Metatron."

The rest of the tape Russell talked about his dream of a past life. At the end, Russell indicated he thought Leo in the dream was DeMayo. *So that's it. He felt Leo screwed things up last time, so he doesn't trust me.*

The tapes had answered a number of questions, but they gave no hint where Paskel would go to hide out. DeMayo began to look through the notes on *Conquering the Ever-Widening Circle*. His head hurt and he felt dizzy, so he laid his head on the desk.

★ ★ ★

Shari woke up still in the tub. The water was cold. She had no idea how long she had been out. She tried to get out but winced in pain with the first effort. *I'm in the trap now, and he has no more feeling for me than he had for the rat.* As Shari sat up, she had a strong sensation that Russell had somehow escaped prison and was looking for her.

Shari carefully got out of the tub, fighting pain with each move. She took two shaky steps and pulled a towel from a hook on the wall. She sat on the commode and dried her feet and legs. Her toes and fingers were all wrinkled. As she patted her chest and shoulders dry, she felt some strength returning. She gingerly stood up, wrapped the towel around her, and walked to the door. She was in an upstairs bathroom off the loft. She quietly moved to the rail and looked down to the living room. *Now's my chance to get away! If I can just get across the meadow.* Suddenly, something grabbed her from behind by the towel and jerked it so hard she went sprawling across the floor. At first the pain in her ribs was so sharp she could not breathe. She looked up, and there was Carl holding the towel in his hands.

"Such modesty ... really, Shari, you haven't got any secrets from me." She felt the carpet on her bare back and concentrated on the rough feel of the fiber as she struggled to remain conscious. "Don't worry, whore. I've got something for you to wear." He threw some pink cloth at her. Shari didn't understand the meaning of the cloth lying beside her. "Put it on, bitch ... or would you rather I do it for you?" Shari struggled to a sitting position and picked up the cloth. It was a pink jumper that looked like a little girl's pinafore. "Wait! First we got to do something about those damn boobs."

"Oh God." The stinging, itchy pain under her left breast seemed to increase.

Carl walked into the bathroom. "Yeah, we can't have them pointing out like that." He came out of the bathroom carrying a wide elastic bandage. He wrapped the bandage from her armpits to her waist. He didn't wrap it tight, but the firm pressure gave her relief from the pain in her ribs.

Shari put the jumper on—it was her size. It was almost comforting to realize he had remembered her size. *What are you thinking!*

"Okay, downstairs." Carl pulled her by the upper arm.

"Okay! Okay! I'm going," Shari cried, her voice shaking.

Shari gingerly walked down the stairs. It would be hopeless to try to run in her condition. The stairs ended in the kitchen. "In the living room!" Carl pushed her violently in the middle of the back. She managed to take two steps before falling on her face in the living room from the force of the push. She started to get up when the wave of pain in her ribs hit.

Carl carried her to a cot in the living room and pulled the jumper above her hips. He spread her legs and bent them at the knees and then took pictures of her. She wanted to move but pain and fear froze her. "It won't do for you to lay there all day like that. Don't you have any pride at all?" He patted her between the legs. "We can't leave that just gaping open … can we?"

"No."

"I thought not." Carl pulled a pair of white panties from the pillow beside her. He reached across her body and put her right foot in. "Come on, whore, help me a little." Shari did not feel like helping him with anything. "You like flashing yourself around? Huh? Is that what you want, whore?" He pulled her legs down and put her panties on. She lay like a rag doll. After the panties were on, he spread her legs and bent them back again. Then he got his camera and took more pictures.

Shari looked up through the hole in the ceiling. The sky was blue gray; it was morning. She would give anything not to have to die the way Carl planned. She suddenly remembered him saying this would be the last time she would see the outside world. She wished she could see Tami one more time—make love to Tom one more time. She strained her eyes at the opening, hoping to see a cloud. *I can die now. It's not so much the dying ... but not that way. Please God, not that way!* Shari was distancing herself from her body. Her body was just a plaything for Carl. She didn't care anymore, and the more she didn't care, the more the pain and sensations of the body lessened. *Is this what dying is?* A peace came over her. *I'm ready then.*

Carl put the camera down. He used handcuffs to attach her wrists to the frame of the cot. Shari had the sensation of looking down from the ceiling at her body on the bed. Her chest looked flat. She could see the white panties and was surprised at how small and skinny her body looked. She did look like a little girl. She felt sad looking at the small body. It was her, but it seemed to be someone else. A voice that seemed to be a part of her, but from somewhere else, came to her. "Shari, you can't go ... you can't let him win. If he isn't stopped now, he'll kill more children. We have to face him and stop him." *But what can I do?* "You could be a beacon." Shari understood. Suddenly, she was back in her body. Carl had left the room. *So much pain. But not yet ... not yet!* Shari consciously relaxed her body as Russell had once told her. First her arms and then her legs, her neck, her back. As she got more and more relaxed, the pain subsided. She felt herself get light-headed but not from pain this time. *Russell, find me. You're my only hope. Find me ... you said you would stop him.*

* * *

Ring-ring. DeMayo jumped from the chair where he had fallen asleep. *Ring-ring.* "All right," DeMayo said, picking the phone up. Every bone in his body ached. It was light outside; he had slept in the chair most of the night.

"DeMayo, that you?"

"Yeah."

"This is Peña at the station. I just got a call from Russell Blaine, the guy you're all looking for. Says to come to Shari's house as fast as you can."

DeMayo's groggy brain suddenly became crystal clear. "He there now?"

"Don't know. Didn't say anything 'cept to tell you to get there … that it was life or death for Shari. Then he hung up. Sounded like he was in a real hurry."

"Okay, I'm on my way. Get the closest squad car there and get Alexander up to speed." DeMayo hung up the phone and ran for the door. In less than three minutes he was speeding down Fifth South toward the on-ramps to southbound Interstate 15. Once on the freeway it was about three miles south to the interchange, where he turned onto Interstate 80 headed east. From there it was another four miles to Shari's off-ramp at 2300 East. When he pulled up to her house, a patrol car was already there. DeMayo jumped from his car and ran to the patrolman. "What's happened?"

"Don't know. Just got here. Ain't seen nothun so far."

"Okay, I'm going to break in. You follow me." DeMayo ran to the door. He was about to kick the door down when he suddenly had a feeling that he should check to see if it was locked. He tried the door—it was unlocked. He ran recklessly through the house. In Shari's bedroom, he noticed the light coming from the closet. Most of the contents of a filing cabinet at the back were strewn across the floor. Several ads for mountain cabins from the time when Shari was still married to Paskel were in the mix. *So maybe he's gone to a cabin. It couldn't be one of these. What's Russell trying to tell me?* He picked up the phone and dialed Alexander. "Yeah."

"DeMayo here. I'm at Shari's house … Russell called."

"I know. Is he there?"

"No … long gone, but he left a stack of ads for mountain cabins on the floor. I think Paskel has taken Shari to a cabin somewhere in the mountains. It's a long shot, but he may have bought a cabin. Have someone check for cabins that have been sold since Paskel got out. He may have used one of his phony names … maybe one we don't know about."

"Let me guess; you don't have a clue where the cabin is."

"Sorry. I suggest we start with an area about eighty miles radius from Salt Lake."

"It's Saturday ... the hall of records isn't open."

"Get it open ... we're talking about Shari's life!"

"Hang on." DeMayo began to pace back and forth carrying the phone. He was anxious, but he was at a dead end unless they found a cabin. "DeMayo?"

"Yeah ... what's up?"

"We just got a fax in from a man who claims someone approached him about four this morning and gave him a hundred dollars in cash to fax this poem to our number at exactly seven o'clock. The guy works in a twenty-four-gas station. The man who gave him the poem said he would get another hundred if it was faxed right at seven."

"What about the poem?"

"Very confusing. It says he's got Shari in a cabin. It says when you get there it will be too late."

"I'm starting for Heber City. Set up a meeting with the man who got the poem. I got to pass right by the Hendrik's shooting range. Call Jerry Olsen and fax the poem to him." As DeMayo walked to the door, the officer stopped him. "I found this letter addressed to a Leo. It's signed by someone named William."

"Leo?" DeMayo took the letter from the officer and read it.

> Dear Leo,
>
> Im sory for the tap on yor head. I wasnt doin no gud trakin Paskel and I rekoned I mite trak Shari from her place but that didn't werk. I spent the nite thinkin and I rekoned I mite cud trak Stella. I new hur all hur life. I ben here al nite thikin on Stella. Ifn I lif the next 12 hours Im fixin to turn myself in. Ive had a feelin for sum time that it was my job to sav Stella but durin the last hours I found out thats yor carma. Yew was late in 1865. I hope yew make it this time. My carma is to

stop Beau. Ill stop him sur nuf, but to late for the ones he already kilt. Beau n me made bad carma back then. Ifn I do die its ok. I deserf it for what I done to that litel slav gal. Beau is a man without feelins but he was my bruther. We make a big fus out uf death but life goes on after. I done gud and bad in this life. As for yew and Stella—I dont know all the threds that sew you together. Ifn yew dont sav her, well I rekon thats okay. Shill jus move to a new fas. I dont fear death. Im getin feelins frum Stella. She saw a sine called Jordanelle Lookout. I dont know wher to go after that. Ifn I dont figer it out Il be waitin fer ya there. Partin now, but remanin always,

Your friend,
William

"What is it?" the officer asked.

"Just the babblings of a crazy man."

DeMayo called Alexander on the car radio as he pulled onto the I-80 Freeway. "Russell left a letter. It sounds like he's gone over the edge mentally, but he says he headed for the Jordanelle Lookout. I'm heading there as soon as I finish at the shooting range."

"Okay. I'll contact the highway patrol and have them intercept Russell."

"No, don't do that. I may be crazy, but Jordanelle is close to Heber, so I think Russell may actually have some kind of psychic connection that's leading him to Carl. At this point, I'd rather take a chance on that."

Less than ten minutes later, DeMayo was parking in front of Jerry's door. Jerry opened the door as DeMayo walked up on the porch. "You got the poem?" DeMayo asked.

"Yeah ... he's using a palindrome."

"A what?"

"Here, check it out," Jerry said, handing the poem to DeMayo.

**If you want Shari to—
live, name no one man evil.**

Was it my fault life abused me with a claw?
I was a victim first—only no one saw.

But now Shari has joined me at my club,
sitting in my power—naked in my tub.

Top this and you'll be getting hot,
but I'm safe—in a cabin smoking pot.

Gas your car, you have to drive, ugly fag.
You'll be late—her limp body will sag.

Nuts to you, your friends, and your stupid gun.
Bring your army—her head I'll stun.

Tons of great clues you have got,
But you can't stop me—stupid snot.

Pots know their place is to hold slop.
I'm above you—Abaddon, you'll never stop.

Abaddon/Apollyon

DeMayo handed the poem back to Jerry. "So, what is this palindrome?"

"The first two lines don't rhyme, and they are bold. I think they're a key to what he's trying to tell us. He puts 'live, name no one man evil' on a line by itself. That's the palindrome."

"What the hell is a palindrome?"

"It means forwards is the same as backwards. The letters in the statement are the same going from front to back as they are from back to front."

"I don't get it."

"Okay, 'noon' is a simple palindrome. It's spelled the same forwards as it is backwards. Look at it, "live, name no one man evil," the first and last letters are both Ls."

"Yeah."

"Then the second from the front and the second from the back are both Is. Then the third letters are both Vs, the fourth letters are Es, then Ns, then As, and so on until you go through the whole statement."

"Okay, I see it. I can't imagine why someone would go to all that trouble. What does it tell us?"

"I don't know yet, but it must be something."

"He's given us a clue where to find him. He thinks I won't figure it out in time."

"Maybe a place that's a palindrome … someplace where if you spell the name backwards it would still be the same."

"I don't think there is any place like that in Utah. Did you check for other palindromes in the poem?"

"I just got it, but interestingly the first two letters and the last two letters of the first line of each couplet are like a palindrome."

"There must be a reason." DeMayo studied the poem. "Look at this. The last word of the second line in every couplet is the first word of the first line spelled backward. Like was and saw, but and tub, top and pot, and so on."

"You're right … they each make a palindrome. It took a lot of effort to construct it. It must be telling us something."

"Why would he go to so much trouble? You're right; there has to be a message in it."

"Maybe it's not a palindrome … maybe the place is a town where if you spell it backwards it means something else, like Levan, Utah."

"Levan?" DeMayo asked.

"Navel …you know, they named it that way because Levan is in the middle of Utah … the navel."

"Levan is in the wrong direction. Russell is headed for the Jordanelle Lookout."

The two men looked at each other and then said in unison, "Kamas and Samak!"

"That's it!" DeMayo exclaimed. "Kamas Samak is a palindrome. Samak is just few miles east of Kamas."

DeMayo called Alexander as soon as he was on the highway. "So, what did you find out?" Alexander asked.

"The cabin we're looking for is either in Samak or Kamas. I'm betting on Samak. Kamas is a farming town, but Samak has just a general store, and the rest is all cabins. The residents call the place East Kamas. I'm headed there now. Get some local police there as soon as possible and tell them to be careful ... Paskel has a hostage."

"We'll do. I have someone coming in records in just a few minutes."

The climb up Parley's Canyon was a 7 percent grade. DeMayo easily maneuvered through traffic on the four lanes going up the hill. Over the summit he passed the Jeremy Ranch area. The speedometer needle was pegged at the top number, ninety. The engine was screaming, and Tom had no idea how fast he was going. He passed Kimball Junction and the cutoff to Park City without slowing. He slowed to make the exit at the junction where Highway 40 split from Interstate 80. He hardly got back up to speed when the Quinn's Junction exit came up. He took that exit. At the bottom of the ramp, DeMayo slid through the stop sign and into the intersection. He turned left onto Highway 248 headed up the Jordanelle cutoff to Kamas. Traffic on Highway 248 was light. He slowed a little as he passed the Jordanelle lookout, but there was no sign of his car or Russell. DeMayo practically flew over the hill overlooking Kamas. As he started down the hill, he got a call on his car radio. "DeMayo here, what've ya got?"

"This is Alexander. We found one cabin sold in Samak four weeks ago. The former owner is one Tyron Mortiz. It was sold to Joseph Hunt."

"What about the sheriff in Heber?"

"Took a while to find him, but he's on the way now. What's your ten-twenty?"

"I'm in sight of Kamas."

"Kamas? You kidding?"

"Hell no!"

"You're probably ahead of the sheriff."

"Kay ... gotta go."

* * *

Shari woke with a start. Someone or something had showered her with cold water. She tried to turn, but she was handcuffed to the bed. She had dozed off trying to send a message to Russell, but there was no sign of help. She sputtered and coughed trying to clear some of the water but lying on her back made it impossible. Carl was standing over her with a bucket, laughing as she struggled. Finally, he unlocked the handcuffs and pulled her to a sitting position. She sat on the bed, gulping air and trying to control the pain. "So, bitch, I hope you're ready for the party."

"What party?" Shari was surprised at how small her voice sounded. She concentrated on everything she could remember about how she got there, hoping somehow her thoughts would get to Russell.

"Before we start with the magnifying glass, you're going to give me some pleasure. It'll be like my angels, but, of course, you aren't pure like they were."

"I don't understand."

A small bar separated the kitchen from the living room. Carl dragged her to a stool at the bar. He poured her a glass of water and pushed it across the bar to her. "Have a drink."

Shari took her time sipping the water. The sun was shining on the wall through the hole in the ceiling. "DeMayo prevented me from getting Azura for my pleasure, so now you're going to pleasure me. You're going to be a slave to my body before we start with the sun. And it's all going to be on video for hold-the-mayo's pleasure."

Shari wrenched to throw up, but her stomach was empty. *I should not have come back to my body.*

"How does it feel to know you're going to give me all the pleasure I want before we start with the fire?" Carl slapped her face. "Answer me, bitch!" She had no control over what he was planning, but she could control how she responded. "Come on, bitch!" He shouted as he slapped her again.

"I'm not playing your stupid games anymore."

"Answer me, or you'll be sorry!"

"I am Metatron, and you will answer to me." The voice was not Carl's. It came from nowhere and from everywhere. The sound filled the cabin, and the contrast of the silence that followed it was as powerful as the sound had been. Carl was leaning over her with his hand back, ready to slap her again. He froze, and Shari saw a glimmer of fear in his eyes. He slowly stood up straight and turned to the door. Something—a silhouette of a man—was standing in the doorway. Shari could not make out the features of his face, but there was something familiar about his voice. His arms were at his sides, and his feet were slightly apart. The fresh smell of pine trees came on a cool breeze through the open door. Carl dropped his arm, stood, and faced the apparition in the doorway. "Who are you?"

"I am the one who stops you. If you are Abaddon, I am Metatron. When you are Beau, I am William."

"What the …? How do you know about Beau and William? That was my dream."

"I'm in your head, Carl. I know your dreams and your plans. I come to stop you."

"How'd you find this place?" Carl took a tentative step toward the bar.

"I'm in your head, Carl. I know your dreams and your plans. You cannot escape me."

Carl darted to the bar and grabbed a gun. "Don't even think about it!" he shouted, but his voice betrayed his uncertainty.

The apparition took a step forward. "I don't fear your puny little gun."

Carl's hand began to shake as the apparition in the doorway took another step forward. Carl quickly put the gun to Shari's head. "Stop right there. If you think I'm Beau, this must be Stella. You fucked up last time, and she died. You want to see her die again? Move over there ... slowly." He indicated the spot where the eyebolts struck out from the floor. As the man stepped out of the light of the doorway, his face became clear. "Russell!" Carl exclaimed. "I thought you were in prison."

"You thought wrong." Russell moved slowly to the spot Carl had indicated. Carl threw a pair of handcuffs at Russell's feet. "Handcuff your right hand to that eyebolt." Russell silently obeyed.

Carl edged closer to Russell, dragging Shari with him. "Lay down on your back and don't move, or I'll kill her." He handed another pair of handcuffs to Shari. "Cuff his left hand to the other eyebolt!" he ordered. Shari put the cuffs on as loosely as possible. Carl pushed Shari aside and tightened the cuffs on Russell's wrists. Carl searched Russell, and then he stood up. "Metatron, my ass ... You aren't going to be able to enjoy the show on your back like that." He unlocked the cuffs on Russell's left hand. "Now you can sit up and see the whole thing. I want you to watch Shari pleasure me. Then you die, and I go on to become the most notorious killer of all time. Soon the sun will shine through the hole in the ceiling right on the spot where you are. I'll have to kill you then so Shari can take your place. She has to die slowly and painfully. I have to balance her account for putting me in prison, and for divorcing me, and most of all for taking up with that prick, hold-the-mayo." Turning to Shari he said, "You are my slave now. I own you, and I'm going to use you as I see fit." Shari had moved back against the bar. Carl kicked her in the middle of her left hamstring. He turned back to Russell. "This has been a real trip for me. You see my power now, don't you? I told you when I was in prison that no one would ever be able to catch me. Now you will see my power. I can do anything I want. I'm too smart for DeMayo or anyone else!"

Carl stood over Russell. "This is the ultimate of Christian martyrdom, don't you think?" Russell made no attempt to respond.

"Shari gets the opportunity to love and forgive her enemy, and then she gets to give her body for my pleasure before I burn her eyes out and cook her nipples off." All the pain was gone now, as Shari let her rage grow and take control. Ever since she had awakened in Carl's car, she had let him have control and power. "I'm making a video of the whole thing," Carl continued. "All the pleasure and the final slow death. Later I'll send a copy to DeMayo so he can see the result of his failure to understand the clues I left him."

Shari could see the back of Carl's head bobbing and his hands moving in rhythm with his words. She sprang forward and rushed him. The impact knocked him to his knees. Shari reached both hands around to his face. Her scream was bone chilling and louder than she expected. As Carl struggled to his feet, Shari scratched him across the cheeks with both hands, digging her fingernails in as deeply as possible, hoping to scratch his eyes out. He screamed in pain and threw Shari back into the bar. She felt something break inside her chest. Dizziness and pain overwhelmed her, but she managed to pick up the keys to the handcuffs from the bar and throw them to Russell. She felt something sharp deep in her side cut as threw the keys. Carl staggered with both hands on his face. When he removed his hands, Shari could see he was bleeding from several scratches but not his from eyes.

"You're gonna pay for this, you bitch!"

In her peripheral vision, Shari could see Russell working with the key in the handcuffs. She knew she had to keep Carl's attention. "You want some more of me, you little pervert? Come on! I'll scratch your fucking eyeballs right out of your fucking head!" Shari was surprised at how strong her voice sounded as she fought to remain standing. As she screamed, Carl paused in mid-step.

"It's over, Beau!" Russell shouted. Carl turned, and Russell started toward him. Carl pulled the pistol from his belt. "Hold it right there!" Russell rushed Carl. At about two steps away, Carl fired his pistol point-blank into Russell's body.

* * *

DeMayo slid his car from the road in front of the Samak General Store, jammed the gearshift into park, and jumped from the car leaving the engine running. He crashed through the door with his badge out. "I need to find a cabin that was recently sold by Tyron Moritz. I'm Detective DeMayo from Salt Lake. A girl's life is at stake."

"You can see Tyron's old place from the front door. Come on, I'll show you."

As DeMayo stepped out of the door of the general store, he heard a muffled *crack*. "That was a gunshot! What's the fastest way to get to the cabin?"

"Your best bet is to go down the road about a quarter of a mile. There's a private road crossing a bridge over the stream. After you cross the stream, just turn back and come this way till you get to the cabin with the two cars."

DeMayo jumped into his car, pealed out, and sped back down the highway. He used the car to break through a gate. Part of the framework of the gate caught the front bumper, causing the car to spin to the right. DeMayo kept his foot on the gas as he tried to regain control. The car fishtailed down the dirt road and struck the bridge abutment, sliding sideways off the road. DeMayo gunned it, but the wheels spun, and the car refused to move. "Shit!" DeMayo grabbed his mobile phone and jumped out of the car.

* * *

Shari saw Russell's body react to the impact of the bullet, but it did not slow his momentum as he rushed Carl. At the moment he reached Carl, Russell's right leg was extended behind him. He brought it forward and caught Carl in the crotch with such force that it sent him sailing in the air like a rodeo cowboy being bucked from a bronco. Russell was holding Carl's shoulders as he flew in the air. He came down, landing on his feet but quickly falling to his knees. Russell grabbed him by the ears and, reaching back with his right leg again, smashed it forward into Carl's face. The force of the blow tore him loose from Russell's grip and sent him sprawling on his back, bleeding from his nose and ears. Russell fell and then staggered to his feet. "You're a man without empathy, Beau. But now you'll experience what you dished out."

Carl mumbled something Shari couldn't understand, but the tone was angry and defiant. He was doubled up on the floor holding his crotch. "Hurts, don't it?" Russell said.

"Fffluck ew," Carl said.

Shari noticed a large amount of blood soaking Russell's shirt and pants. Russell grabbed Carl by the right arm and dragged him to the eyebolt. "How do you think it felt for those little girls to have you rape them?" He cuffed Carl's right wrist to the eyebolt. Russell walked to the bar, stumbling and falling on his way. He picked another pair of handcuffs from the bar and looked at Shari. "Hang in there, girl. Leo is on his way." Before she could answer, he stumbled and staggered like a drunkard back to Carl and fell to his knees. He pushed Carl onto his back and cuffed his left hand to the other eyebolt. Then he fell across him, covering Carl's mouth with his mouth in a kiss of death. The room had begun to spin by the time Carl stopped struggling. The taste of blood was in Shari's mouth and breathing seemed too hard. *You almost made it this time. At least you gave Carl a taste of your anger ... next life, it won't be so easy for him.* Darkness engulfed her. She felt a great sadness, realizing she would probably have to face Beau, or Carl, or whoever he was, another time. And yet she had no fear of him or of dying.

She had lost her sense of place. Gradually she felt herself floating in an existence that had no time or space. She could not say if she had been in this state for five minutes or a thousand years. She could be lying on a cabin floor or somewhere across the universe. She might see Tom and Tami in a future life, but it would not be Tom or Tami. They would be other people with only a shadow of this life. What would Tom do now? She hoped he would recover and have a happy life. There were so many things she would say to him if she could only have another chance.

She had heard of near-death experiences. They all seemed to be accompanied by a bright light of love. Maybe she had not lived her life well enough for that. The darkness got heavy, moist, and oppressive. She was slipping deeper.

Suddenly, she was surrounded and engulfed in a bright light. A voice was calling her name. She could not understand the words, but she could feel the depth of love in the voice. She thought to herself, *I'm ready this time.*

A shadow passed in front of the light, and she opened her eyes. She saw a bright light with the silhouette of a man standing it. *It's time,* she thought. She blinked her eyes a few times, and then she realized she was on a gurney in a hospital. Tom was standing in front of the light. Then she could understand the words he spoke. "Come on, Shari ... you'll be all right. You have to be, but you have to fight, Darling. Please fight!"

I will. Her mind formed the words, although her body was too weak to say them.

★ ★ ★

By the time Tom reached the cabin, both Russell and Carl were dead. Shari was slumped against the bar with pink foam coming from her nose and mouth. Her breath was shallow and with each breath there were gurgling sounds. Tom called Salt Lake and ordered a Flight for Life helicopter. He rode in the chopper with Shari to the hospital.

Russell had been shot in the chest with a twenty-two-caliber pistol. It did little damage except it nicked an artery, causing him to die of blood loss. The autopsy revealed that Carl's testicles were both crushed, and his pelvic bone was broken. There were teeth marks on both sides of his mouth. He had died of suffocation.

Two of Shari's ribs were broken and had pierced her lung. She was in critical condition for several days. She was released from the hospital two months later. She and Tom were married the following March.

Shari finished *Conquering the Ever-Widening Circle,* and Saundrea published it. It was a best seller because of the notoriety of the case. She started a novel about twin brothers born on a plantation in 1837. Many times, her research merely confirmed what she already felt.

On the first anniversary of Marty's kidnaping, Shari asked Tom to take her to Jordan Park. As they walked silently through the Peace Garden, they came to a statue of two young children on their knees playing a finger string game. Shari stopped to look at the statue; tears began to fall down her checks. "Tom, there are some girls walking around in faraway places right now who would be dead if not for the things we did right here. Russell told me once that we would save the lives of girls who did not even know they were in danger."

"I guess one never can tell the size of the ripple."

"I'm pregnant," Shari said.

Tom hugged her. "I love you."

Later, when they had ultrasound, they discovered Shari was carrying twins. "Do you think …"

"Not a chance," Tom stated.

Glen R Stott was born in Salt Lake City, Utah. He is a retired civil engineer who lives in Southern California with his wife. His interests include writing, including novels, short stories, poems, and more. He writes about things that he is deeply interested in. When writing novels, he chooses genres that best tell the story. In addition to the Neandertal series, he has written a psycho-thriller, "Dead Angels," a romance, "Timpanogos," and a general literature novel about a family trying to deal with a child molester, "Robyn."

www.ingramcontent.com/pod-product-compliance
Lightning Source LLC
LaVergne TN
LVHW091531060526
838200LV00036B/567